Praise for *Picture Us in the Light*

"Few books have ever moved me like this masterful story that pulses with love, loss, quiet hurts, and soaring dreams. An instant classic."
—Jeff Zentner, William C. Morris Award–winning
author of *The Serpent King* and *Goodbye Days*

"*Picture Us in the Light* illuminates the intricate bonds that draw us together. Danny Cheng, a young artist growing up amongst Ivy League–minded peers, will break your heart into a million pieces, and then quietly put it back together. Impressively layered and real."
—Stacey Lee, 2017 PEN Center USA Literature
Award–winning author of *Outrun the Moon*

"Heartbreaking and transcendent. Gilbert is a true artist of character, both obscuring and illuminating with each brilliant turn of phrase. In Danny, she gives us a narrator who, in so deeply and completely revealing his own inner life, shows us each other and ourselves."
—Anna-Marie McLemore, author of Stonewall Honor book
When the Moon Was Ours and *Wild Beauty*

Praise for *Conviction*

★"There are no easy answers. Love is both beautiful and cruel. God is both loving and mysterious. And family is both comforting and suffocating. Both hopeful and devastatingly real."
—*Kirkus Reviews* (starred review)

★"A poignant look at the messiness of love, faith, and humanity."
—*School Library Journal* (starred review)

★"Gilbert respectfully and sensitively handles themes of faith, religion, and family . . . [a] moving debut."
—*Booklist* (starred review)

PICTURE US IN THE LIGHT

KELLY LOY GILBERT

HYPERION

LOS ANGELES * NEW YORK

All rights reserved. Published by Hyperion, an imprint of Disney Book Group.
No part of this book may be reproduced or transmitted in any form or by any means,
electronic or mechanical, including photocopying, recording, or by any information storage
and retrieval system, without written permission from the publisher. For information address
Hyperion, 125 West End Avenue, New York, New York 10023.

First Edition, April 2018
10 9 8 7 6 5 4 3 2 1
FAC-020093-18054
Printed in the United States of America

This book is set in 11.35-pt Adobe Garamond Pro, Tekton Pro, Styrene/Fontspring
Designed by Maria Elias

Library of Congress Cataloging-in-Publication Data
Names: Gilbert, Kelly Loy, author.
Title: Picture us in the light / Kelly Loy Gilbert.
Description: First edition. • Los Angeles ; New York : Hyperion, 2018. • Summary: Daniel,
a Chinese-American teen, must grapple with his plans for the future, his feelings for his best
friend Harry, and his discovery of a family secret that could shatter everything.
Identifiers: LCCN 2017034519 (print) • LCCN 2017045797 (ebook) •
ISBN 9781484735282 (ebook) • ISBN 9781484726020 (hardcover : alk. paper)
Subjects: • CYAC: Family life—California—Fiction. • Artists—Fiction. • Illegal aliens—
Fiction. • Immigrants—Fiction. • Chinese Americans—Fiction. • California—Fiction.
Classification: LCC PZ7.1.G55 (ebook) • LCC PZ7.1.G55 Pic 2018 (print) • DDC [Fic]—dc23
LC record available at https://lccn.loc.gov/2017034519

Reinforced binding
Visit www.hyperionteens.com

For Zach and Audrey—

there will always be so much darkness in the world, but may you
never stop finding light and shining it all around you—

and for all the kids living in the shadows

PROLOGUE

Years ago before there was me, while all that cosmic dust that would become my cells was still spinning and cycling through the eons of the universe, there was the image of a life. A better one, I guess, according to whatever calculations my parents were going by then, and so they let go of the world I would've been born into, the only world they knew; they held to the promise of that new life and crossed an ocean and tied our destinies to everyone we'd find on the other shores.

The three of us live in Cupertino now, in the Bay Area—six thousand miles from Shiyan, China, where my parents are from. From what I've looked up, it's pretty there: craggy green mountains rising into the sky, the city cradled between the peaks. You can take a gondola up the mountain. When my parents were growing up, there wasn't too much to do there except work in the auto factories, and they both went to Wuhan University, five hours away, and met when they were just a little older than I am now.

They moved first to Texas, where they were students, and then California, where my dad got a job in a lab for a physics professor, which is what he's always planned to become. By day, he studied indirect excitons—don't ask—but on the side, nights and weekends when the lab was a ghost town and his boss wasn't around to see, my dad was conducting a secret experiment.

The experiment was about quantum entanglement, which my dad explained to me once this way: if atoms interact with one another, then even after they separate they'll keep behaving as though they're still connected. The way they move, or decay—everything will be reflected across the entire entangled system. Once, when I was in third grade, before he'd told us anything about his experiment, my dad brought me and my mom in to show us. We went on a Sunday, after hours. On the drive to his lab my dad was animated, excited and nervous both, and he talked fast and kept looking over at my mom to see how much she was listening and it gave me the feeling that somehow, whatever it was he was doing, it was for her.

My dad's experiment went like this: he'd bring in pairs of people who fell into three categories: people who'd never met, people who'd met a few times, and people who were close family. With each pair, he'd take a picture of one person, and then he'd separate the two people into different rooms at opposite ends of the hall. In one of the two rooms was a screen. He'd set up each person with a blood pressure cuff, a thermometer, and electrodes to measure brain waves and blood volume. When people's vital signs had stabilized, he'd take measurements, and then in the room with the screen he'd flash the photograph of the person you'd been paired up with.

The people who were in there watching the screen, the results were pretty predictable. For the strangers, there was no reaction; their bodies didn't care if they were thinking about the other stranger or not. For the people shown photographs of their loved ones, there'd be some kind of flush—a definite physiological reaction. For the acquaintances, it was more sporadic.

But it was the other ones who mattered, the ones down the hall a hundred yards away without a photograph. Because: for the family members, their physical responses matched their partners'. If you printed out the physical reactions, side by side, they would match perfectly. If it was your mother or wife or son or brother down the hall, when they were thinking of you, you knew. Your body knew, your atoms knew, you felt it somehow when they did. My dad claimed the odds that this would be a random coincidence were so staggering that you'd have an easier time trying to prove the existence of God.

That day, I told my dad I wanted to be the one who was looking at the picture. That part seemed easier, and I was afraid otherwise I'd screw it up, and I could tell how desperately he wanted this to go right. My dad took me next door to the first room, and I sat in the swiveling chair across from the TV screen.

"Your mom's going to understand when she sees the results," he told me. His eyes were hopeful and bright, and maybe nervous, too, underneath that. "It's one thing to hear me talk about it, but when she sees it with the two of you, she'll understand." He finished with the electrodes and patted me on the back. "Ready?"

I nodded. I said, "I hope I do it right."

"You'll do fine. Just watch the screen."

He disappeared again. My heart was thudding as I waited. The screen flashed to life, a picture of my mom appearing. It was her at their wedding reception, dressed in a long red qipao with her hair piled on top of her head; she was turning back over her shoulder to look at the camera and she was laughing. I thought: *I love you.* I thought: *Please work.*

It was a few more minutes before my dad came and brought me back to the main office with my mom. She was quiet the way people get when they want to be alone. My dad had two printouts, and he spread them out on the table.

"Look," he said, and we saw it at the same time: the matching peaks and valleys in the graphs in my chart and in hers. He looked at my mom, and it took me a few seconds to identify his expression: he was shy. "Do you see?"

I saw. I saw it like there was nothing and no one else in the room at that moment. And something happened to me then, and we've never been religious but that was the first time I got what it must be like, how sometimes something happens that takes you past yourself and you feel like your body's not your own—you feel, all of a sudden, like it's somehow much more than that. I think I have spent my life since then, with my pencils and ink and sketchbooks, trying to replicate that exact feeling to give to someone else.

"You see?" my dad said again, and without a word she turned and walked out of the lab, her shoes clicking down the linoleum hallway like she was trying to get out as fast as she could.

Later, at home, my mom begged him to quit what he was doing. They argued about it when they thought I was sleeping, but she won, and extracted a promise from him—he'd dismantle the experiment. They never talked about it after that, and I never found out why it had pulled at her the way it did.

As for me, though, I wanted to believe him that his results proved something. I did believe him. I still believe him. Because if you're tangled up in someone else, if your futures are tied that way, if that's real and if you know when it happens—then it means you know who you belong to, and you know whose fates are tied to yours, whether you like it or planned it or not, whether they still exist in the same world with you or they don't, and I think that's where everything begins and ends. I think that's everything.

ONE

The letter from Rhode Island School of Design comes Thursday.

In the moment it most likely arrives at my house in all its power to alter the course of my entire life, I'm sitting next to Harry in the Journalism Lab, trying to fake my way through the graphic Regina asked me to illustrate for Helen Yee's op-ed. I'm not checking my email, and in fact I've logged out of my account, partly because based on my obsessive stalking of old College Board forums I'm not expecting the decision just yet, but also partly because I know I'll never feel ready to find out and I can't risk getting that email at school in front of everyone.

When I get home that afternoon my dad is back from work early. He doesn't even let me get onto the property line before he's waving the letter in my face. My chest goes so tight it feels like it's splitting right down the middle, my exposed heart pounding in open air.

"That's from—?" I start to say, and then can't say it aloud.

"Yes, yes. It's finally here from RISD." He and my mom both

Maybe muscle memory will take over and I won't have to over- anything. I slide the pen against the page, let a tiny stream of ill out.

nd then: nothing. Nothing comes.

Mostly, I draw portraits. From a distance, if you hold them at length or tack them up on a wall, they look like fairly standard ic renderings, but up close the forms dissolve and you see that you thought was wavy hair or an earlobe is really a tangle of vignettes that make up the person's life—a crumpled sheet of work, say, a discarded candy wrapper, a plate of cupcakes that ut PROM? I've always liked objects left behind.

ut this is what's been haunting me the past two months: I can't anymore. At first I thought maybe it was that I was afraid of ng something better than what I turned in for my applications, would make me hate myself for doing early decision. But then ed, and keeps lasting, and I'm worried now that the truth is omething's empty at the core of me. That whatever well you're sed to draw from to put anything worthwhile into the world— run dry.

nce, a few years after we moved here, my dad came home with pack of sidewalk chalk for me. It was one of the really good with twenty-four colors and sharp ends, and right away I had ea that I'd make a gallery out of the sidewalk in front of the I'd use the lines in the sidewalk as frames.

pent hours out there. I was working on a picture of my old best Ethan's dog, Trophy, when a man walking down the sidewalk d and loomed over me.

miled and said hi (in Texas you're friendly like that, and for a it stuck with me). He was in his sixties, probably, white with air and a gray beard and walking with a cane.

pronounce it like four separate letters, R.I.S.D., instead of *ris-dee.* He's beaming. "Open it, Daniel, what does it say?"

"Okay. Um." I take a deep breath, try to calm my thudding heart. "Okay. Let's go inside first."

"It's the same outside or inside."

Except that inside we don't risk the neighbors getting a live-action shot of my every dream disintegrating. "Well—"

"Open it. Why wait?"

I applied for early decision two months and four days ago, and I've never been one of those people who can just put something so life-altering out of my mind. It's stupid how you can wait for something with every part of you, your every atom aligned toward that one moment, and then when it gets there you want more time. It's just that—if I didn't get in, I don't want to know it yet. I want the safety of hope just a little while longer.

"Here." He grabs it from me. "I'll open for you."

"Wait, Ba, I—"

He's too fast for me, though. My parents are convinced I'll get in. The day I turned in the portfolio my dad brought home sparkling cider and three mismatched champagne flutes he bought that day at Goodwill, and I haven't let myself imagine what it will do to them if I didn't make it. He's already got the letter out, is already reading it. *"Dear Daniel—"*

"Ba—"

Then he flings the letter to the grass. I've lost all vision. The world is a blur. His arms stutter toward me. Finally, I bring myself to look at his face.

He's laughing. Oh God. My heart swells, shoving my lungs against my rib cage and ratcheting my pulse so high I'm dizzy. I did it. All this time, and I did it. It's real.

He reaches out and pats me awkwardly on then—he can't contain himself—crushes me in a back, embarrassed, smoothing his shirt. His eyes

"Congratulations, Daniel," he says, fighting steady. "Everything is going to be all right for you

It's real. I did it. I can picture it: my whole life ra beam out from this one point.

I got a scholarship beyond what I let myself h my parents can't pay a dime, I'm going. Inside, I te of the letter. He doesn't answer right away, and eve it's because he's in SAT tutoring, there's an empty excitement and relief that's waiting for him. A few must be hiding his phone from his tutor—his mes ing in:

Holy shit Cheng!!!!!!!!!!!!!!
You did it!!!!!!!!!!!!!!!!!!!!!!!
I effing told you
Man you were so worried, but I told you
Okay draw me something and sign and date it, go
money off that someday when you're famous
Yo actually draw me like ten things, 10x the $$$$

That empty space fills, spills over. I can't keep t face.

Maybe I will draw him something. There's a pu that's carried over from opening the letter. I pull out

"Crawling all over our sidewalks," he muttered. He jabbed his cane toward me and raised his voice. "You don't own this neighborhood. It's not yours to make a mess all over. That's the problem with you people. You think you can come in here and take over. You tell your parents we don't want you here. You go back where you came from."

The world closed around me. I went inside. I never saw him again.

I never told anyone about it (what would I say?), but for days after that I tried to draw him. I probably had some vague idea that I could turn him into some kind of caricature, just a random old guy frothing at the mouth who didn't matter. Maybe you think if you can take something you're bothered by and make it your own somehow you sap it of its power. So I worked on that sneer on his face as he looked at me, those shoulders puffed up with his own rightness. I drew pages and pages of him, and I named him Mr. X.

But he wouldn't fade away. Now he leers at me from several places on my wall, which I've been drawing on with Sharpies since we moved in, and whispers all the uglier things inside my head. I don't know why I keep him around. I guess I think art should probe the things you're afraid of and the things you can't let go of, but maybe that's just because deep down I want to believe you can conquer them, which might not actually be true.

Anyway. Lately I'm a reverse Midas, everything I touch turning to crap, and so good old Mr. X has been louder lately: *You're a fraud, you peaked, it's all downhill from here. The world doesn't need your art. Get a real job.*

But now I have concrete proof I'm not a fraud, or at the very least I'm an extremely convincing one. Which should change everything, right? The fog should lift.

I just need to start producing again—prove getting in wasn't a fluke. Prove I do have the future I'm supposed to after all. Prove I deserve my future, at the very least. Not everyone gets one; I know that. It isn't something you can squander.

⸱ ˙ ᵒ

"Let's surprise her."

"Huh?" I look up. My dad's hovering in my doorway, joy radiating off him. He's changed into khakis and a collared shirt, his hair combed. I say, "Where are you going?"

"We'll go to dinner to celebrate when your mother gets home. We'll surprise her."

My dad has always loved surprises. Once, the summer I was eleven, he woke me up in the middle of the night and brought me, groggy, into the garage. On top of his car there was a telltale white paper sack, and he pointed to it.

"I went to Donut Wheel," he said. "A bribe for you for after."

"Um, for after—"

"Daniel." He looked very serious. "On Saturday is Robin Cheung's wedding."

My parents had been taking a ballroom dance class at the rec center for a few years; it was my mom's favorite hobby. (Weird, but: she also, every Summer Olympics, arranges her sleep schedule around the rhythmic gymnastics.) Their friends' son was getting married and my mom had at one point expressed a shy desire to show off the fox-trot they were learning at the wedding, but my dad, apparently, was having trouble with the moves.

"So fast," he complained. The naked light bulb swayed overhead, throwing his shadow self across the bare wooden walls. I was barefoot and in my pajamas. "The tango I can do, the cha-cha, but this one—too fast."

"Um, so you want me to—"

"I bought you donuts," he said quickly, seeing the look on my face. "What else do you want me to buy? I'll buy you new pens. Do you want new pens? I'll buy you whatever you want. And I won't tell your friends. I promise."

I am easily bought. I spent all night out there with him, my elbow resting on his and our hands interlaced as he led me around and around the concrete, his jaw tight with concentration. That weekend at the wedding—it was in the banquet hall at Dynasty, steamed bass and lobster noodles and pink neon uplights that made the lines of everyone's faces look dramatic and sharp—I could see him tapping his fingers impatiently all through the dinner, all through the toasts. When the music started, he leapt up and held out a hand to my mom. I watched them on the dance floor, holding my breath, waiting to see if he'd pull it off. He did. Afterward she was beaming and out of breath, and they went to the open bar and came back with Manhattans for them and a Coke for me and they excitedly recapped all their steps, complimenting each other on their technique and form. I won't lie: it was pretty damn cute. I want them to be that way—that sparkling, that effervescent—all the time.

"She will be so happy, Daniel," he says now. "Can you imagine?" He pats his pocket for his phone. "Should we video her when you tell her?"

"Um—no?"

"She might never be so happy again. Maybe we'll want it to look at later to remember."

"That's so fatalistic, Ba." I get up and follow him out to the living room. "You want me to cook something for dinner instead? I think there's pork chops in the freezer." The one thing I can make: turn on pan, drop meat, cook.

He brushes it away. "No, no, tonight we'll celebrate. When she gets home."

My mom takes care of twin six-year-olds and a four-year-old for a family named the Lis up in the hills vaguely by where Harry lives. We wait for her on the couch. Usually my dad watches mostly news, scanning the screen like he can ward off disaster by watching it happen to other people, but today *Planet Earth* is on instead.

I grab a blanket from the armchair and wrap myself in it like a burrito. It's been cold these days, and freezing, always freezing in the house, because my parents refuse to turn the heat on. I wear three layers to bed. Last year, when I drew a portrait of my mom, I made one of her eyes the thermostat, turned down all the way to fifty-five. I pull my blanket tighter and let myself imagine living in a (warm, heated) RISD dorm next year. Of all the people who applied, so many people who've probably been practicing their craft all their lives— they chose me.

My dad keeps glancing at the clock, and I can feel him getting restless as it traipses toward six-fifteen. It's a minor emergency to both my parents whenever the other is late getting home, and I know my dad will take his phone from his pocket and tap his fingers against it, ready to call to check on her, right at six-sixteen.

"They were doing roadwork on Rainbow," I say.

"Hm?"

I motion toward his phone. "If she's late. That's probably why."

"Oh. Yes." But he doesn't look any more relaxed. Then, at six-fourteen, we hear the garage door open, and my dad jumps up, his face lighting up again. "Where's your letter?"

"It's on the table."

"Where's my phone?"

He's still patting the couch cushions looking for it when my mom comes in. He rises from the couch, smiling nervously, and then he whips out the phone—it was in his pocket after all—to record. "Anna—Daniel has news for you."

"News? You have news?" My mom drops her purse and her bags of groceries from Marina. I watch the way their handles go flat, like a dog's ears when it's listening. "You got in?" She clutches my sleeve. "Did you get in? Did you—"

I flirt with the idea of pretending I didn't, of trying to make her think it was bad news, but in the end I can't hold back my grin. Her hands fly to her mouth, covering her smile, and her eyes fill with tears.

"He did it!" my dad yells from behind his phone like we're a hundred yards away, his voice bouncing back at us off the walls and hardwood floor. This video (which he'll watch on loop; I know him) is going to be all over the place, jiggling and blurred. He makes me show off the letter and hug my mom while he's filming. My mom cries.

We go to Santa Clara for Korean barbecue, and I drive, because for whatever reason they always have me drive when we're together. It's not far, fifteen minutes, but you always kind of feel it when you're leaving Cupertino, a bubble piercing. Cupertino's mostly residential neighborhoods and then strip malls with things like the kind of American-y diner that probably used to be big here back when it was all orchards and white people, or the Asian restaurants/bakeries/tutoring centers/passport services/et cetera. It's also its own world—land of overachieving kids of tech titans, of badminton clubs and test-prep empires and restaurants jockeying for Yelp reviews and volunteer corps run by freshmen who both care about the world but also care about establishing a long-term commitment to a cause they can point to on their college apps. When we first moved here from

Austin, I remember being weirded out by how Asian it was. And how everyone has money, too, but mostly in a more closet way than they do in Texas—here you can drop two million on a normal-looking three-bedroom house, so it's not something you necessarily notice right away the way you notice it when someone has a giant mansion on Lake Austin. (Harry's house is an exception—he has two sisters and both his grandfathers live with them, and all of them have their own bedroom and I think there are at least two other bedrooms no one's using.) I don't think anyone I know needs financial aid for college. I don't think anyone I know even needs loans.

It's packed inside the restaurant, but a table opens up just as we're coming in and my parents smile and smile like it's some kind of miracle. Already I'm sad for when the joy of this wears off, becomes everyday. It hasn't been like this with them in I don't even know how long.

The waitress comes and sets the laminated menus in front of us. My dad squares his shoulders and says, to my mom, "Now?" Over their menus, my parents exchange a long look. I say, "What?"

They both ignore me. Then my mom gives a nearly imperceptible nod, and my dad says, "Daniel, we have something for you."

He pulls out a plastic Ranch 99 bag with something inside it. I saw him bring it in, but it didn't register at the time. He hands it to me across the table. "Open it."

"It's for good luck," my mom says. They've taped the bag shut. My family's not the wrapping-paper type.

Inside it's a sweatshirt, the expensive embroidered kind, that says *RISD*. They forgot to take the price tag off. It cost nearly seventy dollars.

"Try it on," my dad says, beaming, so I shove my seat back far enough that I can shrug into the sweatshirt. It has that new look, the creases still showing where it was folded, and it's at least two sizes too big—for whatever reason both my parents think bigger clothes are practical, maybe because you get more fabric for your money or something—and just enthusiastic enough to look dorky. That, or dickish, like I'm the kind of guy who's going to work it into conversation every chance he gets that I'm going to my first-choice art school. My dad says, "What do you think?"

They must have bought this when I applied, must have had it waiting all along. I feel my eyes filling.

"It's great," I say, and put on the biggest smile I can muster. I try to keep that image of the tape on the bag, those creases like he's been clutching it close, to draw later on. "Wow. Thanks. I love it."

"Good." My dad meets my mom's eyes and smiles. "This is so big, Daniel. This is—" His voice breaks, and he swipes at his eyes. "This is everything we wanted."

"You will have the future we hoped for," my mom says. Her eyes are shining at me.

My dad unfolds his napkin into his lap, then smooths it out on the table and refolds it. It looks lumpy and inexact. He glances up at us, like he's going to say something. My mom's eyes are still glittering, but it suspends a little as she looks at him, leaves open space for something like alarm to flash across her face. "What is it?"

He draws a long breath. He looks back and forth between us and starts to speak, but then he stops himself, covering it with a smile. "Nothing. It can wait."

I say, "No, what was it?"

"Another time." He raises his glass of water. "To Daniel. Our beloved son."

"To Daniel," my mom echoes after a second or two, and they clink their glasses against mine.

After that we spend nearly ten minutes settling on our order, and I keep the sweatshirt on until my mom fusses in this proud way and tells me I should take it off, that I don't want to spill anything on it. The waitress hovers by our table, impatient, and I give her an apologetic smile, but I'm not actually sorry. Because these are the best kind of moments: all of us plotting what we'll eat, that comfort you can slip into with the people who know you best, who love you with a fierceness you'll probably never understand.

I'm lucky. I've always been.

T W O

wake up early to get ready for the Journalism field trip to San Francisco that Regina's making us all go on, and there's a note on the kitchen table, my mom's loopy lettering scrawled on the back of a junk mail envelope saying my parents went to Costco. They always come back weekend mornings laden with cardboard flats of frozen chicken breasts and dumplings and greens.

I'm low on cash, like always, so I should bring something to the city in case I get hungry. I'm pretty sure I remember seeing packs of beef jerky in the hall closet, and so I go to look. When I open the closet door, a barely contained twelve-pack of Costco paper towels tumbles out. My parents—I'll just put this out there—are like one Great Depression away from being full-on hoarders. They keep everything. They've always been too Asian to throw away things like plastic bags, but they also keep stuff like expired coupons just in case, plastic utensils and packets of condiments that come with fast food, single socks where the other one's missing.

I start to put the paper towels back. Behind where they were stuffed is this medium-size box labeled with just my dad's name. And something about the careful, centered way my dad's name is lettered on, like someone took the time to do it, and also the way the box is jammed in the closet like it's supposed to be out of sight, catch my attention. I pull it out to look at.

It's taped, and I peel the tape up gently so none of the box comes off with it. Inside there's a little stuffed bear I used to play with that I haven't seen in years. My dad gave him to me when we moved to California, and I named him Zhu Zhu, which at the time I thought was hilarious, a bear named *Pig*. I hold him a moment, finger his synthetic fur, and get that rush of nostalgia, your memories compressed into some intangible feeling mixed with the searing longing you get for a time that's lost to you now. For a long time after I outgrew Zhu Zhu, my dad kept him on his pillow. I'm kind of touched my dad saved him.

Zhu Zhu was resting on the type of piles of clutter that steadily collect everywhere on our counters and in our drawers: a few old carbon copies of checks made out to people I haven't heard of and a handful of what look like some kind of loan documents, a sleeve of pictures that must be from China—some roads and scenes from a car trip, a high-rise apartment building, a pharmacy—and two small unsigned watercolors, good but not quite professional, one of a dark blue bird and one of a multicolored dragon, not at all the kind of art I've ever known my dad to collect. I flip the dragon one over to see if there's anything on the back, but it's blank. Underneath all that is a bulging file in a yellowed rubber band labeled, in my dad's handwriting, *Ballards*. When I slide off the rubber band, a news clipping flutters out onto my desk. It's a real estate article about a house for sale in Atherton, which is where all the venture capitalists live, thirty or so minutes north of here.

I try to lay everything out on my desk, but there are too many papers, and that's where things get—weird. Nearly everything is about a guy named Clay Ballard. There are a few dozen pictures printed off what looks like a Google Images search: some headshots, him at some kind of awards banquet or something shaking hands with a balding man in a suit, a picture of him and his wife at some kind of gala. He looks like a generic white dad—mostly trim, straight white teeth, kind of weathered-looking like maybe he plays a lot of golf. There are all kinds of printouts of public records and also ones that I think you'd actually have to, like, go to some kind of city office to get—a marriage license, copies of a sale of a home in Atherton, a six-bedroom mansion with a wine cellar and a guesthouse that sold for seven million dollars. Toward the bottom there are a few printouts on Sheila Ballard, who I assume must be his wife.

I've never seen either of them or heard their names come up once. I don't know what to make of it. They aren't anyone from UT or either of the labs at San José State that my dad worked with, and the sheer volume of it all, the obsessive detail, is staggering.

In the bottom of the box there are a bunch of letters in Chinese. For all the years of Chinese school I sat through on Saturdays as a kid (and despite the fact that my parents hardly speak English at home), I still can barely read Chinese worth crap, and it isn't until I paw through them, and then in one of them there's a drawing—a child, a grubby fist grabbing a rice paddle—that I realize these must be letters from my grandfather, that probably those watercolors were his too, and this drawing is my sister. I go cold and then hot all over all in a split second, and my heart stutters against my chest. It feels like meeting ghosts.

I'm an only child now, and thought I was one for a long time, but I was supposed to have a sister. Did have a sister, actually, who came and then died before me, a sister who exists now in her absence. I know almost nothing about her except the very fact of her.

I've spoken with my parents about this exactly once. When we moved here in kindergarten, I found drawings of her lodged in one of my parents' old books and brought it to my mom to ask who it was. My mom was in her garden, her garden gloves pulled over her sleeves and her face shielded by her giant plastic visor, when I brought the pictures out to her.

"Who drew these?" I asked.

She froze for a moment and grabbed the papers, the color pooling like watercolor in her cheeks. Her mouth worked without sound. "Where did you find this?"

"In the garage."

She closed her eyes. Her lips were trembling. "It's—that was not for you to find."

"Did you draw them?"

"No. Your grandfather."

I'd never known that any of my relatives liked to draw, too. My parents never brought it up. I'd wished they had. "Who is it? It's not me, right?"

"Another baby."

"Another—*your* baby?"

She nodded.

"And Ba's?"

"Yes."

"So I have a brother? Or—"

"No. Sister. Dead."

All my life I'd been an only child, and in that moment the person I'd been disappeared. The world tilted around me. "When?"

"In Wuhan." She opened her eyes without looking at me. "Before you."

She didn't mean to tell me, and if I hadn't caught her so completely off guard, I don't think she ever would have. Maybe if she'd had more time she would've come up with a better story. She could have told me the baby was her, or my dad, or a friend. I would've believed her.

That was the first time I ever saw her have a panic attack: there in front of me she went clammy and pale, and she rocked forward and dropped her trowel and clutched her chest. I thought she would die. I thought it was my fault.

Afterward she felt bad about it, I think—she was brusque in that way she gets when you make too much of a fuss over her, and she told me not to tell my dad any of it. I didn't. And I never brought up my sister again.

I've never stopped thinking about her, though. The question that most consumed me at first—still does a lot of the time—was what happened. Every time I heard sirens I thought about her, imagining her falling from an open window or getting struck by a car. When I learned to swim, I wondered if she'd drowned. In AP Bio this fall we studied genetic diseases and I spent the whole unit low-key worrying that my parents couldn't bring themselves to tell me that I too had whatever degenerative and fatal disease had killed my sister. Whenever I see headlines of kidnappings or child abuse I wonder if she was old enough to realize what was happening to her, whatever it was.

And I wonder about the rest of it, too. I wonder where it happened. I wonder if they held her body. I wonder when she was born and how much older than me she would've been. I wonder what her name was. When we moved to California, my parents changed our last name from Tseng to Cheng because it was easier for Americans to pronounce (I still remember my mom's tight smile every time white people mangled *Tseng*, the same way she reacted once when some of the other kids spoke nonsense syllables at me pretending it was Chinese or when people spoke loudly and slowly to her like she was a child), and I think about that sometimes now, bubbling in my name on Scantrons or typing it for college forms—how my sister died with a name the rest of us gave up. Sometimes I imagine her older, nine or ten or fifteen or twenty or however old she'd be now. And I imagine her filling all the air in every room of the house.

I look at my grandfather's drawings in the letters for a long time. They're good—confident pen strokes, not a single extraneous one.

The rest of it, obviously, I understand why he'd keep—Zhu Zhu, the letters from my grandfather. But that file on the Ballards is beyond my understanding, and it makes me wonder. I guess I didn't necessarily think I knew their whole story; I knew I didn't. I just never thought there might be that much more to know.

       »   ∾   ๏

My parents come back from Costco weighted down with bags, and I go out to help unload everything from the car. In the back seat there are three paper sample cups my mom saved me: a square inch of coffee cake, seven Jelly Bellys, a teriyaki meatball. That careful way they're balanced there—I take a picture with my phone to draw sometime later before hauling the bags inside.

They brought home frozen burritos, and I microwave one while I'm waiting for Harry. My mom goes out into her garden, and through the window I can see her kneeling to check on her kabochas. She has six raised garden beds my dad and I helped her make, pomegranate and persimmon and citrus trees she planted when we first moved in, an herb garden that runs along the back fence, and in the front yard all her favorite flowers: hydrangeas and gardenias and tuberoses in the spring. Our house itself is old and run-down, and I remember what the yard looked like when we first moved in—hard, parched dirt and dead weeds, the yard of an old couple who drew the curtains and never looked outside. One of my bedroom windows looks out on the backyard and sometimes outside when she thinks no one's watching I see my mom stand up with her hands on her hips and survey it all, satisfied and proud and amazed.

My dad sits down at the kitchen table with the laptop, typing what I can see from the short lines of text is some kind of list. He adores lists. Once, when I was a kid, I found a notepad on his desk with this one: *School. Friend. Sport interest. What are your favorite celebrity. Imagination and opinion.* The list was titled *Question to ask Daniel for conversation.* None of his lists, though, ever felt as obsessively gathered as what I found in the closet.

When the microwave beeps I say, "Hey, Ba, question—who are the Ballards?"

His head snaps toward me. "Excuse me?"

"I was just wondering. I, ah, found a box of yours in the closet with some files—"

His face lights up. Not in the way you say it when you mean someone's happy, but more like an explosion in the night—a sudden flash of heat and noise.

He rises. "Were you looking through my belongings?"

"No. I saw it in the closet. I was looking for beef jerky."

"Why did you go into that box? It was taped shut. You went into my personal things without permission."

I put up my hands. "I didn't know what it was. I thought—"

"Daniel, you know better. I don't want to hear about it again. And I don't want you to ever bring that name up with your mother. Is that clear? Don't ever—"

My mom comes in through the sliding door then, holding a bunch of beets, and my dad stops. Did he say not to bring it up with her because it's something she doesn't know about, or something she does? I hear the familiar sound of Harry's car pulling into the driveway, and hoist myself off the chair.

"I'm going," I say. "Bye."

They both start talking at the same time. "Where are you—" my mom says, and my dad says, "Did we say you could—"

"I'm going with Harry." I edge toward the door. "I asked you already earlier in the week."

"Where are you going?"

"Just to his house."

"What for?"

"Just school stuff."

They exchange that look that means they're weighing something I've asked for against all the threats of the world—a cell network glitch that means they can't reach me if they need to, a blind curve up in the hills by Harry's house. "Well, all right." My mom drops her beets in the sink. "Come back in an hour."

I definitely can't get to San Francisco and then back in an hour. "We have to work on some Journalism stuff, so it's going to take all morning. Maybe until after lunch."

"Aiya, Daniel, I don't like you to be gone so much. If something happens, and we can't call you—"

"I know." I've long since stopped trying to argue or to promise that nothing will ever happen, even when I'm going to be just a few minutes away. "I'll be careful."

"Well—" She makes a *tsk*ing sound with her tongue. "All right. Go study with Harry. Just be careful."

"Wait," my dad says. He looks around, his voice infected with false cheer, like he wasn't just mad at me. "Where's your sweatshirt? Wear it to show Harry. Show it off."

"Oh, ah, right." It's on the kitchen table (I left it there last night, and someone, probably my mom, folded it carefully with the letters facing out), and I shrug it on. "Look good?"

"Perfect." My dad smiles, a real smile; the sweatshirt's worked its magic. "Have a good time."

⋅　　⋅　　　⋅

I make it outside just as Harry's coming up our walkway (Harry isn't the kind of person who just pulls up and honks, even if he's been your best friend four years), and I hustle him back into the car.

"I didn't want you getting all chatty with my parents," I say over his complaining.

"Aw, your parents love me."

I roll my eyes. It's true, though; all parents love him. "Well, too bad for them I'm too selfish to let you."

"You're not selfish."

"In your professional opinion."

"Don't get so sarcastic. You're, like, the opposite of a selfish person. It's a compliment."

I feel the words blooming on my cheeks. "I just didn't want them roping you into a conversation. I know you're a shitty liar."

"What would I have to lie about?"

"I told them we're just going to your house." Harry lives too far up in the hills to walk, so I always get a ride if I'm going up there.

"You know how they are. They'd flip out if I said I wanted to go to San Francisco." Also, it's true: Harry lies terribly. At his core, I think, he's too noble to have any real sense of self-preservation.

Inside the car, Harry unbuttons the cuffs of his sleeves and rolls them in precise, even segments before laying his hands on the steering wheel. A few times—I would die before I told him this—I've sketched his forearms, the map his veins trace over them, the tan he keeps even in winter. He says, "I am not a shitty liar."

I click my seat belt on. "Um, you can't even say that without your voice getting all weird and defensive, so I think I've made my case. Hey—question." As he backs onto the street, I tell him about my dad's files. "That's not weird, right?"

"Uh, a stalkery box of information about some rando? It's definitely weird."

"You think so?" I make a face. I wanted him to tell me I was overreacting.

"Yeah, but your parents have always been weird about things."

"What's that supposed to mean?"

"It's weird how they've never once taken you home to China, for one thing. Haven't you been, like, all over the US and—"

"I think China's probably just too sad for them now."

"I guess I could see that, yeah." He shrugs. "Still. They just kind of seem like people with secrets. You went years without knowing you even had a sister, right? And don't they still never talk about her?" Check and check. "Who were the people?"

"Nobody I know. I don't even know how my parents would know them." It's probably nothing. All the same the road blurs in front of me a second, and I feel a little bit carsick. "So you'd maybe worry at least a little, then?"

"If someone explicitly told me not to? It's like if I say don't picture me naked—what's the first thing you do?"

My cheeks go hot, and then the rest of me. It's enough to pull me back from the ledge, though, back onto solid ground. I say, "I could've done without that visual, thanks."

He grins. "Be nice. Don't make me pull over." We stop at a light on Stelling, and he skims his eyes over me. "Hey, so, uh . . . nice sweatshirt."

"Yep." That was definitely not a compliment. I swear if he says one word about my sweatshirt, I'll kick his ass.

"That new?"

"Yep," I say again. I don't need Harry to confirm for me that in its hugeness and overenthusiastic newness it looks as dweeby as I know it does. I want the gift my parents gave me to be worth what they paid for it, worth how excited they were.

"Rocking those creases. Are you, uh, wearing that when we get there?"

I wasn't going to, I was going to take it off once I got in the car, but as soon as he says it my plans make an abrupt U-turn. With any luck he'll spend the whole ride worrying every single person he sees today will think, *Why is Harry Wong best friends with a loser in a giant creased sweatshirt?* I will wear this sweatshirt at him the entire day. "Yeah. Why?"

"It just looks so . . . new."

I know this about Harry: he thinks it's pathetic in an overeager kind of way to wear anything right after you bought it, or at least to look like you did, so every time he gets something new he washes it twice before he puts it on. "It is new."

He takes his hands off the wheel to hold them up in defeat. "Okay, whatever. You do you."

"You're so generous. Has anyone ever told you that? *So* generous."

"Says the guy getting a free ride to San Francisco."

I roll my eyes. "You'd be going anyway."

"Maybe I wouldn't. Maybe I'm just going because you'd be stranded at home otherwise."

"Okay, (a), you would definitely go because otherwise Regina would kill you, and (b), don't pretend like you're not glad to have an excuse. What would you be doing at home all day instead? Going to tutoring?"

He grins in that self-deprecating way of his, his eyes crinkling up. It is, I'll admit, one of the more charming habits he has. "For *your* information, I'd be probably going hog wild studying for the SAT IIs. So hold up on your smugness there."

He probably would be, too. There is basically nothing Harry won't do in service of Princeton, which is the only Ivy that rejected his sister and, therefore, the only school he wants. It's why he's the managing editor of our school paper, second-in-command to Regina, despite being someone who has no real love of writing and who (I'll just say it) has a crap eye for design. He's also, this year: ASB president, treasurer of National Honor Society, and the director of the Students Reaching Out tutoring club. He got a near-perfect score on his SATs and has a 4.8 GPA and is nationally ranked (low, but still) in tennis doubles. And this is still as true as it's been as long as I've known him: he's always the most popular guy in any room he's in. When I list it all out like that I kind of remember why I used to really hate him.

When he pulls onto Regina's street he looks in the rearview mirror like he's making sure no one's in the back seat listening and says, "Has Regina seemed kind of—off to you lately?"

"What do you mean off? You see her more than I do."

"Yeah, but you guys talk. Maybe I'm just imagining it."

I don't think he's imagining it. "We don't talk that much lately."

"Ah," he says. "Did you know she stopped going to her church?"

"Really? I didn't know that."

"Yeah. And, I mean—the one year's coming up, so—"

I feel that same old catch in my heart. "Right."

"On March seventh."

"I know when it is."

He glances at me in a way I can't quite read. I feel the color rise in my cheeks. He says, "Regina wants to put something in the paper."

"Yeah, no, they will definitely not let us put something in the paper."

"You don't think if—"

"No. Definitely not. Zero chance."

"Yeah, you're right." He sighs. "Such bullshit. She really wants to. You know how she is."

I do know how she is. Except maybe that isn't true; I know how she used to be.

He gets out of the car to go knock, and they come back together. Regina looks put together as always, in bright lipstick, tight dark pants, a billowy white top, and a dark floppy hat that makes her look vaguely 1920s-ish. She has a model's high, angular cheekbones and full lips—she's striking, and I've always liked drawing her. (For her part, she dislikes being drawn. I think it makes her self-conscious.) She's pretty in that way that makes people assume your life is going well.

I open the door to give her the front seat, but she waves me off. I smile hello, hold my breath a little. She slides into the back seat.

"Congratulations on RISD, Danny," she says in a way I can't call anything other than nice, but that also doesn't exactly flood the car with warmth. "You've wanted this for so long."

I say, "Thanks, Reg." And I think how last year I would've told her right away about all those files I found, too.

Then, like she read my mind, she leans forward and touches my elbow. "I knew you'd get in." And maybe that's the most she has right now. Maybe I shouldn't read into it.

"You think this'll be the kind of talk where they have like donuts or anything?" Harry says. "Or you think we have time to stop somewhere?"

Regina rolls her eyes. "No and no. We can't be late. Everyone probably hates me already for making them go to this."

He grins at her in the rearview mirror. "Technically it's not too late to cancel."

"The talk sounds important, right?" Harry was teasing—he's careful around her a lot these days—but Regina says it as if he wasn't. "I just want to make sure we know we have the right to say what we want."

"Pretty sure people are mostly still writing about, like, their buddies on the tennis team," I say lightly. Harry glares at me. I must have gotten the tone wrong.

"Mostly, sure, but what about the times they're not? It's like that stupid story about starfish," she says, adjusting her seat belt. "There's hundreds stranded on the beach and you throw a few back because it makes a difference to those particular few."

"Aw, you think that's stupid?" Harry says. "I think it's kind of nice."

"It's a parable of rampant apathy. Why is there only one guy out there rescuing millions of suffocating starfish? It's a story about how horrible things happen because ninety-nine point nine percent of people can't be bothered."

"Not you," Harry says cheerfully. He twists around and backs out of the driveway. "There is nothing too small for you to be bothered by."

If I'm being honest, I still don't totally get the two of them, and they've been together since sophomore year. I will concede that in a way it felt weirdly inevitable, a mash-up of ambition and popularity and attractiveness, a test-tube match, all roads leading to each other. Harry asked her to homecoming—a flash mob, a bouquet of peonies because that's her favorite flower, a platter of chocolate-covered strawberries with letters that spelled *YOU + ME?*—and then after that they just kind of stayed together, swapped all their profile pictures to ones of the two of them, and in a way it felt weird that they'd ever been separate entities altogether.

But then I always wondered, always still wonder. All that time last year when they were ensconced together—what all happened between them? I can't exactly imagine her breaking down in front of him, pouring her heart out to him, and from comments he makes sometimes I don't think she ever really did. And, like—does he think of her first all the time? She's who he imagines calling first when he gets his letter from Princeton, the audience he pictures when he's collecting all the important and also the stupid insignificant parts of his day to give to someone? When he imagines disasters happening, cancer or nuclear fallout or the Big One we're supposed to get in California, at night when it's quiet and he feels all the weight of his own life pressing in on him, she's the lurch in his stomach and the hand he gropes around for in the dark?

But maybe it's just that I don't want to see it. I would do anything for Harry—and have—and sometimes I picture what it would look like to come up against the hard wall of the limits of how far he'd be willing to go for me.

Which I know is crappy. They're together. And Regina's my friend too. At least, I think she still is.

"Anyway, no one hates you for making us go," Harry says. "It'll be interesting to hear the guy talk."

"It should be. I heard his TED talk about all the things at schools that get censored," she says. "Like banned books and dress code issues. And . . ."

She trails off. We both know what she means, though; there's not a single person in our grade who doesn't recognize that tentative pause, the guilt you always feel plunging everyone around you back into the same dark territory. You always wonder if people just want to forget.

I wait to see then if she'll trust me with what she told Harry, the story she's planning to write. She changes the subject instead, and we talk about personal statements for the next ten or twelve miles north.

We hit traffic then, a sea of red taillights, and Harry swears softly under his breath. He can give a speech in front of all two thousand people at our school, he can go months without saying anything negative about another person, but it's always been the little things that set him off—stick him in traffic, or let his phone run out of battery, and it's like his whole conception of the world collapses: how is this possibly happening to him?

It's clear and cool when we get into San Francisco, the streets swollen—brogrammers in their gym clothes, Asian grandmas carrying pink bakery bags, tourists with their fanny packs and DSLRs, white moms in yoga pants pushing bulky strollers with Philz cups in the cup holders. We park in the Portsmouth Square garage and emerge from the rickety elevator back into the sunlight among all the kids clambering up play structures and the Chinese grandfathers playing chess. Regina, who is excellent at time management and therefore looked up walking directions while we were in the elevator, strides toward the corner so fast it takes me and Harry a few seconds to catch up.

Regina could do anything, I think, become a doctor or an engineer or the lawyer her parents want, but she's dreamed her entire life of going to Northwestern, which has the best journalism program in the nation, and becoming a reporter. She can spend literally hours reading through headlines and going down current-events rabbit holes. She told me once when she was small she knew the names of TV anchors before she did her grandparents and relatives. But reporters make, like, ten dollars, and her parents have made it abundantly clear they have no interest in sending her to major in communications or broadcast journalism. She's supposed to go into pre-law.

"I wish my parents would've moved here instead," Regina says as Google Maps steers us through a back alley, the word *DEFIANCE* tagged across the wall in a bright, arresting blue. I like the lines of the lettering, the way they reach around themselves and keep your gaze captive. "I'm so ready to be done with Cupertino."

"Really? You like this better?" Harry says, gesturing toward a clump of garbage cans. "It smells like piss."

"I don't mean I wish they'd moved *right* here to this alley. But, yes, I like it better."

"Why? It's, like, dirty here. I bet you'll miss Cupertino when you're gone."

We're walking fast still, and she's a little out of breath. "Really? I'll miss driving down the street and seeing nothing but tutoring centers? I'll miss everyone else's parents knowing exactly what I got on my SATs and teachers having to commute from like Morgan Hill because Cupertino is full of rich NIMBYs who refuse to build more housing? I'll miss the hundred percent rule?"

Cupertino's hundred percent rule is this: if you go out in Cupertino, there's a hundred percent chance you'll see someone you know. (Its corollary is the two hundred percent rule, which is that if you're wearing pj's/haven't showered, your odds double.)

"Come on, it's not all bad. Other cities are just easy to romanticize because we don't live in them. It would be a pain to live in San Francisco. There's like zero parking."

"People should use transit more often anyway. Didn't your dad vote against high-speed—"

"Okay, yes, but that's just because the particular proposal wasn't fiscally responsible. He's working on another one." Harry always gets defensive about his dad, even though I know it's not like he agrees with him all the time anyway. (Mr. Wong retired after making a bunch of money and went into politics and is a state senator now, after a term on the school board and two as our mayor.) "But also, people like you there. You know? It feels kind of crappy to talk about how much you hate it when that's where all your friends are."

"When do Northwestern decisions come out?" I say quickly, before she has to answer him—I recognize that slight rise in his voice.

"I don't know exactly when," she says. I'm pretty sure she's lying. "Sometime in the spring. I doubt I'll get in. Even if I do my parents probably won't let me go."

"I'm sure you'll get in. I hope it all works out okay," I say. Which—I can hear how formal it sounds. I feel like that sometimes with her now, stiff and awkward and overly careful. One time in junior high Sandra told me her irrational fear was that she'd drop a diary with all her secrets in it. *You keep a diary like that?* I'd said, surprised—I couldn't imagine her having the patience—and she laughed. *Of course not, loser. I said it was an irrational fear.* But that's how it feels with Regina sometimes now, too, that I'm worried I'll slip and just randomly blurt out everything I'm guilty of.

"You ever been to Northwestern?" Harry says to me. "It's like— rich white kid central. It's different from Cupertino, sure, but maybe it's not better. Most places aren't. Everywhere's just different."

"You've been there?" she says. She knows he hasn't.

"I've looked it up."

"You'd live here forever, wouldn't you?"

"I mean, yeah, it's a nice place to live."

"Nice like what? Nice like easy?"

"Sure." He tries to mask it with a smile, but there's a tightness in his voice. "It makes sense. You know what's expected. I like people to tell me what they want from me, sue me. It's fine here."

We're meeting everyone outside the International Hall on Larkin. I was maybe 30 percent nervous everyone would bail at the last minute, but nearly everyone's there already by the time we show up. Regina slips into what I think of as her Editor Mode—circling the crowds with a smile for everyone and this certain, ardent way of listening to people, even just in throwaway conversation, that makes you feel like she's incredibly glad you're there.

Reemu Kapoor turns around and lights up when she sees me. "Danny! You got into RISD!" She gives me a hug. "That's so awesome."

Harry grins. "I, uh, maybe told people."

And then a crush of people all surround me, jostling and high-fiving and hugging. Harry wasn't kidding. I think literally everyone comes up to me to say congratulations, weaving me into their net of goodwill. I can feel my face going all red, my smile stretching wide enough that it starts to hurt.

I still can't quite wrap my head around the fact that this whole universe we've inhabited nearly all our lives is going to dissolve itself in just six months, all of us flung to the far reaches of the world. I'm not like Regina—I love Cupertino. I love the trees and the quiet streets and the way the hills glow behind everything in the late afternoon; I love how contained it all is, how you can spend your whole life in a two- or three-mile radius and not feel like you're missing very much. I love the people at school. I even love the hundred percent rule.

Maybe Regina blames Cupertino, though. You can play what-ifs forever. Maybe everything would've been different in a different place, with different people, with different pressures. I can't fault her for wondering. I wonder too.

The talk is behind schedule; the doors still haven't opened. There are maybe a few dozen other people here, not exactly the crowd that screams *must-see event!!* Behind me Chris Young and Andrew Hatmaker are getting bored.

"This talk better blow my mind," Chris says. "It better change—"

"Why?" Harry says sharply, whirling around to stare at Chris. His eyebrows go up and stay there.

"Come on, there's nothing else you'd rather be doing with your Saturday?" Chris says. In middle school Chris was in love with Regina. He used to corner me in the locker room sometimes and demand to know whether I was dating her.

"I'm in this great city with a lot of friends, so yeah, I'd say this is pretty good."

"I wanted to sleep in."

"Sucks to your assmar, then, doesn't it?" Harry's tone is friendly, but his expression is hard. "I thought it was a really good idea Regina came up with."

Chris backs down. "Right," he says. "Yeah, okay." He offers Harry a smile. Harry doesn't return it, and stares him down a few more seconds before turning back around. That's new since March with Harry, that hair-trigger protectiveness at the slightest hint anyone might be somehow in opposition to something, anything, Regina wants.

The doors open then, and we go in. At the front of the room there's a thirtyish white guy in a blazer writing something behind a podium. The only three sophomores in Journalism, Esther Rhee and Lori Choi and Maureen Chong, sit in front of me. Esther has a fashion blog, and every now and then I glance at it—she has a good eye, lots of clean text and white space, whimsical outfits with Bible verses Photoshopped along the borders and sale alerts and every now and then posts about fighting child trafficking. She always writes feature stories, usually about people she knows going on missions trips or spearheading volunteering orgs.

I see Esther's expression change when the first slide goes up, the ACLU logo, and she leans over and whispers something to Lori and Maureen. They're all close friends, insular in a way that feels familiar to me. (Also, I'm like 95 percent sure they all have a thing for Harry.) The three of them squint at the screen and duck their heads together, conferring in the way you do when you don't want anyone else to hear what you're saying. I can't tell if Regina notices.

The guy speaking, to put it delicately, is full of crap. Basic slides, mansplanations about legal implications of the First Amendment, and then a long, smug humblebrag about how he represented some school that challenged free speech rules and text message records. I let my mind wander to RISD instead. Regina's watching sharply, a notebook ready, but I never see her actually write anything down.

"Great talk," I tell her as we're filtering out of the theater. "Did you like it?"

She looks around, then drops her voice. "I can't believe I made everyone come watch this."

"Yeah, maybe don't say that in front of Chris."

When we're all back outside, blinking in the sunlight, everyone gathers at the corner and Regina turns on her bright public smile.

"Thanks everyone for coming," she says. "Okay, so the guy was kind of douchey, yes?" People laugh. I see Esther whisper something to Lori and Maureen. "That aside, I thought he had some really good points about how important it is to not let your school or anyone else dictate what you can and can't say." I obviously have no standing to say this since I actively stopped listening, but the parts I did hear— that didn't quite sound like his point. And she's done controversial stories before—one about this mom who always complains to the school board about sex in books we read, an interview with an anonymous classmate (she wouldn't even tell me and Harry who it was) who'd had an abortion. I don't remember getting this same speech any of the other times, even though there were people, Esther especially, who didn't think we should publicize abortion. "I just think it's so important that we—that we be brave in the stories we want to write. And that we remember we have this platform and this influence, and if we aren't using it to tell people what matters, even if it's risky, then what's the point?"

. . ◦

"Every city should be laid out as a grid," Harry says as we're trying to find our way back to the car. "Like, seriously"—he motions to the map pulled up on his phone—"the hell is this?"

"I like San Francisco," I say. "What kind of dull city is all straight lines?"

"New York, for one."

"You're just crap with directions."

He elbows me. We find Jackson Street. I doubt where we are here in Chinatown looks anything like Shiyan; still, it's hard not to draw comparisons to the few things I've heard my parents talk about. When I was a kid my mom used to tell me sometimes about the food they grew up eating there, savory donuts and sea cucumbers and shaomai. We go by clothing stores with touristy sweatshirts spilling from the storefronts, cheap blue Chinese vases and bamboo cuttings and bright plastic toys all laid out on sidewalk displays, and when we pass by a bakery, its windows steamy, Regina turns to Harry and says, "You know the way you were talking to Chris today? Don't do that."

Harry stiffens. "He was just being so negative."

"People are allowed to be negative."

"Why bother? There's so much crap in the world already. Suck it up and find the good."

"You're so . . . optimistic," she says after a little while, and it doesn't come out sounding like a good thing.

Harry watches her a moment, then says, more mildly than I was expecting, "True." He'd never say it, but I think he's a little hurt. And, I mean, I get what she's saying, because it annoys me about Harry sometimes too—in his world there's always a right solution, always a reward waiting if you put in the work, always a pot of gold at the end of every rainbow. But it's one of the best things about him, too. It's nice to have someone in your life you don't have to worry about as much, someone you know will always be okay.

It never used to be like this with her. I would never in a million years describe Regina as mellow, or laid-back, but there was always a kind of easiness to her intensity, too. Or maybe that's the wrong word; maybe it's just that just about anything feels easy when you believe your friendship with someone is unshakable.

And I would've said ours was. I've known Regina forever, ever since I moved here and wound up in the same kindergarten class as her and Sandra. Regina and I were both new to Cupertino that year, me from Texas and her from Taiwan, and I knew I wanted to be friends my first week of school when Mrs. Welton yelled at Jincent Wong for knocking over a stack of papers on her desk and Regina gave her a look of such disgust it would've withered my heart. "It was an *accident*," she said, and then sat glaring at her desk with her arms crossed the rest of the day. At Regnart we were always pretty segregated by gender, and I spent most of my time roaming the blacktop and the field in noisy clumps of boys. But Regina's was the friendship I'll always look back on as the most important one I had growing up, the person who always knew me best and whose opinion I always needed before I was sure how I really felt about anything.

We both went to Primary Plus for after-school care and we'd hang out at the tables and I'd draw and she'd write news stories about the people in our class. Sometimes we'd make little books together (I still have some) and we'd imagine a whole future for ourselves, bringing what we wanted to life on our stapled pages. You know people by what it is they want most. When I broke my arm in sixth grade she bought me a left-handed notebook so I could try to sketch with my left hand; she knew how restless I felt, my mind all congested, when I couldn't draw. And she used to come over sometimes when she was fighting with her parents, which was often. Nothing she did was ever good enough for them, her schoolwork or her violin or her helping around the house or her attitude, the way she looked or the things she wanted for herself. One time, I remember, sophomore year just after she'd gotten her license, it was the middle of the night and she'd gotten into a screaming match with her mom about the future and her mom—who said a lot of awful things to her, but this one always stands out for me—told her she was too ugly to be on TV. I snuck out of the house with a blanket and we lay out on my front lawn and looked up at the stars. It occurred to me to wonder if I should feel guilty (by then she was with Harry already), but lying there like that with her didn't feel like anything, so I didn't. She never liked talking about whatever was going on at home, so after we got bored of star-gazing (ten seconds, probably; not much to stars when you're this far away) we watched cat videos online and laughed about stupid stuff for hours and then I woke up at dawn, damp with dew, and then I had to shake her awake and hurry inside, all clammy in my shirt, before my parents came out and saw us.

The light turns red and we stop at the corner. A pungent, earthy smell that reminds me of my mom's pantry wafts toward us from an herbal shop behind us, sandwiched between a souvenir store and a produce market. I think about what to say. Having to work this hard around them is so foreign to me, like landing in a country I've only ever heard people talk about. A taxi goes by.

"Here's the thing," Harry says abruptly, and we both turn to him. "I—"

But before he can finish, Regina says, "What's that?"

We look where she's pointing. It's a corner of a building painted all black with giant windows that've been elaborately tagged over, and there's a hanging sign labeling the place as NEIGHBORHOOD: A GALLERY.

"You want to go in?" Regina asks me.

I spend a pretty significant chunk of my time following art galleries online and browsing museums' virtual collections, but I hardly ever get to go in person these days. I don't want to drag them, though, if they'd rather not, feel their polite impatience hovering in front of the paintings. "Oh—we don't have to if—"

"No, let's go in," Harry says. And I can feel their earlier tension evaporate; I feel both of them swivel instead toward this thing they know will make me happy. "This totally looks like your kind of thing. Let's do it."

There are more people inside than I would have expected, probably forty or fifty. It's small, not in a way that makes you feel crowded but more that makes you feel a part of the surroundings. And the installation inside—everyone has those moments, I think, that take them out of themselves, when something you come across makes you see everything around you in a new way. Maybe this is how Regina always felt in church.

Whoever the artist is paints on overhead projector sheets and then casts them all over different parts of a room so they overlap and they look different, mingling differently, depending where you're standing. I could stay in here forever, possibly, looking at the way the images layer on each other and also watching people take everything in, watching the projections flash across them. It's a kind of living exhibit, all these real people sliding in and out of the projections, all these lives twined and tangled. The contrast between the physical people and the shaky, flimsy images stirs something in me—lifts from the private recesses of my heart and gives shape to what it feels like to walk with ghosts.

I can feel my mind expanding, all the possibilities filling new crevices in my consciousness. But then I also feel kind of frantic and awful in a way it takes me longer to pin down: it makes me feel desperate. He's done what I always wanted to do and he did it first, and probably better. In fact, standing here, the three of us experiencing this together—this feels like more of me I could show Harry than anything I could ever draw myself.

Harry swivels his head around slowly, then motions toward the wall. "This is really cool."

There's a white guy dressed all in black opening the door for people who I assume works here, and I lean toward him. "Excuse me," I say. "Who's the artist?"

"Her name is Vivian Ho." He points to the other side of the gallery. "She's here today for the opening."

I shouldn't have assumed it was a guy. And I definitely did not expect her to be Asian. I know most of the prominent Asian artists these days because I collect the knowledge of them, imagine myself among them, and I've never heard of her. She's in her midthirties, probably, stocky, with spiky, blue-tipped hair and black plugs in her earlobes, attractive in a guyish kind of way, and she's ducking her head toward a few women who are saying something about one of the projections.

"You should go talk to her," Regina says.

"Nah, she looks pretty busy."

"No, you're into this, right?" Harry says. "How often do you get to meet actual artists? Go say hi. Oh, look, she's coming over by here."

"That's all right. We should keep going."

"Excuse me, Vivian!" he calls. I elbow him and hiss, "What are you—"

But Vivian Ho is coming over and saying, with a friendly smile, "What's up?"

"Hi," Harry says, "my friend is an artist, too, and he wanted to tell you how much he likes your work."

"Oh yeah?"

I can feel my face turning red. "Ah—it's really—"

"He just got into RISD," Regina adds. "On a scholarship."

I hate them both. "Your installation is incredible," I say.

She smiles and crosses her arms over her chest, then leans against the wall. "Hey, thanks for coming. What do you do?"

"I like to draw."

"What do you draw?"

"Ah—portraits, mostly."

"Yeah? The gallery's doing this *30 Under 30* installation next month. You should apply."

"We're going to go find a bathroom," Harry announces. I glare at him. He smiles and waves.

"Nah, I haven't even been to art school yet," I say to Vivian Ho. "Thanks, though."

"So? I never went to art school."

"No?"

"No. I came up in street art." She laughs. There's a warmth and a generosity pulsing from her, which seems about right; I don't believe you can put anything meaningful into the world without having a kind of innate generosity, something of yourself to give. "And I remember what it was like when everyone would preach you that *life experience* bullshit and I was like, fuck that, I have things to say *now*. You get a lot of that?"

"People not taking me seriously because I'm still a kid, you mean?"

"You know the story."

"Nah, I kind of have the opposite problem, honestly."

"You got tiger parents? Is that what this is?"

It's the reverse that's true, really. When I was in first grade, the Cupertino Lions Club had a district-wide art contest for elementary school kids, and I won. The *Cupertino Courier* wrote up a little article about it with a photo of me holding my picture and my mom went up and down the street asking all the neighbors for their copies to give to her friends, and then they started researching lessons nearby, the best art programs I could go to after I graduated. On weekends we'd go to museums. My mom talked about how when she opened her hotel, she'd only have artwork in it by me.

Believe me, I don't take it for granted that my parents have always supported my dreams. I know you don't always get that lucky; I know they could've blotted out the fuzzy outlines of my art ambitions with the sharp clarity of medical school or law school or business school, things that required much less faith in me and that offered a more concrete kind of hope, the kinds of things my friends' parents push them into. And I'm also lucky, I know that, that what they want from me is what I want from myself, too—I'm just worried my talent doesn't run deep enough. And I can't fathom facing the world the rest of my life if it doesn't.

"No, they aren't like that. It's a big deal to them that I'm going next year," I say. "It's more—I'm worried I'm a fraud. Like maybe everyone thought I had all this promise but I'll go through all four years of art school and bomb and my parents will be crushed."

"Well, it's not like you go through four years of school and you're made. You can't just learn your way into it." She pauses. "And you can't do it because of your family, either. You do it in spite of your family."

"You think so? Do you wish you were doing something else?" How could you, though, when you stand in here and see what she made—how could you erase it from the world entirely, stick her behind some desk or podium somewhere instead?

"No," she says. "It's what I chose. But it takes more from you than what it gives back. I wish I'd known that when I was younger. Like, my family all lives in SoCal, and they aren't a part of my daily life.

I just don't have that room. And I know I'll never have kids. Probably never get married." She tugs at her earlobe. "You're going to have to choose, too. You have to look at the world like—you get one shot in it, and at the end you're going to have to look back and see whether you said all you needed to say and gave it back to the world to hear, or if you just let that shrivel up inside you to die with you. All of us have to make that choice."

⸱   ⸲   °

We're all exhausted by the time we get back to Cupertino. On the way back Regina's mood seemed to deflate. I know she thinks *Are you okay?* is one of the most annoying things you can ask people, that it means you think they're being sullen or overdramatic. So I don't ask her. She seems subdued as she says goodbye.

The air in the car feels different with her gone, when it's just me and Harry again. Sometimes I think your truest self is the one that emerges after the day's been scrubbed off you, the way it feels now.

"You going to apply for that gallery thing?" Harry asks, easing around the turn onto my street. The seat belt catches against my shoulder as he taps the brakes. I will be eighty, I think, and still remember that particular sound the seat belt makes. "You should."

"I doubt it."

"How come?"

Someday, maybe, I won't see other art and feel threatened by it; I'll feel in communion with it, part of the same ecosystem. "Eh, I just doubt my odds are any good."

He shrugs. He pulls into my driveway and turns off the engine. "That way it made you feel when you walked in—that really hit you, right? And you could give that to someone else."

Something crackles on my skin like a fire. He felt me in that moment; he understood what it was to me. "Maybe. I probably couldn't."

"Well, not with that attitude." He grins. It's our inside joke—he'll toss it out when Regina says something like *You can't put out a paper with four stories* when everyone's missed deadlines, when I say *You can't get to San Francisco in thirty minutes.* I wonder who he feels the most himself around—if it's times like this, or moments like earlier today with Regina when he has to make a case for who he is. Maybe that's what they have together, that he finds himself more sharply defined around her. Is that what people really want, though?

We sit there a few moments. I'm reluctant to get out of the car, but I can't think of an excuse to give for why. Finally he says, "All those things Vivian Ho was telling you—you think that's true? That you have to choose that way?"

"I hope not."

"You think so, though?"

There's a kind of fear I associate with truth, and I felt it when she was talking. "Probably. She'd know, I guess. What would you do?"

"If I thought I had to choose between my family and what I wanted to do?"

"Yeah."

"Probably my family. Then they wouldn't guilt me about it." He kind of smiles, not in a way that makes him look happy. "Regina's right about me, you know. I always like taking the easy way out."

THREE

It was the summer before middle school, right after the Fourth of July, that my dad first started to slip away to where no one else could follow. He'd stopped working on his experiment years back and I knew he missed it, but he was still working in the lab and as far as I could see, our lives were the same they'd been for years now. Something happened, though, inside him; it was like all the color bled out from the world around him and what was left over was muted and dull. For days every time you tried to talk to him he'd mutter back monosyllabic answers in this flat tone that shamed you for thinking you had anything worth telling him, and anytime you asked for anything you could feel the weight of the burden you were being. It's a profoundly lonely feeling when someone who's supposed to love you doesn't have it in them to be around you. My mom cried sometimes in her room when she didn't think either of us could hear.

And then he'd come out of it again and he'd be sorry, I think, because he'd joke with me in this kind of desperate way or he'd bring home new plants for my mom's garden. Or he'd help her weed, or he'd talk me into coming out there, too, and we'd eat microwaved dinners sitting on a blanket on the grass even the nights it was freezing cold, my dad chattering loudly like he was afraid of the silences, trying to pretend to each other everything was okay. And of course you couldn't talk about all those times you had to spare him your presence, you couldn't blame him for it in case it sent him spiraling again, and so those were almost worse than the times he was just withdrawn.

I'd known about my sister a long time, but that year was the first time I really started to understand what it meant for my parents, and for me, too, that she'd been there and then she'd died. I worried that that was what my dad was reacting to, some kind of delayed grief catching up to him, and that it wasn't something that could ever be fixed. All that summer I looked backward for clues, trying to remember any news stories I'd heard come on the TV that could've been what reminded him: a house fire in Los Altos Hills or a plane crash in Spain or a toddler in San Francisco falling out of a hotel window on a family vacation.

He's just weak, Mr. X would whisper to me. *He's never going to pull it back together. You're not good enough for him, you and your mom. This is it. This is the rest of your life.*

It was the first time I understood what it was like to feel hopeless, for that space you hold inside yourself for good things to close up. I lost whole days to League of Legends, which I honestly don't even really like, and had to watch Netflix to fall asleep. I hated nights, when everything felt amplified, and I got a stomachache each day at that hour when the sun went down but the leftover streaks of color were still hanging in the sky.

But: that was also the year I met Harry.

The first day of seventh grade, my backpack stuffed full of crisp notebooks and a new set of Micron pens, I was in the middle of the pavilion talking with Regina. I'd been telling her how bad things had been at home lately, and she'd put her hand on my forearm and said, "I'll pray for you."

I looked around. "Uh, like, right now?"

"No, no, not right now. I meant for your dad." She looked flustered. "Unless you want me to?"

Regina went to a Taiwanese church by school. Her parents were never religious, but when they first moved here her mom went just to meet other Taiwanese people, so Regina grew up going. A few times she's invited me to go with her, but I never have.

This, I knew, was why Regina believed in God: When she was ten years old her father had gone into his office and found one of his employees, a man named Robert, lying facedown on the floor. The hospital said he was in a stroke-induced coma, and told his family he wouldn't likely survive the night. Regina found out and felt something—a voice in her head that wasn't her own—tell her to pray. So she prayed and she kept praying, and she skipped dinner so she could pray for Robert to live. At nine she heard the same voice tell her she could stop now, and a few minutes later the phone rang. Robert had woken up. We'd never talked about religion all that much, although I knew it was important to her, and even though I wouldn't have minded—I don't think there was much I could've told Regina about myself then that she would've judged me for, and if you really believe in something, on some level it makes sense to want to convert everyone. My dad told me that once, closing the door after a Jehovah's Witness he'd spoken politely with and then offered coffee.

I'd thought back to that afternoon in his lab—my dad has always been an evangelist at heart.

And I wished sometimes my parents believed in something that way. I wished they believed my sister was in heaven, somewhere they'd see her again and I'd meet her someday, instead of just dissipated into atoms circling back into the universe; I wished my dad had something to hope for and I wished my mom had less to fear.

"That's okay," I'd told her, and then wondered if maybe it was a mistake. Maybe I wasn't in a position to be turning anything prayer-like down right now. "I'll pass."

"Okay. I—" And then she stopped talking, and her face lit up, and then there was Harry, bounding in like an aggressive puppy and pulling her in for a hug.

"Regina Chan!" he said. "Where were you all summer? You were supposed to hit me up in Taiwan, homegirl. I was there for like two months."

"I tried calling you when I was there," she said. "You never answered your phone."

"Oh, whaaaaat, that's a lie. It must not have gone through." He was grinning in that almost manic way he has sometimes—I know it now, even if I didn't recognize it then—when he's going to change the subject and just talk at someone so fast all they can really do back is laugh and (nine times out of ten) feel hopelessly charmed. And in that moment, I believed I saw him perfectly.

That was the thing, that back then I was always trying to see people for who they really were because it felt like if you were an artist, that's what you were supposed to do. I wanted to draw people stripped of their outer layers, and so I was always looking underneath for truth. (Honestly, I was probably kind of insufferable.) At any rate, in that moment it felt clear that Harry's trick to getting people to like him was to pretend he liked them: to wield his fake enthusiasm as a kind of currency. I would've bet my life savings that Regina did call him, probably more than once, and that he hadn't given her call a second thought; I bet he hit IGNORE and forgot all about it until just this second, the same way he'd forget about his conversation with her he was having right now. And I would never come up to people having a serious conversation and present myself that way, like a gift. When he was gone I said, "Who's that?"

"That's Harry Wong." She said it like she was surprised I didn't know him already, like it was my bad. Then she added, "It's his birthday pretty soon."

Birthdays in Harry's family, it turned out, were a bizarrely huge deal, and for the milestone ones, like thirteen, his parents went all out. They had (I would learn all this through social osmosis) rented out one of the private banquet rooms at Dynasty that people usually booked for weddings or red egg and ginger parties, and apparently a bunch of important people Harry's dad knew from his years in politics and business were going to be there, and apparently Harry's mother was determined to book a band with at least one radio hit, and apparently the invitations had been custom-printed and had cost eight dollars apiece. Sandra Chang referred to it as Harry's wedding to himself.

I was staying late at school as much as possible those days, stretching out the part of the afternoon where I could avoid going home for as long as I could, and we were sitting on the bleachers overlooking the blacktop. Sandra said, "I heard they're blowing like ten thousand dollars on this party."

"That's such bullshit."

"I heard it from—"

"No, I believe you. I just think it's bullshit anyone would spend that much money on a party. It's gross."

"You think it's gross? I would one hundred percent do the same thing if I had the money. You would, too. Admit it."

"I definitely would not."

She laughed; she didn't believe me, probably. She leaned back so her elbows rested on the row behind us. She tossed her hair and then carefully smoothed it back into place, her nails glinting in the sunlight. She always had elaborately painted fingernails, tiny patterns or colorblocks or sometimes even scenes. One time I'd asked if she did them herself and where she got ideas from. She'd just looked at me in this way that felt condescending and also almost defensive somehow. *Is this because you're all into art?* she'd said. *And you think this counts, or something?* And then she'd changed the subject.

"Anyway," Sandra said, "he invited Regina."

It is exactly how junior high works that whenever someone gets invited to a party, everyone else knows. Sandra and I had a running bet going on his unfolding guest list. I said, "Of course he did."

"I called it." She held out her hand. "Pay up."

I took a dollar from my wallet and handed it over. "That means you're next."

She laughed. "Is that an official bet? You'll earn your dollar back."

"You would totally go if he invited you, wouldn't you."

"Of course I would. You would, too."

"I wouldn't." Obviously I would have. "I don't get why Regina likes him."

"It's because Regina's a nice person," Sandra said. "She has no standards. She likes everyone."

It was true; Regina's always been a nice person. In second grade—we still tease her about this—we had class pet bunnies. A couple months into the year, the one girl bunny got pregnant, and one day we came in for class and found out the mom had eaten all her babies. Regina cried so hard she literally got sent home. Sandra had been Regina's very best friend since first grade, and if you were friends with Regina you understood that was part of the deal, that you'd always be in second place. They had this whole language built on inside jokes and do-you-remembers and vague references that meant nothing to anyone else. They had a way of talking about everything, endlessly dissecting even the smallest interactions, that made it seem like what they were talking about was something important.

I wasn't in Sandra's class until second grade, and at first, I didn't like her. Sandra wasn't what you would ever describe as nice and she had a disquieting ability to hone in on the things you didn't want to talk about, didn't want anyone to notice about you (which Regina always did, too; the difference is Regina never brought them up. But maybe they talked about all those things in everyone else to each other). But she grew on me; she always said things no one else was willing to and she made me laugh, and there's something to be said for always knowing where you stand with someone. She was the only one of my friends who was an only child like I was, and she always complained that it wasn't fair for it to be just you against both your parents, although she said several times she'd trade hers for mine, or for anyone's. Once in fourth grade I saw her arguing with her mom in the parking lot—they were in the car and Sandra had just buckled her seat belt and she said something I couldn't hear, and her mom whirled around from the front seat and slapped her. I never told her I'd seen. She could find the dark streak in anything, in those cheesy inspirational posters hanging around the school or in movies everyone else loved or in people, too. Her house backed up against a creek and once, the summer we were eleven and she was home alone, she invited me over and we went down through the gap in the fence. It was almost dry in the creek bed, just standing pools of water everywhere and crackly dead leaves, and we played with the tadpoles all afternoon. She'd said they reminded her of Mrs. Polnicek—"*Tad*polniceks!" she'd said, cackling in triumph while I rolled my eyes—our teacher that year who I'd liked, actually. "Sludgy and useless," she'd said, chasing one around the water with her finger. "Sound familiar?" I liked Mrs. Polnicek, but, I mean, I could kind of see it; I laughed. Sometimes I wondered if Regina always stuck by her so closely because next to Sandra she got to feel like a better person, the nice one, the one who saw the best in people.

Anyway, at the beginning of junior high, the bulk of my friendship with Sandra was talking crap about Harry. Harry had gone to Blue Hills for elementary school, so this was the first time everyone I knew had been exposed to him, and it was, to put it mildly, a strange feeling watching all the people you thought you knew flock to someone you despised, someone phony and cheaply charismatic. Of Course People Like You If You Con Them Into Thinking You Like Them: The Harry Wong Story.

But Harry was, for whatever reason, completely magnetic. He was (I had to admit it) objectively good-looking, with a strong jaw and high cheekbones and a quick, easy smile that he knew how to aim for maximum effect; he had a friendly self-deprecating way of talking and could, without warning, slip into saying things that were constantly hailed as really deep (once, when Aaron Ishido joked about Brett Lee being the most punch-worthy person in our grade, Harry was like, *Nah, man, violence is never cool,* and I once heard him argue with a straight face that all racism was rooted in misunderstanding). He was forever laughing and joking around with people, always changing the tenor of every circle he walked into. He was the kind of person conversations stopped for. Which was baffling because, to me, underneath the veneer of aggressive perfection, he seemed thoroughly mediocre. There was nothing interesting or different about him; he was just exactly the perfect prototype of everything Cupertino wanted you to be: smart, polished, rich. He wasn't different or unique, he was just what everyone else was, only more so, like someone took the rest of us and turned us up to Technicolor.

Also, a full month into the school year (a school year in which we had not one, not two, not three, but four classes together), we were funneled into the same test-review group in history and he'd turned to me with that plastered-on smile and said, "Remind me your name again?"

I know it all sounds petty. To this day I'm not entirely sure why I took such an instant dislike to him, why his very existence felt so personal to me. In my defense, I was a seventh grader, and there's no such thing as a good seventh grader; all seventh graders are assholes, even the nice ones. Maybe it was just rampant hormones, who knows. Maybe it was how sometimes he bought things at Goodwill and him doing it was somehow cool, proof of him being down-to-earth and unique and environmentally conscious, whereas I knew that if I did it because I didn't have money it would be a different story altogether. Maybe I was jealous.

But when I really think about it, I wonder if maybe it's more than that; maybe it's something that hits close to the deepest core of who I am. I'm not a religious person, but what I have with Harry is the closest thing I have—when I'm with him is when the world is at its clearest for me. I didn't understand that yet, though, sitting on the bleachers with Sandra, blazing with all those ways I hated him.

◦   ◦   ◦

Whenever there's some kind of prize of any kind up for contention, I don't care who you are: you always imagine yourself winning it.

So I imagined Harry saying things like, *Hey, I've always thought you seemed cool. You want to come hang out at this thing I'm having Saturday?* I imagined him bringing up the party at lunchtime. I resented him for taking up so much space in my mind, and resented myself for giving it to him, but that didn't mean I stopped. I also: liked a few of his posts online and then kept checking to see if he'd reciprocated in any way, nodded at him a few times in class, played four or five pickup basketball games with him and some other guys after school.

The last one was the Friday before the party. We were dispersing, sweaty and spent, when I heard someone call, "Yo, Cheng!"

I turned around and Harry was coming after me. "Wait up," he said. "I want to ask you something."

There was a spark in my chest like a lighter. Maybe I'd been wrong about him after all. I would take back all the hateful thoughts I'd had about him and all the things I'd said to Sandra; I would take back my assessment of him as fake. "Yeah, what's up?"

"Do you have the homework assignment for first period?" he said, hitching the straps on his backpack higher. "I was late."

॰ ॰ ॰

The next morning, the morning of his party, Harry posted a selfie of him giving two thumbs up. *Celebrating my birthday at Dynasty today at noon, come on by!* he wrote. *All welcome!!*

That was it for me. My rage ballooned. Harry Wong wanted literally everything for himself, including, apparently, the credit for being friendly and inclusive and magnanimous, which—screw that. No one was going to go and feel welcomed because of some vague throwaway comment online.

Did you see Harry's post? I texted Sandra. *I should go just to call him on it.*

I'm going! she wrote back. *With Regina. You should just come. My mom can come pick you up if you want.*

You're going? What the hell, I thought you hated him.

I don't have anything against him as a person. I just like watching you freak out about it. A few seconds later she texted, again, *You should come.*

My heart plummeted down my chest like it was falling through a trapdoor. I had to put my phone down. The weekend spanned itself in front of me. My mom was at the Lis' house with the twins, who were babies then, because the parents were both out of town on business and so I'd be stuck at home with my dad, who was worse than ever on weekends, answering questions in a grayish monotone voice and staring blankly at the TV, cocooned on the couch in his ratty sweats and unwashed hair.

My dad found me in my room, furiously drawing ugly-looking caricatures of Harry. He watched me for a little while, then patted his stomach. "Want to go get donuts, Daniel?"

"No."

He watched me draw. "Who is that?"

"Just a guy at school."

"You don't like him?"

"No." He waited for me to elaborate. Finally I said, "He had this party today and everyone was acting like it was this huge important thing. I don't know. It's stupid. He's kind of full of himself."

I immediately regretted telling him—my dad can be so advice-y, and I wasn't in the mood. Instead, though, he said, "Let's go on a hike."

"I don't feel like hiking."

"Fresh air will be good for you. Put on some shoes. It'll be fun."

So we drove up into the hills and went hiking at Fremont Older. You drive up Prospect where it winds into the hills and is barely big enough for two cars to fit, park under the oak trees next to the country club, the branches gathering you away from the sunlight, and you hug the side of the hill and pass some shut-off wooden homes and then the trail spills you onto a wide dirt path in a clearing. The dusty path leads up bare grassy hills until you get to Hunter's Point and you can see the whole Bay Area sprawled out below, all gray-green and red-roofed, from so high up blurred in a way that always makes me think of an artist I like named Dashiell Manley, who makes these explosive, haunting oil-on-linen paintings, textured dabs of color that make your eyes feel thirsty and inadequate. I hadn't wanted to come, but my dad was right—it was nice being up here, kind of like being in another world. Literally above it all. My dad was making an obvious effort to be in a good mood, and we saw hawks and a few deer and I watched the way people looked hiking, the lines their bodies made from their tiredness and determination. Any other day it would've been fine; it wouldn't have felt like a consolation prize.

We were headed back to the parking lot, coming around a narrow switchback with a steep drop-off, when he hit a root and stumbled. My mind flashed forward. I could see the accident before it happened—him tumbling down the ravine, the search parties I'd try to flag down, the guilt I'd feel for all the times and all the ways I'd holed up in my room quarantined from his obvious sadness, what it would do to my mom to lose a daughter and then a husband, too. But I was wrong about it—he flailed his arms and grabbed at a shrub, and steadied himself. When he pulled his hand away his palm was bleeding, but he was laughing.

"That was *close*," he said. "Hey, it's not so bad, right? You aren't at your party, but we're not lying at the bottom of a ravine."

My heart was pounding. I was embarrassed by my own fear. "If you say so."

"Say it's better or I'll throw you down this hill. Now I know the way down."

It made me laugh in spite of myself. Afterward, we went to go get donuts at Donut Wheel. My dad ate two. My dad, who deserved a party and a celebration and happiness and instead all that went to Harry, who'd done nothing to earn any of it.

▪   ▪   •

Monday was Harry's actual birthday, a fact I learned when I showed up for school that morning and it was like a balloon store threw up all over campus and Harry's face was plastered all over the halls. People decorated like this for their friends' birthdays, but I'd never seen anyone take it this seriously. There were flyers with his face taped to pretty much every bank of lockers, including my own. When I went to get my books, there was his extraordinarily satisfied face, staring right at me.

I thought: *NOPE.* I pulled my Sharpie from my pocket, glanced around to see if anyone was watching, and drew over the flyer. I edited his features—I made his eyes more leering, more pleased with themselves, and then I zoomed in on his mouth, trying to shape it to make it look self-congratulatory and smug as all hell.

"You didn't like the original?"

I knew before I turned around. I turned around anyway. Harry was watching me, his arms folded across his chest.

"What is this?" he said. "Is this supposed to be me?"

Of course it was. There was no use denying it, either. It looked like him. I couldn't think of anything to say.

He let his arms drop and then reached in front of me and tore the paper off the lockers. The expression on his face—at the time I thought it was disgust. "What is that supposed to mean?"

"Uh—" I tried to grab for the paper, but he held it out of my reach. "It's nothing. I was just screwing around."

"Why?"

What are you supposed to say to that? Finally I said, again, "I was just messing around."

He stared at me a long time. It occurred to me to wonder if maybe he was going to hit me. He didn't, though. He said, "Can I keep this?"

It caught me off guard—it was the last thing I expected—and I nodded before I could stop myself. Anyway, it's not like I could've asked for it back.

He didn't crumple it up, either. He folded it carefully in half, then swung his backpack around and unzipped it and slipped the drawing into his binder. Then he walked away, taking the drawing with him: tangible proof he could fold up and keep of what a petty, vindictive person I was, something that would leave me always on the hook.

My heart was still thudding as Harry rounded the corner out of sight. I had to stop walking to let it slink back into its normal patter. Which seemed like a massive overreaction, except that I think, when I try to re-create that flash of time, I'd done it on purpose for him to see—for a split second there I'd imagined the worst and then wanted it. Or brought it into being, at least, which in the end might as well be the same thing. I'd like to say I lost myself for a moment, and that's why. But that's the easy way out. It seems equally possible that in those moments you just let go, when you give in to your impulses, that those are the moments that are most you.

Originally, my parents weren't going let me go on the eighth-grade science camp trip to Yosemite. My mom was too worried the bus would crash, or I'd get lost in the snow and freeze to death, or I'd slip off a cliff hiking and plunge to the rocky ground hundreds of feet below.

Besides that, things always felt unstable at home. My dad still wasn't himself, although it was starting to feel like this faded version we had to tiptoe around was his real self after all. It's hard living with someone who's never happy—a dark mist hovers over everything that happens in the household and you feel guilty when you want to be happy yourself. I worried about him, and I worried maybe he was going to divorce my mom or that she'd decide to divorce him. I had my cycle down pat: I'd be sullen and quiet around them, upset I had to worry about any of this, and then at night lying awake I'd be guilt-stricken and resolve to do better in the morning. It was draining, and I was pretty close to desperate to get to Yosemite even if for no other reason than to get out of the house.

It was Auntie Mabel, my mom's best friend, who talked them into it, saying science camp was good for my education and that I'd love going. I did love going. Sometimes even now it chills me to think how much of my life would've never happened if I just hadn't gone.

I stayed in a cabin with Maurice Wong and Aaron Ishido and Ahmed Kazemi, other denizens of the group of us who hung out in the middle of the pavilion at lunch—loud, visible, sending ripples into all the peripheral groups gathered around the outskirts. After that drawing I'd kind of thought Harry would muscle me out of his circle, and he could've, too, but he hadn't. Since last year we'd mostly ignored each other, and I always tried to avoid him, but middle school doesn't let you do that; once earlier that year we'd walked into

Geometry at the same time (I'd seen it coming and tried to change my pace, but it hadn't worked), and he'd dipped his head in acknowledgment and held open the door and motioned for me to go ahead. I'd felt him watching me as I went past him, and sometimes in class I would've sworn I felt him watching me, too, although every time I checked he moved his head too quickly for me to see if I was right.

Daytimes in Yosemite we were assigned to hiking groups and we traipsed through practically frozen creeks and did trust falls and foraged miner's lettuce and we were all given trail books to sketch what we saw (I drew portraits of all the other people in my group and gave them to everyone at the end of the week), and ever since then I've been pretty friendly with the random collection of people who were in my group, and I still think of them—Jinson Tu and Jefferson Choy and Helena Heggem and Serina Kim and Annie Chong—as a single unit.

We weren't allowed to take cell phones out on the hikes with us, and Thursday, the day we hiked Yosemite Falls, when I got back to the cabin thirsty and sore before dinner there was a message from my mom.

"Hello, Daniel, it's Ma. I'm taking your father to the doctor. Just so you know. He's all right, but he's very sad."

He's very sad. It isn't fair to resent a dead baby, but in that moment I did.

I wished I didn't have to go back home; I wished I could just stay here and pretend everything was fine. I didn't see a way out of my dad just always drowning in his sadness, and I didn't see a way out of me having to carry that with me my entire life.

It was Thursday night, the night before we'd all get up and stumble bleary-eyed out of our cabins by seven the next morning to get to the dining hall and then check onto our buses, that I couldn't take the feeling anymore. All the guys in my cabin were asleep and it was after midnight, definitely after the nine p.m. curfew, but I figured there probably weren't any chaperones wandering around outside and so I slid as quietly as I could out of my sleeping bag and grabbed my ski jacket and went out into the cold.

It was close to freezing outside, my breath puffing in front of me, the moon behind the clouds turning the whole sky a pale, glowing gray. There were small patches of snow under the eaves and on the ground where even during the day it was mostly shadow, and it was bracingly quiet—no wind rustling trees, no cars. The moon was bright enough to light the snow fairly well, and so I walked past the cabins. I had some vague idea of getting to the clearing by the dining hall, where there were some benches carved out of logs, but I'd only gotten twenty or thirty feet when, from the near dark, someone said, "Hi, Danny."

I whirled around, my heart thudding, ready for I don't know what—and then it was Harry sitting mostly hidden in the shadows on a rock, a scarf wrapped around his neck and his beanie pulled all the way down over his ears. It caught me entirely off guard. I said, "What are you doing out here?"

"Eh, I just couldn't sleep." I could see puffs of air when he spoke. He didn't look as surprised to see me as I was to see him, which meant, probably, that he'd been watching me for a little while. "You?"

"Uh—same."

He jostled his shoulders up and down a few times. "It's freezing out here, though. I can't feel, like, ninety percent of my body anymore."

"How long have you been sitting out here?"

"An hour, maybe. Two."

I raised my eyebrows. "Aren't you going to get in hella trouble if you get caught?"

"Aren't you?"

I mean, yeah, okay. "Touché."

"Well, anyway—" To this day, what he did next surprises me: he reached into his jacket and pulled out a small metal flask and offered it to me. Harry was not—he was absolutely not—the kind of guy you found drinking alone in the snow after curfew, and I blinked at him, my eyes trying to make sense of all the pieces. "Uh—I'm not sure if—"

"You don't drink? Don't worry about it, it's cool. I brought it for my cabin, and then we just—there was never a good time."

"It's not that, I just—" I looked at him closer. "Are you, like, okay and everything? Is something wrong?"

"No, yeah, everything's fine." He flashed an extremely unconvincing smile. He pocketed the flask again without drinking from it. "Everything's cool. I just couldn't sleep."

I could've gone back inside. There were a lot of things I could've done, actually—I could've left him there, or I could've reported him to someone or held on to the information to dole out like currency. And he knew that, I think. It didn't feel like arrogance that had made him say hi or ask me to drink with him; it felt more like, for whatever reason, while he was sitting there on that log knowing I wasn't alone as I thought I was, he made some kind of choice to trust me. Or not trust me, maybe, but at least to put some small part of his fate in my hands. And I owe the past four years to that decision, honestly. I don't think I would've done the same.

Anyway, it felt like I owed him, at least a little bit, for that. I said, "How come you couldn't sleep?"

It felt like a risk. Maybe it always does talking to someone you don't like, because they could turn it on you in any of several ways. I spent the next few seconds of his silence regretting it, picturing a way to extricate myself from this conversation. Then finally he said, "Sometimes—" He stared out into the dark. "Do you ever get tired of all of this?"

"All of what?"

"You know. Just the always—just everything. Like school. Cupertino. You know."

"Tired of it how?"

"Just having to do all of it all the time. Even when you're worried you'll never pull it off or it feels like what's your reward in the end—you just get to do more of the same for longer? You know? And then nothing you do is ever good enough anyway. You ever feel like that?"

"Sometimes, I guess." Then I added, "It never seems like you do."

"Why not?"

"You're so, like—peppy all the time."

He cocked his head and grinned at me. He has a grin that can change the whole mood in a room; I've seen it happen so many times, but that was the first time it happened to me. *"Peppy?"*

"Ah—maybe that's not the best word. I'm just surprised, that's all. You play the game pretty well."

"Peppy, huh." He rubbed his hands over his arms, then tucked them under his armpits. "Regina told me you want to be an artist."

Was he thinking of the picture I'd drawn of him? I was glad it was mostly dark. "Yeah."

"That's kind of cool. It's like a big F-you to the system, right?"

"Nah, it's just that I suck at math."

He laughed. "Like Asian suck, or actually suck?"

"No, like actually suck. I still don't understand how to graph a line."

"What do you mean you don't understand? You just take the slope—"

"I know, I know. Or, I mean—I *don't* know. But I can recite the words like that too. Slope-intercept. Rise over run." This was unexpected—maybe it was just the weirdness of the whole situation—but I was kind of smiling. "I can draw a line. That's good enough."

"No, that's not good enough, what the hell?" He looked around. "Find me a stick or something. I'll write it out for you in the snow. This night is going to end with you learning how to graph a line."

"That's not—"

"No. I'm on a mission. We're doing this." He propelled himself off the rock in an athletic kind of way and went for one of the trees until he found a stick to snap off. This was that same condescension, wasn't it? But why did it feel so different all of a sudden?

He did it, too—he drew his axes in the snow and explained it about a dozen times until—small miracle—I did mostly understand. Then he tossed the stick to the ground and raised his arms in triumph. "Mission accomplished."

And that was the first time I had the same feeling I've felt probably thousands of times with him since then—that small panic about the moment ending. My heart felt kind of strange, sort of galloping against my chest. It made me wonder if maybe quantum entanglement felt like a prickling extra-awareness, like all your atoms poised for action and humming with desire—like a thing between you that'd never quite lie still. I felt hyperaware of how, if I leaned a few inches closer, our arms would brush together.

I wasn't ready to go back to my stuffy cabin and Aaron and Ahmed and Maurice passed out in their grimy sleeping bags, back to the house where my dad was slowly mummifying himself in his sadness that I was pretty sure a doctor wouldn't be able to magic him out of. I said, "I know what you mean about being tired."

His expression changed. He toed at the stick in the snow, then stepped on it with his hiking boot until it crunched in half. "Yeah. Well."

"This week was better, though, right? Like, it was nice to be here."

"I guess. Sometimes I just don't think it's all worth it. Like maybe it would better to just go live in like, Ohio or something and just be a coal miner."

I leaned against the wall of the cabin. I could hardly feel my face. "Is that a thing? Somehow I doubt they're just waiting for some random Asian kid to show up from Cupertino ready to coal-mine."

His eyes crinkled into a smile, enmeshing me in the joke. "I'd do Taiwan proud."

"Okay, then. Represent."

He let go of the smile. "It's probably crappy there anyway. That's the worst part. This is probably all there is. So if you don't play, it's just—" He lifted his arms and then let them fall to his sides.

And I knew exactly what he meant. Any one of us standing out there with him would've, because Cupertino really gets to you. It's not like it's this friendly, squishy, huggy place where mediocrity is fine and it's cool if you fail or just aren't that good at anything, and everyone here knows it. We were all tired and stressed out all the time, all of us worried we'd never be good enough, many of us explicitly told we weren't good enough, so it wasn't like his problems were special or different or more tragic than anyone else's. We all felt it, the relentless crush of expectation, the fear of not measuring up—even me, and I like it here, and as Asian parents go mine are about as chill as they come.

So it didn't have to feel like some big moment between us; it could've felt like talking to basically anyone in my grade. I guess it was just that I knew it wasn't something he ever showed to anyone, but that night, for whatever reason, he did to me. Before I could stop myself, I said, "Hey, Harry?"

"Yep."

I could feel my frozen face turning red. "Hey, I'm, um, I'm sorry about that picture thing last year. Drawing on it."

"Oh—whatever. Don't worry about it."

"It was just kind of a dick thing to do."

"It's cool, really." He kind of laughed. "I think I still have it, actually. Somewhere on my desk. You're really talented. It looked more like me than the picture did. I always hated that picture."

"The picture was fine." I kicked at some snow. "I thought you might try to ruin my life over that."

"You thought what?" He looked legitimately startled. "Why would I do that?"

And I believed him. It was genuine, that confusion, and that was the first time I really saw him, I think—when I understood that his social persona was concealing none of what I'd always thought it was, but actual niceness instead, that there was a kind streak at his core.

It wouldn't be until a few weeks later that I'd understand about the rest of it, but that would happen, too, in Honors History when Mr. DiBono passed back our midterms. I'd see Harry turn his over without looking at it and then sit super still for a long time, his eyes trained on the teacher like he was trying to will himself into not looking. He lasted twenty minutes, and then he looked down and peeled back just the top corner of the page where the grade was written. From across the classroom I saw the way his whole body deflated, and then I saw the way he gathered himself up and hid that, and something about it was so practiced, so automatic, that I understood for the first time how much this was a part of him. I mean, it was a small moment: it was over fast, and it wasn't something we ever talked about. But I saw everything differently after that, I think because it's hard to turn away from someone after you've really seen them. You carry that part of them with you, and it becomes your job to protect it, too.

But that was later. For the time being, in the snow, Harry clapped his hand on my shoulder. I could feel it through all the layers of jacket and glove, could feel it like there wasn't all that fabric in between us.

"We should sleep," he said, and something about the way he said it, something about that *we*—I think I knew in that moment how much I'd want to always be covered by it, how I'd always want there to be a space for me inside it, how I would maybe be willing to do things I wouldn't have imagined in order to make it so.

We walked together back to the cabins. And that was the first night.

◦ ◦ ◦

My dad wasn't seeming very much better by the time eighth-grade graduation rolled around; it had been a rough couple months. The doctor hadn't helped because my dad didn't believe in taking the antidepressants he'd been prescribed or in going to the counseling she'd suggested, so he didn't. All through the ceremony my mom was wiping her eyes, and when I found my parents after on the lawn, all the guys roasting in dress pants and dress shirts and all the girls tottering as their heels sank into the grass, she was crying. I'd been with Harry, taking pictures with different people and all that, but when we saw my parents Harry whacked me on the back and said he'd catch me later. And maybe it was "Pomp and Circumstance" still playing all emotionally in the background, but seeing my mom's tears I felt, for the first time, the true weight of all the dreams they held for me. Those dreams crystallized that day into something hard and heavy, came to rest on my shoulders. Because I felt it in a real way then what they'd lost, that there should've been another eighth-grade graduation before mine, another batch of pictures no one was ever going to look at, and there was never going to be any way to fix what had happened to them. I'd grow up and have my future ahead of me still and still have my dreams out there to reach for, and we'd be different, because I would have the world, I would have my whole life ahead of me, but all they'd have was me.

"Don't cry," I whispered to my mom, and patted her hand. I tried to smile. "It's just eighth grade."

At the graduation dance that night (butcher-paper palm trees taped to all the walls and the lights turned low, bottles of sparkling cider and those Costco three-flavor packs of cookies), when we were tired of dancing, a bunch of us sat on the bleachers and Harry slung his arm over my shoulders. He's always been a kind of handsy person. He leaned close to my ear so I could hear him over the music and said, "How come your mom was crying so much today?"

I held still so he didn't think I was moving to get him off me. "Long story."

"What's the story?"

Back then I never really liked talking about my family with most people—it was complicated, I was worried about fitting in, school was where I got to not think about it, etc., etc. But that night—maybe it was how hard it had hit me seeing my mom crying like that, or how before the dance we'd gone to dinner and my dad had given me a framed signed Dashiell Manley print. He'd watched my reaction eagerly, like he wanted to save it, and when he saw how pleased I was he was proud in a way that made him feel more like himself. Or maybe it was the way it felt to sit there on the bleachers with Harry and for him to have made that space for the two of us that way in that whole big sea of people.

So I told him what it had been like. My voice cracked a couple of times; luckily it was loud in there. I was nervous. I guess I've always believed that's what a relationship is, this space you keep between you where you hold each other's secrets. Or that it's how you build something together, layering the things you've never told anyone else like bricks.

After I finished he was quiet for a long time. Ahmed came over to talk to us and I could see Harry snap into motion, grinning back and laughing, and I wanted to take back everything I'd told him. But then Ahmed went off to ask Sandra to dance and Harry's grin slid off his face and he turned back to me. He put his hand on my knee.

"It'll get better," he said. Harry is an unrepentant optimist, and so I might've been willing to write off what he was saying as a cheap platitude, except for the hand on my knee and also for what came next. "It always does. They'll figure things out and everything will get back to normal. Okay? And in the meantime, I mean—we'll get you through it." And there it was again—that same *we*.

That was when it all made sense to me—why I'd disliked him so ardently at first. It was because something in me recognized how much he would matter to me, all along. I'd just been wrong about the particular way.

I'm not going to try to pass the night off as in any way epic. It was hot in there and everyone was sweaty and you could feel a thousand middle schoolers' worth of hormones everywhere, and everyone had braces and all the girls were teetering around in their heels and the teachers were skulking around in the corners trying to make sure no one was grinding on each other or otherwise getting too gross.

But still. The dance was also a retreat from the fear I'd been living in at that point. My worst fear about my family was that maybe I would never be enough to make up for what they'd lost, that I wasn't supposed to be the one who'd lived, and that they'd wind up broken in a way I couldn't put back together. Maybe they'd break apart from each other entirely. I felt that possibility heavy on my chest every morning when I woke up. By then I could see a future where my family never stopped being a grayer, paler, more trembling version of ourselves, and by then I couldn't shake the possibility that maybe my fate, all our fates, had been sealed before I was even born when my sister died. It wasn't hard to see how our future could get swallowed by the past.

And so it was the way he'd said *we* that felt significant to me—that same *we* from Yosemite I'd been holding on to all these months, the same one I'd been hoping I hadn't just imagined. It's both the best thing that can happen to you and the most dangerous, because what do you have except the people you belong to and who belong to you? But then you can also lose yourself to it; you can do things in service of those *we*s that end up haunting you.

            ˮ   ˎ   ᵒ

Harry was, surprisingly, right: things did get better. Something rekindled in my dad—whether that was purpose or hope or something else, I'm not sure, but he felt like himself again. He'd go to social events again and hum in the shower or while making coffee in the morning and joke around with me. And my mom seemed relieved in her quiet, nervous way—that sort of holding her breath, that sense she gives off that she doesn't quite trust the ground beneath her feet.

I've never told Harry how I feel, and daily, probably, I go back and forth about whether he knows. It's what makes me wonder, too—maybe he's more open than I am and I already know everything there is.

Or maybe not. Maybe he keeps some of that locked up, like I do.

Anyway, though, since Yosemite we've been basically inseparable, but there are ways I don't let my guard down around him. Someday, maybe—I tell myself that all the time. We'll see. Sometimes, actually, he'll say something to me that feels so generous it throws me, but for the most part it's not like we ever said that kind of thing to each other aloud. We always bickered a lot and also, I mean, the things that always bugged me about him didn't necessarily stop bugging me once we got close; I just learned to contextualize them differently. They slid off to the side and allowed room for the rest of it in.

FOUR

All that day after getting home from San Francisco, I think about the *30 Under 30* show at the gallery, and before dinner I finally sit down and look up the submission guidelines. I wanted to just forget about it, but imagining my work being chosen as the *innovative, with a fresh and surprising point of view* portfolio they're looking for fills me with a kind of desperate hope. The submission deadline is January. By then—by then I should've come out from under this slump. I have to.

I look up Clay Ballard while I'm on the computer. I don't know quite what I expected, but he's the same person he seems to be in my dad's files, and you can only scroll through so many articles about seed capital and startups named things like Marquetz and LunchBunch and StumblPAAC. I look up *Clay Ballard Joseph Cheng* and *Clay Ballard Joseph Tseng*, but there's nothing. I wish I remembered my dad's Chinese name. But I really only saw it a couple times in my lifetime that I can remember—as a kid you're not, like, writing

7 5

out your parents' legal names anywhere. And I'm sure my dad would get suspicious if I just randomly asked.

For dinner that night my mom's tried a pasta recipe with basil and the last of the tomatoes from her garden. She's peering at the tomatoes in the sauce, watching for our reactions, when my dad sets down his bowl and says, abruptly, "I will be searching for a new job soon."

The hum of the refrigerator cuts through the stillness. We both stare at him. My mom says, blinking rapidly, "What do you mean you'll be searching for a new job?"

He clears his throat and rearranges the bottles of vitamins on the far side of the table. "Dr. Rodriguez has asked me to search elsewhere."

"Search elsewhere?" My mom sits up straighter. "She wants you to look for a professorship?"

"No."

"Then why is she asking that?"

"Because—" He hesitates. "We had a difference."

"What difference? What happened?"

He ignores that. "So I won't be going back to the lab and I'll find another job instead."

"You'll find another job? Who will hire you?" Her voice is rising. She reaches wildly for the edge of the table and grasps it with both hands. "Joseph, were you fired? You weren't—"

She makes a high-pitched gasping sound. She curls over the table, her hands cupped over her mouth.

I get up, shoving my chair back. "Are you okay, Ma?"

My mom used to get panic attacks all the time. It's been a while, but I have memories of being woken up at two, three, four in the morning to rush to the emergency room because my parents didn't want to leave me at home alone. It was always the same story, my fear that this would be the time something was really wrong, the normal EKGs and pulse oximeters and eventually the doctors sliding from their initial quickness and worry into something tinged with impatience. They'd give her Xanax, but it would always end up jammed into the medicine cabinet, shoved behind the bottle of Kwan Loong oil and the herbs she took for the supposed kidney deficiency she always blamed for the panic attacks.

"I can't breathe," she gasps. Her arms fly out again, flailing, and I grab one and hold her hand.

"You can breathe if you can talk," I say. "Remember the doctor who told you that? She said if you can still talk you don't have to worry, even if it feels—"

My dad, who's been sitting motionless, his hands wrapped around the vitamin bottles, comes to life again. He rubs my mom's shoulders and motions for me to back away, then crouches next to her, murmuring in her ear. She's always felt better with him there, a shield against her own self.

I hover on the other side of the table, my own throat constricting. "Do you want anything?" I say. She shakes her head. I make her tea anyway, partly to try to help, partly to escape into the steps of heating water and steeping and watching for the color to change.

When I set the mug down next to her on the table my mom holds it and takes a sip, less I think because she wants to and more because I went to the trouble of getting it for her. My dad watches her drink. This must be what he started to tell us the other night when we went out.

"Everything will be fine," he says loudly, in English. "Nothing to worry about. All fine."

People change jobs all the time, I know that. My mom greets most news like it's a monster at the threshold, and I don't think her reaction on its own would be enough to unnerve me. It's my dad's expression that does it—that part twines itself around my lungs like weeds. Also, this: at home with us he never uses English on the things that come naturally or from his heart.

I don't say anything; it's clearly not the right time. After a while my mom's breathing catches its regular pattern again. She nods to us, and we sit back down. We finish the pasta, the noodles gone cold, in silence. After dinner my mom unfolds a piece of foil from her stash next to the oven and covers the leftover pasta to put in the fridge, and my dad doesn't offer more details or tell us why he was fired, and we don't ask.

"   "   "

"I love your shoes," Noga Kaplan says to me Monday morning when I come into AP Bio. My lab group's standing Monday morning tradition is a potluck breakfast during class (Mrs. Johar doesn't care if we eat on non-lab days), and Noga's setting out her four red Dixie cups for the bag of Cinnamon Toast Crunch and pint of milk she always brings.

"Hey, thanks." I slide into my seat. I'm wearing my gray Vans, which are now covered in fine-tipped Sharpie miniature portraits, a tiny ground-level entourage. "You're on them."

"Wait, are you serious?" She tucks her hair behind her ears and peers down to look more closely. "Where?"

I'd always kind of wondered if school would matter less once you knew where you were headed next year, but it's the opposite, actually; it feels scarce now. Even small things feel heightened and sentimental, like these potlucks, or how in PE when we run laps I always run with Mike Narvin and he tells me all his obscure and generally X-rated facts about Shakespeare, or how in AP Lit the other day Chris Kum raised his hand in the middle of our discussion on revenge and its limits and said, very seriously, "What do you call a plagiarized version of *Hamlet?*" Mrs. Hogan pressed her lips together—she knew this wasn't going anywhere especially academic—and said, "What?" and Chris said, *"Spamlet."* It wasn't original or even funny—it seriously wasn't—but how often in your life do you get to be in a room full of people you've known since you were six years old all doubled over laughing at the same stupid joke? All that period whenever she tried to get us back on track someone'd whisper *"Spamlet,"* and it was over. Mrs. Hogan laughed, too; she likes us. I spent all of Journalism trying to draw the moment somehow on my Vans, trying (aggressively failing, although apparently not according to Noga) to get down in ink what it felt like to look around and see a variant of the same expression on everyone's face, what it felt like to all be part guardians of a shared joke. I'll miss all this.

I find Noga's face near my left ankle, her shining hair and the dark lipstick she always wears, watch her light up. "It's like I'm famous now," she teases. "Maybe someday they'll auction off those shoes in a museum and I can tell everyone I'm on them."

I laugh. "Noga, if that's your claim to fame, we're going to have to have a long talk about where your life went wrong." To class today I brought trail mix from my parents' Costco expedition, and I put down a paper towel and divide it into four piles. "Wait, is Teri allergic to almonds? Am I remembering that right?"

"Cashews."

"Oh, right." Damn. "I should've brought dried fruit mix instead."

"We should make stricter rules," she says, smiling, neatly distributing the cereal into four portions. She brought, like she always does, four plastic spoons. I love Noga. "Hey, I heard you got into RISD! Congratulations!"

"Yeah, I was really lucky. Still can't believe it. You wanted to go to UCLA, right?"

"You remember that?"

I collect details about people; it's part of how you form the shape of them. "In, um, the least creepy way imaginable, I remember everything."

She laughs, then pauses pouring cereal to put her hand on my forearm. "You can remember it for that long talk we have scheduled."

Harry's told me a couple of times he thinks Noga likes me. She's a dancer with sharp, structured features, probably pretty up there if you're into girls, and for the hell of it I wait to see if anything in me ignites. Nothing does. For a minute there, though, I forgot about my dad getting fired. So there's that.

But it's only a matter of minutes before it all settles back over me. All day, and then all week, it follows me around—my dad at home when I get back from school, avoiding me; my mom darting her eyes around the house like she's expecting some other harbinger of bad news to emerge from the cabinets. My parents have been not quite fighting, exactly, but the form of it's there, if not the substance: the raised voices, tight jaws, that same feeling you need to move carefully around them like waiting for paint to dry.

"He still hasn't said what happened?" Harry asks me Thursday as we're going up the stairs to the Journalism Lab after lunch.

"No, he won't talk about it. And it's definitely not the kind of thing I'm supposed to bring up, either."

"Weird. If it were me I think I'd be trying to tell my side of things, you know?"

"You would literally never shut up about how you were wronged." He wouldn't. "But maybe he knows he deserved it. I don't know."

My dad's car is there when I get home that afternoon but the house is empty, which, if I'm being honest, is always kind of a relief. The laptop's open on the kitchen table, where my dad must've been using it, and he's still logged in to his email. Neither of my parents is particularly great with technology—my mom once leaned over my shoulder when I was on my Facebook page and said, concerned, *How does it know all that about you?*—and I don't think it's ever occurred to either of them to do things like delete their search history or log out of their accounts. But, anyway—obviously I look.

He gets a ton of junk mail. But buried in it I find a message from Laura Yim, one of his colleagues from his lab:

Hi Joseph, I am very sorry to hear you won't be with us going forward. I found your ideas about entanglement very worthy of exploration and I'm sorry about the way things concluded. I hope you can pursue them at your next position. Stay in touch.

Is this—I read it twice more—is this about that experiment he brought me and my mom to see all those years ago? But what would that even mean? He was done with it—he promised my mom. He'd stopped talking about it at home. And he'd never told anyone in his lab, either, because his PI thought it was pseudoscience. And that was so long ago.

Unless, I guess, it wasn't? I look through his sent mail to see if he's said anything (no), and then I scroll through his inbox. There's an email dated three weeks ago from a journal:

Dear Joseph Cheng,

Thank you for your submission to Applied Physics Letters. *We regret to inform you that our board of reviewers is unable to accept your submission.* The submission's attached, and just glancing at it for a few seconds it's clear it's exactly what I think it is: my dad was trying to publish a paper on that experiment. And from the tables and charts of results in the paper, this wasn't just writing about something he was working on ten years ago, either. He'd started it up again.

I sit back against my chair. I wonder if my mom knows.

The back door opens, and I jump so hard I nearly knock the computer off the table. My dad steps into the kitchen and says, "You're home."

"Ah, I just got back." I fumble to close the window before he can see what I was looking at, my heart rattling nervously inside my chest. "Did you go for a walk or something?"

"Yes. Very beautiful outside. All the fall leaves." He's wearing black pants and a button-down shirt—the first time since he got fired that I've seen him in anything but sweats. He fills a mug with water. "I was thinking, Daniel, that tonight we'll go out to dinner. When your mother comes home we'll ask her."

"Oh." I try to catch my breath. I'm not used to them showing up early like this—I used to always have the house to myself until six at least. "Ah, you don't think we should just stay in?" My mom's been worrying over the cost of everything, making passive-aggressive comments about dinner (*Sorry there's no leftovers, but the beef was too expensive*) and scolding us every time we forget to turn off a light or take too long in the shower, so I think my skepticism is justified. "I don't know if she'll want—"

"She'll be glad to." My dad pulls out a chair and sits. There are deep bags under his eyes, his skin heavy. "Where do you think we should go? What would you like to eat?"

I see my mom's face again when she found out he got fired, and I mumble a nonanswer. I pull out some melon from the fridge and make toast. Our toaster is old and glacially slow, and I finish the melon and a pack of dried cuttlefish while I'm waiting. My dad watches me.

I never quite understood why she wanted him to stop so badly. But I don't understand why he would've gone back on his word, either. From what I know of his lab, though, I bet the experiment itself wasn't the part that was a big deal—I'm sure it was that he tried to get this bootlegged project of his published, that he borrowed on the lab's credibility to push what his PI thought was trash science. Did my dad—my incredibly cautious, borderline-paranoid father who uses his turn signal when he's the only person on a residential street—never imagine that getting fired for it was a possibility? Why would he risk that? I think about asking him what exactly happened, except what would I say—*hey, I was just snooping through your emails, and I noticed you got fired because you broke a promise to my mother*? My dad loved his job. Every time his name was listed on a publication he'd leave it conspicuously around the house, hoping we'd read it. He loved waiting for results, loved the peer reviews and 3-D modeling and applying for grants. And most of all he loved the possibility that he'd run his own lab someday—once when I was little he showed me the nameplate he wanted for his door, and he'd typed the name in so you could see it in the model online: *Professor Joseph Cheng*. If he gave all that up because he misjudged the risks, because he made a stupid mistake, I can't imagine what that must feel like.

"You haven't been drawing very much," he says, breaking into my thoughts. "How come?"

"Oh, uh—I don't know. Some kind of dry spell."

"Ah." Then he adds, "Unpleasant."

"Definitely is."

The truth, of course, is that he knows me, that he understands the greed I see the world with. I think he's the only one who does, because he feels it, too. Is that why he went back to that experiment, why he did something risky and possibly incredibly stupid, something I'm

sure he has to regret—because he couldn't let go? Because it would've been like telling me to give up art?

I'm in the middle of buttering my toast, still trying to come up with what to say to my dad, when my mom gets home. She comes in through the kitchen door, staggering under the weight of the grocery bags she's holding. My dad jumps up to help. She drops everything on the floor and turns to me, ignoring him. "What are you eating? Don't eat so close to dinner. I was going to make—"

My dad cuts in. "Let's go out to dinner tonight."

All the air goes out of the room. My mom drops her hands to her sides. "Go out?"

"All day today I thought, *This would be a perfect night to go out.* I've been looking forward to it all day."

"It's a very nice idea," she says, in a tone that means the opposite, but my dad either misses that or pretends to.

"Maybe we'll try somewhere in Main Street Cupertino."

"I have chicken that needs to be used."

"You can freeze the chicken."

I wonder if my mom has said any variation on what flashed across my mind when he first told us, which—I'm not particularly proud of it—was *How could you?* Watching him, his hopeful smile, I think she must not have.

"I'm okay with anything," I say. "Chicken sounds good, too. We can—"

"No, no, we should go out and have a nice dinner together." He turns to my mother. "What do you say, Anna?"

She smiles that tight kind of smile that means nothing is all that happy or funny. "We should be saving—"

"No, no, we have time to save. All our lives to save."

"Rent is due Thursday and the water bill this month—aiya, so high."

His smile falters, but he doesn't back down. My dad's like Harry, in that way: always convinced his own charm will carry him through. "Just one dinner, Anna. You work so hard. You deserve to go out."

And I recognize that for the lie it was. Dinner's whatever, he could take or leave it, but he wants her to not be mad at him. Those pangs of terror she felt when he first told us, all the time she's spent worrying over the checkbook, the past few days he's been looking for some way to fix this: he wants proof that all those will somehow crumble under the weight of their history together.

I think of his desk in the lab, the pictures of me and my mom and the boxes of tea he swore helped him think better and the plaque he was so proud of from when he spoke at a physics conference. I imagine him clearing it out in front of all his coworkers. I pick my side.

"Actually, going out would be great," I say, willing brightness into my voice. "I'm starving. Where do you want to go, Ma?"

She reaches down to pick up her purse and the bags of groceries. There are red lines cut into the backs of her forearms where the bag handles weighted down. We wait, the two of us, a smile pasted onto my dad's face. I can see his shame straining behind it. From watching my parents I think being married or being with someone else in any kind of real way takes a certain amount of bravery, and it's not something I'm positive I have in me. To pluck your heart from your chest that way and hand it to someone, unprotected, and wait to see how gently they'll stitch it back in for you, or not—to wake up all those days you're the crappiest version of yourself and face the person who knows you best, morning after morning, year after year.

My mom sets the bags on the table and reaches inside to put

the meat (the discounted kind; I recognize the orange sticker) in the fridge. My dad stands still, waiting, as she empties one bag, then the next.

"All right," she says finally, refusing to meet his eyes. "Somewhere cheap."

They're not quite speaking to each other on the ride to the restaurant. Or they are, but in the kind of showy way that's meant to prove they're not *not*, which is a different thing.

"Where do you want to go?" my dad asked her when we got in the car.

"Wherever you want. You're the one who wanted dinner."

"The pho place? Or Japanese?"

"That's fine."

"Which one?"

"It doesn't matter."

"Or Hankow?"

"Let's do that," I interrupted, before she could say *It doesn't matter* again.

The restaurant is on one of the strip malls on De Anza, the older ones, not part of all the newer construction they've been putting up lately to give the tech workers their shiny organic fast-casual places. As always, neither one of them will drive us. Sometimes I wonder if my sister is buried somewhere in one of their recurring fears.

My parents like Hankow because it serves Hubei food, which I think—I'm just guessing, because they never talk about it—reminds them of home. My mom thinks her re gan mian is better than theirs, but she loves the dou pi here, sticky rice wrapped in tofu skins and then fried, and the barbecued oysters. The restaurant's full tonight, and we're seated near the front. (Hundred percent rule: a freshman girl I'm pretty sure is named Ami is with her family by the back.) Even though it's not busy it takes forever to get our waters and our menus, and it's kind of cold. My mom pulls her jacket around herself whenever the door opens. I don't think she means it pointedly, but I think my dad might be taking it that way.

He opens the menus and says, heartily, "What should we have?"

"Whatever you like. I'm not very hungry."

I wish my mom would just try. Just say she wants the duck neck or doesn't want it; what good does it do to advertise your anger like this? It doesn't just get at my dad—it knifes me, too. Whenever there's any tension between my parents and I worry I won't be able to stanch it, I feel that hole blown through our lives more keenly. It would've been different if my sister had lived.

"I'm starving," I say, which is a lie. "Ba, let's get like fifty skewers."

He flashes me a look I recognize as grateful, and then we spend a while plotting out the order while my mom stares out the door. It's stupid, because this is my dad's fault and I know that, but something inside me hardens against her. It wouldn't kill her to just try.

It's better after the food comes, though. We eat the cumin-dusted lamb and pork skewers, the pig's ear and the dou pi, and my mom can't stop saying how good the dou pi is tonight. I eat just a few bites so she can have the rest.

"Finish these," my mom says, pushing the plate of skewers at me. Then she squints at the lamb, her mouth full. She swallows. "Cut it into pieces. They cut it too big. You'll choke."

I smile. "I've gotten pretty good at eating, actually. I put it in my portfolio. It's part of why RISD let me in."

She sighs. "Give it to me." She reaches for it and hacks at the pieces with her chopsticks. She always worries about choking; she used to cut my grapes into quarters when I was a kid.

When we're done, and waiting for the bill to come, I say, "Can I ask something?"

My dad says, "Yes." But he gives me a look that means *watch yourself.*

"How long do you think it will take to find something new?"

"Aiya, Daniel," my mom says, a little sharply. "Leave him alone."

"I just—"

"It doesn't help to ask so many questions." Then she adds, "We are on green cards, remember. It's more complicated on green cards. Finish the dou pi. I am full."

I feel a surge of guilt for interrogating him, for breaching the fragile peace we'd brokered over dinner. Probably he just wanted to eat here and pretend things were normal, not listen to his son demand when he'd stop being such a failure.

This is the part I keep coming back to—what did he think the experiment would give him? Was it just that he wanted the fame of it, that he dreamed of himself profiled in all those journals he read, giving TED talks? I can't see it. Or was it something even littler, that he thought publishing the experiment would please his boss and impress his coworkers? I hope not. There's something heartbreaking about the smallness of that.

"I think it matters when people follow their dreams," I say impulsively. They both look at me quizzically, and I feel my face going hot. "Like, if there's something you really care about—I've always looked up to people who went after what they wanted."

"Like you," my mom says. "And your art school."

"No, but I mean—you too, Ba. Do you remember the time you brought us in to show us your experiment? I always—"

I feel it before I understand, the coldness and the noise happening all at once, and it takes me a few seconds to register. Then my mom jumps up with her napkin and I realize my dad knocked over the pitcher of ice water the waitress left on our table. I'm soaked. The table is dripping, our leftovers drenched, a pool of water on the floor.

"Sorry, sorry," my dad says. Except—I look at him closely—did he do that on purpose?

Both of them leave me alone at the table in search of napkins. At the wait station they stop, ignoring the rather prominent stack of napkins there, and my dad says something to my mom. She glances back toward me and replies. Then they stand there, whatever words passed between them caught on both their faces, before they snap back into action.

And then when they're back—I know this play—they're a flurry of motion, mopping everything up, my mom fussing over me, and it's not the kind of activity you can have a conversation around. We leave behind a waterlogged mound of napkins on the table, a slippery wet sheen still coating the tile floor.

FIVE

The Wednesday of midterm season Harry's SAT tutor gets the stomach flu and has to reschedule, so Harry has a free afternoon and we go to the library to study. I love the Cupertino library; it has this nearly floor-to-ceiling aquarium tank, and it's kind of mesmerizing watching all the fish. The library's always crowded, but we find a table and some chairs near the fish tank. When I pull out my Calc textbook Harry makes a face at me.

"Oh, come on, what's that for?" he says. "You got your acceptance letter. Aren't you basically a second-semester senior already? Aren't you supposed to burn all your books or something?"

"Yeah, whatever. Like you're going to let your GPA slip even a millimeter next semester either."

"I'm going to slack the eff off next semester."

"You definitely aren't."

"I might," he says. "You never know." When he smiles it looks like it takes a little more effort than it should.

I can't focus on the equations, though. Instead I keep trying to sketch a toddler girl who's rocking back and forth on her heels in front of the fish tank, squinting suspiciously each time a fish swims near her. I'm better with faces than bodies—I'm not strong enough on anatomy—but even on her face I can't get the light values right, the way the sun reflects off the glass and shines on her alert, wary eyes.

I haven't been able to stop thinking about the *30 Under 30* show. Sometimes—it always seems easier—I wish I could just not care about things, that I could just let it go and not spend the rest of my life wondering if I would've had a chance at getting in. At home I've been watching a ton of workout videos as makeshift anatomy lessons in case one of them might spark some kind of idea I can use as a submission. But every idea seems solid and hopeful until I try to lasso it, and then it evaporates as soon as I try to wrestle it onto the page.

Harry's got SAT worksheets he's ostensibly going through, but he seems distracted, too. He tilts his chair back on two legs, watches a couple little kids pound on the fish tank's glass. The girl looks at them disapprovingly. Then he brings his chair back to the floor, pushes his binder aside, and says, "I told my parents you got into RISD."

"Yeah?"

"Yeah." His phone buzzes and he twists the cap on his water bottle, raising his eyebrows at me in a way that means *don't say it*: he has an app to remind him to drink more water, and I always give him crap for it. "It's funny because if I told them I wanted to be an artist, even if I were as good as you are, they would flip the eff out. Or you know what? They wouldn't even bother, they'd just laugh their asses off because they'd know there was no way in hell I'd get to. But then with you, they were all excited. They even made me show them some of our old papers so they could look at your drawings. They keep talking about it."

It would be douchey to act flattered, I think, since that's obviously not where he's going with this. "Well, what do you actually want to be? Do you not want to go to college?"

"Of course I want to go to college. Maybe like—I don't know. Sometimes I think maybe it would be cool to do something like"—he glances around like he wants to make sure no one's listening—"like maybe acting."

"Acting?" He looks so embarrassed to say it, like he regretted it as soon as it came out, that I know he isn't making it up. "Actually, I could see that."

"Really?"

I grin. "You know how sometimes I tell you you're kind of fake?"

He reaches under the table and socks my thigh. "Shut up."

"No, really, though. Why not?"

"Why *not*? I mean, maybe I'd suck at it."

"And?"

"What do you mean *and*? Maybe I'd suck at it, full stop. Also, I don't have time."

That part is probably true. The drama crowd is forever doing auditions or rehearsals or performances, always siphoned from the outside world into the black paint and velour of the theater. It's why I only ever see Mike Narvin during PE. And Harry's already up until one or two most mornings studying as it is.

"Are you serious about this? It's actually something you—"

"No, no, it's stupid. I'm definitely not serious. It would never work out."

He's lying. "Maybe you could—"

"No, it's stupid. Forget I said anything. I don't know, maybe I'm just too stressed. I just keep thinking how if I don't get in—what was the point of anything I did here? What's the point of anything at all?"

Those dull flashes of heat in his tone—I know he doesn't talk like this around anyone else. "So you're not feeling great about the SAT, I take it."

"It just all seems so stupid and arbitrary. I've worked my ass off the past four years but who knows, maybe the admissions officer I get hates my essay or something. Bam. Done. Just like that."

It's cruel to try to tell someone the most important thing in their life doesn't matter, I know that. I keep picturing my dad having imaginary conversations trying to defend his research to his boss, stumbling over why he didn't just dismantle the whole thing. And what do you say? It matters because it matters to me. That's the worst thing Mr. X always levels at me, that those things I hold dearest just don't matter. You can't mount a solid argument against someone who'd just as soon burn down the things you love, shrugging as they pour the gasoline.

"It's not a great system," I say. "Or maybe it's better if you're at a less competitive high school."

"You're so lucky you're in already. You're luckier than you know."

"Yeah, but—yeah." I stop myself, because he's right; I am lucky.

"But what?"

"Eh—I'm just kind of worried about my parents."

"About those files still?"

"No—they've just been really stressed out."

"Your dad didn't find a new job yet?"

He hasn't. But the other thing is that I went through his search history last night, and it's strange—he's been looking up what feel like totally unrelated jobs. He's looked at Craigslist postings for things like a household manager and an Uber driver, and yesterday he searched *job Cupertino cash only*. He's looked at nothing that feels like a logical transition. "It kind of feels like he's barely even trying. Like he already gave up or he's just going about it the worst possible way, which is functionally the same thing, right? I don't even think he's looking at the kind of job he could actually do. And the weird thing is he's only looking at like—these under the table type jobs. Like the other day I saw he was looking at, like, construction gigs on Craigslist, which makes zero sense. He has a bad back. Do you think what he did was really *that* bad that he can literally never get another job in his field?"

"In the Silicon Valley? Not a chance. I'm *sure* there's like a zillion startups that would see getting fired for doing some secret experiment as all bold and groundbreaking and like"—he makes air quotes—"'*disruptive*' and crap. Why doesn't he apply at one of those?"

"Yeah, that's . . . not a terrible idea, actually." Why doesn't he? My dad's a lot of things, but he isn't stupid. Wouldn't he have thought about all this, too?

"Why don't you just ask him about all this?"

"I've tried."

"Well, why don't you keep trying? How hard could it be to wear them down?"

"Yeah, keep it." Harry always says my parents are Asian lite—how they've never taken me to China, how they barely taught me Chinese, how they're soft. It bugs me every time. Partly I'm sure he really does think my parents are Americanized, and in some ways they are, but partly I think it's just that they're from a random town in mainland China. Harry's a snob. (For his part, he goes to Taiwan, where his parents' grandparents all fled with the Kuomintang, two or three times a year, and he speaks Chinese like a regular adult and not at the first-grade level I do.) "They just don't talk about things they don't want to. I'm not even sure my mom knows why he got fired."

"Oh, she's not violating his privacy like you are, you mean?"

"Shut up."

He smiles. Then he puts headphones in and buckles down to work, scribbling across his worksheets while I draw. We stay at the library another hour or so, and then he has to go home for his tennis lesson, and I fight back that old vague hollowness—that same one you get when a movie ends, or when a storm that's encased you all day gives way again to empty skies.

Harry was wrong: I'm definitely not going to be able to just wear my parents down. There's a certain way they make a room go cold when you tread too closely to our ghosts, and so I don't ask why my dad restarted his experiment or if my mom knows that's what happened or why he's not looking at reasonable jobs. I've been raised to know how not to talk about things. There are shades of answers anyway in the way my mom's lips press together as she riffles through the mail or closes her eyes and lays her fingers on her wrist to check her pulse when she doesn't think I'm looking, in the way my dad spends whole days locked in the study, coming out only to eat.

Without fanfare, we get onto a lower data plan and end the Netflix subscription with all the nature shows my dad loves. We don't go out to eat.

One afternoon when my dad goes to the grocery store I go back to look at that box of files in the cabinet. When I get into the closet, though, the box isn't there. While my dad's gone I go hunting all over the house, but I can't find it anywhere. I should've paid more attention to what was in it.

I take the laptop back to my room and I look the Ballards up again, scrolling through the first few pages of results that I've clicked on already. And then on the third page I learn something that sends a flash through my spine: they used to live in Texas. Or Clay Ballard did, at least, because he has an MBA from UT Austin.

I spend nearly an hour trying to locate him in any kind of specific time frame—I look up his LinkedIn, all his public profiles, every mention of *Clay Ballard UT Austin* I can find to try to find a graduation year. I can't find one. But still—is it just a coincidence that all of us were there at one point? All those files printed out and collected—they have to all point backward to some locus that my dad's private obsession spans out from. It never occurred to me it could've reached back as far as Texas.

I was six when we left Austin. I was born there, and when I was little I expected to live there forever. Even now, the texture and the colors of living there still drift back to me. I remember the velvet-blue nights my dad was teaching class sections and my mom and I would go to the green-lettered grocery store and each pick a brightly colored frozen entrée and a Popsicle and we'd eat them together in front of the flickering TV and she'd let me stay up late so I could see him before I went to bed; I remember the weekends when we'd go with other families to drive out to Krause Springs or Hamilton Pool, all that slate and tree growth and green water that was so striking that later I always tried to draw it and always gave up, because you could never capture the way it felt to be there. We all used to live in university housing together—two-bedroom apartments that all opened onto a common lawn. During the day all the families would leave their doors open and the kids would flow in and out. My best friend back then was Ethan Parker-McEvoy, who lived next door to us but basically lived at our house as much as I lived at his.

I look him up every now and then when the mood hits; there are people so enshrined in your past they'll never stop mattering to you, and Ethan, who was my whole childhood in Texas, is that to me. I found him on Facebook years ago. He looks basically just like he did when he was seven, the same angular cheekbones and crooked smile, his hair (which was always buzzed when I knew him) in an afro now. All his accounts are locked down, so that profile picture is all I've seen. I look at it often. I don't know what's stopped me from reaching out. I guess it's the fear that I won't matter to him anymore or that he won't remember me. At least when you hoard the past for yourself it's still yours. It's like art, really: you tack it down somewhere flat and static, and then no one can take it away from you.

Anyway. This was Texas, the last time—

I was staying at Ethan's place for a few days because my parents had gone out of town on some kind of trip. They'd been excited about it, telling me when they came back they'd have some kind of surprise for me. And I remember beforehand they were in great moods, laughing together over things I didn't understand, and sometimes my dad would catch my mom as she was walking through the house and touch her shoulder or the small of her back. While they were gone Ethan's parents took us on a walk to get tacos at Guero's and let us watch movies and then I slept in a sleeping bag on the floor in Ethan's room and we stayed up half the night talking about how we wished my parents would leave like this all the time and we could live together. I think maybe you're never quite friends with anyone the way you are when you're a kid. I thought of him like a brother.

My parents came back on a Thursday in the middle of the night. I remember them waking me gently, my dad lifting me in his arms. I remember feeling right at that moment how much I'd missed them, how thinking otherwise was only because I'd been so distracted.

At home they must have let me sleep. In the morning when I woke up my room was stripped bare and my mom had a present for me—a gigantic candy bar she'd bought at the airport that said TEXAS-SIZE CHOCOLATE! on it—and she told me that they had a surprise for me. We were moving, she said, to California. My dad was going to get a new job there. Wouldn't I like to live in California? I could see the beach and I could see mountains. I could go skiing in the winter, and see real snow. In fact, we were moving right now.

I fought it as much as you can when you're six years old and your world's been pushed out of orbit in spite of you. I didn't want to leave. And on some level, I think, I was afraid, and over time the fear dropped off because we came here and everything was fine, we've been happy, but I remember that now, that I was scared. That even then I think the way everything was happening felt off to me, how fast it was and how we didn't tell anyone, that I felt that safe, steady image I'd always held of my parents dissolving. I wanted to see Ethan first and my mom told me no, we needed to leave right away. "They'll give away our new house otherwise!" she said, smiling like she was teasing, like it was something I'd be willing to joke about.

I never talked back or argued with my parents back then, but I did that time. Even when you're six, you understand what it means to say goodbye. But they held firm—I wasn't allowed to go see Ethan; we had to leave right away—and when we went to the parking structure, our car was packed. My shirts were stuffed into a plastic grocery store bag.

Sometimes I wonder what Ethan remembers. Nothing, maybe. Maybe he's already forgotten me completely. But every now and then I think maybe I'm wrong and—because he doesn't know my last name now—he's just never been able to find me. I wonder what he made of us just packing up and leaving that way. I wonder if he thought I just didn't care enough to say goodbye.

And I wonder now, and I can't fathom what this would mean,

but the way we left like that—could it have tied back somehow to however our paths could've crossed with the Ballards' while they were there, too?

But I still can't imagine how my parents would even know them, and not just have met them but know them deeply. You don't run into someone a few times on campus and then build a dossier on everything they've ever done.

At a McDonald's somewhere in West Texas, where we stopped early on the way to California so my parents could bribe me with a Happy Meal, I cried so hard my muscles ached. My mom sat down next to me.

"Daniel," she said, peeling the lid off a packet of honey sauce for my chicken nuggets, "do you know something about goodbyes? It's worse if they're long. Otherwise you'll be sad forever and you poison all you have with your sadness, too. It's better not to wallow in them. It's better for you to move on and forget." She dipped a nugget in the honey and handed it to me, then dabbed at my eyes with a napkin. I thought then how both my parents had left behind a whole country, a whole homeland, and how maybe to them Texas to California felt insignificant and small. It was the only way any of this made sense. She smoothed my hair and cupped my face in her hands. She smiled. And I must have been wrong about it all feeling small to them, because it was the first time I can remember, and I remember this distinctly, ever looking at someone's smile and realizing it was fake. "You'll make new friends, won't you? You'll be very happy and you'll forget. You'll be my strong boy."

SIX

On Thursday at lunch, Mina Lee and Grace Leung arrive as emissaries from their corner of the academic court to talk to Regina. They come together, like they need reinforcements, pretending the rest of us aren't there and standing over Regina while she tries to eat her lunch.

Mina and Grace are both part of a group of maybe a dozen or so girls in our grade and the grades below who've all grown up going to Regina's church together. I don't know either of them well—aside from Regina her church group has always been pretty insular—but I've had enough classes with Mina to get the sense that her view of the world is a series of kind of rigid boxes I probably wouldn't fit neatly into. Once, hanging out at lunch last year, one of those days we took for granted, Sandra watched from across the rally court as Mina talked with Orson Lam. She mimicked a narration as Mina looked up at him and giggled—*Oh, Orson, you are just so funny!*— and then when Mina kept tugging down the bottom of her skirt, running her hands over her shoulder like she was checking to make sure her bra straps were in place, Sandra said dryly, "When you want a boyfriend but also your boyfriend is Jesus." Regina was kind of pissed; she always stuck up for her friends from church. I remembered how Mina said once in AP English that girls who wore tight clothes had low self-esteem—it was a throwaway comment, something that was supposed to be a self-evident truth, and I remembered Sandra was wearing this clingy skirt that day. She referenced that comment once or twice as why she didn't like Mina, but sometimes I wondered if the truth was that she was kind of jealous of those friends—all those times Regina vanished into them and their world.

"We just wanted to see how you were doing," Mina says now. "We haven't seen you at church in so long."

Regina puts up a hand to shield her eyes from the sun, squinting up at them. "That's nice of you. I've been good, just busy."

Grace and Mina glance at each other. Mina says, "Do you think you'll come out on Friday night?"

"I think I actually might have some things I need to work on."

"Right," Grace says, like she expected that answer. "What about Sunday? We're probably going to start planning Brothers Appreciation Night. We want to do a progressive dinner. We thought maybe your house could be one station since you live right by the Chiens."

"Sunday I have SAT tutoring, actually."

"Oh." Grace looks at Mina again, maybe for some sort of confirmation. They're uncomfortable in a way that makes it clear if there was any way they could've managed to have this conversation with just her, and not in front of us, they would've. "So, um, how's your walk with God been going?"

Lauren Kao and Maurice Wong, who'd been talking with us, both kind of edge away, drifting toward where Abishek Batra is laughing about something I can't make out. Regina says, "It's fine."

"It's just really been on our hearts to see how everything's been going for you."

Regina smiles. "Things are fine."

"When my mom was in the hospital freshman year it really helped when I was good about doing my quiet times," Grace says, and it comes out in a rush like maybe she's been rehearsing it. "I went through this one book—I can lend it to you if—"

"Sure, thanks."

She's sitting very still, holding the same smile on her face, and you can see them feeling themselves deflect off her. Harry says, "You guys want to sit down?"

"No, we just wanted to say hi," Mina says quickly. She turns a little red. "Regina, let us know if there's anything we can lift up for you, okay? Or let us know if you want to be part of the progressive dinner or anything. And I'll get you that book."

"Great. Thanks."

When they're out of earshot, Harry says, "It sounds kind of nice to have something like that to go to." He says it with a careful, practiced mildness that makes me think he worries about her more than he lets on. "Your church, I mean. It meant a lot to you, right?"

"Sure."

I say, "Sometimes I wish I believed something like that."

She shrugs. "You can."

Is that what people think, that you can just decide what to believe that way? That's not how believing in anything works—you can't always buy in when you want to, even if you know it would be better if you did. It's why leaving Texas was so hard for me as a kid, even as much as I wanted it to be true what my parents told me that it was fine, that we'd be happier.

Harry watches her. He finishes his lunch, some kind of Paleo bowl from one of those meal-delivery services, then crumples up the (compostable) bowl. "Are you annoyed?"

"No."

I can't tell if she means it or not. I also can't tell if she'd answer differently if I weren't here—if she'd open up with just Harry and no one else.

"You were kind of acting like it," Harry says.

"I mean—" She sighs. "No. I wasn't. I don't know."

She's quiet the last few minutes of lunch, and I think she's maybe a little relieved when the bell rings. All day I think about that. Honestly, I'm not the biggest fan of Mina Lee, but coming and finding Regina when she's with all her friends, pressing to make sure she's actually okay according to the terms they always cared about most— when have I done that for her? I should try harder, put myself out there more. I owe her at least that much.

›   ·   ○

This is the thing I keep coming back to: the ASB elections last year. Because of what happened with Sandra, mostly, and because I keep going back again and again to try to figure out how much blame I hold and what it all means.

Harry, of course, was running for senior class president. Harry has been class president every single year since first grade (and I think it says something that I know this, even though I didn't go to first through sixth grade with him).

"You should run for vice president," he said earnestly. "Or like— secretary, or something."

"I'll pass."

"It would be cool if you won and then we were on it together."

"Assuming you win."

"Yeah, assuming I do." He wrapped his fingers into a fist and thumped it gently, pinkie side down, against his palm. "You think I will?"

"Probably." Since I first met him, I'm not sure Harry has lost anything more significant than a tennis match.

"I've tried to do a decent job with it before."

I knew he was fishing, but I also knew he meant it, that it really mattered to him. I've seen how hard he's worked on ASB stuff, how he'll send out memos to everyone in Leadership about inclusiveness and campus culture and peer connectedness. When we have rallies, he spends hours trying to get a good cross section of the student body to call up to participate in front of everyone, and he's always proposing stuff like Tell Someone You Care week or things like that. Every class has its own particular personality, and the class above us was kind of shallow and cruel, the sort of social ecosystem where girls would regularly cry at lunch and if one of the popular kids was talking to you the odds were good it was some kind of joke, and we aren't like that (thank God) in part because of him. I should've just told him that, that I think caring as much as he does and working as hard as he has is something to be proud of, and that if I had to say who the most influential person is on campus it's him, easily, and I think he's actually tried to use that in a positive way because in the truest, most non-throwaway sense of the word, Harry's nice. He is. He's a nice guy.

I didn't, though. I said, "Mm."

You would think, perhaps, that eleven out of twelve would be enough of a run and that it wouldn't matter to him all that much if he got to do it a final time, but you would be dead wrong. I knew how desperately he wanted to win the election. I knew because of how much he didn't like talking about it. He did all the campaign stuff—he made posters, he went around at lunch and talked to people, joking around with the freshman guys and flirting with all the girls. He emailed me about eight drafts of his speech to read over. But then when you actually asked him about it, he'd change the subject. We all have those things, I think—those things we want too badly to speak about aloud for fear someone'll swoop in and tell us we're just dreaming, those things we hold close and fantasize about at night and swear to the world we don't care that much about, the way I feel about art, the way I want to believe my parents are grateful I was the child who survived. What Harry wants above everything else is to know the world is behind him.

Most years I don't think anyone even ran against him, but last year, kind of out of nowhere, Sandra decided to. We had our various cliques-within-cliques but for the most part we had all the same friends, so it felt like a weird move on her part. For one thing, Harry and Regina were going out at that point. Sandra had been the VP since freshman year, which seemed like it was working fine for everyone, but I guess apparently not. "It's all *Game of Thrones* up in here," Ahmed Kazemi had teased, looking between them while they stapled rival posters to the side of the gym. Ahmed had been in love with Sandra forever. I always thought it was a weird pairing—Sandra was a huge partier, for one thing, and even though he went just to hang out, Ahmed was Muslim and didn't drink. And he was always messing around, always at the nucleus of some joke. Once sophomore year he came to school wearing a T-shirt that said DAMN STRAIGHT, and in second period Mrs. O'Neill made this big deal about it being inappropriate. They argued back and forth until finally Ahmed wrote an *R* on a Post-it note and taped it over the *M* on his shirt. "Darn straight," he announced, flinging his arms in a come-at-me-bro motion, and everyone applauded except Sandra. Mostly Sandra acted annoyed with him, and Ahmed tried to make her laugh. But all the same it seemed like there was a kind of happiness between them, or at least a comfortable set of roles to settle into.

Anyway, the election was something people talked about a lot—who they'd vote for, whether Sandra was being a bitch by running against him (public verdict: yes, if you already didn't like her, which a lot of people didn't), whether it was going to be really embarrassing for whoever didn't win, etc. It was, I think, borderline agonizing for Regina, who always just smiled when Sandra would link arms with her and say, "Regina's my campaign manager. Hos before bros." Regina came over once that week and we sat at my kitchen counter drinking the chrysanthemum tea my mom makes in hot weather and discussed whether there was ever going to be any form of competition that Harry would look at and decide he didn't care if he won. No, was our consensus. Probably not.

"Is that exhausting to be with someone like that?" I said. I couldn't quite look at her when I said it—I swirled the tea around in my cup and watched the little whirlpool it made instead.

She shrugged. "You're his best friend. You're probably with him more than I am. Is it exhausting for you?"

"It might be if I were as success-driven as you are."

"I'm not success-driven," she protested, and it was such a ridiculous statement I laughed out loud. I teased her about sitting here in my house this way and lying to my face, and she got all snappish the way she always does when you tease her. I remember thinking, in that moment, if my sister had lived it would've felt like it always has with Regina.

"It's not because Harry doesn't like other people," I said. "It's the opposite. It's because he wants them to like him."

Regina said, "I know."

Something in her tone—there was something static about it, something I couldn't relate to. "Are you happy with him?"

"Yes."

"Really?"

"Everyone has good and bad to them."

"Whoa, whoa, let's keep it PG, can we? Get a handle on those hormones, Regina."

She kind of laughed. "It's true, though, right?"

"I guess, sure. I just think that's a weird way to look at things with your boyfriend."

"Maybe. It's probably the most fair way to look at everyone." Then she said, apropos of not very much, "You know, I really think you and Sandra could be pretty tight again if you got over your feuding," and I got up and cleared our empty cups. I said, "Mm."

My relationship with Sandra was, at that point, nonexistent most days and awkward/residually negative the others. This is what happened, or at least this was the first thing: The day before school started freshman year, I was supposed to hang out with Sandra. Since none of us could drive yet and Regina and Harry were way up in the hills, she and I had seen a lot of each other that summer. Which is what I told myself when Harry called me that day—he'd just gotten back from a few weeks in Taiwan—and I told him I was free, and a few minutes later I let Sandra's call go to voicemail.

Harry got a ride down the hill from his dad and at my house we decided to walk to Pearlbubble. We'd gotten to the end of the street when my phone buzzed with a text from Sandra: *What are you doing? I'm bored.*

I could've just said *I'm with Harry, we're walking to get boba, you want to come?* But the truth was that I didn't want her there. Not even her in particular, nothing personal; it was just that it had been weeks since I'd seen Harry and I didn't want his attention pulled away.

Busy right now, I wrote back. And then, because it felt too abrupt, I added, *You get your class schedule already? What is it?*

She didn't answer, and I pushed away the twinges of guilt. A few seconds later Harry pulled his phone out of his pocket and glanced at it. There was a plummeting feeling in my stomach; I knew already, I think.

"It's Sandra," he said. He lifted his head and looked around. "Doesn't she live right by here? I'll tell her to meet us."

If there was a plausible reason I could've given to say no, I couldn't get there in time. We waited for her on the corner. She found us five or six minutes later—her house was just on the next street over.

"Well, *hi,*" she said, giving me a cold smile, her lips pressed together. "So nice of you to let me join you."

I could feel my face going hot. "I thought—" And then there was nowhere to go with that one, obviously. I mumbled something about being glad she could make it. She ignored me the rest of the walk as much as you can ignore one of the two people you're with. But—I always think about this—she could've made a scene in front of Harry, she could've revealed me as the person I was, and I would've deserved it, and she didn't.

We had homeroom together the next day—it's alphabetical, and at MV there are so many Changs/Chens/Chengs I barely made the cutoff—and she cornered me while everyone was milling around inside before the bell rang.

"Why did you ditch me like that yesterday? I thought you hated Harry, anyway."

"He's—" I hesitated. "He's not the worst person ever."

"Not the worst person ever. Right." She crossed her arms and glared at me, for so long I felt the rest of the room fade back, all those new binders and new outfits and all that first-day-of-school energy. I wished we were outside so I could squint, hide my eyes under the guise of it being too bright. My mouth was dry. The irony was that in basically every other circumstance I always wanted to talk about Harry, wanted to feel his name on my tongue and fill the room with my thoughts of him. Sandra said, "Why did you say you were busy? I was just sitting at home. We were supposed to hang out."

I'd had the past night to come up with a better story now. "I just thought you wouldn't want to walk. It was hot. You hate sports."

"Walking's not a *sport*. Are you serious?"

"Well, it's not with that attitude." I forced a smile. She didn't. "Fine, next time if we walk somewhere I'll tell you. Okay?"

"I just think it's weird you didn't want me there. And by weird I mean you were being a dick."

"It wasn't *you*, I just—"

"I also just really didn't want to be alone."

She'd been like that as long as I could remember, the kind of person who gravitated toward noise and commotion and who scored off the charts in those *How Much of an Extrovert Are You?* quizzes online. In elementary school she used to always get in trouble for talking to other people during class, and in high school she'd go to anyone's party even if she didn't know a single person there. I said, "I'm sorry."

"Yeah, whatever. Keep it."

"I'm just—"

But she was done with the conversation; TianTian Chien had come in and Sandra was bounding over to talk to her without a backward glance, which was a rebuke, I knew, even if no one else in the room would notice. I sat down heavily, a simmering feeling in my chest. It had been *one* afternoon, I thought. And for all she knew I was going to hang out with her later in the day. She was overreacting. But even at the time, I think, I knew that what was masquerading inside me as pure resentment was more complicated than that, something maybe closer to a form of guilt. Which made it worse, actually. I held that against her.

Later, by the time Harry's and my friendship was pretty widely established, Sandra told a bunch of people she thought I was a social climber. I never got past it, and a coldness filled the distance between us. If I was talking with Regina and Sandra showed up I'd usually go somewhere else, and a few times Sandra had made a big deal out of it. "It's okay, go ahead," she'd called after me once. "Go find someone better to talk to. Go for it. That's right, keep walking. You'll get more popular that way. Keep going." That was the time I'd turned around and snapped, "Bitch." I hate myself for it still.

By that point, Harry and Regina were going out, which seemed like a double standard given that she and Sandra were still best friends (hadn't we both chosen Harry?), but I guess it wasn't; it was more that Sandra thought I'd been a hypocrite, I think. Regina liked Harry from the beginning, so Sandra never judged her for that the way she did me. And maybe Regina didn't make her feel like she'd chosen against her; I'd always suspected Harry came second for her, after Sandra. Or maybe we all just forgive the people we love, because we love them, and for no other reason than that.

But anyway, so Sandra had made it clear what she thought of me, and someone's opinion of you isn't the kind of thing you can exactly confront someone over or defend yourself against, especially when that would mean bringing too many things you'd rather keep hidden out into the open; it's just that every time from then on when you see them (which in my case was kind of a lot) you know that they think you have no principles, which, cool. Especially because loyalty matters a lot to me. I'd still do Ethan any favor he asked, and it's been twelve years. But as far as Sandra was concerned I was someone else completely, and I'd always resented her for it.

I told myself that, anyway, because it let me off the hook. But maybe it was always more that I couldn't ever quite face her. Maybe it was just that she was a witness to a part of myself I'd rather bury. That's probably why I let things stay that way—I was always afraid she'd expose me, even if just to myself.

·   ·   ·

I was hanging out in the library after school waiting for Harry to get done with a lab group meeting one day after school last year, right in the middle of the ASB elections, when Sandra came and slid into the chair next to me. I was drawing (I was forever working on my RISD portfolio; I probably slept five hours a night all year) and I looked up. She said, "Hey."

I probably couldn't quite hide my surprise. "Uh—hey?"

"Could you sound less excited to talk to me? That would really make my day."

"I wasn't—" I pretended to clear my throat. It was probably no use pretending. "What's up?"

"I have a proposition for you." She leaned forward. "Who are you drawing?"

"No one. Just doodling."

"Regina said you're just applying to art schools."

I put my pen down. "Yeah. Ideally just one, actually."

"Oh, gross, you're doing early decision? If I only applied to one school I literally don't think I'd be able to get out of bed in the morning. Just thinking about that kind of pressure makes me want to die.

It's like colleges were like, wait, how can we possibly determine your self-worth in a way that's even more stressful and even more degrading than it already is? Boom: early decision."

I smiled in spite of myself. The truth is that I missed her—all along I'd missed her. I was just too much of an ass to do anything about it, too much of a coward to make a first move. "So you're applying more than one place, I take it. You know where?"

"Everywhere. Like literally everywhere. I have no chance." She laughed a little, not like she actually found it funny. The sad thing was, it was possibly true. Sandra worked hard, but she wasn't someone everything came easily to, not a Harry or a Regina, and her parents refused to forgive her for it. She'd probably get into the lower UCs. Irvine might be a stretch. "But I'm avoiding thinking about it. Anyway, I'll save you the suspense. I wanted to talk to you about the float."

"Oh, right." It was homecoming season, and Sandra was in charge of our class float. Sandra loved floats. She'd spearheaded the efforts every year since we were freshmen, one reason I'd always avoided it. The theme that year was Around the World, which I knew because a side effect of Sandra being in charge meant Regina spent a disproportionate amount of time talking about homecoming, and for a few weeks we all had to pretend we cared about our preternaturally ungifted football team. (Should've made homecoming during a badminton game. At least then we might've won.) "What about it?"

"I want you to design it."

"You want what now?"

"Design it. I think we have a really good shot at winning this year instead of the seniors. Their float last year sucked—remember their sixties theme and it was, like, three girls in poodle skirts? That whole class is super mediocre. So if you design it and we build it, there's no way anything they come up with will—"

"Who's going to build it? You know there's probably like ten people in each class who even care about winning, right?"

"But I count as twice as many people at least. Hence, our win. You'll help, right? I'm wearing you down?"

I was never going to say no to her. I mean, she was offering me a chance to literally stick my art on a wagon and parade it in front of hundreds (okay, dozens) of people. Of course I was going to say yes.

The three years since we'd talked had given me a while to pretend she was someone she wasn't—someone it didn't matter if I lost, I guess. But I understood: this was a peace offering, after I'd proven I didn't deserve one. I said, "Yeah, whatever you need." I should've said more.

"Perfect. Draw something and give me plans by Friday." She'd picked up her purse and turned to go when I said, "Can I ask you something?"

She turned back around. "Maybe."

"Why— This is going to come out badly. But how come you're running for president instead of vice president again?"

She looked evenly at me. I thought she wouldn't answer. After a while she said, "Does Harry think I'm a bitch? I asked him if he cared before I decided to run."

"Nah, he doesn't think that." It was news to me that she'd asked him. What was he going to say—*No, don't run*? *Yo, I actually need this to feel good about myself*? "I was just wondering, that's all. Forget it."

"Oh, you know," she said finally. She smiled; I don't think I realized it at the time, but there are people who always smile when they're upset, and she was one. She pitched her voice in an imitation I knew was supposed to be her parents. "You don't win. Too lazy. Never best in anything. Don't waste time trying if you don't win. College don't want to read about number two."

"That's messed up."

"Well." That smile again. "It's not a big deal either way. I probably won't win, anyway. Everyone loves Harry, right?"

It felt like a loaded thing to say, and I think she meant it that way. I could feel my face turning red and I mumbled something about the float, how I'd get ideas and draw up plans, and then I pretended to have to check my phone so she'd take off. Which, I mean—she was probably teasing. How hard would it have been for me to just laugh it off, or say the truth, which was that everyone says stupid shit when they're freshmen and it's not something you're supposed to carry with you?

The election was a week later—speeches in the gym while all of us were cramped in on the bleachers, Mr. Hartwell getting on the mic to remind us this was supposed to be about people whose achievements we admired and trusted and not just a popularity contest (one of the white stoner sophomore guys sitting near the front booed, which made everyone laugh). Harry's was about the importance of inclusivity and kindness and diversity and all the other things he's been saying our whole lives (in other words, practice for if he ever runs for political office someday). Sandra's was about how whatever else we did that year, we should make sure we also did things to just relax and live in the moment.

Mr. Davidston, who taught my Honors History class, taught the Leadership class too and was giving extra credit for the first five people to sign up to help tally the votes, so I signed up. I didn't know Regina had, too, until I walked into the teachers' lounge and she was there.

"At least your civil war's almost over, right?" I said. And Regina said—I've never forgotten this—"I've been getting stomachaches thinking about how one of them's going to lose." Then she looked around the room. "Can you keep a secret?"

"Yes."

"I think I might break up with him."

"You're what?" I grabbed her sleeve. "When?"

"I don't know. My parents would kill me if they found out I had a boyfriend. And I always feel weird about it at church. But mostly— I've just been thinking about it. For kind of a while."

Then Mr. Davidston got there and I was spared having to come up with the right thing to say. We all took an honor pledge not to share numbers with anyone outside the room and split the ballots into five piles to tally. I thought about how Harry would take it if he lost, and I thought about how all year so far he'd been letting me cheat off him in Advanced Geometry because otherwise I'd be tanking. I thought about him having no idea right now that Regina was thinking about dumping him. And I thought—it physically hurt to think—about how hopeful he was. The force of someone else's hope can be completely crushing.

It was much closer than I would've expected. Leaving the room I felt kind of sick, and I told Regina my mom wanted me to go home and I hurried off before she had a chance to say goodbye. We weren't supposed to tell anyone results, but I texted Harry to tell him— Davidston was going to call all the people who'd run, but I wanted to be the first. I waited until I was home and then I closed the door and waited until I heard my mom go out into her garden, which was stupid, because it was just a text, but I was nervous. His phone did that ellipses thing that meant he was typing, then it stopped, then he typed again, then stopped, like he couldn't figure out what to say. Finally he wrote back, *Fuck I was nervous. Just been sitting here trying to calm down. Thanks for telling me, buddy.*

In the morning they made the announcement. I told myself not to look at Sandra, but then I did, and I saw her eyes fill with tears, and

I saw how long it took her to wrest her expression into something presentable in public. She clapped for Harry along with everybody else.

He was so happy; I caught him sneaking off at lunch to call his dad to tell him, his hand cupped over the phone like he didn't want anyone to hear. I avoided Sandra, and I avoided Regina a few days, too. And I waited for her to break up with him, and I thought about warning him, and in truth the only reason I didn't was that I never knew how to bring it up. And then, of course, Regina never did.

I have never told anyone this. I wanted to at the time—I wanted to immediately, mostly because I felt like garbage—but who was I going to tell? The truth is, though, Harry was supposed to lose. I lied tallying up my votes.

I still can't say exactly why I did it. I knew it was wrong. And deep down I think I only even partly wanted him to win; watching him smile modestly at everyone the next day I was filled with this rush of something that definitely wasn't happiness. Maybe I wanted to give him something and that was the best I had. Or maybe I wanted to let Harry have something I might've, maybe, wanted for myself—not the election itself, which I didn't care about, but just the idea that you would want something or want some version of yourself and you would get it. Maybe I wanted to hang on to the belief that the world worked that way for as long as I could.

Or maybe it was none of that, maybe it was something much shallower and less nuanced. Maybe it was just that between him and Sandra, obviously I wanted Harry to win.

SEVEN

The SAT is a couple of weeks later, and Monday Harry's still in a weird mood, worrying about the test. He's taken it twice already—first he got a 1580 and then the second time he dropped down to 1540, which really rattled him.

"The worst part is, I know I'm always bad with dangling modifiers," he says as we're heading to the rally court for lunch, talking loud over the echo of all the footsteps and conversations in the concrete hallways outside the math wing. He's holding his books against his waist, and it contours all those lines of muscle in his arm. "I swear I miss every single one of those questions. So I studied them all the night before, and I think I still missed them anyway."

"You dangled modifiers in public? Have some decency."

"Yeah, yeah." He smiles, but in an obligatory way. "I wish I remembered the questions so I could look them up."

"You probably got it this time," I say. But I kind of hope he didn't, that somehow his scores will magically be exactly good enough for Brown and no better. We'd be just miles apart.

And then we're at the planters and everyone's milling around and eating—no Regina today—and Harry marshals himself for lunch, teasing Priya Dev about something that happened when they were both taking the SAT, sitting cross-legged, his hands on his knees, nodding sympathetically as Margie Rhee talks about how she's gotten maybe four hours of sleep a night all week. He's soothing for a while, and then—he has impeccable instincts—knows just when to pivot into joking around again, teasing her about the time she made wristbands with the solubility rules printed in five-point font sophomore year when we all took Honors Chem.

I know him well enough to know he's still down about his test, though. I've never brought up the thing that I always felt like, underneath everything, knitted us together early on: that the truth about Harry is that he's always felt like he has to distract the world from noticing he doesn't measure up, that deep down he believes that if you take away the GPA and the test scores and everything he put on his college apps, there's nothing left.

I wonder where Regina is. I have a goal today, after watching Grace and Mina come find her last week: I want to talk to her. Really talk, not the way we've been navigating around each other since last year. I want her to know I miss how it used to be between us and that I'm here for her. I was lying awake last night thinking about all these convoluted ways to try to lead into it, but really probably the easiest thing to do is just say, *Hey, I hope you know I really care about you, and I hope things with us are okay.*

Regina comes back ten minutes before the bell rings. Harry looks up at her from where he's sitting on the steps, putting up a hand to shield his eyes from the sun, and says, genially, "Where'd you go?"

"I was just looking at some things for story assignments."

"Anything juicy?"

"I was just—no, not really. Just trying to figure out—some things."

She sits down next to him. Regina and Sandra used to always sit next to each other at the very edge of the planters, sometimes cross-legged with their backs to each other, leaning against each other, or sometimes with their arms linked together, Sandra peering around the rally court and murmuring things darkly into Regina's ear as Regina laughed or sometimes rolled her eyes in disapproval. They always pooled their lunches together, so you'd sit next to them and not be able to pick out what belonged to each of them. A few times I tried to draw those lunches but I could never quite get the details right, never get it to look like more than just food.

I practice mentally: *hey I hope you know I really care about you and I hope things with us are okay.* I have the words ready, all arrayed in order like a paint palette, but as soon as I open my mouth they dry out. Regina reaches into her backpack, pulling out a container of soy yogurt and a plastic spoon. I'm eating a satsuma, and I hold it out for Regina to tear off a segment. She either pretends not to see or doesn't.

I've never said this aloud to anybody, and I resist letting the thought form in my own mind, too. But this is the thing I'm most afraid of, the fear that fits its lens over everything Regina ever says or does to me: that she blames me. Even if she doesn't know the whole story—and it would be so much worse if somehow she did.

I wonder sometimes which moments are the ones where she misses Sandra the most. There's a case to be made, I think, for when things are rough, when nowhere else in the world is a safe harbor and all that history you built with someone collapsed—every fight she has with her parents, every time the grief overtakes her. But I think there's something to be said for when it's just moments like this, too, the mundane ones that you can't talk about with anyone else because they don't matter all that much. One time sophomore year after Harry's sister was already away at Harvard he texted her a picture of their dad casually walking around in a pair of skinny jeans he'd gotten himself. *I'M DEAD,* Evelyn texted back, and then like twenty skull emojis. *DEEEEEADDDDDDDDDDD.* And I missed my sister all through middle school when my dad was struggling, sure, I missed her every time things were tough at home, but after that I felt cheated by her absence in all those small things and in all those times that were various opposites of hard: how one Christmas my parents, who never buy each other presents, both independently bought each other the same Costco garage opener as their sole gift, or the way my mom looks driving in her gigantic sun visor when no one else is in on the joke. Who does Regina text now about those stupid things that don't matter enough to tell anyone else, when she sees twin puppies on a walk or when a pair of shoes she's been eyeing go on sale or when she reads a mildly interesting article and wants to talk about a single line in it—is it Harry? Or do they just wither in the ether?

Talk to her, I tell myself. Do it now.

The bell rings. "I'll meet you guys," Regina says, getting up. "I need to stop by the office first."

Harry lifts his hand in a wave goodbye, then grabs his backpack kind of roughly and jostles it onto his back. When the rest of our group trickles out into the crowd he lets his public smile, the one with the crinkle around his eyes, slide from his face, and then he just looks tired after that.

.   .   °

It was March of last year, March seventh, that Sandra died. We found out in first period. It was a Wednesday, so it was a block day, and I was in AP English. When we came in and sat down we could tell Ms. Lee had been crying. When the bell rang she sat on the edge of her desk, a piece of paper in her hand, and said, "I want you to know that I love every one of you." Then she read the letter from the principal: *Dear Monta Vista community, it's with deep sadness that I have to inform you that junior Sandra Chang died yesterday by suicide. Counselors are available to help you process the news. Please notify a staff member immediately if you are having difficulty coping or if you believe you might harm yourself.* That was the whole letter, and when she finished it broke open a wall of silence that froze us in place.

Regina was whisked away by one of the counselors and we didn't see her the entire day. After school we all ended up at Harry's. Both his parents were gone on business, his mom in Taiwan and his dad in Singapore, and a steady stream of people trickled into his front room. Ahmed was there already, and he stood up when he saw me.

"What are you doing here?" he said, his voice hard. I'd never seen him look so angry. "You weren't even friends. You're just here because everyone else is, or what?"

I felt my face burning. "No, I'm—look, man, I'm sorry, I know you guys were—"

"You didn't even like her. Why'd you even come?"

Before I could answer—and what would I have said?—he'd turned away. He set himself down roughly on the couch, and said to Lisa Teng, who was sitting next to him, "He's never even liked her. He wants everyone to think he's this deep sensitive artist, but all he is is some asshole who can draw." Then he buried his fist against one of the cushions so hard the sound, even swallowed by the leather, made a sickish thud I felt in the pit of my stomach. I recognized the look Lisa gave me: she felt bad, or at least awkward, but also felt trapped by the moment, and that look was all I'd get from her. Harry was seeing Aaron and Maurice in at the door, and I don't think he heard. I escaped to the bathroom, my face stinging, my heart carved into shreds. I washed my face and toweled it off and stared at myself in the mirror. My eyes were red.

When I came back I settled myself on one of the leather chairs in the far corner of the room, opposite the couch where Ahmed was sitting, Regina next to him. Harry was standing by the wall, still shell-shocked. Susan Tung had taken a bottle of Xanax from her backpack and was passing it around. I took one. My parents had been calling, and I was ignoring the calls.

Later more details would trickle down to us—how she'd taken pills, how she'd been drunk at the time, how it was late at night. But that day it was all a gaping mystery. No one knew why. That was what we talked about. We knew she was worried about next year, we knew she sometimes seemed unhappy, we knew she had it pretty bad at home. But then everyone was worried about next year, everyone was sad sometimes, so many of us had problems at home. And even if it was worse for her at home than for almost anyone else—which I'd believe it was—we couldn't make that somehow fit cleanly up against death.

We still tried, though. All afternoon we kept trying to come up with some way to force the world into making sense.

Regina was staring at the wall, blinking rapidly, her face a mask. I watched her from across the room. There was an aura around her, something like a force field that made you afraid to get near her. Even Harry wasn't near her, although I guess constantly having to get up and open the door was his excuse. Next to me Susan was shaking so hard she was struggling to put the lid back on the bottle of Xanax. I reached for it and twisted it on and then touched her hand a second, which she didn't react to. It's a strange and uniquely painful thing when you try to reach someone and instead you pass right through them, like a ghost; it makes you feel not all the way there yourself.

After ten or twenty minutes—or maybe it was shorter than that, maybe it just felt like an eternity—Regina jumped up and announced she'd make everyone coffee. I followed her into the kitchen. She was a whirlwind, flinging open cabinets and pouring water and staring daggers at the coffee maker while it dripped, pouring the coffee into cups roughly, so it splashed over the side. I touched her elbow and said, "You need help?"

"No."

Her hands were trembling. I took the coffeepot from her, and even after I set it down the coffee still sloshed up the sides for a few seconds. Regina leaned against the counter and folded her arms against her chest.

And she almost said something to me. I could see how much she wanted to, and I was afraid I knew exactly what it was. She had the words formed on her tongue, and I could see them, and I put my hand on her elbow and I was ready for whatever it was she was going to say, I was determined to hear it and face it, and then she stopped herself. I could see her deciding not to tell me, deciding to hold it in. She took a deep breath that looked like it ached. "Open the cabinet over the oven, will you? Get me a tray and I'll put the coffee on it."

"Reg, are you—"

"*Get* a *tray*," she hissed. Her voice was streaked through with hatred. I got a tray.

We all sat there in Harry's living room as it got dark, clouds rolling over the hills and obscuring the treetops of Cupertino below.

Every now and then someone would start crying. A couple people went home, and each time someone did it hurt, kind of, in this lonely way I was pretty sure everyone else felt, too, or maybe I was wrong and it was just me. Around dinnertime we ordered pizza. Well, Regina ordered it, and when people tried to chip in, she refused. No one ate any when it came.

It was around six when Regina broke down—the only time I've seen her do it. Ahmed was the first one to grab her and hold on to her, whisper something in her ear, grip her shoulders and rock back and forth with her. When he did it I could feel a kind of tightening in the room, like someone pulling on some kind of string that knotted us all together. I cried, too.

I was the last one to leave that night. I helped Harry straighten up, and lingered until I couldn't anymore. I would be okay as long as I was here with him, I thought, but as soon as I left it would all hit me. When all the pillows were back in place and all the uneaten pizza slices thrown away and I was at the door to go, my mom waiting outside the gate, I said, "Ahmed thinks—" and then I couldn't go any further with it, couldn't say it aloud.

Harry didn't make me. I have always loved him for that.

"No, I know you," he said. "He's wrong. I know you better than Ahmed. I know you better than anyone."

That saved me in that moment, I think, that absolution. I've never told him that. It wasn't enough to erase the rest of it—a part of me still shrivels whenever I'm around Ahmed, that same part that worries the universe chose wrongly in keeping me here—but in that moment it was enough to hold me. I said, "Okay." I turned to go.

"Wait." He reached for my hand, and then he put his arm around my waist and pulled me closer. "Promise me you won't ever do that. What happened to Sandra, I mean."

My mind had flashed blank for a second when he'd touched me like that, and it took me a second to recover and answer. "I won't."

"No, Danny, I mean—" He looked frantic. "Promise me."

"I meant it. I promise."

He scanned my face. There was a heat creeping into all those cold places I'd been sinking into all day, and a tingling that ran through me like a shock. I held myself still and let him look. I wanted, in that moment, to give him the entire world.

Finally he said, quietly, "Okay." He dropped his arm. When he did it was like a cold gust of air blew over me and I wanted, kind of desperately, to ask if he'd found whatever it was he was looking for. He repeated, "Okay."

I would have stayed there forever. And it didn't mean anything, I don't think, it was just that the world had spun out of control around us and when that happens you reach for literally anything you can to steady yourself. But the moment had moved on, and also maybe part of me was scared of it, or maybe scared of ruining it, which is a different thing. I wished I wasn't, though, because the thought of leaving and being home without him felt like a small death.

Right before I closed the door behind me, though, something happened. Harry said, "Danny, wait—"

He stepped over the threshold and stood there for a moment in front of me. His breaths were shaky. He opened his mouth and I thought he might say something, but then he didn't. Instead he reached out and cupped his hand on my cheek, then he held it there, and then very gently he brought my head closer and touched his forehead against mine.

"You promised," he said finally, stepping back. "I'm not going to forget."

EIGHT

There are twenty-eight of us in Journalism this year and we're pretty self-sufficient; people mostly trust a bunch of kids stocking their transcripts with a UC-approved elective course. Our advisor, Mr. Renato, primarily teaches AP English and has a never-ending stack of essays to grade in his classroom next door and is in there at least 50 percent of the time, including today. We put out one paper a month and it's mostly Regina running everything, assigning stories and cajoling local tutoring companies and restaurants into buying ad space, badgering everyone not to write stories directly in InDesign and to remember hairline framing around photos.

Today is story assignment day. Most people always want to write, like, profiles of their friends or movie reviews, but Regina likes big, demanding stories: refugee crises and hate crimes and police brutality, all the deep fissures in the world. I've always thought they give her energy and purpose, and—paradoxically, I guess—a place to rest.

She seems a little nervous perched in front of the room—her

voice is pitched higher and she keeps running out of breath. She's wearing a striped blazer with the sleeves rolled up, tight jeans and heels, and she looks professional and adult, and she makes me wish everyone else here cared as much as she did. In here I can imagine a whole future around her—a life where she got out of Cupertino and built something else for herself, where I can turn on my TV each night and watch her distill all the chaos of the world into measured, narrated segments.

"As we know, we're coming up on the anniversary of Sandra Chang's death in March," she says, holding her hands still in her lap, "And I know that's still a little while out, but I wanted to see what everyone thought of doing a tribute to her in that month's issue."

Twenty-seven people go quiet. This is the first time since Sandra died that I've heard Regina bring her up in public voluntarily.

Here's the thing. When someone at your school dies by suicide it consumes you, not just you as an individual but corporately, the whole campus. Theories swirl and everyone looks for a reason, for something or someone to pin the unthinkable to. (Was she bullied? Too stressed out? Was she abused?) Parents start to flood school board meetings and the teachers panic, pulling you aside to ask if you're all right every time you're quiet or tired in class. The administration calls in experts and you take anonymous surveys about whether you've ever been depressed and psychologists come talk to your second-period advisory classes about calls for help and about healthy ways to deal with stress, and they don't let you all wear her favorite color on the same day or dedicate anything to her. You aren't allowed to post pictures or notes on the person's locker or have any kind of memorial service, and the family's funeral is private. And the places you once believed were safe—your school, your world—feel hostile and fragile and uncertain.

"What kind of tribute?" Advaith Jagtap, our news editor, says cautiously. After Regina, Advaith's probably the most invested in the paper; he's the guy you go to when you want to talk politics or current affairs, because he always knows what's going on and always has opinions and has probably already written a thirty-part tweetstorm on the topic. He hangs out with a group of mostly robotics-club-type guys and wasn't friends with Sandra.

"That's a great question," Regina says brightly. "Any ideas? I was thinking maybe we could interview different people so they could share memories, or—what does everyone think?"

Harry's sitting very straight, looking around the room protectively like a hawk, like he's just waiting for someone to say something out-of-bounds so he can pounce on it. Esther leans over and whispers something to Lori and Maureen, and Harry's eyes hover over Esther. She's crocheting something, a ball of bright blue yarn getting tugged around on the tabletop.

"That's a nice idea," Advaith says. Harry whips his head around to watch him. "I think what I'm wondering is—there's no way Renato will approve it, so like how would we—"

"Well, we don't run all our story ideas by him anyway," Regina says. "So this would fall under that same category."

Another silence. We all know how to rebel in standard, practiced ways: how to take Pepcid to hide Asian glow when we drink and how to lie to parents about having a boyfriend, who to ask to take the SAT for us or Photoshop a report card. But that's a different thing than blatant, public rebellion. The last time I cut class it was literally to go with Harry to the library so we could research our AP Lit projects, and even that made him nervous.

"Could it cause problems?" Esther says, not looking up from her yarn. Harry goes on high alert. Esther's crochet hook flashes back and forth. "I don't think we should do anything too risky."

"It's not risky," Regina says smoothly. "I mean, that's a really good question, but you don't have to worry—it won't have everyone's name on it. I'll be responsible."

"What if we just put it on the website?" Lori says. "Then we can take it down if we have to. Putting it in the paper is so permanent. Some people save every issue of the paper."

That startles Regina; she laughs. "Do they? Who? Even I don't do that."

"You totally do," Marvin Chu says, grinning. "Admit it. You probably have a special filing cabinet and everything."

"A special filing cabinet? You don't know me at all. Obviously I have them all framed on my walls." Everyone laughs. I've always both admired and worried about the breeziness she exudes in front of other people even when we're circling around everything that happened. "But the point is that it's permanent. Also, no one looks at our website."

"It's true," Advaith says. "I think there was a month when we got thirteen hits. Thirteen. And probably twelve of them were me."

Lori raises her eyebrows at Esther's cascade of yarn. "Well, I'm just saying."

"No, those are really great points, Lori, thanks. But, yes, everyone should know it's not really a question of *risk* to anyone. I just want to make sure, you know, everyone's on board with whatever we decide to do as our center spread."

"Technically," Advaith kind of mumbles, as nicely as possible, "according to that lawyer you made us go listen to, school papers don't have First Amendment rights. So I wouldn't say there's *no* risk. Just, for what it's worth."

"I just think," Regina says carefully, "that we have these resources here, and we have these voices, and we could just use them to write yet another profile of the boys' soccer team, or we could also use them to write things that would actually affect people in a meaningful way."

"Right," Advaith says. "Well, yeah, that's a separate issue, then. That's what we decide is morally right."

Esther sits back in her chair and taps her crochet hook on the tabletop. The door swings open, and we all kind of freeze, but it's just Francesca Deeths walking in late, not Mr. Renato. Esther puts her crochet hook down and folds her hands on the table.

I stay quiet. There's a cold dread spilling into me, that same feeling I get when I sit down to draw and start panicking or when I imagine my dad just never finding another job, and I don't know why. I don't know why I want everyone (or even someone, even just Esther) to say we shouldn't do it. Maybe it's that I'm not sure what Regina wants from this. Or I'm not sure it will fix anything or do anything, and when you think you want something, and you do it, and then it turns out it wasn't what you wanted—where does that leave you?

"What about her family?" Advaith says. "Will this violate their privacy?"

"It won't be anything new," Regina says tightly. "This isn't, like—reporting. It's a tribute. It's not really about privacy. Should we vote on it?" She looks at Harry uncertainly. "Or—"

"I don't think we need to vote," Harry says, looking around the room to dare anyone to argue. After he says that, of course, no one will. Everyone knows Regina was Sandra's best friend.

"Regina, it's admirable that you're taking a stand on this," Harry says. "It really is."

Something twists in me, watching him say that, and almost immediately I'm ashamed of myself. Because, what—do I not want them to be happy? They're my best friends.

Maybe I'm just not convinced by his performance. Harry loves rules, the safety of them around him, context to operate within or—rarely—against. And why shouldn't he? Rules have always been kind to him.

Regina says, "What do you think, Danny?"

I sit up straighter, my heart lurching against my chest. I didn't expect to be directly asked.

"Ah—" I say. "I think, um—" I imagine Sandra unimpressed, tainted by the cheapness of our gesture. Regina would mean it, of course, with all her heart. But there are definitely people in here who wouldn't. Kathryn Liu, I mean—did she ever talk to Sandra in her life? But you can't say that, definitely not to the whole class. I of all people can't say it.

"I think yeah, definitely," I lie. "If that's what you think we should do, then yeah."

"Will you draw a portrait of her?"

I blanch. Regina's gazing at me evenly, her expression carefully constructed, and I can't read enough in it to know whether this is supposed to be some kind of punishment or some kind of test.

But, again, how can I say I won't do it? There's only one answer here. Regina knows that, too. She could've asked me in private, she could've not asked me at all, but she chose this.

"Yeah, sure," I say quietly. The muscles in my back bunch together, a slow sort of cramp. "Just tell me whatever you want."

鴛

On the night of your birth in Wuhan the moon is a sliver in the sky, and you slip into the world beneath a fraction of moon. It's an omen, perhaps, a banner unfurled over you to declare that your life, too, will be marked by fractions, divided into pieces of a whole.

Your parents are nervous, young, excited. Your mother is running on no sleep and an adrenaline high, staring at you swaddled in your tiny bassinet. Your father is afraid to hold you. He keeps breaking into incredulous giggles, then trying to make himself sober and solemn again, especially when the nurses or doctors sweep into the room. Nine months has been a long time to wait, long enough to make you seem a fiction of their imaginations. And yet here—warm and wriggly and perfectly formed—you are.

Already, this night you enter the world, many are leaving it; it's possible, in a sense, to imagine that you have displaced them. You arrived on a wave of joy, dispelling old ghosts from the room you entered, and for now it's easy to miss the ways time is already etching itself into your new, tiny body. But people vanish every day. They vanish into new towns and countries, into death and illness, into the past and into different presents; they vanish all around you, they vanish sometimes slowly and sometimes with no warning. And so too it will soon happen to you.

But that first night, the three of you there on your very first night into the world, no one knows this. Your parents marvel at you. They inspect you, your tiny perfect fingers and toes, a hundred times. Perhaps, holding you there in her arms, amazed at the heft of you, the fact of you, your mother can fool herself into believing she'll hold on to you like this all your life.

NINE

Before Christmas break we have a group video project in Spanish, which I hate for the tediousness of the editing but like for the excuse to hang out with people I wouldn't otherwise. I spend a week at Ruby Lau's house after school darting around in a Harry Potter costume we appropriated from her little brother and saying we hope for dinner Hogwarts will serve cacahuetes (we all found the word irrationally satisfying to say freshman year, all find excuses to work it into our dialogues still) to hit our four examples of the subjunctive tense. On the last day, we go into Ruby's bedroom to find something Allison Dannon can wear as Hermione and there's a picture of a junior-high-aged Ruby and Sandra on the desk. The picture's carefully angled and there's a moat of emptiness surrounding it, separating it from all the papers and photos and two crumpled sweaters tossed haphazardly onto the desk. I didn't expect to see Sandra here. I'd never thought of her and Ruby as good friends.

"This works, right?" Allison says, holding up a gray sweater, and I look at her, startled.

"Yeah," I say. "Perfect."

I get stuck in a dream sequence that night. I'm in first period again and Ms. Lee is reading the letter about Sandra, and I'm feeling again that very beginning of what it means to lose someone forever. But then—this is the part where I get trapped—Ms. Lee reads it again and this time it's Harry, and then again, and this time it's Regina. I'm trying to get up to run, to find them before it's too late, but my legs won't move.

I wake up panicked and suffocating, a feeling like a boot on my chest. I gulp down air and wait for the night to settle over me. Outside my window the plum tree is rustling in the wind, the leaves brushing against my window. I try to root myself back in the world, the real one, where Harry and Regina are both still here, both fine. I reach for my phone. It's 4:43, and as I'm still looking at the screen the numbers blink to 4:44, and my stomach folds in on itself. I've never been one for any of the things my mom thinks are lucky or unlucky and I'm never superstitious except, apparently, in the middle of the night when the whole rest of the world is shuttered away out of reach and it's just me and my phone blinking three numbers that in Chinese sound almost exactly like the word for death.

I should call them. They would understand. Isn't it better to wake someone up in the middle of the night than to be left wishing you had? I have my finger on their speed dials a dozen times, maybe more, and my heart never quite settles down. But I don't do it; I can't tell Regina *I was worried it would be you this time* if she picked up. Your fears at night aren't something you can carry out past the walls of your mind.

I can't go back to sleep. Finally I get up and slip out of bed. I'm too old for this—I've been too old for this for like a decade—but I slip quietly down the hall to my parents' room. Their door is open, like I'd hoped it would be, and I sit down cross-legged outside it.

I used to get nightmares a lot when we first moved here, and my mom would always come rushing into my room. That sound, her footsteps flying down the hall toward me, would hold the night at bay. She would lie down next to me and stroke my back until all those dark worlds looming in the shadows had retreated and I could sink back into sleep, and I'd wake up in the morning and find the blankets pulled tightly over me, my pillow straightened and my pajamas buttoned up. (When I drew the portrait of my mom I submitted in my portfolio I drew those blankets as part of her forehead, the lines taut from being tucked in.) My dad's always been a noisy sleeper—he has mild sleep apnea—and I'm grateful for it tonight. I sit silently, the wall cold against my back, scrolling aimlessly through the internet on my phone and wishing it were dawn.

I've been sitting there almost twenty minutes, the dream still clinging, when I drop my phone. It clatters onto the hardwood, the noise exploding against the quiet of the house. In the near dark I see my mom bolt upright in bed, her hand flying to her chest. I scramble up.

"Sorry," I whisper loudly. "Sorry. That was just me."

"Daniel? What are you doing out there?"

"Um—" Their bedroom is all the way at the end of the hall, and I can't think of a good answer. "I was just—"

"Are you sick?" My mom pulls a blanket around herself and swings her legs down to the floor and then comes padding toward me, peering into the dark. "I'll make you—"

"No, I'm not sick," I say, before she can tell me she'll boil herbs for me to take. "Just—just up."

"Aiya, Daniel, it's so late. You should be sleeping."

"I know."

Already I can feel the total, swallowing loneliness of her going back to sleep. She squints at me in the dim hallway, and something almost imperceptible shifts in her expression. "You should eat something. It's not good for your stomach to be so full of acid all night. Come."

She heads down the hallway toward the kitchen, and I follow, weak with relief: she'll turn on a light and for as long as she's in there with me, I won't be alone in the dark.

"Why are you awake still?" she says, flicking on the kitchen light.

I shrug. I've never talked to them about Sandra. It felt too distant from their own lives, a chasm I couldn't bridge just through repeating the facts—I could feel how they'd get mangled and shrunken in my telling. When they asked about her I'd lied and said I'd barely known her and that we had never been friends. I don't know why. My mom probably remembered me going to Sandra's house as a kid, and maybe they knew I was lying, but they left it alone, even though—I saw them read it—there'd been tears in my mom's eyes when they read the letter the superintendent sent home.

I sit down at the kitchen table. I have that vaguely nauseous ache in my stomach you get when it's the middle of the night and you're awake. I didn't notice it earlier, underneath the dream hangover—like when you clean a dirty dish and then it's broken anyway. "Just couldn't sleep."

She makes a *tsk*ing noise. She pulls out the leftover pot of pork and lotus root soup from dinner and ladles some into a bowl to microwave, then puts the bowl in front of me.

What am I going to do next year when they're on the other side of the country? I imagine a roommate watching me struggling to pretend everything's cool after a nightmare or when I have the flu or something. I imagine my parents coming back from their weekend Costco runs to a quiet, empty house. Maybe it'll be different in the daylight, but right now I hope they're the kind of parents who call a lot. Probably they will, probably for things like reminding me to register for classes or demanding to know whether I'm eating enough vegetables. "Thanks, Ma."

We eat quietly. The soup is hot and salty and sharp with ginger. Food tastes better in the middle of the night, I think—more soothing.

I think how much my mom would've loved to have an adult daughter, someone who'd come over and drink tea and gossip with her at night, someone to go shopping with or maybe to Napa or something on weekends, not that my mom ever really does either of those things. She would've loved having a daughter to feed when she dropped in.

"Is everyone coming over for Christmas?" I say, raising the bowl to my chin and sipping the broth. We all love Christmas, and it kind of snuck up on me this year—it's just a week and a half before break.

"Yes, I think so. Everyone as usual."

"Are you excited?"

She kind of laughs like I said something bizarre; it's the word *excited*, I think, the idea that she'd pin it to herself like a name tag, describe herself that way even if it's true. "So much work."

"What? You love Christmas. You like cooking."

"I'm getting too old."

I roll my eyes. "You're not old. I can help you cook, though."

"Aiya, Daniel, you don't know how to cook. Worthless in the kitchen." I grin, and she takes my empty bowl. "Are you hungry still?"

"I'm good. Thanks."

She puts the bowls in the sink and reaches for her rubber gloves. I'd offer to wash them, but if she does it that means she'll stay here longer and I don't have to go back to my dark, quiet room. I guess I could at least turn on the lights. She scrubs and rinses the bowls and puts them in the dishwasher to dry, and I say, impulsively, "Do you ever miss Texas?"

She looks surprised. "Texas? It's been so long."

"But do you ever miss the people from there? Like the Parker-McEvoys, or"—I almost say the Ballards, but I stop myself—"or anyone else?"

"It's much nicer here." She pauses. "I miss the Freshtival."

I laugh, startled—I'd forgotten all about that. It was this garden festival, and we used to go every year. Kids got free plants if you dressed up, so my mom used to gather up as many of the neighborhood kids as possible and pin green leaves to our hair, and you could enter the Fruits and Vegetables show. My mom entered her cai tai, but they didn't know how to categorize it and no one knew what it was supposed to taste like, so she didn't win anything. "You got robbed," I tease. "Your cai tai should've won."

"They don't eat it. Americans don't know how to prepare vegetables. Next year, Daniel, you'll have to cook them for yourself. Make sure you eat five servings a day."

"You never miss Auntie Monica, though?"

"You meet new people." Does she really feel that way? I don't get how a person can. She peels off her gloves and busies herself wiping down the countertop, moving the bottles of sauces and oils out of the way. "People are the same everywhere. Some good. Some bad." She yawns hugely, then switches back to Chinese. "It's so late, Daniel. You have to be up in less than two hours. You should go try to sleep just a little bit more."

Back in my room I make myself imagine she's still awake, reading or thinking about her garden or watching the night pass by so I can stave off the dark primal fear of being the only one up. Finally a little before six, forty minutes before my alarm goes off, I fall asleep.

Still, the uneasiness from my dreams stays with me all morning, and I don't feel better until I see Harry and Regina walking together by the cafeteria—silently, like they aren't speaking to each other—and tap both of them hello to feel them solid under my hand, to reassure myself they're real, alive.

＊　＊　＊

All day, though, I think about what my mom said about the people we knew in Texas—*some good, some bad.* I only knew the good ones. I didn't know there were both.

I look up every connection to Clay Ballard and Austin I can think of. I google some of the surrounding cities, too. And I find things— the street he used to live on, although I can't find the dates and it's not an area of town I remember—but nothing to explain a connection.

It's close to midnight when (let it not be said that I learned nothing in all my years of Journalism) I look him up in the archives of the *Daily Texan*, the school paper. And there's an alumni profile of him in there, something that didn't show up in a Google search. His MBA was, it turns out, a few years before my parents came to Austin, which means he could've easily still been in Texas when they got there. The article says he graduated near the top of his class and went on to start a debt collection company, which I think must have been right before he moved to the Bay Area. He saw an opportunity amid a housing crash, apparently, and jumped on it, purchasing debt from lenders.

How do you purchase debt? Regina would know all this, I think— there were a few weeks last year when she talked about things like redlining all the time. But I have to look it up. I'm kind of stunned, reading through a few websites, that this is a thing—that you can, without any connection whatsoever to someone who owes money, spend a fraction of what they owe and go after them with all you have and take them for whatever they originally owed someone else. And I'm stunned at how far you're allowed to go in ruining someone's life to take what's now, legally, owed to you.

My skin feels prickly. I should've paid more attention to what was in my dad's files. I remember checks made out to names I didn't recognize and I remember loan documents, but I should've looked more closely at what exactly those things said. At the time I wrote them off as unimportant. Because you never see the whole picture, maybe—you just sculpt the world around you so it fits into the box you've made for it, so it matches everything you already know. Or maybe that's not true, either—maybe you just see what you choose to.

T E N

Christmas this year dawns cold and clear, a sharpness infused into the whole world. I go for a run in the morning, all the Christmas lights in the neighborhood dulled and faded in the bright sunlight, and when I get back my mom is in full holiday prep mode.

At heart, I am a child about Christmas. I believe it will fix everything. The act of it, the coming together and the goodwill—I always expect big things from it. And it always manages to flatten all the problems lurking around it, too; if we can shelve whatever's wrong for the day, then nothing can be quite as bad as it seems.

Tall order, this year. Four days ago, my parents sold my dad's car, which they tried to spin to me as no big deal, which didn't work because I'd been hearing them argue about it the past two weeks. When my mom came home from work she was tight-lipped and quiet, aiming most of her conversation toward me in a way that felt pointed, and my dad retreated into himself, eating dinner in silence and then doing the dishes without saying a word. Two days ago they got into a fight over my dad buying two bottles of name-brand mouthwash.

I've been trying to escape into drawing the way I always used to. I wanted something new to submit to the *30 Under 30* show and I also wanted to forget about it altogether, but the deadline was coming up and I couldn't tamp down that force of how badly I wanted it and so I gave up a few days ago and sent in the pieces from my portfolio I thought had the best shot. And I've been trying to come up with something Regina can use in her tribute in our March issue, too, but every time I find a starting point, try to trace that line of her cheekbones or the dark curves of her eyebrows, a sick feeling comes pouring into the room the way heat comes through the vents, that same feeling I get when I think about being at school the day of the anniversary, and I have to put my pencil down.

So the mood at home had been dark overall, I guess, with all three of us. But now: Christmas.

My mom always makes sea bass and duck for Christmas and starts planning in the summer, deciding what herbs and vegetables she'll plant to serve with dinner. This year she found whole chickens on sale a few weeks ago and now four of them are defrosting in pans on the counters, lined up like a small chicken army, and she's out rooting around in her garden. She's been worried about the weather all week, worried it'll be too dry or too cold, always checking the temperature online and going outside to finger the plants to see if there's been any damage.

We don't have any family in the area—or really anywhere, I guess, since both my parents are only children whose parents are gone—and we've always done holidays with their friends. They mean a lot to my parents, my mom especially. She was lonely here for a while when we first moved, always asking me about my classmates' parents. I remember when she found out Uncle Benson and Auntie

Mabel listed us as emergency contacts for Harold and Anson's school, it meant so much to her she cried. I always think how she probably would've loved to have a big family. I wonder why they never tried for any more after me.

By four, an hour before everyone's supposed to arrive, my mom's flying around the house getting stuff ready, dusting and straightening and pulling the plastic covers off all the furniture. Also, she's turned the heater on for once. It's legitimately balmy in here.

"Finish wrapping the presents for the kids," she says over her shoulder on her way to Windex the bathroom mirrors. My dad's been tasked with sweeping and vacuuming. I wrap the toys she got for everyone and doodle drawings on the wrapping paper with Sharpie. Sometimes when the kids were younger and we'd go out to dinner—always Chinese places with the giant lazy Susans and paper place mats on the table—I'd entertain the kids by drawing on the place mats. One time Harold Chiu carefully tore off and saved a drawing I made him of a robot.

But even trying to draw random crap on present wrapping that'll get crumpled up and thrown away—I've got nothing. I resort to drawing a bunch of cartoony dogs that look like Sushi, the Lims' collie, which will make the kids happy, at least.

"Do you think there will be enough food?" my mom says when I come back into the kitchen to get more tape. "I'm worried there isn't enough."

"What are you talking about? There's always way too much food."

"I should have gotten fish, too. Maybe I can send Baba to—"

"There's plenty, Ma. I'm sure everyone else will bring stuff, too."

"No, I told them not to bring anything."

It makes me laugh. "You're kidding, right?"

"I told them I would cook everything."

"Okay, cool, I'm sure they totally listened and will all definitely show up empty-handed."

"Should I send Baba—"

"No."

"Maybe I should get—"

But I'm already out in the living room with my tape. "Not listening!" I call back. They're all Chinese; obviously they're all going to bring something. "Can't hear you!"

At five-forty (which is basically five, Asian time) the doorbell rings. "Aiya, Daniel, the door," my mom cries from the kitchen, rushing to the hall mirror with her lipstick. The Lims and the Chius come pouring in, their arms weighted down with the pink bakery boxes and oranges and Saran-Wrapped platters of spareribs and noodles and braised abalone my mom insisted they wouldn't bring, and everyone's greeting each other in the hallways when the Pons come, too (also, for the record, bearing food), and with them that flood of goodwill that makes me feel a little safer in the world.

My parents' friends' kids are all younger. I'm four years older than Harold, who's the next oldest. The Huang kids brought iPads and plop down in the living room, and Chelsey Lim and Anson Chiu crowd around to see what they're doing. I sprawl out on the floor and talk with Harold, who's in seventh grade now, about whether his school's robots club is a sham (spoiler: it is; the advisor keeps trying to tell him drones aren't robots and as far as Harold's concerned, all credibility has been lost). Harold's this nerdy kid with giant glasses that keep slipping down his nose and a total lack of social awareness, and he's a genius. He takes practice SATs for fun. I get a kick out of him. Sometimes when I think about the kind of kid my parents would've chosen, if it worked like that, I think Harold is who my dad would've picked, and I wonder if my sister would've turned out that way.

My mom comes to recruit me to help her in the kitchen, the counters overflowing with steaming plates and bowls, and in between her hurried orders—*get a cup for Mabel a yi, put Lin a yi's cake in the refrigerator*—the aunties descend on me, chattering about how big and handsome I've gotten (sure, I'll take it) and asking a million questions about RISD. They pinch and pat me and plot out a future in which I'm famous and rich and successful until my mom pulls me aside, her smile gone.

"Go find Baba," she whispers, which is when it occurs to me that ever since the doorbell rang he's been in the back of the house. "Tell him to come back out here."

I assumed he would be doing—what, exactly? Getting ready or something, but when I find him he's lying on his bed watching TV. My hope flattens a little, loses dimension. I say, "Uh, Ma wants you to come out there."

He kind of grunts and pretends to be watching really intently. It's a commercial. "Are you coming?" I say. "What are you doing in here?"

He waves his hand. "I'll come out."

"She said—"

"It's okay. I'll come right out."

I close the door behind me. When my mom sees me come back without him, something in her expression collapses. An image of the two of them next year, the space without me here echoing between them, floods me with sadness. I wrestle the sticky rice into a serving dish and joke around with Uncle Benson and Uncle Fred. Convincingly, I think, even though in truth I have a sick feeling that maybe I should've tried to talk to my dad, or tried to alert my mom.

It's ten or so minutes before my dad comes back out. I see him coming down the hallway before he sees me, his face drawn, and just before he comes into the living room he plasters on a smile, folds himself into the back-clapping and loud exclamations of his friends. He relaxes, I think, a little bit. Christmas is back on track.

And it stays that way until my dad's pouring drinks and Uncle Benson asks, "So how is the lab? When will you move up to professor?"

Auntie Mabel makes a jerking motion with her head at him. My dad starts to answer and then stops, and then waits a beat too long, and then the silence stretches out until you feel it around you like a cloak. My mom's smile slips away. Auntie Mabel and Auntie Lin exchange a look. I realize, when they do, what happened—my mom already told the aunties what happened, but the uncles don't know yet.

"Why isn't he answering your question?" Calvin asks. He's five. Auntie Mabel motions at him to be quiet. Calvin frowns. "But—"

"Calvin."

"But you said—"

Auntie Mabel smiles apologetically around the kitchen. That could've been my dad's out; he could've made some joke about kids, or something. But he fumbles, isn't sure what to say, and then that awkward silence rears up again.

"Well, that's all right," Uncle Benson says loudly, realizing, I think, why his wife was trying to motion to him to shut up. "Always next time, right?"

"Right." My dad clears his throat, and stretches his lips over his teeth. "Yes. Next time."

 ·   ·   ·

Everyone leaves early. I can feel my mom frantic to keep them there, frantic for everyone to be having a great time, but as soon as presents are opened and red envelopes handed out the parents all quickly gather their kids, making excuses about getting everyone home to bed. When they're gone I find my mom sitting in the kitchen, staring blankly at the mound of dishes and the chicken carcasses strewn all over the counters.

"I'll do these," I say, trying to paint brightness into my voice, trying to ignore the pit in my stomach. "You should go rest."

My dad comes in. "Such a mess," he says, surveying the kitchen. My mom swivels her head toward the wall, fast, but not fast enough to hide the way tears well up in her eyes. Something in my dad's expression retreats. He holds up the half-empty wine bottle from dinner and says, roughly, "Should I dump this?"

My mom blinks at the wall and then wipes her eyes. "Okay," she says, fighting to keep her voice steady.

"Or should I refrigerate it?"

I glare at him. He doesn't look at me, though, and lifts the bottle a little. "You want me to just throw this away?"

"I don't care what you do with it, Joseph, I had no money for the fish and the duck, and we had to serve our friends chicken on Christmas, and—"

There's a cold feeling that starts in my stomach, spreading out to my extremities. "The chicken was great," I say quickly. "Auntie Lin kept saying how good it was."

They both ignore me. My dad starts to say something, then gives up—he dumps the wine into the sink, and it glugs loudly through the bottle's neck like it can't escape fast enough.

"It was fun to see everyone," I say. I can hear the desperation in my voice. What I want to say, of course, is *Tell me it's going to be fine with you two, with all of us.* "The kids are so big. It was great to see them, right?"

There's a looseness in my mom's expression, like she might come apart and never find her way back together again. My palms are sweating. She starts to say something, then stops. Then she puts her hand on my shoulder a moment. "Merry Christmas," she says, and that's all, and I hear her footsteps falling all the way down the hallway.

. . .

When I get up late the next morning, nearly afternoon, the laptop's missing from my desk—one of them must have come in when I was still sleeping—and when I find it on the kitchen table and look through their search histories there's a whole trail there of one of them looking up divorce.

The world bottoms out around me a second or two, wavers around the edges before it slowly balloons into place again. Which of them looked it up? Was it that one of them wanted or was even think- ing about a divorce, or was afraid the other did?

I try to calm my breathing, then call Harry. "What are you doing? You want to hang out?"

"Right now? I was going to wait in line at Din Tai Fung with my parents. You want to come?"

I'm careful to mask my disappointment. "That's all right. I don't want to crash your family thing."

"It's not a big deal. Actually—you want to come over? I'll just stay home. I'm not in the mood to sit around waiting in the mall for two hours. It'll be packed today anyway."

"No, you should go to lunch with them."

"Nah, they'll be glad to get rid of me. Just give me a couple min- utes. I have to shower."

He's still toweling off his hair when my dad drops me off— Harry takes the longest showers—and a few beads of water cling to his calves. Not everyone gets this: someone who'll drop everything for you, no questions asked. I know how lucky I am.

I will not think about my parents. I will not think about my parents.

And, mostly, I don't. We eat leftover prime rib from the Wongs' Christmas dinner and then play Skyrim while the food coma has its way with us, and then Harry wants to go outside and play basketball. They have a half-court out back next to the tennis court. We play one-on-one. I get my ass kicked.

"It's only because you never do anything you don't already know you're good at," I say over his gloating as we head back inside. "That's why you always want to play basketball."

"Damn right that's why."

"Uh, that was not a compliment."

"Anything is a compliment if you take it as one."

"That's definitely not how compliments work."

He laughs. Then he holds the smile, trains it at me until I feel something at the core of me start to liquefy. I can feel my heartbeat in my ears. Maybe it's from the exercise. I take the water he's holding out for me and drain it quickly, averting my eyes.

When we're back in his room he sprawls out on the floor and then says, "Oh, hey." He sits back up. "Regina got into Northwestern."

"She did? She found out?"

"Yeah, she heard the day before Christmas Eve."

"She didn't tell me." I would've expected her to. Knowing she didn't—what am I supposed to make of that? The distance unfurls like a carpet, rolls itself longer and longer, and a weight sinks against my chest. *It's exactly what you're afraid of,* Mr. X hisses to me. *She sees you. Sees right through you like a window.* "Was she stoked?"

"I don't know if I'd call it that. That program is damn hard to get into, too. It was kind of weird. I thought she'd be happier."

"Maybe she's just worried her parents won't let her go." They've always said she has to go to whatever is the best-ranked school she gets into, and I doubt Northwestern will end up being it. Even if it is, they've always said they'll never let her major in journalism. I hope she does it anyway.

"Maybe, yeah."

"Regina's parents are garbage." I always think of how he told me that after Sandra died Regina's parents made her take down all her pictures of the two of them and get rid of anything of Sandra's she still had in her room. *I think it just freaked them out,* Harry said. *They're scared. They're scared she'll—you know*—which was, I always thought, overly generous of him. So what if they're scared? Some things don't deserve the benefit of the doubt.

"They're definitely—complex."

"Yeah, yeah." I take out my phone to text her congrats. "What are you going to do, then?" I say, not looking up from the keypad. "If she goes, you'll be really far away from her." And: me. The thought of having whole states between us next year feels like someone took a hole punch to my heart. "You think you guys will stay together in college?"

"Maybe." He kind of laughs. "Or maybe she'll want an upgrade when she gets there. Who knows. We've never really talked about it. She might not want to do long-distance."

Sometimes (okay, a lot of times) I wonder whether she and Harry are sleeping together. Harry never says anything about it, which could mean they aren't or could just mean talking about it isn't his style. It feels like another lifetime that she told me how she was going to break up with him. I've never asked her about it since. For a while I kept waiting for it to happen, but it seems clear now it isn't going to, and I should probably be glad. It would be a stain on anyone's character to wish more loss on someone like Regina. The easiest thing to imagine is that after Sandra died she just couldn't do it—she needed him too much, and she couldn't endure another loss on top of everything else.

He reaches for a basketball shrouded by the edge of his blanket. "I'm scared I'm not going to get in anywhere."

"That's definitely not going to happen. But what about like University of Chicago or something?" I say. "I bet you'd like it there."

"Yeah, maybe . . ." He's too polite to say he would view that as complete and abject failure, but he would, obviously. It isn't that I want him in Chicago, either, I just wish he didn't see it as Princeton or bust. I guess what I wanted to say was *You could do a lot worse than Brown.*

"When you turned in your portfolio," he says, "did it feel like, I don't know, like you were ripping off your clothes so they could judge you naked? I don't know what I'll even do if I don't get in anywhere good."

"You'll probably get in everywhere you applied."

He hooks his leg over mine and then, without warning, rolls over so he's pinning me against the ground. I can feel his heart beating against mine, which means, probably, that he felt it when mine picked up. He grins in my face.

"Get off me," I say. My voice comes out kind of squeaky. I move feebly underneath him, not enough to actually shake him off.

"I'm trying to open up here and share my genuine fears and you're just brushing me off. You're probably going to get to RISD and find a new best friend, huh? Just replace me?"

I am hyperaware of every centimeter of him against me. And at the same time my mind is a raging mess of color and chaotic form, a Jackson Pollock painting splashed across the whole thing. I manage, "No." Then he rolls off me.

I'm out of breath. What am I supposed to make of that?

He looks unruffled. Why did it feel like a lightning bolt to me, then? My whole body is still tingling.

Harry palms the basketball and tries to lift it. "I'm starving. You want to stay for dinner? My mom said the cook got crab."

I do want to stay for dinner; I'd want to if the cook had gotten cardboard. I wait until I'm sure I won't sound out of breath. "I'll ask my parents."

He lies down on his back, tries to twirl the basketball around on his finger without it falling and clocking him in the face. He keeps having these near misses, swerving his head out of the way. "You're an idiot," I say. Today the emptiness of life without him feels more real to me in ways it didn't when I got the RISD acceptance. When my mom picks up, I say, "Hi, Ma, Harry asked if I could stay for dinner."

"For dinner? No, Daniel, come back home. We have to eat all the leftovers."

"I can have those tomorrow inst—"

"Don't stay for dinner. They'll think you don't get to eat enough at home."

"They won't—"

"Baba is home. I'll send him to get you." She hangs up.

"No go?" Harry says.

"Nah, another time. Thanks, though."

The ball thumps millimeters from his face again. He sits up, grinning, his arms stretched wide.

"What are you doing?" I say, my heartbeat not yet back to normal still. "Why do you look so smug? You're terrible at that. You have nothing to be smug about."

"It never got me, though, did it? I always got away."

At home: tense silence, a cold—the heater's turned off again—that slithers up against my nose and neck, my mom ensconced in her garden, tools arranged around her like armor. She's out there another hour at least (an hour that, for the record, I could've stayed at Harry's) and she comes back in wearing her sun visor and with her arms laden with some carrots and a bunch of greens. She fills the sink with water and plunges the vegetables under. The water swirls with dirt.

They've had all day to work things out together. I hope they did exactly that.

"Go get your father," she says without looking up. "Tell him it's time for dinner."

He slides into his chair without looking at anyone, and his unhappiness spreads through the room like a fog. My mom shakes out her napkin and smooths it over her lap. For dinner she spooned mushrooms and pickled vegetables over rice, and the chicken from dinner last night is waiting on the middle of the table on a plate. There's a tightness in my stomach.

"Lin still hasn't called me back," my mom says. Something about her tone, like using just the tip of your finger to touch a pan to see if it's hot—it makes me think they haven't spoken to each other much all day. My hope that they've reconciled fritters into nothing. "Anson left his jacket here last night."

"Did you leave a message?" my dad says.

"No."

"So maybe she doesn't know why you're calling."

"That's what I mean. She doesn't know why I'm calling, so she isn't calling me back. That's not like her. That's what I'm telling you."

"Well, how long ago did you call?"

"This afternoon."

My dad raises his eyebrows at his plate. "Maybe they're not home."

My mom tightens her lips. She reaches for a piece of leftover chicken. "I called her cell phone."

"Maybe her phone is turned off. Maybe they went to see a movie."

My mom takes a very deliberate bite of chicken, then another one. I say, "Good chicken, Ma."

She ignores me. To my dad, she says, "Anson might need the jacket."

"He's fine."

"He might not have—"

"He's *fine*," my dad says sharply. "Don't waste time worrying about it. It's not consequential."

The look she gives him feels like a knife. I remember that jolt I felt looking at the search history this morning.

Our chopsticks clink against our dishes. I chase grains of rice around my bowl. Brown rice, which none of us particularly likes, but my mom made the switch a few years ago after reading some article about diabetes.

She wants to say something else, I can tell. What I can't tell is whether my dad is oblivious to that, or is acting oblivious because he knows better. Maybe it doesn't matter. Either way, he's making everything so much worse.

"Regina got into Northwestern," I say.

My mom turns to my dad in a way that makes it abundantly clear they both plan to ignore me. "It's going to freeze tonight. That's what the forecast says. It will drop below freezing."

He sets his cup down harder than necessary and grunts.

"In the hills it may even get down to—"

"It's not going to freeze."

"The forecast says it's going to—"

"Don't worry so much about your garden," he erupts, his face going red, with a suddenness that I think even surprises him. "Of everything else—it's not important. You shouldn't be so attached. It's only plants."

. . .

This time they don't save the fighting for when I'm out of the house. When I get out of the shower I can hear them in their bedroom, their voices carrying down the empty hallway like a freezing wind.

"It's because you made last night so uncomfortable for everyone. You were hiding in the bedroom, and then you—"

"No one was uncomfortable, they—"

"Yes, they were uncomfortable, Joseph, because you hid in the bedroom and then you didn't speak to or look at anyone and then you pretended everything was fine at work, when they already knew you were fired."

"I was only being polite. I didn't want to ruin your dinner."

"No one likes to see other people's private business. And if they worry we're struggling maybe they would feel obligated to try to help. How can I see them now? I can't talk to them because they'll think they have to help."

A pause, which gives me brief hope it's over. Then my mom says, "Our savings is already—"

"You're overreacting. You—"

"I knew this would happen!" She's the first one to yell, and her voice is shaking, I think with tears. "I *knew*. I told you it was danger-ous. I told you it was going to ruin us. You wouldn't listen."

So she knows, then, what it was that he did. But that was the thing I haven't heard her say yet, the thing she keeps biting back. She hasn't outright blamed him. I stand in the foggy room, hugging myself in my towel. Outside the door there's another silence, one I feel inside my eardrums, my rib cage. When my dad speaks again he sounds drained.

"That's not what ruined us," he says. "You know that."

"We've been so careful all this time. How could you just—"

"It doesn't matter, Anna. You know it doesn't matter. We always knew it couldn't last forever."

* * *

I fall asleep with their words ringing in my ears—*that's not what ruined us, you know that*—and I don't know what time it is when my dad wakes me up. I garble something unintelligible, still half-trapped in sleep, and my dad whispers, "Wake up." He shakes me gently. "Wake up."

It's freezing. If my eyes weren't so bleary, I bet I could see his breath in the dark.

"What's wrong?" I say. And then my heart slams against my chest, because it's the middle of the night and he's wearing a jacket: he's leaving. This is him saying goodbye.

"Here." He holds out my ski jacket. "Get up."

"What is this for? Ba, I'm not—I can't—" I'm not going with him. If he's asking me to take a side, expecting me to choose him, I can't do that. I'm not leaving this house.

"Put it on and come with me."

"But—"

"Just come with me."

I get up. I'll go with him to the door, at least, try to talk him out of it. My knees are weak. I scramble for the right thing to say.

We pad down the hallway. He opens the door to the hallway closet and gathers an armful of towels and sheets, then slides the sliding door open onto the backyard. That part confuses me—maybe I'm reading the situation wrong.

The cold hits hard. My mom is outside, kneeling in the moonlight. She looks up, surprised to see us. "What are you doing?"

He goes and kneels next to her and puts his mound of towels on the ground, then plucks one from the pile and drapes it carefully over a row of her cai tai plants. It's one of the things she loves best in her garden—you can't find it in grocery stores here and it took her years to grow any that she thought were as good as what you could find in Wuhan. My dad tucks the ends of the towel carefully over the stalks. It looks like a ghost in the shadows.

I feel stuck in place, bronzed in my relief. "What is this?"

"The freeze will damage the plants," my mom says, holding out a sheet toward me. "The sheets will keep moisture from the ground. Maybe it will save some of them." The anger from earlier has slid away from her voice.

"Come help," my dad says quietly. He meets my gaze, and when he does I understand that he knows I overheard them earlier.

We work side by side in the freezing cold until I can't feel my fingers anymore and my eardrums ache. We swaddle her whole garden as the moon sinks toward dawn, and afterward I'm so cold I can hardly feel my hands. I bury myself under my covers and wait for the warmth to spread, for sleep to come. In the morning, all her plants made it through.

鴛

Your parents first meet in college, at Wuhan University, a castle-like building with green roofs on a campus teeming with trees, like a green-jeweled island among Donghu Lake and the Yangtze River. It's beautiful, made for postcards and glossy brochures, a stunning backdrop for your father to notice the quiet, graceful young woman sitting by herself eating dinner. Your father: decent, good-humored, ambitious. Your mother: loyal, anxious, bright, determined. They are young and beautiful and hopeful. They have both been met with tragedy, both lost parents far too young, but on such a beautiful campus it is possible to believe that the future now belongs to them. It's hard to begrudge them this—they're so appealing, this young couple shyly making their way toward one another—even though that future, later on, will leave no room for you.

You were not supposed to come yet. Not for years—you were an accident, and your timing was off. You were supposed to wait until your parents were settled into careers and felt ready for you, and maybe if you'd done that, if you'd somehow not come into existence that moon-slivered night, it would have all gone differently. Your fate will hinge on small choices. Starting with that one—your parents could have been more careful.

Your parents are just out of college when you're born. Your father dreams of becoming a professor, your mother of opening a hotel. Their dreams back then have form and shape and texture—the gleaming lab equipment, the silky bedsheets, those lives out there waiting for them. And then crashing unbidden up against those dreams is you, and life takes the sudden form of long nights of you squalling in your crib and all your small toys and clothes slowly burying the rest of the apartment.

As a baby you're utterly attached to your mother. You sob when she leaves the room or when someone else picks you up. In the mornings when she leaves for work it takes your grandfather thirty minutes to console you. When she's home with you you whimper, unmoored, until she scoops you from the vast, heedless universe and wraps you safely in your mei tai. You nestle yourself in the hollow of her chest and gnaw on your small puffy hand and examine the world from your safe perch, moving with her, a part of her, tethered to all you hold beloved. For now you believe in your mother's love as a talisman, that it will keep you safe.

At night she holds you next to her in bed. A palm seeking reassurance rests on your tiny chest to feel it rise and fall. Your mother imagines all the fates that might befall you, and recognizes that at least one of them will. Someday you will die. This, somehow, did not occur to her until you were here and she was confronted with the fact of you, but now when it's dark and quiet the knowledge consumes her.

It's possible that she's too attuned to this fear. That it's slithered through her heart and bitten through all those parts that might fuse with your own. That it poisoned her faith in your permanence, and because she never believed in it, she couldn't shape her life around it. That it made her surrender you before you were ever fully hers.

ELEVEN

I find out at the end of January that the pieces I submitted to Neighborhood were accepted for the exhibit. I'm shocked. I didn't really think I had a chance. They have me write up a bio and they send out a press release with all the contributors, and I read their email (*we were particularly intrigued by your treatment of shadow*) about a million times. I hold it in my mind all week, pulling it out to marvel at.

I won't lie, though—there's a sense of asymmetry at having something like this happen when I still can't draw the portrait for Regina. In a fair world I don't think it would've gone this way.

But, of course, it's not like I'm going to say no. Harry drives me into the city over the weekend to deliver my submissions. I lie and tell my parents, who are anxious and distracted but at least in ways that don't seem aimed at each other, that I have Journalism stuff.

"I'll be gone all afternoon," I say. My mom's going over a pile of bills again, and my dad's eating shrimp chips and watching TV.

"Be very careful," my mom says, not looking up.

"Okay."

"Be home for dinner," she adds. "We'll have—" She frowns at a line in their ledger, pulling the checkbook up closer and squinting. "Joseph, what does this say?"

I swallow my guilt and slip out the door, squinting when the light hits, the sunlight bright against my guilt.

In the car, though, Harry's excited—it's infectious, like it always is, especially because it's about my art. He's pumped it got accepted, pumped people are going to see it, pumped he gets to be there to see it, too. Turning off my street, though, he glances at me. "Why aren't you totally flipping out about this? I would be."

"Eh, I don't know." I reach up and pull the sunshade down. "Just stuff at home. I'm pretty sure as soon as I left my parents started fighting again. My mom just had that tone."

He winces. "That sucks."

"I really thought it was going to be, like, this thing that sucked for a few weeks, maybe a month, and then he'd be on to the next thing. I really did not expect it to be this complicated. And also—"

I hesitate. Harry says, "And also what?"

"And also I found out—you remember the files my dad had? I found out the people in them have this debt collection company and I've been reading up on how the whole system works and it's, like— extremely easy to get taken for all you have. And I'm worried my parents got tied up in something ugly. They keep making all these ominous comments that feel sort of out of proportion for one person losing their job."

"You think?" He makes a face. "I kind of doubt that. Your parents are smart, right? If they were in financial trouble why wouldn't they have just declared bankruptcy or gotten a loan or something?"

Something hot stirs in my chest—the kind of flippant way he

says it, maybe, like he knows anything at all about bankruptcy loans. "Yeah? They teach you about that at your country club?"

He laughs in that way he does when he's embarrassed. "Okay, fair enough. I'm just saying. I don't think it makes sense."

"Yeah, well, that's because you always want these neat elegant explanations for things. You think the world is an orderly place where everything eventually works out."

"No, I don't."

I roll my eyes. "Yes, you do. You have as long as I've known you. And my parents are the perfect counterpoint. Sometimes they just react in the worst possible ways and torpedo their own lives because they can't do the most basic logical things to change course. They're in debt in Texas, so they move to one of the most expensive places in America and my dad gets fired."

"But you think they'd really do that? You don't think that in itself is weird?"

Obviously I think it's weird. We're having this conversation because I think it's weird. But *weird* can mean so many things, most of them innocent, most of them just that people aren't always rational, that sometimes you don't hit on the right path the first time you go into the woods.

And, mostly, I'm done talking about it. I shouldn't have brought it up.

"They're just like that," I say. "It'll be fine. It's always been fine before. They'll figure it out."

We pass through the hills on 280, the grasses all tawny and golden from their winter deaths. There's fog creeping over the Santa Cruz Mountains, pouring between the soft peaks. I watch the movement of it, try to still each moment in my mind. It would probably be like everything else, though: nothing I could tame from the world long enough to get onto paper.

"For the record," Harry says around San Mateo, his voice quieter than usual, his eyes trained on the road, "I don't believe everything always automatically works out."

In the city, we find parking a few blocks over after circling for a while and driving past three spots Harry swears are too small (they aren't; he can't parallel park). It's bright out today, the city closing in as soon as we get out.

Harry jabs me as we're walking in. "You excited?"

"I guess." I am, obviously. I'm also scared. What if it's not enough, or what if it was all some joke, or what if they made a mistake and next to all the other work it becomes clear I'm a fraud, etc., etc. Or what if my dry spell doesn't wear off in time for RISD and in fact never wears off and this is when I peak and I will literally never pull this off again.

I take a few long breaths. I wish, kind of, that I'd figured out a way to get here by myself first, to see how everything looked once it was up and make sure it was actually something I'd want people seeing. But it's too late; we're already inside.

It's more crowded inside than it was the last time we were here. It takes a few seconds for the faces to emerge from the blurry crowd, come into focus, but then all at once they do: Aaron Ishido and Edwin Chen, Steph Sakamoto and Annette Lu, Noga Kaplan.

I can feel the shock etch itself into my face. It's at least five minutes of greeting everyone before I can whisper to Harry, "What the hell?"

He's smiling. "I, uh, may have told a couple of people about this."

"There are like thirty people here."

"Thirty? That many? I swear I only told one or two." He thumps me across my shoulders. "Good thing you suck at math."

The guy I remember from last time is there to shake my hand and take the portraits I brought in and fit them into gallery frames. We watch. The first piece is one of my mom. And then there it goes, up there on the wall: my art.

It feels like someone gently peeled back my skin and muscles, my rib cage, and carefully lifted out my heart and made copies of it and pinned them all over the building. My eyes well up, and I turn away so Harry won't see. He punches me on the shoulder.

"Damn, Danny," he says. "Look at *you*."

And everyone watches with me as the next one (this one's Harold Chiu) goes up. The portraits lit up in the clean, bright quiet, all of us held in a shared stillness—I feel it then, that power I think some part of me is always after. Or maybe it's not power after all, this feeling, and instead it's just a place to rest.

This is what Vivian Ho meant when she said you have to choose what's important to you and how far you're willing to go for it. When the universe zooms in on all that space I take up inside it and asks me why, this is the only answer I've ever known.

⸻

At home after the gallery showing, as soon as I've come in to tell my mom I'm back home, I go to my desk and pull out my Bristol pad.

I'm going to do it. This is all I am. I'll do this for myself and for my class and for Regina, who wasn't there today, but messaged me as we were driving home: *Hope it went well, sorry I couldn't make it. Harry spent like all week orchestrating this.*

I go back into the kitchen and make myself some coffee and then come back and roll a piece of paper into a blending stick, sanding the edges with a nail file I stole from my mom. I fold the pad to an empty page, and for a second the blankness of it sucks all the air from the room. These used to be the best moments, that wide open space where the whole page was possibility still, where it could be anything at all before I narrowed it into one thing only. I miss how alive and expansive it always made me feel.

But maybe it's like seeing a friend after it's been a long time, how you trust that when you brush away those webs of awkwardness the old friendship's still there underneath, the way I've always kind of thought it would still be with Ethan.

You have to start somewhere. I imagine a light source coming from behind her—all the lines dark and shadowed, Sandra backlit. It's been so long since I've drawn anything my strokes are choppy and short at first, feathering the lines and blurring her outline. I tear out the piece of paper and start over. It's the most expensive kind of paper I use and I almost never sketch on it, but I tell myself it's fine, even if I go through the whole pad it's worth it to be back in the game. This time—I haven't had to do this in years—I practice the strokes through the air first before I lay them down.

My palms are clammy. I drink some of my coffee. It's now or never, isn't it? All of today at the gallery still coursing through my veins—I feel wired. I feel buoyant. And everything you take in from the world becomes a part of you that flows back through you into whatever you draw, I know that. There won't be a better time than now.

I don't like to look at photos of people I'm drawing; I like to hold them in my thoughts and reach past any one static image of them, and I call her face to mind. I draw her eyes. I tilt the pencil and arc wide swaths of lead to color her ever-present eye shadow, lightly stipple in the dark circles under her eyes she always tried to makeup over.

It's ten minutes later that my heart squeezes against itself, drops off a beat, and then pounds back against my chest so hard it knocks my breath away. It's a different panic than the one that's started to feel like home to me these past months. It's not that it feels empty or that it doesn't look like her—those things I expected, those things I could manage—it's that it does.

I put my pencil down and toss the blending stick into my trash can, a queasiness vibrating like guitar strings through my heart. I could've done it if it didn't look like her. But it does, and I can't.

*   *   *

On Monday Mrs. Mosher lets us out a few minutes early for lunch, and I park myself outside Ms. Sharma's classroom to wait for Regina. She comes out talking animatedly with Joel and Rachel Pruitt, the twins, and after they head for the cafeteria I say to Regina, "Walk to my locker with me?"

"I have to go see Mr. Renato."

"Can I walk you there?"

She hesitates a second too long, and I feel that closed-offness again. "Sure, if you want."

Part of me wishes she'd said no—I'm not exactly looking forward to this conversation. I reach out to take the books she's carrying. "What do you have to see him about?"

"Oh, I emailed him yesterday to make sure it's okay to switch the date with the printer so the March issue comes out right on the seventh, and he emailed me back last night saying we should just stay on schedule and keep it for the twelfth like it's scheduled." She runs a hand through her hair that way she does when she's a little stressed.

She always gets like this in the final few days before we go to press, but it's early this time. "I should've just done it without asking. He probably wouldn't have noticed."

"Why doesn't he want to change it?"

"I think he just doesn't want to have to deal with the printer. But I'll tell him I'll do it."

"Ah. You don't think he'll find out, do you? About the center spread?"

She shrugs. "When was the last time he looked at something before it went to press?"

"Fair enough." I fight back the part of me that would keep her talking about the press logistics or about anything else, really, until we're out of time. "Hey, I, ah, wanted to see how it's going with all that. With the tribute, I mean. I keep meaning to talk to you about it."

"It's going all right." There's a tiny shift in her posture—she stands straighter, and her voice brightens. "I'm working on my piece, and Margie and Helena are getting quotes from people. I think they're going to just get as many as they can and then we'll pick the best ones. How's the art going? When do you think it'll be ready?"

"Ah, yeah, the art."

"I was thinking it would just be your art and a lot of white space, and—"

"Right. Yeah." I balance the books against myself with one hand and rub the other on the back of my neck, where the muscles feel tight. "About that, that's kind of what I wanted to talk to—"

Her expression shifts. "You're not going to do it?"

"Reg, I think I have to pass this time. Could you use a photo instead?" My palms are sweating. "It's just that my parents have both been such wrecks lately, and if I get in trouble for anything—I really think it might push them over the edge."

"I see."

She knows about what happened, obviously, even though we've been talking less; if nothing else most of the details about our lives channel back and forth through Harry. "My parents are both stressed all the time because my dad still hasn't found anything and my dad is, like—not doing well. I think he's depressed. And it's been really hard on my mom."

"Right."

Why don't I just tell her the truth? "I also just—I don't think I could do it right. You know?" I swallow. "I've been off lately. With drawing, I mean, and I wouldn't want to give you something crappy for this, of all things." Her expression hasn't softened. My face feels hot. "Reg, I swear to God, it's not that I don't care about Sandra or anything, or about you, it's just that—"

"I understand."

"Reg, come on, don't be mad. I'll help edit layout. Or I'll do whatever you want, as long as it doesn't have my name—"

"Oh, that's fine," she says, her voice like shards of sun. "I understand. It's fine."

⁕   ⁕   ⁕

For a long time after she died it didn't feel like we'd ever find our way out of the initial shock and horror of it. It was the way everything reminded you, the way it would wash over you without warning when you were sitting in class or buying fries in the lunch line or lying in bed when the rest of the world had already gone to sleep. The ordinariness of the world, the same trees swaying, the same murals watching from the walls of the gym and the same hills gold with haze in the late afternoons, all felt like they'd been placed there specifically to mock us. Because nothing was ordinary, nothing was the same.

And we were all scared. I wouldn't have expected that from Sandra in a million years, and then you start to worry whether it could happen with other people you knew. Whether it could happen to you.

For the rest of the school year, I felt sick walking into first period and seeing Ms. Lee every morning. Or we panicked whenever someone posted sad lyrics or whenever our calls went to voicemail, or I'd text Harry and Regina at odd hours and be jittery and anxious until I heard back. Sometimes Regina just wouldn't answer and I'd freak out and make Harry check on her, and then the next morning she'd act like nothing had happened.

At the first of those assemblies we all had to go to, eight days after she died, a psychologist told us that the vast majority of people who survive attempting suicide regret those attempts almost immediately and are thankful they survived. When she said it I got that sharp flash of pain above my heart that you get sometimes and you have to breathe past (precordial catch, my dad told me once when I was little), but it hurt so much I took shallow breaths to spare myself. There was a loosening feeling in my head. When I looked around the bleachers, a lot of people were crying. Harry was sitting stiffly next to me, and him sitting there was the only reason I was able to gather myself back together. I pressed my hand against my heart and breathed all the way past the pain until it released.

This was the part I couldn't stop thinking about then: If there was a moment, before it was all over, that she regretted it. If she saw what she was losing and tried to clutch the whole weight of the world in her hands as it all drained away.

When you draw something it matters every time that you're the one who drew it. I've always believed that. Like, what did you glimpse in a person's expression? What do you have to say about them? Why is your perspective, yours of all the billions of people on earth, worth trapping on a piece of paper and showing to everyone?

Harry read somewhere once that the reason your life flashes before your eyes when you die is that your brain always responds to information with all the knowledge it's built in the past, and so when you're about to die it shuffles frantically through everything it knows for clues about what's happening, what it's supposed to do. I always wondered if that happened to my sister, too, if she was still too small for that or if maybe it was just that her images were small too: her mom, her dad, her favorite toys, the view of the ceiling from her crib. (I drew those things once, in a strip.) Anyway, in that final burst of Sandra's memory, I can't help thinking about how maybe I would've flickered in and out and how I wonder if she ever knew I didn't mean for things to go the way they did.

But of course not. Of course more important thoughts would've fought for her attention before they went dark, and of course I didn't matter to her any more in her last minutes than I did during all those years and years with her I threw away. Of course she didn't forgive me.

I wish I could do the drawing—I wish a lot of things—but there are lines you don't cross. That one's mine.

T W E L V E

The thing about high school is that no matter what happens between you and someone else, you still get up each morning knowing you're going to face them approximately eighty times that week—all of it resurrected there in the hallway between periods/in the rally court at lunch/in class.

Which is to say that Tuesday morning I see Regina coming down the hall and I lift my hand to wave, but she turns away fast without acknowledging me and goes in the opposite direction. My face catches flame. I look around to make sure no one saw.

All week Regina avoids me as much as she plausibly can, and all week it knifes me every time. It's striking how fast the glow from Neighborhood disappears.

But something happens at the end of that week: I get a call from Araceli Padilla, who runs Neighborhood, to tell me that one of my pictures sold. I'm so surprised I can't think of anything to say for a good ten seconds. I knew it was technically a possibility, but I think the things you dream about most sometimes seem less possible—you imagine them so much, so many different ways, that they take on a kind of otherworldliness you only recognize as fantasy.

"Wow," I say finally, recovering. "That's—wow. Thank you so much. Which one was it?"

It was the portrait of my mom I drew last year—one of the dozens and dozens I've drawn trying to capture that expression on her face the day she told me about my sister. It's imperfect, and her expression's off, but I like it because I think there's something cohesive in all the small vignettes that I drew to compose her face, and because I think even if I didn't quite nail the expression, something about her, some essential quality, still comes through all the same.

Araceli doesn't know who bought it; it was one of the new cashiers who rang it up. All day, all through the Calc quiz and the AP Econ group project and the in-class essay for Lit, I think about that, imagining that picture going home with someone. It's dumb, but part of me misses it. I should've taken better photos of it. I didn't expect anyone to actually buy it.

I wake up Saturday morning weirdly determined to believe everything will be all right. Maybe every artist has dry spells. Vivian Ho made it sound like it'll never be easy, that the struggle is part of things, and maybe that's okay, maybe I'll be better for it someday.

I decide I'll tell my parents about the picture, mostly because I know how excited they'll be. It'll be instant gratification. I'll have to lie and say I learned about the exhibit online—they'd hate that I went to San Francisco without telling them—and that I mailed the pieces in.

When I come out to the kitchen they're both sitting there at the table like they're waiting for me.

"Sit down," my dad says, motioning. When I do, slowly, my

mom sets down a bowl of re gan mian in front of me. She never cooks breakfast anymore. Alarm bells go off in my head.

"We have something to tell you," my mom says.

My mind flashes back to that search history about divorce and my heart stutters against my chest so hard it knocks my breath away. I shouldn't have sat down. I press my fist against my chest to try to steady my heart. "What's going on?"

I can name the exact tacit negotiation taking place in the way they look at each other: which of them it will be to break the news. My mom gives in first.

"You should remember that in fall you go to RISD," she says in English, then switches back to Chinese. "That is the most important thing. You will work hard and achieve your dreams there. Your future is secure."

She looks at my dad for help, but he's staring down at his noodles. She inhales sharply through her nose. The freezer is making its clattering sound and the light overhead is flickering.

"Daniel, we're moving. You're already accepted to RISD, so—"

Another heart palpitation, this one so hard I feel it down to my palms. "What do you mean we're moving?"

"The rent is too high here."

"What? But—" The words get jumbled on their way to me; I have to untangle them and even still they barely make sense. "But we—"

"We have no choice. It's too expensive."

I have grown up in this house. My life is literally written on its walls. I know this kitchen so well I don't even see it anymore; I have to look around it and focus in order to ground myself. "Can't we get a loan? Just until Ba finds—"

"That is not an option. We can no longer afford it."

"But, I mean, you're just never going to find another job or what?"

"Daniel," my mother hisses.

My face is hot. "Can't you talk to the landlords? They probably don't want someone else to—"

"We've already spoken to them."

I never even think of the landlords, shadowy beings who occasionally appear when a pipe bursts. I don't think of our home as theirs. "Can you talk to them again?"

"There's nothing more to talk about."

"But we don't—then what are we even supposed to do? Just move into some random apartment or something?"

My parents exchange another look. "Daniel, Cupertino as a whole is very expensive. Apartments are no more affordable. Cupertino is a terrible value for the money, and we don't need to pay for a good school district anymore because you have already been accepted for next year. So we will move to San José."

"San *José*?" Technically Cupertino shares a border with the west part of San José, on the other side of De Anza. "Like where, where Los Dos is? Like by Westgate?"

"It will be . . . less close to here."

"Okay, then where? Like by Valley Fair or what?"

"Not by Valley Fair. More . . . past the airport. It's all we can afford."

"The airport? I can't live all the way over there and go to MV."

My mom flinches—they knew that already, of course. She pushes my noodles toward me. "Aren't you hungry?"

This can't be happening. What the hell. What in the absolute hell. An old panic rises up, that same trapped feeling I remember from when they told me we were leaving Austin—the world trailing away from me as I struggle after it.

"I'll get a job," I say. "It can't be that much of a difference, right?

In rent? I'll get a job and—" I remember. "I just sold a drawing. I made three hundred dollars."

They both look surprised. "Where?" my dad says.

"At this gallery—it's kind of a long story. I found it online, and someone bought one of the drawings—"

"Where? How did—"

"It's kind of a long—anyway my point is that I just made three hundred dollars. That can help, right? And maybe I'll sell more. Or I can get a job and—"

My mom's face is pained. "It's already done. We've already signed the paperwork."

"Like where exactly?" I let my phone thud onto the table. "Show me on a map."

My mom does, reluctantly, pointing to an area northeast of the airport that I've never been to in my life.

"That's like forty minutes away." People go eat in that area or Milpitas sometimes, there's this hot pot place Regina's family always drives out for, but that whole lower curve under the Bay always felt so irrelevant to me. And I've been perfectly happy with that. I love Cupertino. I never wanted a reason to know where anything else was.

"It's really only thirty minutes when there's no traffic."

"Okay, fine, thirty—that's not—don't you have to give at least a month notice to the landlords?"

"We gave notice two weeks ago."

Two *weeks*? The past two weeks I was finding out my portfolio was accepted at Neighborhood. I was driving to SF with Harry for the installation the past two weeks. I trusted my parents when they said everything was going to be fine. "You've known about this for two weeks?"

She looks away. "We didn't want you to worry."

"But I could've gotten an after-school job, or I could have—"

"No," she says firmly. "Your job is to prepare for art school."

There's a film over my eyes. The refrigerator buzzes louder. Everything I can think to say swirls around like mixing paint. Finally I say, "So all this time you've been lying to—"

My dad gets up abruptly, making me jump. The suddenness of it makes me back away, but he's not headed in my direction after all—his footsteps fall through the living room and then down the hallway. His door slams.

My mom gets up from the kitchen table.

"Later this weekend we'll find moving boxes," she says. "You can start packing your things."

. . .

"You're *moving*? You're moving *where*?" Harry blinks at me, nothing computing, his mind not awake enough yet to process the information. It's just before seven-thirty and the bell hasn't rung yet, and we're huddled by Regina's locker, Harry and Regina holding hands, all our sleep-deprived classmates walking zombielike past us in the early morning cold. I took the news to bed with me last night; I didn't have the energy to call Harry after trying to make myself invisible, cloaked in my anger, all day. I forgot at first this morning when I woke up, and then it all crashed back over me again.

"San José," I repeat. I peek at Regina, who hasn't said a word. Maybe I should've waited to get Harry alone.

His jaw tightens. "And you're doing it when?"

"Two weeks."

"They can't put it off just until the end of the year?"

"They said we can't afford it."

"Did you ask if—"

"Believe me, I asked."

"Danny, that's horrible." Regina looks stunned. I'm not above being gratified by her expression—it means she doesn't hate me. "Aren't there renter protections? I think if you just refuse to move out they have to go to court to make you leave."

It's such a Regina thing to say it makes me laugh in spite of myself. "Well, there's an option."

"The important thing is that there *are* options," Harry says. "Right? That's shocking, but it's—it can't happen. We'll figure something out."

That *we* again; it blankets me. "Maybe. I hope you're right. But like—" I swallow. "Okay, this is going to sound like I'm losing it, but do you think it's a lot worse than I thought? Like—what if they bailed on their debt completely and someone is actively after them? What if they owe money and they just ran off and that's why we left Austin? And changed their names and everything—they could be in so much trouble. I feel like they wouldn't be that stupid, but at the same time—I don't know. They've always been so paranoid it almost makes more sense if someone's after them."

"You really think that's possible?" Harry says.

"I don't know. I need to find out."

"Do you think—" Regina smooths the hem of her shirt. "Do you think that's a good idea?"

"What's that mean? You don't think it is?"

"I just think that—I don't know that it's always better to know more."

I smile a little; I can't help it. "That would go well on some business cards. Regina Chan, reporter: SHIELD YOUR EYES FROM TRUTH."

"Mm. I'll put it in our masthead." She raises her eyebrows a little. "But really, Danny—haven't you ever learned something you wished you never knew?"

So all day I think about that. It's true, probably, and she's right, but it's also true that that almost never matters—you'd find out again anyway; you wouldn't turn down answers. Maybe it would be different if it only affected my dad and his career, if it were something that could exist in a sphere apart from me, but obviously that's not the case.

In Journalism sixth period, Harry pulls me aside.

"Listen," he says, "I don't want to embarrass you or anything, but—I can ask my parents to loan you money. It can't be that much, right? I'm sure they'd say yes."

I wish he hadn't put it like that, because of course I'm embarrassed. But that's nothing compared to the gaping emptiness I feel when I think about moving. "Really?"

"Yeah, they like you. And it's the kind of thing they'd do anyway. And it—" He clears his throat uncomfortably. "It wouldn't be a problem for them. No big thing."

"Okay. That would be—I mean, that would be great. I promise we'll pay you back. And—"

He waves it off. "Don't worry about it. I'm just being selfish, anyway. I don't want you to move."

That reaches through the blur I've been trapped inside all day. Maybe what you need most in life is people who will fight for you; maybe that's all that matters. I want to tell him something like that, what it means to me. I don't, though.

.   .   .

"Daniel, what are you *thinking*?" my mom cries that night when I tell my parents. We're eating gai lan and leftover noodles from the weekend, and they're gummy. "We are not borrowing money from your friend! How could you ask him that?"

"I didn't ask. He offered."

"I am humiliated that you asked him."

"I just said I didn't—"

"I will not have you begging your friends for money. Tell him absolutely not. And you are forbidden from speaking of this with anyone ever again."

I turn to my dad. "I'll help pay it back. I'll get some kind of job and—"

"No. Our decision is final."

The walls press against me. I force a deep breath. "You can't do this."

They exchange a look. When my dad says "Daniel," it's a warning.

"It's one thing if it's just completely out of your control, but I'm offering a solution that—"

"You will not speak to your parents this way."

I slump back down in my chair. My heart is pounding and I feel fuzzy and hot, like a hangover. I last forty seconds, maybe, before I can't help myself. "How did you let things get so bad that—"

"Quiet," my dad orders.

"But why didn't you—"

"*Quiet!*"

He never yells at me, and it feels like being struck. Whatever I might've said back dies in my throat. His voice roars against the linoleum floor and old sand-colored paint of the walls, and he stands and points a trembling finger at me.

"You will never bring this up with us again." His voice is shaking. With anger, I think, but when I meet his eyes I realize I'm wrong: it's fear. "You don't understand as much as you think you do and I will not have this. We're moving. That's it. You'll accept it or you won't, but it's happening either way."

鳶

You are a year and a half old when change sweeps into your tiny kingdom. Change comes in the form of a letter: your father has been accepted into a master's program in physics in the United States. It isn't the PhD program he has always dreamed of, but it's enough to fill his mind with dreams of models and graphs and charts.

They don't know this yet, but your whole life is bound up in their decision. If they decide to go, they will cede you to the abyss. Small choices accumulate like snowflakes; enough of them, and the avalanche buries you. But for now you sit contentedly in your parents' arms, oblivious, while your future is dissected on the table. Your parents argue. They're quiet arguers, the kind to wall off rather than yell, and so for weeks the house is bathed in silences. Your mother doesn't want to go. She would have to work full-time to put your father through his program, and—there's no visa for your grandfather—there would be no one to care for you. Your mother cradles you and imagines you screaming, left in a stranger's care.

Your grandfather, who disappears when your parents talk about the letter, is in the other room. Weighing your fate, your parents aren't minding you. You are sitting on your mother's lap when a mound of steamed yam lodges itself in your throat. Shock and terror overwhelm your system. You flail your arms. They ignore it. You grab at your mother's arm, and she peels your fingers off one by one, not pausing as she talks to your father. You try to cry, but it's a wheezy, quiet disturbance. The oxygen drains from your bloodstream, and your skin turns red, then blue. You fling yourself back in her lap, your head butting against her chest.

Your father sees. He peers at you, confused—disaster can be coy to reveal itself—and then understands. He shouts. He lunges for you, flips you over and beats at your back, yelling for your mother to call for help. Your mother is frozen. All the broken promises of the world, all those ways it's exactingly cruel, sear her vision. She cannot see.

But then your father is pulling you upright, and you're crying, wailing really, and your grandfather has run into the room and is grabbing your face, needing the physical reassurance of you, and it's okay. Their hearts are pounding. They snap at each other, all panicked at what could've happened (what will happen, in a sense, sooner than any of you realize). Your mother's skin crackles with electricity, and then those knockout heartbeats, the blurred vision and the constriction in her throat—she has to hand you to your father to try to struggle through the panic attack. She doubles over, gasping for breath.

It's your cries—you're still crying—that pull her back to gravity. She reaches for you again, and you burrow yourself into her. She closes her eyes and tries to match her breaths with your own. You're both fine, she tells herself. She cradles you. You're soothed against her. You're all right, you're safe, you're all right.

THIRTEEN

The next few days feel like some kind of surrealist painting, segments of the world darting back and forth in front of me with nothing chained to any sort of meaning or reality. In AP Econ I bomb a test because I don't even think to flip over the last page. I nearly run over a pair of sophomore boys going down the stairs.

On Wednesday in Journalism Advaith drops into the seat next to me. "Hey, Danny, I wanted to ask you. Can you do an illustration for my article?"

"Um—"

"It's the one about the Talent Search."

"Oh, right." A girl from our class, Monica Agarwal, won the Intel Science Talent Search for research on some kind of bioinformatics test of cancer markers in stem cells or something like that. Advaith's been pumped to write the article. "So I was thinking it would be cool to have a picture of her with a clipboard surrounded by life-size cells, and she's looking up at the cells. What do you think?"

What am I supposed to say? Actually I can't because I'm moving, because for reasons they still refuse to disclose my parents fucked us over? "Ah—"

"I know you must be really busy with everyone asking you to do illustrations for them."

"Right. Um." I can't even fathom making the announcement that I'm shearing myself from this entire life. "Yeah, sure, I can do that for you."

All week I wonder if I could convince my parents to just let me keep going here. People do it—everyone knows Megan Gee lives in Campbell, for one. And sometimes the school sends people to check (I remember a few classmates who got kicked out), but it's so close to the end of the year it's hard to imagine they'd even bother.

In the meantime, pointlessly, I've been trying to draw. I don't know why. What am I going to do—draw my parents a picture of my feelings? Draw my feelings for the landlord? The world spins on capital and power; it doesn't bend to drawings. This is what Mr. X tried to tell me all along, wasn't it?

And yet this is the thing I plan to structure my life around—this is all I have. I can't believe how less than three months ago getting into RISD made it feel like my whole life was set. I might be willing to give all of that up to keep our home—to have it for the rest of the year, to have it to come back to after that. We belong here.

Or we don't, I guess. Not in the only way that matters.

The packing, this segmenting of our lives and the smell of the cardboard boxes and the *ckkkkkerrrrrk* of packing tape—it all brings back those old feelings I guess I buried years ago. I hole up in my room trying not to hear my parents scuttling around their room packing, the drawers rolling open and closed like tongues lolling.

The house gets scavenged. I remember this from Texas, too, the visual shock of familiarity stripped for parts. First it's all the pictures I drew that my parents had framed and hung on walls. Then it's the junk drawers I never realized I had any kind of attachment to—but home is the place where you can always find the scissors and the batteries and the earplugs without having to poke around. Then it's the spare sheets and blankets and towels, and then it's the dishes and silverware, and that's when it starts to feel real: when I first start reaching for things that are no longer there, whole segments of our lives vanishing piece by piece.

◦ ◦ ◦

I hear them Thursday, nine days before moving day, when I wake up in the middle of the night, my half-asleep mind scrabbling around to root myself back in the world I know.

"Maybe it would be safer there," my mom says. "There's no record of me being there. Then, if anything happens, I'll still be here with Daniel."

"How do you know you're safe there? The Lis—"

"They wouldn't tell anyone. They've never asked me."

There's a silence. Finally my dad says, "If you think it's best—"

They're quiet after that. But the night—it has its hold on me, the kind of night when shadows feel menacing and the morning feels far away and anything feels possible at all. So I lie awake, a coldness wrapping itself around my shoulders, replaying that conversation. I think about it so long I wonder if I made up the whole thing, if it was a dream that bled into those moments where I was almost but not quite awake. In the morning I look up pictures of Clay Ballard again, looking for signs of ruthlessness or danger in his pleasant, practiced smile. Have I just missed all the parts of his history that make him someone to run from?

In the morning—eight days before moving day—my mom tells me that because it will be too hard to get to Cupertino and back each day with one car, she's arranged to stay with the Lis as a live-in nanny during the week and just come to San José on weekends. She says it offhandedly, the way she'd mention she was stopping by the grocery store on the way home.

And I push away my misgivings from last night and think about asking them if I can keep going to school here. It's a perfect parallel, even—if she can stay in her job in Cupertino, can't I do the same?

I tell myself to count to five and then ask, to count to ten and then just say it, and I stand there in silence trying to rally. But I can feel already—I recognize the anger wafting and curling around me like steam—how she'll immediately shut it down, how she'll act distressed and disappointed that I've even brought it up with her, the way she did when I told her Harry's offer and every time I ever asked about my dad's job. And then I'll feel guilty about asking to begin with, I'll spend the rest of the day second-guessing whether asking was a selfish and thoughtless thing to do. So I don't, and a resentment blooms in the space where the question could've gone, choking out all the air.

If they're really afraid—and even if they aren't, things are still objectively bad enough for us to lose our home—why didn't they do anything about it? They could've talked to a lawyer or to the cops, even. They could've talked to a bank. I offered to get a job. Harry offered to loan them rent. It's my whole life, is the thing—and they weren't willing to fight for it even a little bit.

When I get home from school Friday afternoon my dad's sitting on the couch, not watching TV, just sitting. His face is all red. He's drinking a glass of wine. I almost never see him drink. When I come in, he lifts his glass toward me. He says, "I got a job."

"You got a job?" The news roars through me like a waterfall. Oh, thank God. They weren't just cowering after all, and this was just one of their overreactions, their worry clouding the actual—

"Security guard," he says. "At the mall."

"At—oh." I never saw that coming. I try to imagine him donning a uniform, chasing a bunch of kids away from overpriced bags, and my chest pinches with guilt. Maybe every night when he comes home with a little more of his soul stomped down by the Claire's and the Banana Republic he'll remember all those times I badgered him about getting a job, how much I complained about having to leave. And maybe every night he'll look at me here in this house still and think how it wasn't worth it. Maybe things will get as bad as they were in junior high again. I swallow. "That's—well, that's great, Ba. I'm sure it's just for a little while, and then—"

"Eastridge Mall." He takes a sip, grimacing. He's never liked the taste of wine. "It's closer to the new apartment."

"But we—if you got a job we don't have to move, right?"

He looks at me for the first time then. His face makes me forget, just for a moment, what it's felt like to be this angry with them.

"No, we're still moving," he says quietly.

"But you just said—"

He drains the rest of his wine. His eyes are bloodshot. "It's not a good job, Daniel. It doesn't pay enough. So everything is still the same."

FOURTEEN

My mom takes me to see the new place the day before we move in when she goes to sign the rental agreement. By car, which I'll never get to use anyway because they sold my dad's, it's almost half an hour without traffic, off a freeway exit I've only ever driven past. It's on a street with four lanes and a forty-mile-an-hour speed limit, all gray, everything gray, and cars that barrel past so relentlessly it's a full five minutes before I can make the unprotected left turn into the parking lot.

The apartment has linoleum floors and stained matted carpet, a single bedroom and bathroom and all of two closets, a cramped balcony off the living area that overlooks a collection of dumpsters in the parking lot, and locked stairwells that feel like somewhere you get murdered. We're on the third floor. Noise from the neighbors above and around us seeps through the walls: a faucet turned on, a toilet flushing, a short burst of laughter, and then nothing. I think, until seeing the place, I didn't actually fully believe this was happening.

"You get the bedroom," my mom says. She tries to smile. "Baba and I will sleep out on the couch."

She's nervous. I can tell she was dreading showing me this.

"Where are you even going to put your stuff?" I say stiffly.

"There is another closet outside on the balcony, too. It's very big."

"What about your garden?"

"I am writing an instruction manual for the next renters. Maybe sometimes after I leave the Lis' I can stop by and check on—"

No one wants some random woman coming into their yard all the time. "What about your friends? How are you going to have everyone over for holidays now? What did they say?"

"We aren't telling anybody."

"What do you mean you aren't telling anybody?"

"You never know what people—" She hesitates. "It doesn't matter. Maybe we won't see them so much anymore. People are busy, you know."

She's just not going to tell them and then, what, ghost them? Those are her best friends. I can't imagine keeping something like this from Regina and Harry.

But maybe it shouldn't surprise me at all. Apparently it doesn't bother them to keep things from the people who need to know.

"I think your bed could go right here. Yes? Then if you put your desk right here you can look out the window while you draw." She's watching me, hopeful in a way that feels bracingly obtuse. She thinks I'm going to draw here? Like my life just went on the same way as always? I don't answer.

"The closet is bigger than your closet at home, I think."

Great. Perfect. Woo, a better closet. I have to leave my friends and my life and my home, but at least my *closet* picks up a few more square feet. " 'Kay."

"And the bedroom is nice, isn't it?" she says. "It's small, but has the big window." She scans my face hopefully. "We thought about getting a studio apartment, because it's less expensive, but then we thought, *No, Daniel should have his own room.* So we chose this instead."

I don't have it in me to answer that. I shouldn't have come with her. I pull my phone from my pocket and pretend I got a text. At the door she pauses.

"It isn't so bad, right?" she says. "Not as bad as you imagined."

"Are you *kidding* me?"

I expect her to raise her voice in return, but she's quiet. "You can stay here while I turn in the deposit," she says finally, but a few seconds later I hear her slide the balcony door open instead. When I go into the living room I see her out there, her face in her hands, her shoulders shaking.

And right on cue comes the same ugly feeling I always get in the aftermath of arguments, that guilt hangover. In the heat of the moment whenever we fight I want to hurt them, want to say something barbed and incisive, and it works for as long as they're angry back, as long as my words have no powers of weaponry. When I do actually hurt them, my heart crumples like a piece of paper. I've heard it said the worst thing in the world is to get exactly what you want, and I don't know how true that is, but it's true when you win a fight with someone you love.

I should go out there and tell her it's fine and that the bedroom is fine, is great, the window or whatever it was she pretended to like about the room is great. I should do it. I know what it's like to look back on all those times you wish you'd said something different, chosen kindness so at least later on you'd still have that. I swore to myself I'd never do that again.

A train rumbles past. I stay in place, my chest tight. Outside a car goes by. A headlight flickers over her, illuminating her for one brief moment—she looks like a statue—and then casting her shadow, long and dark, back across the bare apartment walls.

▪ ▪ ▫

Saturday night. My last night at home.

The walls in my bedroom are a ghostly, empty white again. My eyes keep forgetting—the space where my drawings used to pulse with life keeps catching me off guard when I see it in the corner of my eye. When my dad came in with the quart of paint he wouldn't look me in the eye. He offered to help—I said no—and then he told me to make sure I took pictures of my walls so I had them someday. I know it cost him something to say that, to acknowledge what I was losing. Which is worse, actually—at least if he were flippant about it I could get pissed. It would feel at least briefly satisfying to just blow up.

Harry calls at seven. "What are you doing?"

I tell him I'm packing.

"I'll come help you pack."

"Don't do that," I say, but he's hung up already, and he ignores my *seriously, don't come* text, too. Fifteen minutes later, while I'm stuffing the contents of my dresser into plastic Ranch 99 bags, the doorbell rings.

My dad makes it to the door while I'm still coming down the hallway. He peers through the peephole first. "It's Harry," he tells me, then opens the door and says, in a jovial tone that feels like someone spilled bright paint all over a finished portrait, "Hello, Harry!" My dad's always liked Harry. Parents always do.

Harry lifts his hand. "Hey, Mr. Cheng." He ignores me. I always liked when he did that—not ignored me, obviously, but ignored me with the tacit understanding that it's because I'm the one who matters, the default one who doesn't require the pleasantries that intimacy replaces.

"Harry," my dad says, and squares his shoulders in that way that means he has a speech to give, "you've been a very good friend to Daniel."

I hiss, "Ba," by which I mean, *Stop.*

He ignores me. "A very good friend, all these years. Friendship is a very important thing. But you'll still see each other sometimes. And you can talk on the phone, so it's essentially the same as before."

"Sure, yeah, thank God for phones, right?" Harry says easily. He smiles, a friendly smile, but I know him well enough to know which smiles are fake. "Danny's been a great friend to me, too. Good luck with the move." He's probably the only person I know who could say that without it coming out snarky.

My dad starts to say something else, but I say, "Okay, I have to keep packing," and motion Harry down the hallway.

My dad says, "Harry, would you—"

"I said I have to pack," I snap. My voice comes out ugly.

My dad's smile flickers. He stops himself from saying something, I think, and nods wordlessly and shuffles off.

"Well," Harry says, and pats my arm a few times in a way that makes me pretty sure he thinks I was an ass, "let's do it." His footsteps echo behind me, all the creaky spots rising up on cue—those sounds that form the backbone of my childhood, the kind of thing you never realize how much you'll miss.

"Aren't you grounded?" I say when we get into my room.

"Yeah. But my parents are out tonight and Cindy promised she'd cover for me."

I didn't believe him that he'd actually help—I envisioned him sprawled out on my bed watching me do it—but he gamely tapes boxes together and pulls clothes from my closet and folds them like the perfectionist he is. It's an odd feeling having him all over my closet that way, like showing more than I meant to. And maybe it's that—or maybe it's everything, that tomorrow I'm leaving home—that makes me feel off-kilter, like the center of things has melted and the rest of the world is teetering around the edge of the sinkhole. After a while my dad pokes his head in to tell me he's going to buy more packing tape. I say, "Okay," in the most neutral voice I can muster.

The house feels different with him gone, with just me and Harry in it. We're both quiet a little while, and I feel a little like I did that first night at Yosemite—all my atoms buzzing at a higher frequency, spinning on their axis, or whatever it is atoms do. It's the first time we've been alone alone, not just alone in those spaces you carve out in a crowd, in a long time.

Harry touches the silence first, the words like how it used to feel jumping into the water back in Texas when we'd go to swimming holes. "When did you paint your walls?"

"I did it yesterday."

"Did that suck? It seems like it would suck."

"It sucked."

"Yeah, sounds about right." He abandons the box he was filling and sinks down on my bed. "It's definitely going to suck here without you."

"You have Regina."

"Right, but—" He cuts himself off then, and I want—desperately—to know what worlds would've unfolded inside that *but*. "Right, yeah. She's going to really miss you, too. I bet your new school is going to suck ass."

"I bet so too."

"I'll come drive down there every weekend."

"Please do."

Then quiet again, a fragile, crackling quiet. I'm pretty sure that, even all the way across the room, I can physically feel him here. He doesn't move back toward the boxes. That molten center expands, sucks up a little more of the firm ground around it. I say, "Can I ask you something?"

"Yeah."

My mouth feels dry. "Are you in love with Regina?"

He looks at me sharply. "Am I what?"

"Um—" Shit. "Never mind. Forget it."

"No, why?"

"No reason."

"You don't just ask someone that without a reason." He trains his gaze at me, his eyebrows raised, until I have to look away. My insides feel like water. He says, "Do I act like I'm not?"

"Seriously, forget it. It's not my business. I'm sorry."

"No, I want an answer now. Do I act like I'm not? You think I'm not good to her?"

"You're good to everyone."

"Just less good to my girlfriend? Is that why you're asking?"

"No, I just—you know. You guys are my best friends. I just want you to be happy."

"You don't think I am?"

"Harry, I'm sorry, okay? I shouldn't have said anything."

"Do you think I'd seem happier if I were with someone else?"

I force myself to swallow. "Like who?"

"Hypothetically."

"I think—" I have an excuse ready, the way they argue sometimes, but it evaporates before I can get to it. I clear my throat. "It's not my business. Forget it. As long as you guys are both happy."

"Right." He leans over and grabs the nearest box from the floor—my jeans—and stacks it roughly on top of a box of shirts. "Yeah, I mean, of course I'm happy. Hopefully I make her happy too."

"Well, good. That's good."

"Right." He propels himself off the bed. "I should get going. My parents will kill me if they find out I left."

"Oh—" Shit. Shit, shit. "Right, yeah. Um—thanks for coming."

I walk to the front door with him, my legs shaky. I'm desperate to keep him here, desperate to try to fix what I said. It isn't even what I meant. Not completely, at least. But I can feel my face prickling with the heat of whatever words I wanted to say.

Or didn't want to, I guess. Didn't want to badly enough.

. . .

I text Regina to see if she can/will talk after Harry's gone, right away, before I can descend into that hell of picking apart all the things it's too late to unsay. Maybe—for multiple obvious reasons—she's the last person I should talk to. But the only other person I want to talk to is the only one I can't, so. Part of me doesn't expect to hear back, but she calls a few minutes later.

"Don't squatters have a lot of rights in California?" I say when I pick up. "Didn't you tell me that once?"

"Packing isn't going well, I take it? Harry told me he was going over to help."

"Packing is not going well."

"I'm sorry."

"Yeah, well." I sit on my empty desk. Harry's boxes are lined neatly against my bed. I feel shaky still. "Thanks. Hey, look—I wanted to see—I know it's not like I won't see you again or anything, but are we cool?"

"Are we cool?"

"I know I kind of let you down with the paper tribute."

"Oh." There's a pause. "It's fine."

"You sure?"

"I understand."

"Do you? Because your voice kind of sounds like when you say *I understand,* you mean *I understand you're a shitty excuse for a friend.*"

If my voice comes out too charged, shot through with desperation—I can't lose both of them in one night—she doesn't let on. "You're like my brother, Danny. We're always going to be fine."

"All right." I exhale. It's not everything I wanted to ask her, obviously, not the whole story, but it's not nothing, either. I'll take it. "Thanks, Reg."

"Do you ever go to San José? It's actually a pretty great city."

"Not the part we're going to live."

"Ah."

We're both quiet a moment. I wish I could ask her if she thinks I wrecked things with Harry. And I wish I could be honest about what I'm really asking her, if she's forgiven me for how I treated Sandra. But I'm not brave enough. In Austin we used to go camping up in hill country with the other families, and one of the dads would build campfires and show us how fire suffocates and dies out when it can't get oxygen. Your worst fears are like that; you can't expose them to the air or they'll flare out of control and consume you.

"Harry—I'm not supposed to tell you this," she says. Oh, God.

My heart skitters across my rib cage on his name. He told her, he's finished with me. Then she says, "They said no, but Harry asked his parents if you could move in with him the rest of the year."

I feel an instant relief, the kind that burns off, and then a more lingering comfort. You don't ask that and then abandon the person altogether, right? Maybe there were a lot of ways he could've taken what I said to him tonight. "Really, he asked that? But they said no?"

"They didn't think it was right to do that to your parents. They told him they would never be okay if someone else offered to take in their kids, basically. They'd be insulted. They had a gigantic fight over it. That's why he's grounded. Harry didn't talk to them for like three days."

My heart swells. "When was this?"

"As soon as you told us you were moving."

I tap my fingers against my desk. I'm glad, in the moment, that we're on the phone and she can't see my expression. "I guess it shouldn't surprise me, coming from him."

"Right," she says, and I can't quite parse the tones in her voice.

I still can't believe the way the days ran out right in front of me, how we're really doing this. Someone else will move into our house, hammer some cheap IKEA print over my mural wall, rip up my mom's garden. "I wish my parents would just come out and tell me everything. You know? Everything just snowballed and I still don't even know exactly why it all got so bad so fast."

"I . . . don't think you do."

"You don't think I do what?"

"I don't think you do wish they'd tell you. If you really wanted to know you'd be pushing harder for it. But you aren't, because you don't. It's easier not to know."

"Aren't you the one who told me sometimes it's better to just let the truth exist on its own or however it was you put it?"

"Yes, but not necessarily better in general. I meant better specifically for you."

"Specifically for me? What's that supposed to mean?"

"It means—" She hesitates, and something in the way she does it makes me think that whatever she's going to say, it's something she's been holding on to a long time. "It means, among other things, that I know you rigged an election to help your best friend win."

Twin flashes of light in my peripheral vision. "You—what?"

"Are you going to deny it?"

"It's not—" But then I don't know where I'm going with that, and then my body betrays me, my heart clanging against my rib cage, my breaths catching shallow in my throat. You always catch up to yourself in the end; you can't hide who you are. "Shit." Finally I say, "How do you know that?"

It's a long story—something about how her numbers had been different enough from mine that she'd wondered, and after we'd all left she'd gone back into the teachers' lounge and found the ballots and recounted herself. All this time she knew.

"All right." My breathing hasn't recovered. "Well. All right. You'll make a good journalist someday. Did you—you didn't tell Harry, did you?"

"No."

"Are you going to?"

She doesn't answer right away. I say, "Please don't. Reg, please. It'll kill him to know that he—to know that I—"

"It wouldn't *kill* him."

"You're right. I shouldn't have said it like that."

Then I run out of words. Regina makes zero attempt to rescue me from the silence. It's hard not to lose your foothold when someone peers inside you, sees all those things you tried the hardest to keep hidden, all those ugly shames you've tried to tell yourself aren't really as bad as they seem. All those lies disintegrate in the light; I could never tell Regina I didn't take anything from Sandra, that I only ever wanted the best for her.

My lungs pucker into themselves, shrinking against the air I need them to hold. I'm getting a headache. Finally I say, "Do you hate me?"

"Of course not," she says, and I can't locate any of what I'm looking for in the flatness in her voice. "How could I? Now you and Harry are my best friends."

I'm still reeling when I get off the phone and go out into what's left of the living room. My dad is stretching packing tape over all the boxes stacked up to the ceiling, and my mom is working on the binder she plans to leave the new tenants with instructions for the garden. How foreign it feels that just a few months ago I was worried about leaving them behind next year—worried that I'd miss them, that the house would feel empty with just the two of them in it.

"I will do anything if you let me still go to MV," I say. "Please. I'll do anything."

They exchange a long glance across the dining/kitchen area. My mom says, "That isn't possible."

"I'll take the bus, I—"

"It's against the rules."

"But it's so close to the end of the year. I'll be so careful. They aren't going to care this close to June. Did you already do the green card notification?"

My dad looks at me blankly. "What do you mean?"

With a green card, you're supposed to notify officials within ten days of moving—I learned that when I went to look up whether it was true what my mom said that it would make his getting a new job more complicated. (A little, maybe, but not the way she was implying.) "The address change. Can we just wait until June? Then it won't be on any records that I stopped living in the district."

"Daniel—" my mom says.

"I looked up what happens if you get caught, and it's a misdemeanor in the absolute worst-case scenario. But it said nothing ever happens because they don't have time to go around prosecuting people for forgetting to give their address, and if you get fined, I'll pay the fine. Just—please. I won't ask for anything like this again."

I feel a little sick, the corners of the room wobbling. I stare at where the living room couch used to be. And Regina was right, I think—because I start to ask the other questions, too, but then I don't.

My mom turns away. She folds her arms and she's staring at the wall, so I can't see the look on her face. Finally my dad says, "You have just three months at this school and then you'll be at RISD, Daniel. Think about that part instead."

FIFTEEN

The new school is enormous and ugly, all gray cement and darkened windows, an island of a city block on a street made up of long flat houses and a faded medical complex. There is nothing on this street worth looking at, no surprising colors or trees that twist up into the sky or building angles that demand a second glance. At MV I always loved that view of the hills, how out on the fields for PE they rose up like a backdrop behind you and made you feel like you were out on the edge of the known world.

My anger at my parents is a hard lump in my throat. My mom's already at the Lis' for the week, and my dad was still on his night shift when I left this morning. I would've had nothing to say to either of them anyway. There was a note placed carefully on the table and eleven creased one-dollar bills (*Daniel, approximately three-quarter of a mile from here is Q Baguette, which is close enough for you to walk. Go only there after school to purchase banh mi and then come directly home. I will be home by nine*). It was still mostly dark when I woke up, and

I took a shower with the door open because it felt safer to keep close by to any alarming noise from outside. The whole way to school I kept checking over my shoulder. I'd thought maybe the feeling would break open when I actually got here, that the place would carry that bland bureaucratic reassuring schooly feel schools sometimes do even when they aren't yours, but this one doesn't. Even the mascot (a mustang baring its teeth in a giant mural painted on what's probably the gym) looks menacing. I've never trusted horses.

I keep hoping to hear something, anything, from Harry. Last night I finally gave in and texted him *thanks for helping me pack*, but he never wrote back. My stomach's been in knots all morning.

I didn't text Regina. I started more than once, but every time I lost my nerve.

A bell rings, the sound tinny and sharp compared to our bell at home. I make my way down the hallway toward where I think the office is, hating everything about this place. The other kids here feel different, too, all blurred into that indistinguishable mass of thousands of people utterly indifferent toward you.

"Yo homo," someone calls across the hallway. Something in my heart seizes, some fist clutching all the chambers of my heart. I tell myself not to turn my head. Then in my peripheral vision a slim white guy in fitted jeans ducks his head and tries to walk faster. He passes me.

"Hey, come back, I'm talking to you." It's another white dude, one with a casually merciless grin. His voice is pitched unnaturally high and cruel, a mocking lisp inserted like a skewer. "Come back." The other guy walks faster, toward an open classroom door.

"Come—dammit—" The guy's already gone in. He yells toward the door, "How come you never call me back, huh? How come you never pick up my calls?"

The people around me kind of laugh. Mostly not, though—mostly, in a way that tells me everything I need to know about this place, everyone ignores it. Something cracks in my resolve. Maybe it's because everyone I know is too stressed out about actual things that matter, or maybe it's because I go to school with two thousand people who are probably considering running for president someday, who knows, but the people I know are better than that.

Unexpectedly—this is embarrassing—my eyes well up. I think on some level I always had some idea that living in Cupertino and going to a school like MV was a bubble—that if you whisked any one of us away and plunked us down in some high school in, say, Indiana, the rules would be so different that all the things we'd worked so hard to build ourselves would crumble. You felt it sometimes at away games if you went to go watch and you could feel all the ways you wouldn't belong there, that hyperawareness of how to an outside eye you'd look exactly the same as everyone you were there with, that same feeling I remember getting sometimes when my family would take road trips and we'd drive through Podunk middle-of-nowhere towns and I'd feel that same mix of superiority and self-consciousness, that simultaneous need to prove my separateness from my family and also my belonging to it, that sense it's the group of you versus the world. But I've never felt all that so keenly as I do right now. It's difficult to breathe.

The office is at the end of the hall, its windows looking out into the hallway. When I go in the person at the front desk doesn't look up. I stand there in front of her desk for five minutes, watching them play out on the clock, trying to psych myself up to hand over my forms and consign myself to a life here. My heart is pounding and I feel that pressure behind your eyes you get when you're about to lose it. She never glances up.

And right then, just as I'm about to say something, my phone buzzes and I get a feeling and I know without even checking it's Harry. I'm right. It's a selfie of him making a sad face, his lower lip jutting out, and he's written: *this sucks. Fyi.*

A rush of pure, euphoric relief. All the worry that's been coursing through me lifts. There's a tingling feeling that runs up my legs. And—here in this god-awful place I have no business being in, this stupid detour my life has taken—some part of me zooms back to that day in my dad's lab and how I watched all those people's atoms revolting against their own aloneness, leaping into a tandem existence with the people they loved. And that's what this is. I was thinking of him, and he felt it. I was terrified I ruined everything, but we've been through too much together. I'm forty minutes and however many miles away, but he still felt me. And I've never been more certain of anything in my life: I need to figure this out between us. I need to see it through. I can't just fade out of his life like this, not in these last months we have before the future. Whatever it is with us, whatever it's going to be—I need to be there for it. I am not trashing my best shot at happiness for this shitty building full of shitty people.

So I do the only thing that feels reasonable, which is: I turn back around and walk out the door.

Walking home I work out what I'll do, and then I spend the rest of the day trying to draw. It's Mr. X's face that keeps emerging from my pen no matter what I try—the hard set of his eyes, his sneer. Finally I give in and draw him talking to me, looking at me like I'm a filthy and disgusting thing. I try to, at least. I work on shading in the area around his eyes, trying to make it look like he's staring you down. It just makes him look like a raccoon. The conversation goes roughly like this:

Mr. X: *What if they're really trying to hide something? They're hiding out from Ballard, and you're fucking it up? Your parents will kill you if they find out.*

Me: *I'm sure it isn't like that.*

Mr. X: *No, you're not sure. You aren't sure of anything. You don't know shit.*

Me: *Well, I'm sure they're handling all this in the stupidest way imaginable. I'm definitely pretty sure of that.*

Mr. X: *What, exactly, do you think they should do? Huh?*

Me: *I mean: get a loan, or—*

Mr. X: *That's what you think? You think they should ruin their own lives and their own plans so you can hang out with your friends at school a few more months? Probably won't even talk to any of them after you graduate. You want your parents miserable because of you?*

Me: *The school was terrible.*

Mr. X: *And?*

Me: *I can't go there.*

Mr. X: *You think you're such a special snowflake you're too good to go to anywhere but your one precious school? You think the world owes it to you to pay your way when you can't do it yourself? News flash: you can't go there. You're too poor. You literally cannot afford to go there.*

Me: *I'll figure out a way. This is important to me.*

Mr. X: *The world is not lining up to give you the things that are "important" to you. The world owes you nothing. You want*

something, you earn it yourself. You don't freeload off the rest
of us.

Me: *No one needs me to go to a new school. I don't owe that to the*
world.

Mr. X: *You owe it to the world to follow the damn rules and stop*
telling yourself you're entitled to something you couldn't pay for.

I don't know what to tell him. The world owes us nothing, maybe; you could look at it that way. Or you could look at the world like you love it and you expect something from it because of that, because that's the only reason you can ever expect anything from anyone.

Or something. Maybe that's not quite what I want to say, but it's something. The drawing, though—it's nothing. It's flat and lacks any kind of heat or energy. It's technically fine, as in obviously the guy has a nose and a mouth and all his parts, but there's nothing to it. This is what keeps happening—a total lack of perspective, I guess. It used to work, and it doesn't anymore.

᠂   ᠂   ᠂

At 3:23, long enough after the last bell's rung and he's had time to talk to the millions of people he always has to talk to every day but not so long that he's already driving, I call Harry.

"Day one," he says when he picks up. The sound of his voice feels like home. "It sucked about as much as I thought it would. How about you? How was the new school? Was it trash?"

I don't think Regina told him anything—he'd sound different, I think, or he'd say something. "Right. Um, about that—on a scale of one to ten, how bad would it be if I just . . . kept going to MV?"

"Wait, did your parents say yes?"

"Not . . . exactly." This is my plan: I'll tell my parents I signed up for zero period, which starts at 6:15, and every day I'll take the bus to Cupertino and just keep going to MV. It's only four more months.

I've never taken the bus in my life, so I looked up how it works, and that was the first hurdle: to get to Cupertino by 7:35, which is when first period starts, I have to get on the 5:09 bus (which: eff). They wouldn't believe I need to be leaving the house at like 4:55 to get to school, and so I landed on this: I'll say I joined the swim team. I wanted to meet people at the new school and the swim team lets everyone join.

"That's a stupid idea," he says immediately. "Probably your stupidest ever."

I guess I could've predicted that it would be too far outside the rules for him, a breach of the system. "Yes, but—"

"Do it anyway."

"Really? You think I should?"

"I mean—no, technically, I don't think you should, I think it's risky and probably really dumb, but—I mean, Danny, come on, you expect me to tell you I'd rather you wait out the year in some crappy school forty minutes away? You want me to say it doesn't make a difference to me whether or not you're here? If that's what you wanted someone to tell you, I'm not the person you should've called."

᠎   ᠎   ᠎

A little after nine, I hear carpet-muffled footsteps in the outside hall and then a key jostling against the doorknob. My heart forgets itself, going quiet for a beat in my chest. Funny how your whole day can be angled toward waiting for someone to get back, and then when they do, you wish you had more time.

It's not like you can hide in an apartment like this, though, as much as I'd like to stay holed up in here permanently, so I go out there. I do a final run-through of the lies I've been rehearsing all day.

My dad's sitting on the couch/pullout bed, and his belt with the walkie-talkie is sprawled across the couch like taking it off was the first thing he did. He says, "What happened with school?"

He has dark smudges under his eyes and his hair is stringy, and there's a new hollowness carving itself out under his cheekbones. I can feel how badly he wants not to have this conversation, wants not to have one more thing to worry or feel guilty about. "Did it go all right? You're enrolled?"

"All enrolled."

"Do we have to sign anything?"

"No."

"Was there any trouble?"

My palms are sweating. I try to force my voice to come out casual. "No, it's all taken care of. They just needed the forms."

"Well, good. Did you get all the same classes?"

"Ah—yeah. Pretty much."

"Did they give you a schedule?"

"I think I find out the first day I go."

He frowns. "You didn't go today?"

"Oh—no, they told me to come back tomorrow. They have to like process the paperwork and everything."

"I see." He leans back again. "Is there any left over from your sandwiches?"

"Oh—sorry, I didn't know you wanted—"

"That's okay." He glances toward the kitchen like maybe he'll go see if anything materialized, and then gives up, sinking deeper into the couch like he would meld into it if he could, shed his tired body.

A good person, the kind of person I've always wanted to be, would feel compassion for him. Would offer—having sat at home most of the day—to maybe put together something for him to eat or go out and get him another sandwich. Maybe that's the kind of daughter my sister would've turned out to be.

And I know that's my duty, since she never got the chance. And I also know that if there's any kind of real karma in this world I'm not exactly in a safe position to nurse my anger.

But still. Looking at him there, exhausted, like his day and probably the past months won't leave him alone and like probably he regrets all the off-ramps he could've taken away from this last stop, all I can think is: *Good.*

SIXTEEN

An hour-and-forty-five-minute bus ride starting at 5:09 every morning is, if possible, even more exhausting than it sounds. When my alarm goes off my whole chest cavity feels hollow and aching and I have to drag myself out of bed. I don't know if I can do this every morning.

But then on the bus I text Harry to complain and he tells me he'll get there early to hang out. At 6:54, when the bus stops, I see him stopped on the side of Stelling with his hazard lights on, his car spilling over the bike lane halfway into the street. He's reading on his phone, oblivious to the stream of cars displaced around him when I get in.

"Pretty sure you aren't supposed to be parked here," I say, right as someone honks.

Harry waves it off. "It's practically dark out still and there's no one on the road. They can go around me."

The relief I feel at seeing him in person balloons around me, filling the car so thickly between us it actually makes him seem farther away. I can't stop smiling. I imagine my alternate-universe self making my way through the other school right now, how miserable I would be. This was the right choice. This was the only choice.

Harry has a long external monologue about whether we have time to go to Philz and back before first period starts, finally settling on no (*you're already breaking the rules, so let's not tempt fate*), and so instead we go hang out in the Journalism Lab. It's mostly dark when we go in, the soft on-off dimming of the power lights glowing like forty tiny heartbeats across the computers. Harry runs his hand up the bank of light switches, and the room wakes up. I kind of miss the darkness. You feel closer to people inside it.

"You look tired," I say. In the fluorescent lighting I can see the dark circles under his eyes.

"Yep."

"You up studying or something?"

"Nah. I was just—I couldn't sleep. My parents were on me about next year."

We both settle into the chairs in front of computer stations. The school sprung for the nice kind of chairs, swiveling padded ones, except they're constantly getting poached into other classrooms so we're always half a dozen short, and we fight over them. I always lose. I don't fight hard enough. I say, "They're on you how? It's too late to do anything now. Your applications are all in."

"I know. They're just worried I didn't do enough. My mom keeps saying I should've done more SAT tutoring."

"You did so much SAT tutoring, Harry."

"Yeah, but I really think I could've gotten a perfect score. I just kept choking on test days."

He missed the perfect score by ten points, in the end. "I really doubt that's going to break you."

He shrugs. "My mom thinks it will."

I know what his parents can be like, but still, it defies the imagination that anyone could know Harry and wish he were somehow different or more. I want to tell him that, want him to know I mean it. I clear my throat. "Harry, you know—"

But at the exact same time he starts to talk. "They definitely—"

We both stop, and he motions for me to go ahead. But it's too late; my face has gone hot, my courage dissolved. "Nothing. What were you going to say?"

"I mean, they've definitely backed off some compared to last year, but I don't think they're actually like any more cool with me going to like Irvine or something. They're just worried about me going over the edge."

"You're definitely not going to end up at Irvine."

He grins. "Who knows, though, right? I could drop out and become a pro surfer."

"You hate the ocean."

"That's true." He swivels his chair toward me and kicks lightly at my ankle. "You know dolphins don't need to sleep for days? And they play with their prey before they kill—"

"Yes, I know, you've told me that like six times." He has a thing about dolphins. "But you're definitely not—"

The door pushes open, and we both go quiet. It's Regina, backlit by the morning sun. She blinks at us. "What are you guys doing in here?"

"We got to school early." Harry stands and kisses her forehead. Maybe I'm just imagining it that he deflated a little when she came in.

Just projecting, probably, because of those times I feel it myself, that urge in me that resists other people wedging apart a moment I didn't even realize I was so invested in. "What are you doing?"

"Working on my piece for the center spread."

I knew I'd see her, obviously, but I didn't think it would be yet, and it feels like staring into an eclipse. I say, quietly, "Hey." What I don't say is *Please don't think I'm a terrible person. Please don't think what happened to Sandra was even a little bit my fault. Please don't tell Harry.* When I meet her eyes, I can tell—I know her—she knows exactly what I'm thinking. That's the hardest thing to walk away from in somebody: those spaces where you're known and mirrored back.

"Hi, Danny," she says. Her real voice, the one she uses in private, is pitched lower than her public one—plain and unadorned, missing all the embellishments she has when addressing a roomful of people, or a group. And I trust it, less because of that and more because, in all the time I've known her, it's how she sounds when she's at her most vulnerable. "Harry told me about your plan."

I bring my chair-swiveling to a halt. "Ah—yeah."

"You're going through with it? You're just staying here?"

"Assuming I can pull it off."

I have been through a whole lifetime with Regina; I could never untangle her from my history even if I wanted to. You always think people will give you a sign, that when you know them as well as I know her you'll be attuned to it, that even within those secrets hanging between you you can parse meaning in a look, a careful word.

Regina gives me more than that, though. She sits across from me and touches my wrist, and when I meet her eyes she offers a tiny smile, one that means—I know her—we're okay. "I'm really glad you're back."

It's funny how almost losing something makes you see it all differently—makes it rise up in your vision all shining and bright.

I miss my house and my old life, my real life, constantly. Whenever I go by our old street the anger that's always burning in me flares up, the flames licking at my lungs. But at least here I have friends, a place I belong, a world I've made myself a part of that I can find myself in. We're knitted together, all of us, in our history and hopes and grief and guilt and all those things we saw each other through and in twenty years any one of the people I know from here could call me up and ask me a favor, and I'd do anything for them. I would. In Regina I have someone who knows probably the worst parts of me and still thinks there's enough left over worth keeping, who decided to keep our friendship even knowing what she knows, which I will never take for granted. And in Harry I have—still not sure how I'd put it, exactly, but what I do have I managed to keep. For now.

So there's a part of me that, when I'm at school, is always something close to euphoric, the way it feels when you slam on the brakes right in time and can see over the ledge. When you're with the right people you can feel like you're hidden wherever you are. But every morning, as soon as I wake up, that dull gray patch that retreated in the night flies back to me and spreads itself expertly and efficiently over my whole body. It dims the light around me and pulls a dark film over my eyes. Mr. X watches, grimly indifferent, reminding me, always reminding me, that I deserve nothing more than this, demanding some objective proof of what I think I'm worth, why I should've been the one who lived.

I'm scared all the time—all the time—of losing this. It could be anything. Maybe some kind of important mail will get sent home and I'll miss it, or I'll accidentally say the wrong thing in front of a teacher or one of our old neighbors saw the moving trucks and will call and report me to the school. (The real Mr. X still lives there, probably, if he hasn't white flighted himself somewhere free of Ranch 99s and Tapiocas Express.) And I'm terrified I'll slip up and my parents will find out.

My parents have, by all appearances, accepted the course of our new lives as inevitable. We don't talk about my mom living with the family she's paid to be a part of; when she spends the night here on weekends and my dad's gone we say nothing as she checks the deadbolt dozens of times and peers motionlessly out the peephole when we hear footsteps coming down the hallway. And when they ask me about the new school it's only questions you're supposed to answer like you're happy: *Your new school has less homework, that's nice, huh?*

Their determination to pretend everything is fine is starting to mess with me. Have I just developed some inflated sense of entitlement—I think I'm too good for anything but the best schools, the best cities? There are always people who have it worse. That, I think, is the implication lurking behind every look my parents give me: it could be worse, and I should be grateful for what I have. And maybe both those things are true. And so we don't comment on any of it like it's anything strange or surprising or wrong. Your eyes adjust to the dark.

My dad comes home from a shift one night when we've been there a little over two weeks, and I'm awake still because every time I heard a sound outside I had to get up, my heart galloping, to check the hallway outside.

He opens the fridge. It's still mostly empty, and he takes the last of a pack of frozen dumplings from the freezer and microwaves them and then slumps heavily into one of the kitchen chairs. The gray of his uniform pulls out the grayish tones in his skin. And maybe it's that soft, desperate mood you fall into waiting at night, that stage it builds for all your fears to come alive, but in spite of everything I feel a surge of tenderness toward him, a twin surge of guilt for all the ways I've been lying to them. This is what being in a family is—how your home holds all those things, the whole spectrum of everything you feel toward them. You can't always hold on to everything at once, but the rest of it is always right there so close to you, ready for you to pick it up again. It's the opposite of a blank page, how you can feel pissed off and guilty and nervous all at once, how you can remain angrier at your dad than you've ever been at anyone and at the exact same time still feel seared by the sight of his pain. Maybe he never deserved all the ways his life has unraveled, whatever those were. I say, impulsively, "Can I tell you something?"

My dad shoves a dumpling into his mouth, then wipes his lips with one of the paper napkins my mom took from the Ranch 99 deli. His voice is flat and tired. "What is it?"

Maybe it's not the right time after all. "I forgot."

"You didn't forget."

"Um—do you like the job?"

It's not what I wanted to say—I wanted to say something affectionate, but I lost my nerve—and my tone comes out strange, almost flippant. And the look on his face right then—he swallows hard and fights to get control of his jaw, which is quavering, and it's then that I realize: he thinks I meant that to make fun of him.

My heart tears in half. "I didn't—I didn't mean—"

He tries to smile, tries to act like he's in on the joke, but his voice comes out harsh. "It's great. Just what I always dreamed. Why your mother and I came here."

I never meant it that way. Couldn't he hear that—didn't he feel that same softness I was feeling?

"Then why did you let all this happen?" I say, my voice low with anger. How could he think that about me, that I'd say that to him?

"Excuse me?"

"Why did you tell Ma it wasn't your experiment that ruined you? Are you in debt?"

This time I recognize the look that flickers over his face before he chases it off—that same fear again. This time, though, I see how deeply rooted it is, how easily it's pushed to the surface.

I shouldn't have brought it up. Maybe you only ever say aloud the things you want easy answers for, the fears you want to be laid to rest.

My dad stands up abruptly. "It turns out I'm not hungry after all." He shoves the bowl of dumplings across the table at me, mostly untouched. "Have the rest."

⸱　⸱　๏

Latenights for our March issue start that Tuesday, and the paper will come out on the seventh, next Thursday. Watching the anniversary come nearer, like a plane on its final approach, makes me claustrophobic. I can feel the walls inching closer each time someone brings it up.

Regina's gone into her Latenight Mode early this cycle, holed up in the Journalism Lab lunchtimes and after school. On Tuesday she comes into the lab with cookies she baked everyone—I saw her online at four-thirty in the morning when I got up and figured she just hadn't slept yet, and the cookies make me think I'm right—and two bottles of coffee. Minuet Lam, who's always in charge of getting snacks, has scattered bags of chips and jerky and Pocky around all the computers, and there's a fruit platter at the tables.

Things always pick up like this toward the end of a production cycle—everyone blows off deadlines in favor of studying for AP tests or finishing lab reports (everyone gets an A in Journalism anyway), and then in the last days before we have to go to press that loose panic of failure descends and we all bring sweats to school and set up camp in the Journalism Lab every night until after dark. A few times we've stayed right up until 11:59, the last possible minute before the alarms switch on for the night and we have to be out of all the buildings, holding our breath as we shut the doors behind us.

I like watching people be good at things, and so from within that noise and chaos of the latenights I've always liked watching Regina roam all competently around the room, how effortless she makes it seem to give advice and tweak layouts and cut stories down to fit into their allotted column inches. I know she's always kind of stressed in the way you are about things you care about, but still she makes latenights a place you actually want to be, that same particular amalgam of frenetic and cozy you get with group projects that go really late into the night and that I wonder whether you ever get again after high school. That I'm glad I didn't give up.

Harry's late today, at an ASB meeting, and it's different without him—more industrious, I think, less like we're all hanging out. I keep watching Regina's computer to try to see the center spread she's been working on, but she's turned the screen's brightness all the way down and angled the monitor toward the wall. She's quieter than usual, too, tucked away in the corner, and it's at least an hour before she gets up to go around the room checking in with everyone. When she does, Chris Young covers his screen with his hands and orders, "Shield your eyes, Regina. Go check on someone else."

She peers at what he's doing. "Are you just writing your story straight into InDesign?"

He brings a fist to his chest, grinning. "Regina. Stab me in the heart. You'd accuse me of such betrayal? When I know how much you hate when people write straight into—"

"Just make sure you spell-check."

Chris lets his eyebrows go up a little, watching her pass by. Andrew Hatmaker flicks a pencil at him. It hits him on the shoulder. And I'm kind of watching them, and also glancing back at the door each time it opens watching for Harry, and because of that I don't hear what happens just before the noise level in the room dims all at once. Then Regina says, "What?"

She's in the first row of computers, Lori Choi standing next to her, something defensive in Lori's posture. Lori says, "Esther wants to tell you something."

Esther says, "Lori, shut up." She's sitting down still, not looking away from her screen.

"What?" Regina repeats.

"No, I don't."

"Yes, she does." Lori nudges her. "Tell her."

"Lori—"

"Esther doesn't think the center spread is a good idea."

All the rest of the noise is plunged from the room. Next to me, Emily Chien puts her pencil down.

Regina frowns. "Are you really that worried about—"

"I'm not *worried*," Esther says. "It just feels too political to me. It feels like using someone who died just to make your point about free speech, and I don't think it's right."

"You think—" Regina says flatly. "You think it seems like using—"

But then her control slips, her voice giving out on her. She closes her eyes like she wishes she had somewhere to hide.

The lights buzz quietly above us. Advaith shifts in his seat and bites his lip, staring hard at his screen.

"I'm just saying," Esther says. There's a tremor in her voice I don't know her well enough to translate, but my best guess is this: she believes that. And she's felt this way long enough to have been seduced by the idea of her own rightness, with the image of herself as the one person in the room willing to stand up for what's right.

And, I mean: what in the absolute hell. Everyone knows—*everyone* knows—Sandra was Regina's best friend.

I can't get down quite enough air. Next to me Megan is blinking rapidly at her screen, and everyone's waiting, and it's all such a glaring, enormous silence for Regina to fill.

"I think," Regina says, her voice shaking, "that we can't—" She stops.

I know—most of my life I've known—what it's like to have so much to say to someone who isn't there. It's that you can't defend yourself against all those ugly accusations that crop up in your own mind—that you didn't care enough, that you don't deserve to be the one surviving. Or you can, it's just that you can't defend yourself to the one person who matters most. Regina knows perfectly well it's a garbage suggestion that her ulterior motive is to make some kind of political statement, I'm sure, but Sandra doesn't; Sandra will never know anything again. But it's her opinion and her approval and her recognition that Regina actually cares about. It was always like that, the way they'd text incessantly about even the smallest things like sending each other pictures of what they were going to wear to school or the way they'd read books together so they could call each other at midnight and complain about characters they hated or the way Sandra would sometimes say things like *Ugh, I'm such a bitch*, and

Regina would just laugh and link her arm though Sandra's and say *No, you just pretend you are,* and you could tell that meant something real and vital to Sandra, that she trusted and also needed the way Regina saw her. And Regina needs all that to matter still, needs Sandra to understand it matters still, and that's the part—that maybe that's why she's been wanting to do this tribute—that wrecks me. All our doomed, desperate dreams.

Esther says, "It isn't okay for us to—"

"This isn't your call," I say. I tilt back my chair so I can meet her eyes over the computers. "You weren't there."

"Yes, I was. I was here last year. And it doesn't feel right to—"

She doesn't understand, that's entirely clear. And, I guess, how could she? She was a freshman last year. How do you explain Sandra to someone who only ever knew her, reduced and clipped and faded, from that letter they read us all in first period?

So I should—can—reach past that first flash of anger and rummage around for some measure of generosity. "Esther—I get that you're trying to do the right thing. And that's cool, that's good, but by any possible metric that could matter, you weren't there." I say it as gently as I can, but I don't wait for an answer; it doesn't matter what she'll say. This isn't hers to care about. "Regina," I say, before I can talk myself out of it, "I'm in. Whatever you want me to do, I'll do anything. You wanted a portrait, right? You still want one? I'll do a portrait for you. Whatever you want. Count me in."

SEVENTEEN

I draw so many iterations of Sandra. But my fear comes through in all of them, and she looks saintly and flattened, leeched of her real self. I draw for days, all through the first two of the four latenights and then at home in the apartment all night, my dad asleep in the living room and my mom gone, the building quiet. I've never choked like this before—just had nothing right up against the last minute. It makes the whole world feel slippery and thin in my grasp.

I can't shake the certainty that I'm a fraud. A lucky fraud, up until now, but luck runs out eventually, and then you have to face yourself.

The night before our last latenight it's nearly one in the morning and my eyes are burning. I don't put my pen away yet, though; once I do the accusations on the periphery will come oozing back in. I feel desperate. I draw Mr. X—Mr. X sneering at my lack of talent, Mr. X pleased about my family leaving our neighborhood, Mr. X in the principal's office telling them he has some information about a student's fraudulent enrollment that they might like to know. I imagine how he'd look to them, they who don't know him—a polite neighbor, a clean-cut elderly gentleman. I draw him a mild, deferential I'm-in-public-talking-to-other-white-people expression. And that's when it happens.

This is what I've been doing wrong all along with him, why those drawings never came alive over all these years despite how vivid he's been in my head: I've tried to turn him into a cartoon. I've tried to make him look evil. But the real power he has over me is that there was nothing especially extraordinary about him. The worst things you fear aren't the rare or distant ones. The worst things you fear are the ones so close they take up residence inside your head and whisper to you in the background all the time; the worst things you fear are that there's so much darkness lurking inside the nicest people and the safest places that you know. I sketch him out (his face is so familiar to me) and I keep the hard anger of his eyes, but this time I make him kinder-looking, his smile genial, and then, only then, does he finally look as menacing as he always has in my mind.

And that's it. After all this time, after all those moments I was afraid I'd never draw again. When I finally check the time it's past two o'clock in the morning. My eyes are burning and my hand is cramped. I have to be up in just over two hours.

But this was it. It's lifted.

I flip to a new page, shapes forming in my mind. And I think of something else then, too, the thing I've been trying to draw my whole life: that look on my mom's face when she told me about my sister. Maybe that's the reason I could never capture that one, either: because I kept trying so hard to make her look so sad. I missed the other dimensions, the guilt and maybe the hope, too, that it would be better with me, it would be different with me, because after everything, that was the part that crushed me. Those things you want to capture in someone else—the darkest ones hide.

I think about how Sandra was mean sometimes, and funny, the things we used to laugh at together, and then I let myself think about all the horrible things you think about that never go away. I think about her parents and how they have to wake up each day and do crap like—get honked at in traffic, or get guilted for not flossing better at the dentist, and how pointless and enraging it must all feel.

I've grown up knowing how when you leave the world—however it happens, however it went with my sister—you take a part of it with you, like when water dries up in a creek for the summer and it's silent and lonely and parched. This is something I know now that I didn't then, though: that almost all of us have wanted to leave it before. Maybe you always do when your days feel like one endless night closing in on you and you lose the light, grope around in darkness before it starts to feel easier to just let it swallow you altogether.

But I also know you can try to rope off that idea that somehow you'd be better off gone and set your compass to some shore beyond it. I know it can be done. Since March I've seen it more than once. Like how Ahmed's parents made him go see a counselor and he thought she was a hack, and then he went through three or four others until he finally landed on someone he liked and now he literally lists her number in all his profiles in case anyone else needs it. Or like how Mina Lee started taking antidepressants and it made her feel like herself again. Or how—he told me this a few days after she died—that night I found him outside at Yosemite was one of the times Harry felt that same darkness creeping over him, and plans starting to form. Maybe it takes everything you have, every last atom, to sail past that dark idea, and then on arrival all you have to offer the world is your exhausted, battered self. But that's everything. You know? It's enough.

I rub at my eyes with the heel of my hand until they're dry. I pick my pencil back up.

I don't have time to draw a portrait made up of all the carefully pieced-together objects I usually do, but somehow it doesn't feel right this time, anyway. I leave gaps where I can, as much empty space as possible, and draw with spare, quick strokes. And I watch her emerge.

Afterward I feel hollowed out, not tired so much as drained, kind of the way it feels to give blood. I tape the picture to the wall and look at it, trying to imagine what Regina will think of it and whether it's the kind of statement and impact she wants. I make a few small adjustments, then lie in bed, my whole body aching, and watch the sun come up.

Art doesn't change the ending. It doesn't let you lose yourself that way—the opposite, really; it calls you from the darkness, into the glaring, unforgiving light. But at least—this is why it will always feel like a calling to me—it lets you not be so alone.

That's what I can do here. I can give form and shape to what everyone's feeling, a picture of her that feels as true as anything else has this past year. Maybe that's the only way you heal.

Or maybe that isn't quite true, either—you never quite heal. But at least you get to say you're sorry.

EIGHTEEN

I pull Regina aside at the latenight to give her my picture, all nerves. She doesn't say anything for a long time. Finally I stick my hands in my pockets and say, "What do you think?"

Her eyes go wet. "Oh, Danny."

I nudge at a rip in the carpet with my foot. "It's all right?"

"Thank you," she says. "I mean it. Thank you." Regina's not a hugger, but—impulsively—she hugs me. When she does, something lifts off my shoulders, the ground leveling underneath me. She lets go and wipes her eyes, and then I can see her gathering herself, plunging whatever was behind those tears and that hug back down inside. "I'll go scan it. I'm almost done with the layout."

We'd talked about all the different things we could include in the center spread, interviews or hotline numbers or a photo collage, but in the end Regina wanted something stark and simple, lots of white space. Before we send it off Francesca guards the door to make sure Mr. Renato doesn't come in and we all gather around the computer to see how it came out. There's an essay Regina wrote about the day she watched from across the academic court as they cleared out Sandra's locker, shoving everything into a garbage bag that they knotted closed, and on the opposite page, the full page, is my drawing of her. We left my name off it, just in case, and it feels better that way, too, less like I was doing it for my own sake.

Our gamble is that the administration will let it go. (And maybe a part of Regina's gamble, I think, is that they'll feel shamed by the knowledge that they would've stopped us if they'd known about it. Or maybe she doesn't care either way, maybe she wouldn't mind getting in trouble for it.)

When we're finished that night, all the lights off and all of us dispersed through the dark parking lot, Harry drives me home. We still have to look up how to get to my new place.

I'm exhausted. Usually getting the paper sent off to the printer in time is a rush, but it was more subdued this time, and my energy is sapped. Harry's quiet as we drive down Bubb toward the freeway, and at first I think it's just because he's tired, too, but then when we turn onto Stevens Creek he says, "You know Regina knew, right?"

"She knew what?"

"Sandra talked about it sometimes." He stops at the light before 85, and when we go under a streetlamp the shadows carve deep lines in his face. "She'd say things like she'd rather be dead or how it would be easier to just kill herself. Regina never thought she meant it."

My organs all constrict. I don't have to ask why Regina thought that. It seems obvious now, now that we've sat through all the assemblies and panicked every time anyone seemed especially down about something or bombed a final or had a bad breakup, but before that I couldn't count the number of times I've heard someone say basically the same thing. I probably wouldn't have taken it seriously, either.

"No, I didn't know that."

"Yeah. When she told me—it was a few days after—I had this feeling she was just never going to be okay again."

"You still think that?"

"I don't know." The light turns green, and he eases the car onto the freeway. "I think Regina keeps thinking about—you remember that one woman who came to talk to us from Stanford psych or whatever? The lady who made everyone put the crisis hotlines in our phones? Honestly, partly I think she was full of shit because she doesn't understand what Sandra's family was like, but I think Regina keeps thinking how she said if you're depressed enough to kill yourself it's a treatable illness. So Sandra died of a treatable illness. And, I mean, how do you get past that, right? How do you not just lose yourself in all the ways it could've gone differently? I hope—" His voice cracks and he smiles a little, embarrassed. "I hope Regina gets what she's looking for in this. You know?"

I do know. I say, "You think it's a good idea?"

"No." He taps the fingers on his left hand gently against the steering wheel. "But I still want her to have it."

If they really love each other, if they're right for each other and they flood all those empty spaces around one another with enough warmth and light to hold at bay all the worst trappings of the world, then if I care about them, that should be enough for me. I know that. And I hope I'd be a big enough person to let it lie.

But I just—I don't see it. And I know you can see things as you decide, shift the objects in your world so the light falls on them the way you want it to, but there are different ways to love someone and I'm pretty sure Harry feels the same way toward Regina as I do.

We go by the Vallco exit, a few minutes later the exit for the Winchester Mystery House and Valley Fair. "Okay, seriously," Harry says, his voice lighter in a way that seems not forced, exactly, but something maybe closer to determined. Harry believes in positivity. "How are we still not to your house? We've been driving like thirty years."

I don't quite have it in me to match that level of jokiness, but I give it my best shot. "We've been driving, like, four freeway exits."

But then we both lose the energy for it, I think, and we're quiet again. We pass the 880 interchange, the point where it always starts feeling like you're leaving the boundaries of the known world.

"Every now and then at night," Harry says, "when I'm trying to sleep, I'll feel all weird and I swear to God, it's knowing that you're, like, ninety miles away."

Something catches in my heart. I try to keep my voice steady. "It's not even twenty miles. It says it right there on your map."

"It feels like ninety."

"It does." Except there are only ten more minutes now before I'm home and he drops me off and leaves. I wish it were ninety, just for tonight.

I lean back against the seat. We go under an underpass, into what starts feeling like the heart of San José to me. I feel that same spreading, frightened sadness of being home by yourself after dark, something I don't usually feel when he's there.

"So you still don't know why, huh?" Harry says. "You never found out if you were right about your parents trying to run out on their debt?"

"No."

"Did you ever find out more about those people your dad was obsessed with?"

"Not really."

"Who are they? I wanted to look them up."

"I did that already." I reach out to change the radio station, but Harry swats my hand away.

"So who are they?"

I give him their names only because Harry's stubborn; I can't imagine actually saying no and then expending the necessary energy to stave him off until probably the end of time. When I do, a weird expression goes over his face.

"Like, Clay Ballard as in that billionaire guy in venture capital or whatever?"

"Yeah, that one."

"Dude, I know them, kind of." He sits up straighter. "Or my parents do. The guy donated to one of my dad's campaigns."

For some reason this never occurred to me—that Mr. Wong might know them. I should've wondered. He knows everyone, and, especially if you're up at a certain level, I think, the Bay Area's only so big. "You know him? You've talked with him?"

"I met him once at one of my dad's fund-raisers. He was hosting it at his house. That's . . . really strange it would be him. He was kind of weird."

"Weird how?"

"Just like, socially awkward. He has this really harsh laugh that sounds like a machine gun." Harry demonstrates: *ehh-ehh-ehh-ehh-ehh*. "And he cornered me and gave me this long spiel about how he has Chinese American daughters and how important it is for his daughters to get to see Chinese American leaders and how he's very passionate about China and Chinese Americans in America. I was like, um, all right, thank you?"

"That's awkward. How well do your parents know him?"

"Not very, I don't think. I can ask. I'll ask."

"Yeah, no, don't. You ever see him besides that one time?"

"Not that I can remember."

I think about that fear that sparked in all the lines of my dad's face when I asked about their debt. "Did he seem threatening? Can you picture him trying to ruin someone's life if they owed him money?"

"I didn't get that vibe. Maybe a little bit cutthroat like every VC ever, but he was also kind of—earnest. He's that guy who genuinely thinks the startups he's investing in are going to change the world. He was weird but in the way that like—I don't know, like Mike Narvin will probably grow up kind of weird. Like a rich white guy kind of way."

"I love Mike Narvin."

"I know you do. But he's a little weird, right? Picture him twenty years from now with a shitload of money and a hot wife and a job where all day people tell him he's all smart and important, and that's Clay Ballard." Harry pauses. "Honestly, he doesn't really strike me as the kind of guy your dad would know. He was like . . . really Silicon Valley."

I take a second or two to answer that. "What's that supposed to mean?"

"It means—" He winces. "Come on, Danny, not like that. You always think I'm such an elitist. He was just like extremely venture capital-y, you know? I can't imagine your dad, like, getting steaks with him in Palo Alto or whatever. Do you think maybe your mom— didn't you say for a while your mom—"

I stare at him hard until he looks away. "Didn't I say my mom what?"

"Nothing. Forget it."

He means, obviously, did my mom ever clean their house or something. Mrs. Wong is the VP of some tech firm, and I remember how she tried to cover her surprise when she asked what my parents did. At the time I definitely kind of hated her for it, but in a way she was right—my mom runs herself ragged working and look what good it did her, did any of us.

Harry chews on his lip for a few seconds, then he says, "Danny, I didn't mean—"

"Forget about it." I guess it's not entirely outside the realm of possibility. "I should just stop speculating, probably. What's the point."

Harry starts to say something, stops. I say, "What?"

"Nah, never mind."

"Okay." I know him well enough to know if I don't take the bait he'll probably just say it anyway. I'm right; it takes about forty seconds. He clears his throat. I say, dryly, "There it is."

"Yeah, shut up. I was just going to say if it were me and I really thought it had something to do with why my parents moved me to the boonies or if they were really trying to hide out, I wouldn't let it go. But I guess you're you."

"What is that supposed to mean?"

"Nothing. It doesn't mean anything. I can just see you letting it go, that's all."

"I'm too tired to feel insulted, but check back in the morning after I've slept."

He laughs softly. "You don't sleep anymore. You have to be up in like four hours."

We're on my street now (it will never feel like mine) and he turns into the parking lot. The unprotected left I hate is easy when it's late at night, when you wouldn't mind it taking longer. I say, "Thanks for the ride."

"Yeah, anytime."

"You won't fall asleep on the way home, right?"

"Nah, I'm good."

I'm reaching to shut the door when he says, "Hey, Danny, wait."

And I turn back, something in his voice drawing my pulse faster a few ticks. He says, "Ah—I go right out of the parking lot, right?"

"Yeah."

"Okay. Thanks."

He was going to say something else, I know. I heard it there. But he doesn't; he smiles kind of tightly and then lifts his hand in a good-bye and waits for me to close the door instead.

。　.　。

When I get home it's empty, and there's a note on the table saying my dad won't be home until three in the morning. I am, it turns out, more hungry than tired; also, I have a hard time sleeping when it's just me here. I boil water for instant ramen and crack a few eggs into it, and then throw in some frozen broccoli, too, which always feels kind of like a bid for karma. I microwave some frozen dumplings and then lose my appetite two in. They're better when my mom cooks them. She actually uses a pan.

There are two stairwells going up to our floor and they're usually propped open, which defeats the purpose of them having a lock. The street we live on is mostly businesses, and everything starts closing down around five or six—by nightfall the street has emptied, gone thin with stillness. Out the window the streetlights make everything look darker, somehow, like the yellowish light is only there to show you all the shadows, and there aren't any sounds tonight from the apartment next door. It's strange how in a building of so many people—it's three floors—you can feel so completely alone.

I never even had to realize how safe it always felt in Cupertino.

Idyllic, even: there were literal deer wandering around our neighbor-hood sometimes—they'd come down from the foothills and scavenge in people's yards, garden pests—and I never fully absorbed how com-forting it was to live in the center of my life, my school and all my friends and all the places I frequented all huddled together in their safe, tight radius.

I take a shower—I hate showering when I'm by myself here; it creeps me out—and brush and floss and turn on all the kitchen and living room and bathroom lights and get into bed, and then I lie awake listening to cars pass by outside, watching their headlights trace swaths of yellow across my walls. I wish every noise from the hallway didn't remind me of overhearing my mom say she'd be safer at the Lis' house and of my dad's practiced, instinctive fear.

But this is stupid. I am eighteen years old. I'm a legal adult. People my age fight in wars and have kids and work full-time. I can vote, and buy cigarettes, and I can damn well sleep in an apartment by myself at night.

Three hours until my dad comes home. Less than three. I picture him walking through the dark empty parking lot at the mall, coming up those unlocked stairwells here. I picture someone closing in on him, the stack of files he collected to protect himself hidden uselessly in a box somewhere. My heart is going kind of wildly, and I resent it, especially because I know all this would feel so different if it were daylight now.

Back in Texas, Ethan, who was a year older than me, was afraid of the dark. Afternoons in Austin all the kids would play out on the common lawn and I remember the day I announced that and watched that wave of glee roll over everyone, that immediate consolidation of forces against him. It was the first time I remember understanding that something someone told you in implicit trust could hold so much power, and I wish I could say I understood it only after the fact. A second grader named Stan Smith latched on to a chant of *Ethan's afraid of the dark, Ethan's afraid of the dark* that he kept running, almost methodically, while he climbed on the monkey bars and chased after a soccer ball, and all day two of the older kids kept running after him and putting their hands over Ethan's eyes and laughing, asking if he was scared. He was someone who got quiet when he was upset—maybe he still does—and his face turned hard and finally, when the parents who were out there that day (they all traded off teaching sections and writing dissertations and watching all of us) weren't paying attention, he kneed me in the crotch. By then I understood I deserved it. His expression was pure betrayal as he surveyed me rolling on the ground and said, quietly, "You're afraid of the dark, too."

I was. He knew because the day before when I'd played at his house he'd summoned me into the bedroom he shared with his baby sister and, from inside a tattered box of Star Wars Legos, pulled a roll of wintergreen Life Savers.

"Are you scared of the dark?" he'd asked. When I'd said yes, he'd carefully peeled the wrapper away and plucked one Life Saver and handed it to me.

"If you chew it really hard in the dark and look at a mirror, it lights up. That's what I do when I'm scared." I'd tried it that night. He'd been right—the wonder of it, the unexpectedness, were strong enough for the moment to banish the dark. Sometimes, every now and then, I try to draw him. Usually when I do it's him in the dark staring at a mirror, Life Saver in hand.

I wish my parents, both of them, would just come home. It's hard to hold on to your anger when you're scared and lonely, when you miss someone at night.

It's around two in the morning and I'm still awake when I get out of bed, finally—it's clear it's a losing battle anyway—and open up the laptop. My search auto-completes for me as soon as I type *eth*. Guess I look him up even more than I realized.

I could just keep not doing this forever, I guess, just like I've been doing, but lying awake here I've been telling myself I'd go through with it. So I send him a friend request, regret it immediately, google whether you can undo a request, find out you can't, refresh the page a billion times to see if he's accepted even though it's the middle of the night, and then all night and all the next day—through my Spanish quiz and lunch and the bus ride back to San José—live in that very specific hell of waiting for someone to see something you can't take back.

It's five-thirty California time, and I've just gotten home, when Ethan accepts the request. I have just a few seconds to catch up on his profile—he goes to Howard University and has an extremely pretty girlfriend, a serious-faced Black girl with close-cropped hair and the kind of frame that makes her look tall, although it's impossible to scale her next to someone I haven't seen since I was six—before he messages me: *Hey, sorry, who's this?*

My heart does its plummeting-elevator thing inside my chest. I am the loser king of Losertown. No one cares what happened when you were six years old; I bet he didn't spend a second thinking about me after I left. I waste too long thinking of the least pathetic way to get out of this, and finally write back, *Are you the Ethan that used to live in UT family housing? Came across some old UT stuff and just wondered what you were up to these days. Looks like you've done pretty well for yourself.*

He writes back about three seconds later: *DANNY TSENG, HOLY SHIT.* And then, right after: *What's your phone number???*

I send it over. Almost instantaneously my phone rings.

"Danny Tseng. I can't believe this," he says. I haven't heard that name in years. I wouldn't have recognized his voice, I don't think, but maybe I can still hear him inside it. "Danny, I swear to God I never thought I'd hear from you again. We never stopped wondering what happened to you. Seriously. My family still talks about you guys. I can't wait to tell my parents you found me on Facebook after all these years. They won't believe it. Where have you been? And how come you changed your name?"

I tell him how we've been living in California. He seems surprised in a relieved kind of way, like he'd expected much worse, and then he tells me what he remembers and what he learned from his parents over the years: how that last time I stayed at his house my parents had told his mom, Auntie Monica, they were flying out to California. They didn't say much about the trip—every time Auntie Monica asked about it my mom laughed it off and said oh, it was nothing, just a little jaunt. She'd been happy and excited about it, and had gone to Monica's the day before they left to borrow a few pieces of clothing. Monica had thought it was some kind of anniversary trip.

The strange thing, though, was my parents hadn't bought tickets back yet, and hadn't been able to say exactly when they'd be home to get me. It was unlike them; usually they were hyperorganized. They called a few times a day to check in on me and it wasn't until the last day, last-minute, that they'd booked a flight back to Texas. When they came back they were rushed; they got in after my bedtime and Auntie Monica had offered to let me stay until morning so I wouldn't have to wake up in the middle of the night, but my parents said no, no, they wanted to come right away. Auntie Monica thought it was sweet that they'd missed me. She offered to pick them up from the airport so they could all have drinks together and the Parker-McEvoys could hear about their trip, but my parents took a cab and came back rushed and quiet. They woke me up and thanked Ethan's parents for taking me, and said goodnight. It was the last time his parents ever saw us. My dad didn't show up to the lab that Monday. At first everyone thought my parents were probably just tired out from their trip, but when people knocked on our door no one was there and then a few days later the university started cleaning out the apartment to give to the next family on the waiting list.

I have that growling, acidic kind of pain in my abdomen you get when you're up too late, and it surges then. I say, "Huh."

"You know, something else kind of weird happened, too. Someone came around a few weeks after you guys left. I was, what, seven? So I had no idea until a couple years ago when we were talking about you and my parents told me. The guy wouldn't say who he was with. Like, if it were a police detective, he would've just said so, right? But he was all hush-hush about it, so my parents didn't tell him anything. They didn't think your parents were the criminal type. Plus they still thought they were going to hear from your folks again."

"Folks." In spite of my lungs compressing at what he said, all the air squeezed out in a *whoosh*, I can't help smiling. "You sound . . . really Texan still."

"Oh, sure," he says, and I can hear that he's smiling, too. "Sure. You vanish into thin air and call me up out of the blue twelve years later with no explanation, and you make fun of my accent? I see how it is."

It's surreal to be talking to him. I'll worry about what he told me when I have the space for it, because I think it'll take a lot. For now I ask Ethan to fill me in on his life since we left. He tells me when he was eleven his family moved to Ann Arbor, where his parents both got jobs at UMich, and he's at Howard now, wants to intern for a congressperson, loves DC. And then for a long time we stay on the phone, excavating old memories from Texas, and that world I lost takes on shape and form again—the humidity bearing down on you in summers, the way the gravel in the landscaped pits outside felt against bare feet, the Popsicles Mary Peelen's mom used to give us when we played outside. It's like being given back my childhood, and it reminds me what I always felt I had in drawing: how it can hold this same power, can capsule up that same rush of texture and memory that we all carry and can never fully share.

"You still draw?" he asks. "I remember how good you were at drawing."

"I do. I'm going to design school next year, actually."

"No way, man, that's awesome. You're going for it all the way, huh?"

"Something like that, yeah." That small flash of joy each time in claiming it aloud for myself, the way it shines through the haze of everything he told me about us leaving—I hope that never goes away.

"What about your parents?" he says. "How are they doing?"

Less joy. I tell him.

"Your father's a security guard?" he repeats. "At a mall?" There's a long silence, and my shame blooms bright and hot inside it. I want to explain it's not like that, but, I mean, it is like that. "He could've gotten a job anywhere," Ethan says. "My mom always said he was so brilliant. And wasn't your mom taking business classes? Didn't she want to open a hotel?"

"Yeah, well." Not much else to say there. "Hey, Ethan, this is going to sound really stupid, but do you remember their names? My parents?"

"Do I remember your parents' names? Sure. Anna and Joseph Tseng."

"Or—right. I mean their Chinese ones they used. I've never been able to remember, and they stopped using them when we moved."

"Why don't you just ask your dad?"

"Ah—it's kind of a long story."

This is a tribute to our past together: all these years later, Ethan accepts that as an answer. "Ah, I got you. I can ask my dad. He'd probably know."

"All right. Hey, tell him hi for me, will you?"

"Yeah, of course. He'll be thrilled. He'll never believe I actually found you."

He texts me about ten minutes later. Mr. Parker didn't know my mom's legal name, but he knew my dad's: Tseng Huabo.

I google it. And there staring back at me is the truth, what they've been hiding from me all this time: for the last twelve years, since right around the time we moved here, my parents have been wanted for false imprisonment and assault.

NINETEEN

The paragraph is from an archived article on an Atherton community website. *Huabo Tseng (may also go by Tseng Huabo) and an unknown female accomplice wanted in connection with an incidence of assault and false imprisonment in the 800 block of Watkins. Huabo Tseng is described as an Asian American male, five foot eight inches and a hundred and sixty pounds, with black hair and brown eyes. His female companion is described as Asian American, five foot four inches, a hundred and ten pounds, with long black hair and brown eyes.*

I look up everything else I can think to, every iteration and misspelling I can imagine white people making of my dad's name, everything I can remember from his files. It gets me nowhere. I go to the pay phone outside the 7-Eleven on the corner so nothing can be traced to our apartment. My hands are sweating, and my throat feels like it's swelling shut. The phone rings once, and then a dispatcher picks up. "Is this an emergency?"

"No, I wanted to look up an incident report?"

"You wanted to what?"

Immediately, my resolve weakens. "Um—I'm allowed to do that, right?"

"I'll transfer you to records."

On hold, I picture the person on the other line frustrated with me, picture pretending not to notice as I make my demands, and I almost hang up. The person I'm transferred to doesn't sound much more thrilled to hear from me. "You want to look up an incident report," he repeats, in a grumbly voice. "All right. What is it."

None of his questions have question marks at the end. I read him the date from the police blotter, and there's a long silence that means I'm not sure what. Finally he clears his throat and says, "All right. What is it you want to know."

"Is there any information that's not in the police blotter? More of what happened, or anything?"

Another long, irritated silence. I can feel his annoyance radiating through the phone line. "You want me to read it to you?"

"That would be great."

"Every word?"

"Um—that would be great."

He reads it flatly in his low, grumbling voice: *Received a call about an assault and false imprisonment. 807 Watkins Ave. Suspects fled before officers arrived. Suspects previously known to the victim and believed to be Huabo Tseng and female companion.*

"Is there anything else about Huabo Tseng?"

Another long pause. I can hear others talking in the background. "We have no other records on that individual."

"Um, who made the report?"

"The report was made by Clay and Sheila Ballard."

"Thank you," I say. I knew this—as soon as I saw the article, as soon as I saw Atherton, I knew. "Thank you very much."

You live with someone so closely—you share toothpaste and soap and loads of laundry, and all your thoughts and dreams and private shames and secret hopes tumble back and forth across each other over and over in the five hundred square feet they're trapped in—and you'd never think someone could hide so much of themselves. But they can, apparently, and maybe it's just the sleep deprivation, but I feel sick.

Does it matter if someone isn't who you always thought they were? If they let you know them a certain way and whatever else existed in their world, they kept it locked out—which part actually matters?

But that's a cop-out, and I know that. People hide themselves until they don't, and then whatever you believed is irrelevant. Maybe you believed you were an only child, or that your home was yours, or that someone you used to call a friend would be there to wake up each morning. Maybe you believed in the life your parents constructed for you.

All week I literally don't see either of them—my dad picked up extra shifts and sleeps while I'm gone at school, and my mom's at the Lis' and I can never bring myself to interrupt one of her *What are you eating? Did you finish your homework?* calls and texts to ask if it's true. It feels absurd, actually, that in the space between her saying how dumplings were two-for-one so she bought extra, and will bring them home over the weekend, that there could be any kind of darkness lurking, that they're criminals.

I go looking all over the apartment for the box on the Ballards, and then I keep looking. Even though there aren't many places you can hide something in five hundred square feet, it's gone. I would be lying if I said part of me wasn't relieved.

鴛

The scene: the four of you, your parents and your grandfather and you, suspended in time, locked in a moment that will vanish all too quickly. Your parents hover over their decision, unable to land. Your father— who calls you his little empress, who brings home the most unblemished yams for you to eat because they're your favorite—wants to go. He can see nothing but the future. He imagines himself at the head of a classroom, all his gathered knowledge flowing through the air like oxygen. He imagines all the papers his name will head. He imagines you going to the best of American schools.

Your grandfather, your lone surviving grandparent, your only link to your own history, pretends not to listen. But at night he lies awake in his cold bed, staring at the ceiling, imagining his empty life without you and your parents in it. He no longer works—he's an old man already, was already old when he had your father—and it's he who cares for you during the day while your parents work, mashing yams and eggplants to feed you, putting you down for naps and carefully bundling you to take you on walks outside. Each day when your parents leave it feels like a tiny death. You cry when they go, and every time it's like a sword through his heart. He would never say this aloud, it's not his way, but he would rather die than have you taken away from him.

Your mother has never wanted to leave China. Even moving to Wuhan for college, five hours from her home in Shiyan, left her homesick. She doesn't wish to cross an ocean and set down roots in a strange country full of guns and cheese and nursing homes packed with abandoned elderly parents. When she first met your father there was a restlessness to him she tried to tell herself she liked. She tried to tell herself that it would stir the same in her.

But with both her parents gone now she feels adrift, like her own past here has been released into the universe. (How easy it is to vanish, how fragile are the ties that tether you to your world; your mother should recognize these things. This is her first duty to you.)

Your father plays his trump card: in the United States you could have siblings. Your mother has always loved American stories and shows about big families. Your grandfather, finding his voice for the first time, terrified of being left behind alone, speaks sharply against this. Children shouldn't have to fight for their parents' attention, he says. You deserve better than this. But a seed has been planted—the mechanisms of your destruction have been set in motion. Still, though, it's not too late.

Your grandfather prepares your parents' favorites for dinner one night at the height of your parents' discussion, dresses you in your mother's favorite outfit. Over the meal, he makes a proposition: he will keep you here in Wuhan with him. He'll care for you until your parents build up a life with room for you in it, and you can join them then.

It's practical—the obvious solution—but your mother is hesitant. Maybe you won't remember her all those months later. Maybe you'll miss her too much. She imagines you sobbing for her, imagines you wondering why she's abandoned you.

If she says yes, though she doesn't know it, it will spell your end. She has a week before your father's paperwork is due to decide. The arguments of whether to leave you behind play out every moment in her mind. She imagines going; she imagines staying. She wishes her parents were here to offer advice.

In the end, though, isn't every lengthy decision just a way of contorting reality to fit whatever one wants it to be? If history has shown anything, it's that humanity is rotten at its very core. There is a screaming emptiness where goodness might reside; instead of empathy and principle there is fear and greed and stunning, breathtaking hypocrisy. People will believe themselves good in the face of all evidence to the contrary; people will smile and cling to their own respectability in the face of atrocity. You should have expected no better from your mother, perhaps. But there was a time, that time when your fate was in her hands, that you did.

In the end you are no match for their ambition. The future they constructed in their minds was built too strong and rigid, so that when they tried to slip you into it the structure toppled.

Your mother assents. Your fate is sealed. Your father accepts the position and purchases plane tickets, just two, and they will go to the United States. You will never join them.

TWENTY

March seventh, the anniversary of the day Sandra died, falls on a Thursday this year. You can feel it going to sleep the night before, and I text Regina around ten to see how she's doing. She starts to type something (I get that ellipsis) and then stops, and two hours later finally writes back: ¯_(ツ)_/¯

I'm beyond tired, at that stage of sleep deprivation where you start to feel more like a limbed id than a real person, but I lie awake most of the night. My dad's sleeping here, which I'm grateful for in spite of myself—I don't think I could handle being alone tonight. I try to sleep and try not to think about anything; my mind is too tired. It doesn't work, and all the thoughts I try to box out come stampeding by, taunting me.

It wasn't just Ahmed who said something to me. There were two separate times, right after she died, when I walked up at lunch and everyone went quiet. I knew what that meant. And you can't say *I swear I actually liked her, I swear it wasn't like that* because no one will believe you; they'll think it's cheap for you to say it. And maybe it is.

In the morning I stumble out of bed and shower in the hottest water I can stand to try to wake up. Thursdays are late-start days and it's light out already when I wait for the bus, but even so I'm so tired my head feels stuffed with helium. The whole ride to Cupertino, I feel sick. It's early still when I get to campus, but the newspapers are here, stacked outside each classroom like sentries. I don't pick one up.

The first person I see this morning is—thank God—Noga, who gives me a sad smile and then—I think she debates it with herself first—a hug.

"I'm glad I know you," she says. "I told myself today I'd tell everyone I care about that they matter to me." Her face starts to crumple, but she catches herself. "I can't believe it's been a year."

I hug her back and tell her I'm glad I know her, too, that it won't be the same next year without her, and then I lie and say I need to go make up a quiz, because my eyes are welling and there's a greater than zero chance I might just lose it. I text Harry to see if he's at school yet. He doesn't answer, which means he's probably driving. It'll be better when he's here—the frenzy I feel locked into will settle.

A cluster of freshmen I walk by on the way to my locker are reading the paper. At my locker, I borrow my mom's ritual when she feels a panic attack coming on—long breaths, inhaling as far as your chest will expand. I'm getting books from my locker, my lungs mostly normal again, when someone says, "Hey, Cheng."

I turn around. It's Ahmed standing there, the paper in his hand. My heart dive-bombs into my stomach. But whatever I'm feeling, I know it's so much worse for him, so I force myself to say, as kindly as I know how, "Hey, man, how you doing?"

He holds up the paper. "You drew this, right?"

I shouldn't have. I should've just told Regina to use a photo. But it's useless to deny it. I've had pictures in the paper every month for the past three years, and anyway, there's not another person on campus, probably, who could've drawn that. I think I might throw up. "I did."

"Nice picture."

My face must go blank for a moment. "Uh, really?"

"Yeah, it looks good."

"Oh." I can feel my expression trying to rearrange itself, failing. "Well—thanks. You doing okay today?"

"Kind of. Yeah, I mean—" He reaches up and pushes back his Yankees cap. "I kind of didn't want to come to school today because people would be all weepy, or people who didn't even know her would act like they had some right to be sad. But then I was like, okay, the administration pretty much made sure no one's allowed to talk about it, right, so I thought it would be fine. And then I saw the paper, and I thought I wouldn't want to see anything, but—"

He kind of chews on the inside of his lip. I reach up and wipe my forehead.

"I'll be honest, I know you guys had your deal with each other, but she also talked about you sometimes like she missed you. I think she wanted you guys to be cool again. And when I saw the picture you drew of her—I guess it's nice to know that there was actually something there, you know what I mean? Like that she meant something to you all along. Because if she thought that and she was just fooling herself, that would be pretty fucking sad. Maybe she knew she was right. I hope so."

If I were to paint what it feels like right now to have him stand in front of me and say that, it would be this: dark splatters shoved aside by some kind of glowing center. "That, ah, means more to me than you know."

"It's just what I thought when I saw your picture. I'm going to hang on to it." He offers me a smile, his eyes crinkling. I always thought he had a great smile. "I'll save it for when you're rich and famous. I'll say I knew you when."

▫ ▫ ▫

I'm still replaying that smile walking into first period, keeping it close by to make myself feel like today's going to be okay after all. When I walk in, Mrs. Sachdeva comes toward me like she's been waiting for me.

"Danny," she says, her expression sympathetic. She puts her hand on my arm. "Mr. Denton would like to see you in his office. Why don't you take your things with you? He's waiting for you, so go ahead and go."

▫ ▫ ▫

Regina's mother is there in the AP's office, her face pinched with anger, Regina sitting rigid and silent next to her. Mr. Denton, the assistant principal, stands when I come in, his hands splayed across his hips.

Mr. Denton went here for high school back when it was a different place entirely. He's probably my favorite of the APs—he's always seemed the most human—but he's also always seemed baffled by us and all the ways we aren't the white jocks and cheerleaders in his old yearbook photos, always casting himself as wearily, benignly bewildered by us and by our parents who come to argue with varying amounts of English about our grades and complain about our teachers.

"Danny, thank you for joining us," he says. "We've called your folks, so we're just waiting on them."

The room spirals in front of me, a whirlpool that sucks in everything in my field of vision. "They can't come, they're both working, but I can just have them call you, or—"

"They're on their way. We'll just go ahead and hang tight until they can be here too."

"I told him that was unnecessary," Regina says sharply. "I told him the drawing was anonymous and it wasn't you, and that—"

"Regina." Mr. Denton gives her a tired smile. They know each other; she was one of the National Merit Semifinalists and he wrote all their letters of rec for college, and she's in his office a lot doing interviews for stories, too. "We've been over this. Let's just—" He holds out his hands in a *whoa-there* gesture. Regina folds her arms across her chest and sits back against the chair, her lips pressed together. Her mother glares at her and snaps something in Taiwanese. And her tone—it's that panicked anger everyone who's ever had a parent recognizes from the way you get yelled at when you cross a street without looking or reach toward a hot burner, and it makes me think I misjudged her when I first came in.

My throat is slowly closing. I thought maybe we'd get in trouble, but I figured it would involve a slap on the wrist and that since my name wasn't on it I'd be fine. It didn't occur to me that without any warning my parents would be called here. My worst-case scenario was how I'd intercept a call home.

When they burst in they look frantic. My dad's wearing his security uniform and he's clutching his phone, and both of them are out of breath like they ran from the car. Next to Mrs. Chan they look disheveled and whole magnitudes more panicked.

"Thanks for joining us," Mr. Denton says, sticking out his hand for them to shake.

"We're very sorry," my mom says. "We can work out whatever—"

He gives them the same hands-out gesture. "Let's just sit down and have a conversation together here. I think that's the best course of action."

They sit. My mom presses two fingers against her wrist, checking her pulse. And I realize, seeing them next to Mrs. Chan that way, that their fear is aimed differently: Mrs. Chan's, it's clear, is about Regina and probably, I think, about Sandra. My parents' is about Mr. Denton.

"First off," Mr. Denton says, "just want to cover all our bases here and check in and make sure you two are doing all right. I know it's a tough day. You feeling okay?"

Regina says, flatly, "Oh, I'm great."

"Danny?"

"I'm fine."

"All right. If at any point you feel like this is too much or you need to talk to someone, you stop me, okay? We've got our counselors right here in the office. Deal?"

Regina glares at him. Mr. Denton says, "I'll take that as a yes. All right. Let's just take a look here—" He reaches across his desk for a copy of the paper and shakes it open, and then launches into an explanation for our parents' benefit of how we went behind our teacher's back to print it/how hard the school's working to protect all its students and be sensitive to everyone's needs/why it's supposedly necessary to have such clearly defined guidelines in place/how said guidelines have been made abundantly clear. And how we must have understood that, which is why we did this covertly instead of asking permission, right? He looks between us, his eyebrows raised.

I don't answer that one. But I have to fight to keep the anger off my face. Someone you grew up with dies, someone whose history is inextricable from your own, and you're supposed to what, exactly—talk to random counselors about grief and acceptance, feel proud that you've gotten over something you really should never get over? Regina says, "Talking about suicide isn't the same thing as glorifying it," and there's a crack in her resolve—her voice is shaking.

"We don't want you to not talk about it, believe me. We want you to have every resource at your disposal. Whatever you need. We just want you to be careful how and where you talk about it. If you think of something contagious, like a flu, and you think about the precautions you'd take—"

"Daniel is very sorry," my mom says. Her breaths sound shallow. So all right, then; there it is—they aren't going to take my side. She smiles a desperate-looking smile. "He will never do anything like this again. Daniel, tell him you're sorry."

My dad is sweating. His temples are gleaming. "Very sorry," he echoes.

That flame in my chest flares higher. They both turn to me, staring me down until I finally mutter, "I'm sorry." The lie tastes like ash.

"I'm not sorry."

"Regina," her mother snaps.

But Regina's blazing. She turns to Mr. Denton. "You're not going to turn this into something we did wrong. It was something we all wanted to do, and if there's a single person on this campus who thinks it was somehow *hurtful*, then they can come and tell it to my face."

"Whoa, whoa, let's just take a step back. Let's take a step back," Mr. Denton says, and when Regina tries to answer he raises his voice to talk over her and keeps doing it, loudly, until she finally goes quiet, her face like stone. "Look, no one's getting in trouble today. We care about all our students and we want to make sure you feel taken care of. But we do—Regina, Danny, I want you and your parents to understand that we take this very seriously. We have a lot of kids on the edge here, lots of kids under extraordinary pressure at home, all that cultural pressure I'm sure you're both familiar with, and when someone's teetering on an edge like that, we want to do whatever we can to pull them back in. And that goes for both of you, too, all right? We treat moments like this as cries for help. Given that, we think it's appropriate to ask you to take the rest of the day off, which I hope you'll both take as an opportunity to assess your own mental health and ways you might be struggling with Sandra's choice. To that end, we're recommending—requiring, actually—that you both meet with our trained psychologists moving forward. They're great, very understanding. They'll put you right at ease. You know, no one wants to meet with me." He cracks a smile. None of us returns it. "And we wanted your parents to be very aware of the situation. You know, it's hard to remember sometimes as a teenager, but Mom and Dad love you and want the best for you." He reaches out and pats both of us on the shoulder simultaneously—Regina recoils—and then palms the edge of his desk with both hands and exhales. "Okay? My secretary will get you hooked up with those psychologists. I think we're done here."

· · ·

When we get outside my mom grips my arm hard enough to leave marks. She's trembling. "Hurry up," she orders, motioning toward the car.

Regina and her mom come out behind us, her mom yelling at her in Taiwanese. Regina's face is entirely blank, like it took all she had to be lectured and now there's nothing left.

"I need to talk to Regina," I say, shaking my arm free.

"Listen to your mother," my dad hisses.

They just sat through the same talk I did; how could they watch what they just did and tell me not to talk to Regina? They know Regina's been my friend nearly all my life. "I'm going to see if she's—"

My dad whirls toward me so violently I actually flinch. *"Go get in the car."*

It's clear there's no choice. I obey.

"We can't stay here," my mom says to my dad, her face pale, as they hurry me across the bus circle. "They'll find us. The school will notify—"

"Try to be calm, Anna, and—"

"I will not *try to be calm*. We can't stay here. You can't go back to the apartment. They'll find you."

I say, "What are you talking—"

"Quiet," my dad orders. "You clearly cannot be trusted."

I can't be trusted? *I* can't? There's a warrant out for his arrest, one he's kept hidden over a decade, and I can't be trusted?

"How could you do this, Daniel? If we're caught—"

My dad looks around the parking lot nervously. "Get in the car, Daniel. Right now. We'll speak in the car."

I get in. Through the window I see Regina sink onto a bench. Her mom grabs her by the elbow, her face contorted in what looks from here like anger, and Regina yells something at her and then bends over, burying her face in her hands.

"I need to go see if she's okay." I reach for the door handle, and my dad yanks me back so hard my shoulder nearly wrenches out of its socket. I look at him, shocked—he's never rough with me. He stares back, daring me to move again. I don't. My shoulder throbs.

"Drive," he orders.

"But Regina—"

"Drive."

When he says it something snaps inside me like a rubber band. I do it, though, watching Regina in the mirror as long as I can. Her mom has sat down next to her and is saying something, and as I watch she pulls tissues from her purse. And then I turn, and I lose them in my rearview mirror, and for as long as I live I don't think I'll ever forget what it feels like for my parents to forbid me from being there for one of the people I care about most in the world.

Once I've pulled out of the parking lot, my parents explode. I've ruined everything. I've betrayed our family. I have put all of us at risk. My duty is to our family and yet I've lied and disobeyed and broken their trust. I grip the steering wheel as hard as I can as we pass the 7-Eleven, their words rattling around in my eardrums. We pass the Ace Tutoring building, the Apple extension. And then a barrage of threats—

"You won't go back to Cupertino," my mom says.

"And we're taking your phone."

"Yes. You won't talk to Regina or Harry or those others from there again. They're bad influences and you don't know who you can trust."

"You're going to come to work with me and sit in the car as you obviously can't be trusted to be home by yourself."

They have left the land of rationality. And now what? The paper's finished and Sandra's still gone, and whatever it was Regina needed today, she couldn't have found it in Mr. Denton's office or sobbing in front of the school on a concrete bench. The road wavers in front of me, then holds again.

"You knew it was wrong," my dad's saying now, low and furious and also kind of disbelieving, like he's stunned I could do this. "Do you know what could happen? I can't believe you would be so selfish." His face is pinched white. "What if they try to send someone to the house now? Or they look at your records more? What if—"

"Why did you get arrested for assaulting the Ballards?"

It's like drawing a shade, the completeness of the silence, the void it leaves behind. They stare at each other in the rearview mirror. Then my dad says, his voice low and dangerous, "Quiet."

"You didn't tell me you got arrested. You didn't tell me we were losing our house. You've never even told me how my sister died."

My mom makes a choking sound. We've just passed the police station when she says, "I can't breathe. Daniel, pull over and—"

"Don't pull over now," my dad orders. "We're right by the police station. Keep driving."

"Who cares if we're right by the police station?"

"I said keep driving."

"She said she can't *breathe*. I'm pulling over."

"I said—"

My heart is pounding in my throat. I can feel myself careening past control and I can feel, too, the lure of obliterating whatever part of me might still feel regret or shame. When your anger is big enough you can let it swallow you, and then there's nothing left of you to have to face it. And maybe it's a relief. "I don't care what you said."

He reaches for the steering wheel. I wrench it back, hard, so hard the car fishtails across the lanes. The wheel feels hot under my hands. And even as it happens I can feel how many times this scene will play across my mind and how even after that I still won't quite be able to separate the sequence of events, break them down into discrete moments. I know my mom screams, and I know she says, *Daniel, watch*—and I know my dad curses and then there's a loud honking and that I panic but that by then it's too late, and then the feel of the impact, how you feel it all the way down to your teeth and the door I've opened flaps all the way open and then slams back, pinning my shirt so I can't twist around.

I wish I could say that it was just an accident and that accidents happen, and I wish I could say that even though I was angry I never meant for anyone to get hurt. But that's not true. The truth is that I saw the telephone pole, and in that split second I understood what I was doing, that if I swerved, just moved my hands a matter of inches, I would cede control, and for an infinitesimal amount of time that felt like some kind of out. And I wanted to cause damage. I wanted the crush and chaos of metal on metal, and the pain, and their panic. You could've run the future past me, given me a chance to stop it, and I think in that moment I still would've said *Yes, play it out.* I wanted them to be sorry.

I meant for it to be me, though. But when you light a fire you don't always get to choose where it burns. The car spins to a stop and then there's a stillness, and then people start running toward us, shouting. There must be someone who pulls my mom out, there must be calls to 911, but for a long time all I'll remember about this part is those seconds of my dad screaming *Anna, Anna, open your eyes.*

TWENTY-ONE

Galaxies die and climates change and eras end while my mother lies on the sidewalk motionless. It could be ten seconds, maybe, I don't know, but each one stretches out whole lifetimes. I watch through the window, frozen in place, and even after she opens her eyes and squints at the strangers standing over her, groggy, I don't come all the way back to the world until my dad yanks me out of the car so quickly I stumble, my legs giving out against the pavement.

"Can you breathe? Is anything broken?" He's frantic, patting me all over for injuries. I tell him I'm okay, but he doesn't believe me. I'm shaking so hard it's hard to stand up.

My mom is hunched over on the sidewalk, two strangers crouching next to her trying to talk to her. I was only going thirty miles an hour and I thought, maybe, that it didn't feel that fast at the time, but the car is totaled—the hood crumpled like paper—and my mom's eyes are squeezed shut in pain. She can barely speak.

I can feel my blood pounding through my arteries, spurts of pressure in my forehead, and I have to sit down and breathe until the world has leveled off again. The sirens don't break through into my consciousness until my dad snaps his head up at the sound. "We didn't call—"

"I called," one of the people by my mom says, a white woman waving her hand at him and speaking loudly. "You're lucky it happened so close by. They'll just be right here."

"No," he says. "No, we don't need—we don't want—" And my mom, grimacing, manages, "No police." But then they're there with two cars, lights flashing like strobes, striding toward us and barking questions, and it's just a minute or two later that a fire truck comes, too.

When I was a kid I used to love whenever we pulled over for emergency vehicles. It was before I knew it was a law—I thought it was a reflex people had that spoke to some common goodness, everyone's shared desire that help arrive. But the way it feels today when they come, the way my parents visibly brace themselves—this is not the help I imagined on the other end when I was a kid.

"You were the one driving?" one of the officers says to me. "You have your driver's license already?"

"Yes, sir."

"Were you speeding?"

"No, sir, I—"

"He never speeds," my dad says quickly. His face is stricken. "Never—"

The cop holds up his hand, and my dad goes silent. "Were you on your phone?"

The cop's a small white guy, shorter than I am and thinner, too, but I can feel how impervious he is to me, how the force of every strong need or feeling I've ever had in my life would glance right off him. I say, "No, sir."

"Tell me what happened."

"I don't—I don't know what happened. I lost control of the car."

"You just lost control going thirty miles an hour?"

I can feel it falling apart for my dad then, too, even though he doesn't say it. Of course I didn't just lose control. The road's straight here. "Yes, sir."

"He just swerved," the white lady puts in. "Going straight and then, bam, all of a sudden."

"My foot slipped."

He rakes his eyes over my face. I can't help it—I look away. Maybe that was all he wanted, though, because he mostly leaves me alone after that. They make measurements on the road, take my phone and look through it, and dismiss me to go help my mom.

Which I can't do. I can't talk to her, can't get close to her. I hang back and watch as my dad talks to the firefighter paramedics.

"It wasn't a concussion, just fainting," he insists, my mom grimacing and trying to nod along. "At the hospital, what would they do? They would send us home and tell us to keep an eye on her. We'll just do that already."

"You sure?" one of the paramedics, a white guy with an enormous neck, says skeptically. "You're probably dealing with some cracked ribs here, best-case scenario. It were me, I'd go get checked out."

"Yes, yes," my dad says, nodding vigorously. "Very sure, thank you, yes, she's fine."

"You should go get checked out," I say. "You—"

But the look my dad gives me, urgent and terrible, silences me. "She's okay," he repeats. "No need for a hospital. We just go home."

"Do you remember losing consciousness?" the other paramedic, a slim Black woman, asks her. "Did you wake up confused?"

"I am fine," my mom whispers, her face white. "I will go home and rest."

So they write on the report that my mom is declining medical treatment, and the cop rips a sheet of paper from his clipboard and hands it to my dad and says, "Call in a couple days to get the report for your insurance company," and they all leave—the paramedics and the cop cars that came swarming around us and the people who stopped when they saw the crash. We sit on the curb watching as the tow truck comes, my mom curled in a fetal position and my dad blinking rapidly at the space in the street where the car used to be, the asphalt covered in cubed greenish glass from the windows like bloodstains, and then the taxi comes.

. . .

We don't speak to each other on our way back home. In the taxi my mom sits in the front seat, her breath coming in short catches. My dad, watching her, keeps leaning forward and begging the taxi driver to slow down. As for me, I got off easy: I ache all over and have a splitting headache, but nothing broken, nothing worse. My dad, who was sitting behind me, came out about the same.

The driver turns up the radio and hums to himself. Whenever I glance back at my dad he's cradling his arms around his sides, but except for telling the driver to slow down every time we hit a bump and my mom gasps my dad says nothing, and never looks back at me. The fare passes thirty, thirty-five, and I have a sick feeling in my stomach as I watch it go up past seventy.

We've gotten off the freeway when I finally understand what I should've as soon as I saw the assault charge and what I should've understood, maybe, all along. And then everything comes together like an avalanche—the way they were always so careful before opening the front door. The way they always acted like they weren't sure they'd still be here when I came back. How they always have me drive, how I've never been to China and how it's been years since they were on a plane. How panicked they were at the police.

I don't know why I never put it together before this. And now—what have I done?

We're back home. I can feel the lines of my life like watercolor blurring and starting to bleed. My dad gives the driver four twenties and tells him to keep the change.

Inside the apartment it's stale the way small places get when you leave them for a long time, those scents of your life distilled and amplified back at you, and the squeak of our footsteps against the square of linoleum in the entryway echoes accusingly, all our shoes lined up in the entryway staring at us.

My dad helps my mom to my bedroom. I hover in the doorway, my head pounding, my chest hollow. My dad goes into the bathroom and I hear him open the medicine cabinet, and then he's in the bedroom for what feels like a long time. When he comes back out he closes the door behind him.

I can't speak. My dad folds his arms across his chest and stares around the apartment, and I wait for him to say something. For the first time in my life I'm afraid of him. Not that he'll lose his temper, not that he'll hurt me; it's that he'll confirm for me that I'm exactly the person I'm afraid I am.

I'm shaking. Outside a car honks, and a truck shudders by. My dad stands still. Finally I can't stand it anymore and I say, "Ba—"

I mean to say *I'm sorry, I'm so sorry*, to say *I swear to you that somehow I will fix this*, and maybe also I mean to beg him to tell me things will be okay. I don't get even halfway there. Instead I break down and cry, and whatever punishment I deserve, my dad spares me. Instead, he awkwardly pats my back and says, sternly, "Stop it. She'll be fine. She's strong," and he doesn't mention the car, or what happened to my mom, or what I've done. He doesn't ask me if I meant to do it.

And then, painstakingly and clumsily, because he so rarely does it, he cooks me dinner. He starts the rice cooker and stands in front of the freezer a long time, staring at it, then defrosts a package of ground pork and makes mapo tofu from a box mix and sautés wilted bok choy with garlic and ginger while I try to pull myself together a thousand times, a thousand ways. Then he scoops everything into bowls and puts them on the table and comes to where I'm still standing in the entryway and puts his hand on my shoulder. He says, very gently, "Come sit."

"   ˎ   ˳

I ask him when we're finished eating, which for me happens a third of the way through my bowl. And he's going to lie to me, I can see the words forming, but then he massages his temples with two fingers and says, quietly, "Yes. Your mother and I are in this country illegally."

Small fireworks light up in the edges of my vision, the room around me going hazy. "It's both of you?"

"Both of us, yes." His eyes are glittering. "But you have RISD now. You've achieved everything we dreamed for you. So you don't have to worry anymore. Your future is secure."

"I can't believe you didn't tell me."

"We never wanted to worry you."

All this time. It's been years—years—and I had no idea. "And you can't apply for citizenship because you were charged with a crime."

He catches his breath. "Yes."

I lean over and rest my head against my knees, trying to let blood rush to it. I'm light-headed. I wanted him to tell me I was wrong.

"But we have been very careful since then," he says quickly. "And so—"

"What happened?" My voice comes out muffled, trapped against my knees. I sit back up, all the files in his box spilling back into my mind. "Who are the Ballards?"

"They're—they are no one. They're strangers. They stole from us and I confronted them. It was a very brief mistake. But afterward we realized our status was in jeopardy. Green cards are revoked in the case of certain crimes committed."

"But what—"

"It was when we were living in Austin. Your mother and I came to visit California and it happened while we were here. So then we knew—we knew it was important to act fast. We returned here to California and I interviewed for jobs right away, hoping that if I received an offer it would all be too quickly for the background check to reflect what had happened. And then we were very lucky. I received the offer at San José State, and after the background check, I simply told them I wished to be called Joseph Cheng and I changed various pieces of information on my hiring papers. The university never investigated further."

And then, of course, their green cards were as good as useless at that point, and they couldn't renew them ever again. "Did we—" I swallow. "Did we move because you're afraid of someone finding you?"

"No, no, Daniel. We moved because we knew we would need the

money, as much of it as possible, to save. We are still facing uncertainties. It's better to have the money in savings than to pay it in rent. That's all."

He's lying. By now I know his face when he lies to me. Regina's made us read accounts of immigration raids before, ICE officers with assault rifles and kids cowering in fear as the world closes in on them, screaming for their parents as they're yanked away. There's an unraveling feeling in my stomach, the world going soft at its edges, and in that blurred space Mr. X rises up to leer at me, his mocking smile aimed triumphantly at the terrified kids, at me, at my parents; he'll toast to our removal, he'll cheer our terror and heartache, he'll go home and sleep in peace. And my dad's not unaware of any of this, obviously, he's just trying to make me feel better. I start to say it. But what would that do—force him to admit it aloud, pull the fear from the depths of his mind and sculpt it into something hard and ugly to set down on the table between us? I say, "Okay." And then: "Do your friends know?"

"No."

The rest of it will hit me soon, I know, all of it, but right now that's the part that sinks through me: that they've always had to keep this from their friends.

"Daniel, there was nothing you could do. Listen to me. Look me in the eye." He takes a long breath and then forces a wobbly smile. "We have been careful all this time. We have taken every precaution. We have many plans in place and have prepared for every scenario. And now you are going to RISD and you have a very bright future and you will be very happy. Okay? So don't worry. Everything will be all right."

265

When I wake up it's dark outside and I feel the collision in all my bones. I'm on the couch bed, and when I sit up, the springs creaking angrily, there's a note next to my pillow:

Get rest, my dad's written in his messy scientist's scrawl. *Take care of your mother. If you feel any symptom of concussion such as: nausea, dizzy, double vision, excessively tired, call me RIGHT AWAY.*

I still ache all over, like someone unzipped my skin and wrenched each bone thirty degrees out of place and then zipped me back up again, but otherwise I'm fine. My mom's the one who paid for what I did.

I texted Regina before I fell asleep. *Are you okay?* I wrote, and when she wrote back that she was I said, *You promise?* and she said yes. Harry's been texting and calling me—there were like fifteen messages the last time I checked, and then I stopped checking and then I turn off my phone. I know I'm breaking the code we've lived by since Sandra died. I should call him back. Except everything that happened yesterday (I can't believe it was just yesterday) isn't anything I can tell him. I feel hollow inside, and I can't fathom talking about any of this. What is there to say?

When I peek into my bedroom now my mom's sleeping on my bed, her hair splayed across the pillow. On my nightstand next to her there's an expired bottle of Vicodin from years ago when she sprained her ankle, and a cup of tea I don't think she touched. I stand in the doorway as the crash flashes over me again, and with it all its alternate-universe endings—my dad and I coming home without her, my dad planning her burial—that I was so close to bringing about. I watch her there, remind myself she's breathing, steady myself back in the world.

Around lunchtime my mom wants to move back out to the living room. I help her to the foldout couch and then hole up in my room, lying down and trying to nap or trying to lose myself on the internet. She calls for me an hour or so later.

"Can you—bring me—water," she says, biting off the end of each syllable like it hurts to talk. "Time for—another pill."

I get her a glass of water and bring it over. She shakes out a pill from the orange bottle and swallows it, and then sinks back down onto the bed, wincing, then lies flat and tries to catch her breath. "The medicine makes me so tired."

I don't know what to say to her—it feels wrong to be talking at all without having first apologized. But everything I try to imagine saying sounds so impossibly small, wet cardboard trying to hold up a rooftop. There's nothing I can say in my defense, nothing that can possibly make the situation any better, in any way, and I can't bear the thought of hearing that made solid and loud and permanent by admitting it. Right now that truth is a hard knot in my stomach. I say, "Okay."

And I can hear right away how it comes out all wrong—I sound hostile and sullen. She looks at me, wounded and maybe a little angry, and I should say it all then, at least try, but I can't. I go back to my room instead.

。　.　°

All afternoon and all evening I draw Mr. X. This time I draw him on a couch, hungrily watching immigration agents pointing guns at my mom on his TV, his blood pumping like his team just won the Super Bowl. It's dark out and I'm shading in his knuckles (he's holding a beer, enjoying himself, his cane lying next to him on his couch), when a knock on the door shatters the quiet, threatens to detonate my heart. I sit frozen at my desk for a good ten seconds, waiting, the room contracting and then expanding around me in time with my heartbeat. When I lean forward and look into the living room my mom is out still, the medication pulling her under the surface. Another knock. I get up silently, cold all over, and look through the peephole.

It's Harry. I close my eyes and try to breathe past that feeling like a belt cinched around my chest, wait for relief. It doesn't come. And the realization crests over me then, my eyes still closed: I can't go to Providence next year. There is nothing I don't owe my parents now, and I can't leave them on the brink of emergency like this each time someone knocks.

I open the door and step into the hallway, closing the door behind me. "What are you doing here?"

"What am I *doing* here? I came to see if you were all right, which, apparently, you are. Where the hell have you been?"

His jaw is tensed. And something about the way he has his arms folded tightly against his chest—I've never thought this, ever, but I'm pretty sure he wants to hit me. I say, "I was here."

"And you couldn't take five seconds to pick up your phone? I've been calling you since yesterday."

"I know. I saw. I just—"

He lets his arms fall. He takes a step toward me and shoves me toward the wall, not hard enough to make me lose my balance, but not exactly gently, either. "You saw and you, what, just couldn't be bothered?"

"You know it's not like that. It's—it's kind of a long story."

I say it quietly, and something in him deflates. "Okay, look," he says, closing his eyes a moment, "I got kind of—it was a pretty bad night."

"You want some tea or something? I can make you some."

"No, I don't want *tea*, I want—" He composes himself. "No, thank you."

"You want to come in and sit down?"

"All right."

I hold the door open. He comes inside, slipping his shoes off and shoving his hands into his pockets and looking around. I close the door behind us.

I can read the shock on his expression; it's his first time inside. Failure always makes him uncomfortable; he always tries to gloss over it in anyone else and stamp it out in himself. But this apartment is unequivocally failure. I see it again through his eyes, the grimy carpet and '70s appliances and boxes and bags stuffed with our things crammed into all the corners, rising up the walls. I see him start when he sees my mom, too, sprawled out on the pullout bed.

I lead him into my bedroom, which at least has the distinction of being reasonably neat and unpacked. His eyes flicker sharply over the bare walls. He plops down on my bed. Even furious there's an almost aggressive perfection to the way he holds himself—impeccable clothes, hair artfully arranged, a chiseled profile that's highlighted, somehow, by his anger. For the hundredth time, I think fleetingly how nice it must be to be him.

Even in the dim lighting, though, his cheeks look flushed. I say, "Are you drunk?"

"A little."

"What the hell, Harry? You drove here drunk?" I'll kill him.

"Of course I didn't. My parents would've heard the garage open anyway. I took Uber. Don't tell Regina."

"Ah." Regina thinks Uber is evil. "She's okay, right? I should've called her, but . . ."

He lets me trail off. There's nowhere for me to really go after that *but*. I should've called her, full stop. Finally he says, "Yes," his tone clipped.

"That's good. I was worried."

"Were you."

"I mean—yes."

"Cool. It's great you called her, then. It's great you didn't just go dark on her overnight. It's great you answered your phone all the times I tried to call."

"I know. You're right. I'm sorry."

He raises his eyebrows at the wall. "I didn't mean to yell at you earlier." His voice is stiff. "I didn't—actually, you know what, screw it, I did mean to yell at you. Why the hell didn't you answer any of my messages? I wouldn't have done that to you."

I want to tell him the truth—about the accident, about everything. But I picture him getting up in horror and disgust and leaving, never coming back, and my heart curdles. There are some things you can't bring yourself to risk.

"I wasn't trying to piss you off," I say. I sit down next to him, my back against the wall. We're close enough that our knees brush against each other. It feels like the Pop Rocks candy Ethan and I used to hoard sometimes when we could talk our dads into buying it for us, those small explosions I can feel all over. I wait to see if he'll shift away. He doesn't.

I tell him about crashing (I don't say how) and how my mom got hurt, and I tell him everything my dad told me after. I didn't realize it until just now but I kind of subconsciously assumed, when we moved, that I'd never bring anyone I knew into this room. And him solid and angry next to me—it sets him in sharp focus and blurs the rest of the room around me like he uses up all my vision, all my atoms rushing to align themselves toward him in a way that leaves behind so many billions of lacerations. I'm still exhausted enough, and every-thing I'm telling him is still surreal enough, that the room has the filmy, detached quality of a dream.

He's stunned. When I'm done he's silent a long time. Finally he says, "*Illegal* is a messed up way to put it. You're supposed to say—"

"Dammit, Harry, you think I care right this second? Does it look like I care?"

He swivels to face me. His hand hovers over my knee, and I think he's going to rest it there. I want him to so badly I can't breathe. But then he drops it to the comforter instead. "What are you going to do?"

"I guess what they always do. I mean, what is there to do?" He opens his mouth and I recognize the look on his face, that one where he believes he can architect the right outcome in any situation if he just tries hard enough, and I say, quickly, "No, trust me, they've already thought of everything. This isn't something you can fix."

He looks panicked in a way I've never seen him look. "You aren't, are you? You were born here?"

"I was born in Austin."

"So no matter what you're good, right? You get to stay here?"

This is why *illegal* is a shitty thing to call people, because it shifts the goalposts on you—suddenly the things about yourself that you want to matter don't anymore; nothing matters. I imagine trying to defend them to Mr. X. This is why I had to stop reading the com-ments sections to everything a long time ago, because I couldn't stop thinking about the real people lurking behind them harboring all that ugliness, sitting beside me in class, waving me on at a stop sign, in line next to me at the store.

"I don't mean it's not terrible," he says quickly. "I just—okay. As long as you—okay." He exhales. "Okay." He catches his bottom lip with his teeth for a second like he's considering something. "Also, I wanted to tell you something. I got into Princeton."

"You—what?" The words come as if from another lifetime, folded like those origami notes all the girls used to give each other in junior high. I have to fumble to unfurl them. "You just found out?"

"I got the letter yesterday."

"What'd they say?" Stupid question.

"The usual. Congratulations, welcome."

Was this why he came, so he could tell me this? Am I supposed to be thrilled for him? A heat starts to spread behind my eyes, prickling across my cheeks and the bridge of my nose. Why the hell would he tell me this right now? "So that's it, then? You're moving to New Jersey next year?"

The look he gives me—he wants me to understand something, but I don't know what that is. "I have to, right?" He yanks at the string on his sweatshirt, knotting it into something elaborate he probably learned as an Eagle Scout. "I'd be stupid to turn it down."

What was it, exactly, that I was hoping for—that for how impeccably he's crafted his application package the past four years he'd somehow only get into the one exact school that's close to me? That he'd get in nowhere at all and would move to Providence just for the hell of it? That he'd decide, suddenly, the thing he's wanted all this time doesn't really matter to him? That now that I can't go to Providence after all he'd say, oh, what the hell, I'll just stay in Cupertino then? Still, I can barely speak. "Yeah."

"I didn't think I'd get in."

In some parallel universe where I just left the election alone—then what? Would that have hurt his application enough that he wouldn't be destined for a future he only wants because it's in the one place he thinks will feel all his? Would Sandra be here still? Sometimes when it's dark and I'm alone I torment myself with tests of my own morality: Could I say, honestly, that if it meant bringing Sandra back, I'd give up Harry forever? Could I do that? But in the end, it turns out, I get neither.

"What about Regina?" I blurt out. It's not even what I meant to say. My skin feels hot all over, ragged at its seams.

"Assuming her parents let her, she'll go to Northwestern. If not, she'll go to UCLA."

"So you'll just—be in completely different parts of the country? You'll never even see each other?"

"I mean, if we can somehow find some kind of transportation device that will lift us through the air and—"

"Yeah, but what, three, four times a year you'll see each other? Are you really in love with her?"

"Why do you always ask me that?" He takes his eyes off his knot to look at me, but I can't read his expression. Then he returns his gaze to the knot, and I feel like someone shoveled out the contents of my chest.

"I just want you to be happy."

"I'm happy."

"Are you really in love with her, though? You never actually answered me."

He starts dismantling his knot. There's a tremulousness in my voice that I hate, that I can't scrub out, but his tone stays low and steady. "Yes. Right? I think so. But I started thinking about asking if she thought we should break up before college and I almost broke out in hives. I can't do that to her. If she wants to break up, that's fine, I'll get over it, but you don't break up with someone whose best friend died a year ago. You just don't."

Not with that attitude, I think wildly. There's a porousness in my head, like words might starting leaking out too fast for me to stanch them. "You're really just never going to break up with her? What if she never wants to break up?"

His smile feels forced. "Then I'm a lucky bastard. Regina's a ten."

"You'd literally get married to her and spend your whole life with her just because you don't want to break up with her?"

"You've made promises to yourself, right? I know you have." He drops the strings and doesn't look at me. "That one was mine. Right after Sandra. Anyway, I could do a hell of a lot worse than Regina."

Of all the stupid scenarios I always imagined where I'd find the limits of his loyalty, it's the most obvious one that I'll have to live with: he'll stay with Regina and move across the country, probably make a bunch of new fratty friends, let me fade from his life. And maybe not even because he loves her, but because it feels like the right thing.

I don't know why I can't think of anything to say, or why he can't, either, but the silence holds us, descends over us like a tarp. I sit next to him, still touching him, without moving, and I think how strange it is that you can know someone so well and feel them threaded through your life in more ways than you can count and then still they build out these places inside themselves that they retreat to and you can't follow, can't even really see.

I feel light-headed. A car backfires outside, making both of us jump. The spell evaporates, and Harry reaches out and thumps me gently on the back. "I gotta get home. I'm still grounded." He pulls his phone from his pocket and navigates it with his thumb. "There's an Uber four minutes away."

I slide off the bed. My legs are numb.

It's just that I love my life here. Loved it, at least. And now so little of it is left.

I walk down the stairs with him; I know Harry well enough to know both that the shadowy gated parking lot probably freaks him out and that he'd never say so. As we go I imagine him moving further and further into a life that'll always be too distant for me to be a part of, all those unfamiliar days building up like fence planks while I'm stuck in a picked-over version of our old life, the one he shrugged off and left behind. I didn't even realize how much I'd been clutching that hope that we'd end up in the same place after all—I thought I was more of a realist than that—but I feel it now, that sharp pain spreading into a dull ache like a fistful of hair being ripped out.

I wish he'd just stayed home. I didn't need to find this out tonight.

"Listen," he says, his voice echoing through the stairwell and coming to swell in my eardrums. "I just—I needed to see you with my own eyes. I had to make sure you were okay. Next time please, please just get off your ass and call me, will you? Please don't do that to me again."

Something unspools inside me like a kite string. "What does it matter?"

He frowns. "What do you mean what does it matter?"

"I mean—" I'm trembling in that way you start to when it's late and the night has bleached all traces of the day from you and you're depleted. "Who cares, right? In a few months you're moving to New Jersey anyway. I'll probably never see you again."

"What the hell? Why would you say that? Of course you'll—"

"Did you really have to come here and tell me this tonight? I've had literally the worst two days of my life."

At first he looks startled, like he can't believe he heard me right, and then his voice goes hard. "Yeah? Maybe I would've known that if you'd bothered to call me back."

"I was a little bit busy."

We're on the ground now, and we let the stairwell door slam shut behind us. His Uber's waiting there, a vehicle summoned from the darkness to whisk him back to his perfect life that'll funnel him into the future he's always planned for. Harry jams his hands into his pockets and turns to face me.

"You guys need anything?" he says tightly. "You want me to run to the store for your mom tomorrow or anything?"

I can't say why it's that, of all things, that does me in. "Just go."

"Just *go*?" He lifts his hands in an angry, empty kind of way and then lets them fall. "You know what, thanks for all the support. I really appreciate the congratulations. Thank you, as my best friend, for not trying to guilt me about the most important thing I've ever done with my life. It's not like I've spent the past four years or anything trying to—"

"You weren't even supposed to win that election."

He squints at me. "What?"

"Sandra won the ASB election." My heart is careening through my chest, pounding sideways and upside down and in every direction, roaring in my ears. "I changed the number of votes."

His face changes, slowly at first and then all at once. "What?" he says again, and this time I don't answer; I know he wasn't really asking. And immediately regret billows around me like steam, condenses on a mirror, and my skin feels hot and damp. I didn't plan to say that. I was never going to tell him.

"You would've gotten in anyway," I say quickly, even though I know that's not the only part, even though it's too late. "You—"

But he puts out a hand to stop me. And I always thought I would hold that secret because of what it said about me, because it would expose me in those moments I was emptiest. I was wrong, though: it was because of this exact look on his face.

The Uber driver, a white guy in his twenties, rolls down the window and leans out. "Is one of you Harry?"

"Yep." He breaks himself from the moment, turning toward the driver to lift his hand. "Thanks."

I say, "Harry, wait—"

He doesn't, though. He climbs in and before he closes the door I see him manage a mostly convincing smile for the driver, hear him say, "Hey, man, what's up?" Then the door closes, and the car starts. In the dim light of the parking lot I see him lean his arm against the shotgun seat and rest his head in the crook of his elbow. I watch the car drive away, the taillights staring back at me like bloodshot eyes as it goes down the street.

鴛

Your grandfather loves birds. He loves to point them out to you, loves to tell you their names and habits, loves to try to teach you to distinguish between their calls. He likes to draw them for you. When he was younger he nurtured a private dream of being an artist. He was a factory worker instead. You sprawl on the floor next to him, playing busily and watching wings take form and life on his papers.

You love birds because he does. You dream of them at night. You're a jealous, greedy watcher of their flight. If you could fly, you would follow your parents across the ocean. You imagine your mother looking up at the sky in shock and surprise, seeing you coasting toward her. Sometimes you practice. Your grandfather finds you climbing onto shelves and counters and tabletops. You defy him and climb and jump, your arms aloft, when he isn't looking.

The house is empty without your parents here. It feels cavernous to you, its dark corners treacherous, even though if you'd ever had the chance to see it through older eyes you'd find it small and cramped. Your grandfather worries all the time. A dark cloud hangs over him. He worries about your parents overseas, about you here without them and how you seem withdrawn sometimes, about financial crashes and the tightness in his chest and intruders and natural disasters. Once a seawall has been breached the floods pour in: his son is gone, and maybe worse is still to follow. Once fear takes a foothold it consumes you.

There is a young man who lives with his parents across the hall from you who makes your grandfather particularly uneasy. There is a frightening self-containedness about him, a sense that always, always, he is holding back. There is a menacing watchfulness he wields easily against the world. When news comes one day when you're nineteen months old of a mass knife attack in Xuzhou, it's the neighbor whose face your grandfather superimposes over the assailant's. He seems not to fit into society; a quiet rage he swallows sets him apart. At night (your grandfather doesn't know this) the young man goes online to complain about his life: he deserves a beautiful girlfriend. He resents the women who don't realize this. He has worked hard all his life and for nothing. He is alone through no fault of his own. Sometimes your grandfather believes he sees the man watching you with something like a hunger. In those moments he feels a rage and a fear at his own frailty. He hurries you past the man, feeling the man's eyes boring into his back. But who can he tell these things? The man has done nothing to him. Maybe it's all in his imagination.

Every night your grandfather shows you pictures of your parents or plays recordings of them for you. Sometimes it makes you weep for them, but he wants you to remember. He misses your father. He wants to remember, too.

On the last day of your grandfather's life, he wakes up early. There's an alertness to his waking, as if maybe his body understands what's coming. You're still sleeping—you sleep with him in bed the way you used to with your parents—and he lets you sleep.

He shaves and gets dressed. It's been warmer lately, and he wears short sleeves, although he'll still bundle you in layers: the last outfit he'll ever dress you in. He cooks you eggs, your favorite.

He will take you to the park today, he decides. (It's hard not to wonder about this day in particular, to imagine how much weight each small choice, no matter how lacking in malice, takes on.) He packs the things you'll need. There's a heavy feeling in his chest, that heaviness that settles over him sometimes in the middle of the night—he has night terrors—that never evaporated.

He scolds you for spilling milk at breakfast. Then stops midsentence, puts a hand on his chest. You, small as you are, notice the fracture in the air. You slide your hand back onto the table and push your cup toward tipping, watching him to see if he'll return to normal. He does; he drops his hand from his chest and swats your hand away. You're relieved. Things are fine.

There are birds all over the park. You brought bread for them, and you tear it into pieces and lay it out in careful patterns and watch as they descend. Your grandfather points out the different species. The sun on your face, the flapping of so many wings that feels like it could lift you along with it—you are happy.

You're back home, almost inside your door, coming down the hallway (him pushing your stroller, you walking next to him, running your hands against the wall and thinking about the birds), when a clot builds in his coronary artery. He coughs, pounds his chest. You reach for his hand. The young man next door has opened his door and sees the two of you there. Something like alarm flickers across your grandfather's face, and you sense it, and move closer to his side.

And then it all happens at once—your grandfather clutches his chest and slumps, then topples over, dragging you down, your hand still clutched in his. You both hit the floor together. You land on top of him. You scramble off.

The man springs to action. He leans down and yells in your grandfather's face. He pats your grandfather's cheeks, trying to rouse him. Your grandfather's eyes are locked open. You are silent, frozen. You know what this is. You know what it is to be left behind.

The man puts his fingers on your grandfather's wrist, waiting. The man's face is red, and he's breathing hard. He waits a long time, moving his fingers around. Finally he drops your grandfather's wrist. He straightens. He tries to catch his breath.

He looks around the hall, pausing, listening. He watches you for a long moment. He looks over his shoulder. Something changes in his face.

Then he squats down next to you. "Are your parents gone?" he asks you.

You know what *parents* means. You say, brokenly, "Mama."

"Is she here?

You hug your arms around yourself. You say, "No Mama."

The man slides his hands into your armpits and lifts you. "You can come with me."

TWENTY-TWO

Regina doesn't pick up when I call her that night after my mom's taken another round of medicine and passed out again. I try twice. It's late enough that she could be sleeping, but I have a feeling I get sometimes that she isn't, that same tugging certainty I first learned of in my dad's lab. I text her: *Really need to talk. Call me? It's about my parents.*

My phone rings a few seconds later (and even then, even though I know who it is, there's a part of me that hopes it's Harry). She asks what's wrong, and I ask how she's doing. "I was really worried about you yesterday when—"

"I'm fine." From her clipped tone, I don't think we're having that conversation right now, maybe ever. I wonder, briefly, if Harry told her anything. I don't think he would've; I think it's a wound he'll tend to alone. "What happened with your parents?"

So I tell her. For a long time afterward she doesn't say anything. I can hear the clock we brought from the old house, shoved uncerimoniously on top of the fridge, ticking invisibly. Next door the neighbor's toilet flushes. Then Regina says, "Oh, Danny."

"I didn't mean to call and dump all that on you. Or, I mean, I did, obviously. Thanks for listening. But I mean, I didn't want to call and upset you. I just wanted to hear what you thought. It won't be that bad, right? They've made it this far."

"They have," she says, and then she's quiet a long time.

I hear a noise from outside and it makes my skin shrink around me. I get up with the phone and check the lock and the deadbolt on the front door. "Do you think there's anything I can do?"

"Do they have a lawyer?"

"They don't have money for a lawyer."

"You could try to find someone to take their case pro bono, maybe."

"But then what—they'd like go to the police with their lawyer? They obviously can't do that. They're better off just hiding out like they've been doing. Except—" I swallow. "I mean, now they probably have years of falsifying records and stuff, so if they get caught, they're really screwed."

"Danny—" Her voice sounds strangled. Maybe I shouldn't have asked her to call.

"It's all right," I say, to make her feel better. "I keep thinking like—okay, they lived in China before, so *worst*-case scenario if they end up there again—"

"It's not just like you get put on a plane to your home country and there's a life waiting for you there," she says softly. "You get jailed in a detention center. And those places are awful. They're privately run and there's basically no oversight, and they take all your belongings and assign you a bed and make you wear prison uniforms. If you have kids, you don't always get to keep them with you. Your parents would probably get split up and they wouldn't be able to talk to each other and they probably wouldn't be able to talk to you, either. And then they'd hold them there while they're waiting for a hearing, and maybe in theory you have a few rights left, but in practice you really don't. There's no accountability for the guards, and they're really terrible about getting you medical care or even food sometimes. I mean, Danny—people die in detention facilities."

My knees stop working. I imagine my cartilage dissolving, like in a soup, leaking out my pores. I sink onto my bed. She says, "Are you okay?"

"Not really."

"Yeah." I hear her exhale. When she takes another breath it's shaky, and I realize she's crying. "I'm sorry, Danny."

"Oh, Reg." I feel like crap. "I shouldn't have called you. I didn't mean—"

"No, no, I'm glad you did. I'm going to research it for you."

"You don't have to—"

"No, I'm going to. I'll look for lawyers. I'll read up on it more." She rattles off a list of things she'll look up, orgs she'll contact, and something about the plan of it—it's soothing. If nothing else there's a comfort in knowing someone's holding space in their own life for what's hurting you. That's the thing that's makes life bearable sometimes, I think: that you can feel more than one thing at a time, that it floods into you from so many directions at once.

‸   ‸   ‸

I sleep late Saturday morning, the exhaustion catching up to me. When I struggle into consciousness I can hear that my mom's up and moving around.

It's a good sign, a relief. I should be glad. I knew she wouldn't sleep forever; I knew eventually I'd have to face her.

I fumble around on my nightstand for my phone to see if there are any new messages, but there aren't. The laptop is open on my desk when I get up—my dad must have come in while I was sleeping. He left all his tabs open, searches about bus routes and broken ribs and pain relief. I close them one by one. The last three are searches, too:

what happen to son if parents deported
18 year son no parents
illegal immigrant deported can you delay for son

If what Regina told me is right, I hope to God my parents have never googled all of it.

I find my mom rummaging through the kitchen cabinets and brewing one of her herbal medicines for herself, wincing in pain and catching her breath each time she moves too suddenly. I try to gather up all the things I know I need to say to her. This is what I like best about drawing, that you can retreat to a space where the moments are infinite and you don't have just the one shot to get it right. You can say what you need to, with your whole self, in the way you want.

It doesn't work like that in real life, in real time, and I'm struggling. But my mom lets me take the coward's way out. She looks up when I come in and says, "Are you hungry?" and when I say yes she starts discussing places she's driven by around here, and I answer all her questions about the neighborhood and about what I'd like to eat (true answer: nothing ever again), and in this way she never makes me face the worst of what I've done. All day, all night, she never complains about her pain in front of me (even though I hear it when she thinks I'm asleep and weeps in the bathroom), and she never says a word about the accident or about the fight we had in the car or the newspaper or even about me changing schools, and we don't talk about any of it again.

Or in another way, I guess, it's all we'll ever talk about from now on—it'll be there every time my mom panics about me being in a car, in the way she'll grip her seat belt when we're on the freeway or how she'll call me to make sure I'm okay, every time her ribs seize in pain or she gets one of the massive headaches I read you can get months after a crash, in every Craigslist ad they pull up for cheap, rickety cars. It will be there, always, in everything.

All the rest of that night I wait for her and then for my dad once he's back, too, to come out and tell me so. I wait for them to tell me that my truest self was revealed as the car curled around the telephone pole—that you're not some kind of greatest-hits collection of your best moments, the kind you like to show off for other people, you're just the lowest point you ever let yourself sink. Either or both of them could so easily say *You're a pathetic excuse of a son, and shouldn't it have been you instead of your sister who died?*, and I would believe them.

They don't, though, and by the time night falls, I understand that they won't. Which means the question is now mine to answer for the rest of my life.

TWENTY-THREE

Sunday afternoon I get a call from a number I don't recognize, and I answer only because of the tiny chance it might be Harry. Instead it's the art gallery: the exhibit's coming down, and I have to go pick up my work.

I completely forgot about this. Once upon a time I knew I had to go do that this week sometime, but I lived in a different world when that was still true. It's disorienting to know that it is, after everything, still true.

That night my dad tells me I'm to stay home this week and help my mom. I don't know if she's going to go back to work for the Lis after this, and I'm afraid to ask; I don't know if they meant it that I'm finished at MV, or finished with school in general, and I'm afraid to ask that, too. I say, "Okay, sure, Ba."

"I will call you in sick."

"Okay. Does that mean—" I hesitate. "Okay."

He reads my mind, though. "We don't know if it's better for

you to stay there or not. If someone finds out—however, in thinking about it further, if any questions come up when you try to register at a different school—we don't know. For now I'll call the office and say you won't be in."

Which means I can't sneak off to San Francisco. My mom told my dad she's adjusted to the medication more and it doesn't knock her out the same way, and anyway it's not like I could slip out knowing she'd wake up alone for hours.

I think about it all night and finally in the morning I just come out to where she's sitting on the couch/bed to tell her.

"Your artwork?" she says, sitting up straighter. "They chose it for a contest?"

"I could take the bus to Caltrain. If I just go there and come right back it'll be like four hours. Five, tops."

I can see the panic rising up before her, shoving away whatever excitement had started to gather. "Aiya, Daniel. That's so far away."

"If you need me to come back sooner, I can get a ride—"

"Can't they send you—"

There's a loud, sudden knock on the door. Her words tumble away like rocks. We're quiet. The knock comes again, sharp and insistent. The way watercolor washes from the page if you pour water on it—that's how the color leaves her face.

Neither of us speaks. Before I can stop it, my mind runs ahead to what it'll be like after it all ends—my dad's leftovers waiting for him in the fridge still, my mom's clothes still strewn across the empty bed. I'll be lost. There's another knock, louder this time—a more insistent rapping. The sound is like a thousand knives laid against my skin.

"Don't move," my mom says, so low I can barely hear her. She sits perfectly still. I don't know if that's the right thing to do—if it were my dad here, I think he'd be trying to figure out a way to climb down the balcony, and I know she can't do that now but should I be trying to find a way to get her out of here? "Don't move. Maybe it's the wrong address. We'll see if they go away."

I can't breathe. We wait. My mom is pale. I can see her pulse in her neck, the skin flickering in and out in a way that makes her skin look fragile. And then there's the sound of footsteps going down the hall, and the terror webbing us tears open and together we exhale.

My mom slips two fingers onto her wrist, and her eyes flit away like she stopped focusing. I say, "Are you okay, Ma?"

She draws in a long breath, then nods. But then she doesn't move and she holds her fingers there on her wrist, making sure her heart's still beating. She's shaking.

It's another five or ten minutes before she gets up and opens the door. When she does there's a flyer taped to it. My mom tears it down and reads it, then crumples the whole thing into a jagged ball. I say, "What is it?"

"Nothing," she says. "An ad. Buy two pizzas and get five dollars off."

TWENTY-FOUR

The deal was this: I can go to San Francisco, but not by myself; my mom wants to come, too. A four-hour stint on public transit is clearly beyond her, so we're getting an Uber. (*Goober*, she'd called it when she suggested it—"You know, Daniel, when you put something on your phone and a car comes"—which, after everything, made me laugh. Regina, forgive me.) It'll cost over a hundred dollars round-trip just to get there and back, and I tell her I can ask Regina or someone for a ride, but she wants to go.

It takes a good ten minutes to help my mom down the stairs. She's wincing the whole way, and once she draws in a sharp breath and tears spring to her eyes. When we're on the freeway, my mom tightening her seat belt around herself and taking a long breath, staring over the driver's shoulder at the speedometer like she can keep the car inside the lane lines, I think about all the dinners she's made for me, about that stupid sweatshirt they bought me, about the way that knock on the door stilled her in her fear. I deserve whatever bad things ever happen to me.

The first of which, I know, is having to withdraw my RISD enrollment. I keep trying to find a way around it, but there isn't one. I can't sail off across the country to a place I've always dreamed of, to seize the life I always wanted, while my parents—who I put at risk, who I physically harmed—cower inside a faded locked apartment. I can't put myself hours away by plane when it could mean, conceivably, that something could happen to them while I'm gone. I imagine it: my mom coming back from the Lis' one weekend and finding the house empty, my dad vanished.

And I know it's the right thing and that I've signed away any right to complain, I know that, but the whole way up to the city I feel like I'm riding to a funeral. I wish I'd realized somehow at the time when I saw my work up on the wall at Neighborhood it would be the only time. I wish I'd stayed longer, maybe taken photos or something. Maybe I would've tried to hold on to it all a little differently.

We go through Brisbane, where when you're going north on 101 the hills rise out your left and the Bay comes almost right up to the passenger side windows. "It's very pretty," my mom says.

I force a smile. "Yeah."

"Daniel, I never imagined you would already be having gallery showings even before art school. I never expected that until next year."

"I got lucky, I guess."

I watch as a flock of seagulls lifts from the surface of the water and fills the sky. It's beautiful here, I remind myself. The Bay is part of me, my history and my blood, and maybe I was just never meant to leave. And Harry and Regina will come back for breaks, probably, at least at first, and there are worse places to spend your life. You can choose to be grateful, to remind yourself that life is still a gift, and I'll do that. Dreaming about something all your life doesn't mean it's yours.

"But Rhode Island is very beautiful too," my mom says.

"Sometimes I look up pictures. Very picturesque. You will be very inspired there."

"Right," I say. I turn back toward my window and watch as the road veers away from the water and back through the city again.

When we get there the gallery's closed to the public, and they're in transition: a few of the walls are already blank, a constellation of holes where there used to be an installation of cutout books nailed, crucifixion-style, to the wall. My mom spots my section immediately. I see it happen, that moment she finds mine: her whole face transforms, something in it opening up. She takes a few steps closer, transfixed, and puts her hand over her mouth as she takes in the collection, the gallery lights they have shining on each piece, the placards with my name.

"Oh, Daniel," she whispers, almost reverently.

I can feel my face turning red. "Looks better here like this than all stacked up on my desk, huh?"

"I wish Baba could see this."

I should've brought him. "I'll take some pictures with my phone."

"He would love this." She points to a picture I drew over the summer of Harry, one of my favorites. "I like that one."

"Thanks."

She looks at me and then, fast, back at the picture. "I like your friend Harry very much."

I nudge at a loose nail on the ground with my shoe. "He's a good guy."

"Relationships are very important," she says, still looking at the picture. "Your life will change next year, and you should be careful to remember who you are and the people who care about you."

"Mmhm."

"Sometimes—sometimes you think you have more time for a relationship and then things change. So sometimes it's important, Daniel, not to wait."

"What?" There's a tightening feeling in my chest, a heat trickling from my cheeks down my neck. What is that supposed to mean? I can barely handle watching movies with my parents where people so much as make out—I've never been able to imagine myself having that conversation with them. "He's not—he's just—"

But she turns hastily toward another picture, the one of Harold Chiu, and starts chattering about it, and then goes—slowly, with effort—up to the wall to look at them up close.

"Which one sold?" she asks, turning back to me.

"It was the one I drew of you. Remember it?"

"That one? Aiya, they should have picked another one. Someone not so old." She waves her hand dismissively. But she's pleased, I can tell.

One of the employees, a slim white guy wearing dark clothes and a thin gray tie, comes over to ask me how I want to carry everything out, and my mom hangs back. I'm aware of the clock running, the Uber fare racking up while the driver waits outside.

My mom's still staring at the pictures when I turn back to her. "The Li children—they grow up so coddled," she says. "They have everything. But you—" And then she surprises me; she reaches up and wipes her eyes, opening her mouth the way she does putting on mascara, like maybe she's about to cry. "We never taught you this. You did it on your own. You are strong and independent and you work hard. You have accomplished so much already." Impulsively, and fiercely, she hugs me—another surprise; I can't remember the last time she did. "Daniel, you make us very proud."

It takes them fifteen minutes to wipe all trace of me from their walls. The driver brings the car around again, and my mom goes to sit while I make a couple trips back and forth to carry everything. On the last one, I stop one of the girls working today. "Can I ask you to look something up?"

She smiles and leans a little closer. "Sure, what?"

"Mrs. Padilla said someone bought one of my pieces, and I was wondering if you could look up who. I'm just curious."

"Sure." She goes to open a cabinet and comes back with a ledger. "What was the name of the piece that sold?"

"It was called *Ma at Home*."

"Do you know the date it was sold?"

"It was last month sometime." It's hard to believe it's only been that long.

"And you're Danny Cheng, right?"

I won't pretend I'm not flattered that she knows that. "Yeah."

"I like your work. It's deceptive. When I first saw the installation I thought, *Okay, so they're tricked-out portraits*, but they made me feel so weird I couldn't stop looking at them. I couldn't believe it when they told me you were eighteen." She runs her finger through the notebook. "Okay, here we go. C. Ballard."

I feel the little flare of shock pass over my face.

"Thank you," I manage. "You weren't here when he bought it, were you?"

"No, I was off last week." She straightens and smiles at me again. "Hey, good luck with everything, Danny Cheng. I'm going to keep an eye out. I think the world will be seeing a lot more of you."

TWENTY-FIVE

I should've taken pictures of everything my dad had in that file. I don't remember enough of it. But when we get home and my mom, exhausted, passes out on the pullout bed, I look up everything—everything—I can think that might have any connection at all.

C Ballard San Francisco. C Ballard assault. C Ballard Tseng Huabo. C Ballard Danny Cheng. Nothing, nothing—either too many results, or too few. I can imagine my dad tapping out these same internet trails on these same keys. *C Ballard Neighborhood.* I get desperate: *C Ballard art.*

And I can't say what it is that makes me click on a link from a few months ago, an academic paper from *Ecology: Age-related variation in reproductive output and success in Sandhill Cranes (Grus canadensis) breeding at low latitudes.* The paper's behind a paywall, but there's a list of names that begins: *C. Joy Ballard. Art Gomez.*

C. Joy, huh.

Searching *C. Joy Ballard* and then just *Joy Ballard* hands me pages of meaningless results; it's the same on Facebook, too much to wade through. I go back to the bird paper again. I am my father's son; I know the last author listed on any academic paper (in this case: Jonathan Perez) is almost always the PI. I look up *Perez lab* and am rewarded: a sterile-looking UC Berkeley page with grad student mug shots. C. Joy is halfway down the page: *Joy Ballard, a Kim Geefay Tu Rogel Fellow, is conducting research at the Tule Field Station in Modoc County, California.* She's Asian (didn't Harry say Clay Ballard was talking about Chinese American daughters?) and something about her face—it looks familiar. I can feel the room around me dimming, and my eyes start to burn the way they do when I get too locked into something on my screen.

When I look up Joy Ballard on Facebook again I add *Berkeley* this time, and this time I find her. Most of her profile is private, but a few people have tagged her in pictures that're public. I scroll through them. I feel overheated, even though I'm pretty sure it's cold in here. The nagging idea coursing through my head seems on the one hand ludicrous, but then what about the past months hasn't been?

The picture I think I was subconsciously looking for is posted by a person who must be her sister (Ruth Ballard; she's Asian too, and looks nothing like Joy). It's a small kid sitting on a counter, eating some kind of batter off a spoon: Joy, according to Ruth's caption. She's young, probably three and a half or so, with short-cropped hair and wearing nothing but polka-dot shorts and a huge smile. And because every face has its share of the generic you can see what you want to in anything, in any image, any situation. I know this. I have taken advantage of it my entire life to draw the things I have. But seeing her there something in me lights up all at once, something primal and electric, like bioluminescence—the plankton my dad took me to see once in Santa Cruz during red tide, that shock of water throwing off a glow where there should've been nothing but dark. And I can feel bright blazing lines slicing across all the vastness of the universe between me and her and I can feel how those lines sink coordinates into the gallery, our footsteps and fingerprints there crisscrossed over each other's, the time that separated us distilling and flattening into a single heavy point. And I am certain—I am certain—that the person who bought my picture is the same person in that picture my grandfather drew in the letter home to my parents.

I get up and leave my room before I can talk myself out of it. The apartment is wavering around me like heat rising off asphalt. My mom is lying on the couch still, and when I come in she stirs and opens her eyes.

"Ma," I say, my voice coming out shaky. "I need to ask you something."

With visible effort, she hoists herself up. "What is it, Daniel? What's wrong?"

"Who is Joy Ballard?"

I won't ever forget the look that goes over her face—her features frozen sharply in place and the well of pure pain that pools in her eyes. "I don't know who—"

"Joy Ballard is the one who bought my drawing."

"She what?"

"She bought my drawing."

My mom grips the edge of the blanket thrown across the couch/bed. Her hands are trembling. "You spoke to her?"

"No, the gallery told me."

She presses a hand against her chest, hard, and holds it there. She takes a long, shaky breath, and then another one. She's shaking still.

And I don't know what makes her decide. Maybe it's that I already know the rest of it; maybe it's that you can only bury things for so long. Whatever it is, she finally drops her hand and says, "Come sit down, Daniel. I'll tell you."

Hu Yongyu is the name of the man who lives across the hall from where you and your parents and your grandfather all used to live together, your whole world contained in a single apartment. He is a factory worker who lives with his elderly parents, both of whom suffer health problems and are descending into dementia, and his life with them, stuffy and cramped, is filling him with rage and terror at the trajectory his own storyline seems to be hurtling toward—that this will be his own future, too, dying alone cooped up in a tenth-story apartment somewhere, only he'll have no child to care for him or cook for him or bring him books and postcards and bootlegged DVDs from the outside world, no wife to meet his needs. Or, worse, he'll work his factory job until he no longer can, and then he'll probably be reduced to begging on the streets, taking his last gasping breaths ridiculed and alone.

There are dark villages in the internet, and Hu, who has never been able to feel all the pains and heartaches and graces of the outside world, travels toward and then through them, absorbing their languages and culture, their ideology. It's easy to distill the universe into the imbalance he finds in their embrace—what exists in the world versus what of it he can personally claim, which is far from enough. And it's in there that he learns about how much money the Americans will pay for babies, and in those faceless worlds Hu meets people—people who know someone, people who know someone who knows someone. He hears of the mindlessly easy fortunes amassed, the jobs quit, the fancy cars bought and cities visited and of course the women everywhere.

How lucky to change one's entire life in a single move that way. People, he has learned, are useless; he is not skilled enough to extract from them the life he deserves, and absent that, they provide him nothing. His own parents, whose duty it is to provide him with all he is entitled to, have failed. But the things he read online fill him with hope and promise, and he files away the names and locations and details.

It's a few months later that Hu comes home to the commotion inside his building. He is stunned at first, unable to believe what's happened. But this is the opportunity he's been waiting for—it is easier than he ever dreamed—and he brings you inside his apartment. (Later the investigator will find your DNA inside; Hu's fast-deteriorating parents, who will let him look at Hu's computer, will not register what this means.) His parents are delighted by you. His mother asks to hold you, but you thrash your way out of her arms, frantic. His mother coos over you, unreached by your screams, and pads to the kitchen to find you a snack. You are trying to open the door—you understand that your own home is outside it—but you're too small, and his mother, smiling, holding a bowl, finds you and pulls you away.

Hu goes to his computer. It's easy to go back and find that online village—always open, always populated—and track down all the information he needs, reach out to his contacts and make arrangements.

He takes you by taxi—multiple taxis, to make it harder to trace, as has been suggested to him. He has no car seat, so he has to hold you on his lap. You have never liked strangers, and you are afraid. You beg for your grandfather and your parents, ask for milk, for a snack, for the stuffed bird your grandfather gave you. Hu is irritated. He snaps at you to be quiet. You break down into sobs.

The orphanage whose location and details he's siphoned from the internet is four hours away. You scream most of the way—he is furious—but finally fall asleep sprawled across the back seat. You stir as he pulls you out of the taxi.

"Hello," he says to the woman who appears before him in the orphanage when he pushes open one of the doors. "I heard you might be able to help me."

TWENTY-SIX

The adoption agency was on the second floor of a four-story building, above a pharmacy. The sign outside the door was in English. My parents arrived nearly a year after my grandfather died and the investigator they hired, who'd cost them their entire savings and drained the loan they'd managed to take at the bank, had finally pieced together what had happened to their daughter.

They'd retraced all her steps, spoken to the people he'd fingered as being involved, and so far they'd been met with denial, evasion, and stonewalling at nearly every turn. It had been impossible to pin down any one person. Hu had vanished—his parents, in the throes of dementia, were confused by his absence, sometimes forgetting he was gone at all and incoherent when my parents tried to speak to them— and no one from the factory knew where he'd gone. At the orphanage where Hu had brought my sister the staff had acted confused, claiming not to remember her, then claiming the baby had been dropped off by her destitute father and released to an aid worker. (It was all lies, probably, but what could they prove? According to the investigator, the orphanage was desperately poor and needed the money to care for its older children, who were unlikely to be adopted; it asked no questions about the money it was given in exchange for the babies dropped here for a few days and then taken again. One of the staff there remembered my sister only because of how she'd screamed and screamed when she was taken away.) At every step they'd hoped beyond hope the inspector had been wrong and that they'd find my sister waiting. They imagined over and over what it would feel like to burst in and scoop her up and have her melt into their arms, cling to their chests with her little fat hands, bury her face in their shirts, how she'd feel relieved and safe. She would know them, after all these months. They had gone multiple times to the police, who told them their daughter was probably long gone—that twenty thousand kids were abducted in China every year, most never to be heard from again. *Stop looking,* the police told them. *You won't find her.* One of the officers, trying to be kind, had added, *It's better not to know.*

And now they were at the adoption agency. On the way here they'd assured each other it would be fine. She would be taken care of; no one paid twelve thousand US dollars for a child and then harmed her. It could've been worse, my dad said; she could've been sold into—

But my mom cut him off. There were places her mind wouldn't let her go.

My mom smoothed her hair and practiced a smile for her child. Her heart was pounding so hard she put her hand against her chest to try to calm it. My parents clutched each other's hands and my dad knocked.

A smiling white woman opened the door. "Hello!" she said loudly, the way people talk to you when they aren't sure if you speak English, like maybe half shouting will help stamp the words into your brain. "Can I help you?"

It was an office building—there was a reception area with lounge chairs and magazines, and there was a front desk and then three open doors leading into offices. There were no children. Their daughter wasn't there. The awful possibility my parents had refused to speak of all this time—that she was forever lost to them—reared up like a shadow behind them in the night.

"Our daughter was brought here," my dad said. I didn't know him then, obviously, but I know the way his accent gets more pronounced when he's nervous. He held out the picture of her—now a year and a half out of date—they'd brought along. "We've come to get her."

The woman's smile wavered. "Well!" she said brightly. "How nice of you to think of us—I'm not sure if . . ." Her voice trailed off, and she glanced behind her toward the rest of the office. There was no one else there. "I'm not sure I understand your question, but I can put you in touch with—"

"We know she was brought here. She was sold here."

The woman's smile slid off. Nothing of the sort happened here, she insisted. This was an organization that provided homes to the orphans of the world, rescuing them from lives of suffering. They were bringing light and hope to children, not snatching children away from their parents. When my parents told her they knew about Hu and about the orphanage, they knew about the babies bought and sold, she denied it, her voice rising higher and higher.

I've never known my dad to be anything remotely approximating violent, not even close, so I can't imagine what happened next. He lunged forward and caught the woman by the throat, squeezing until her face turned red. This time it was my mom who screamed.

"My daughter," he said. "Tell me where she is."

He let go. The woman doubled over, gasping for breath. She clutched at her neck. She tried to reach for a phone, but my dad caught her wrist. "Tell me where my daughter is."

The woman gave in. Her hands trembled as she went to a filing cabinet and pulled out a stack of files.

"These are just the files on the children. The adoptions are closed. The information about adoptive families isn't kept here."

She let my parents comb through the files, looking for their daughter. In the bottom third of the stack, there she was: Baby Girl, with a photo. According to the file, the unnamed man who'd brought her to the orphanage was her father. He had chosen to relinquish her for adoption to give her a better life.

"This is her," my mom said. "This is our daughter."

The woman was having difficulty breathing, less because of any injury and more out of fear. She stared at the file.

"You have no proof," the woman said, her voice shaking. "You have an outdated photograph, and that's all. We were told the man who brought her to the orphanage was her father. We would never participate in stealing children."

My dad was trembling. His fingers burned from where he'd used them to hurt another person. "Tell us where she is," he said. "This is our daughter. We have proof. We'll tell the authorities you're trafficking children."

"Please believe me," the woman said. She reached out a hand to my mother, imploring. "Please. I have two children. I'd tell you if I could. The information isn't here."

"Then where is it?" my mother said. She didn't feel some kind of shared maternal bond, if that's what the woman was getting at—she felt rage and injustice, since the other woman had her two children still, and my mother had none.

"We don't store it. Some of our adoptive parents don't want their children coming back to search." She looked at my dad again, and shrank back. "I can—I can give you the names of everyone who's done business with us. That's all I can do."

And so she let them go through all the files and make copies of all the charges billed to adoptive parents from the past year. It was nothing. Compared to the feeling of their daughter safe in their arms, it was less than nothing.

They wanted vengeance. They wanted someone to pay for the loss of their child. But the woman was young and had children herself, and in the end it was impossible to blame only her. So they left her there, the same way they'd left the baby and their homeland to begin with, the same way they'd leave so much more. That was the beginning, maybe, of how my parents had grown so skilled at leaving things behind.

They were going to tell someone, but who was there to tell? Back in the US, my parents looked for a lawyer, but they had no remaining money and no real case. Their daughter was gone, that part was true, but it was going to be next to impossible to prove that any kind of crime had occurred on US soil. Likely none had.

There were forty-seven families from the accounting statements. And that was all there was—just names and routing numbers. They were common names, mostly, the kind of names where googling didn't narrow anything down but did the opposite: suddenly the world exploded with Susan Cerras, Helen Starks. They remember the names still.

For seven years they searched. They posted her picture in private adoption forums; they worked their way through phone books; they scoured blogs and public Flickr albums and newspaper articles. When they could afford it, they took trips to try to find the families they'd tracked down, each time staked out somewhere watching for their daughter, only to find an adopted Chinese son, or a girl the wrong age. It took seven years to find the Ballards, another two years to save the money to go see them. I was six years old.

That was the trip from Texas, then: to go to her. They'd flown to California and gotten a car and made their way to the Ballards' house and watched from the street, waiting to catch a glimpse of my sister. They were parked there on the side of the street when two girls came out of the Ballards' house, and their hearts nearly stopped. They were convinced it was her, the eleven-year-old, the older of the two: their daughter. After all these years.

They thought that if they talked to the Ballards, the Ballards would understand, and would relinquish the child. They would find a way to come up with the money the Ballards had paid for her, if that was the case. They would do whatever it took.

The girls disappeared back inside. My parents knocked on the door. They clutched each other's hands while they waited. My mom was tapping her feet up and down, picturing what it would feel like to finally hold her baby in her arms, trying to practice holding her face steady so she wouldn't burst into tears at the sight of her daughter. Would she recognize her parents right away? Would they recognize her?

The woman who answered the door was small and blond, well-dressed and perfectly made up.

"Hi there," she said, giving them a practiced smile. "What can I do for you?"

My parents introduced themselves. My mom's voice was shaking in anticipation. The woman's eyes went wide, and she stepped back. "Clay!" she yelled. "Clay!"

While Sheila Ballard was standing there, frozen in place, my parents stumbling over themselves to explain the situation, there were soft footsteps in the entryway and someone came up behind her. And there she was.

My mom gasped. My dad's eyes filled with tears. They both started toward her, crossing the threshold into the house, but then before they could touch her Sheila Ballard yanked the girl back. *"Clay!"* she screamed. "Joy, come here!"

This time he showed up, his footsteps quick and heavy. "Who is it?" They were all talking over each other, my parents trying to get close to Joy, and finally my mom grabbed for her, and wrapped her arms around her. Her daughter; the first time in ten years she'd held her. Joy yelped in fear and reached for Sheila Ballard, crying *"Mom, Mom,"* and my own mom's heart shriveled into something hard and small and parched. She clung tighter, desperate.

Clay Ballard lunged for my mom. My dad crouched and rammed his elbow into Clay Ballard's solar plexus as hard as he could, and Ballard doubled over in pain, struggling for breath. Then he went around behind the half wall and came back holding a gun and a camera.

"Let go," he yelled. "Sheila, call the cops. Let go of my daughter this instant." He took a picture of my parents—my dad lunged at him, knocked the camera away, but he raised the gun higher. "Let go or I'll shoot you."

Joy was crying, and when my mom let go, uncertain, Sheila Ballard swept Joy into her arms. She held her fiercely. Joy melted into her, and my parents felt that rift in every one of their cells.

I was the reason they left. If Joy had been their only child, they would've stayed there; they would've fought to the death. But without talking, they each thought about me back home, playing obliviously with Ethan Parker-McEvoy, and so they stepped backward, and they let themselves be chased out with the gun, let themselves feel cold and afraid and panicked. Clay Ballard slammed the door behind them. They could still hear Joy crying inside.

On the porch, on top of a bin of well-loved toys, was a small stuffed bear. My dad picked it up. He felt numb and hollow, ice coating him from inside. He thought he might be sick.

On the way home, on the plane, my mom said, "I won't lose another child."

My parents understood they weren't the kind of people who would win this case in court—what did American courts know of leaving a child behind to work at a better life, of children traded on the black market? The Ballards were white and rich and well spoken and well connected; they'd given their daughter American clothing, an American bedroom, an American name. They had, in the eyes of the United States, legally adopted her and made her their own. No laws had been broken in the US, except by my parents, who'd broken into a house and attempted to kidnap a child who wasn't legally theirs and who'd assaulted that child's parents. It would be very easy for them to be deported. If the woman from the adoption agency had reported them in China, surely they'd eventually be caught there too.

And that was no life for their second child. They would lose me to the foster care system if they were both incarcerated; I'd grow up shipped off from house to house, in and out of group homes, maybe, unloved and unwanted; they might never get me back. Maybe they'd never be permitted inside the US again, and then they'd lose me altogether.

On the plane, the two of them sitting stiff and frozen in their seats, their grief too huge to fit into the whole vast land beneath them, my mom said, "Our daughter is dead."

My dad protested. He wanted to try again. But my mom insisted: now I was all they had in life. I was their only child. Their daughter was gone, and now they had a son who needed them, who had no one else in the world, and so they would give her up. They would consider her dead, and they would bury her.

They didn't know whether the adoption agency would have contacted the parents whose names were given out. Maybe they did, and maybe that's why the Ballards were so instantly wary of my parents. Either way, the Ballards had gotten that photo of them; they'd gotten a picture of the rental car's license plate. It was only a matter of time before the authorities showed up at their registered address in Texas.

And so they went to California, where they weren't expected, to be close to her. Even if they could never see her, even if their paths would never cross, something in them pulled them closer. California was big enough and Asian enough that no one would find them there; no one would think to look for them. They would go and change their names and change their identities, and they'd give up everything for their son. For me. They'd hope to cross paths with her someday, maybe, but then life went on, and that dream sputtered and died.

They knew the Ballards were still looking for them. There was the plainclothes detective who'd come by right before we left Texas, the police report they saw. There was the blog post Sheila Ballard wrote and then deleted (then deleted the whole blog) about how they'd never feel safe and she'd never relax until my parents were behind bars.

It's not that I didn't feel my sister there, even before my mom told me she was dead, because I did. I felt the way they grieved, but I was always wrong about what it was for. I thought it was for a dead sister whose body had long ago broken down, her molecules dissipating back into the world, but I was wrong. It was the grief of parents who chose one child over another, who chose me as the one who lived.

TWENTY-SEVEN

It's six in the morning when I slip past my mom, who's passed out on the couch, and walk out to the concrete stairwell and call Harry. He's probably not up yet, but it's the longest I could possibly wait. I haven't slept all night.

He's groggy when he answers. I say, "Did I wake you up?"

"No."

He's lying. I can't tell from his voice, though, if it's just that or that he doesn't want to talk to me. Maybe, unlike me, he hasn't been waiting for his phone to ring.

I tell him all of it, keeping my voice low, watching a pair of birds descend onto the dumpsters in the parking lot below. I feel like I'm talking forever. I can feel the force of his silence emanating back at me—that he's stunned within it, at a loss, for once, for words.

Or maybe I'm wrong there. Maybe it's just that I already lost him.

"I need to know if it's her," I say. "I can't just sit here and wonder."

"What are you going to do? Are you going to talk to her?"

I found out she's stationed at the Tule Field Station on a fellowship. It's in the Modoc National Forest, just outside Alturas, way up in the far northeast corner of the state four hundred miles from here. "She's in California. I have to find a way to get to her."

Silence on his end again. "Where is she exactly?"

"Near Oregon. It's seven or eight hours by car."

"Ah."

The thing about asking someone for something huge is that you can't take back the request—if they turn you down, you can't ever pretend away that gap between what you stupidly thought they might give you and what you're actually worth to them. I jam my free hand into my pocket and kick at a pebble on the concrete. "Will you take me?" I say to him, before I lose my nerve. "I know it's far, but if it is really my sister—"

"It's eight hours?"

"Yeah."

He could hang up on me, and I'd probably deserve it. He could also make me wait, or he could try to extract something from me first. He does neither one.

"Yeah, sure, of course I'll take you," he says instead. "Just say when."

◦　　◦　　◦

I shower and pack an overnight bag just in case while I'm waiting for Harry. I try to contain the noise as much as I can, peeking out every couple minutes to check whether my mom is still sleeping.

In my room, I write a note: *Going to Alturas with Harry. I'll be careful, I promise. Don't be worried.* My phone lights up with Harry's text telling me he's downstairs.

I haven't lived here long enough to learn the creaky parts of the floor, and I stay light on my feet. I hit a loud spot near the kitchen and freeze. My mom stirs, and my heart explodes against my chest. I stand perfectly still. She stays asleep.

I get to the door and reach for the deadbolt, turning it slowly and cringing at its soft metallic click. My mom stays asleep.

I turn the knob and the door creaks open. The couch springs groan.

"Daniel?" My mom sits up, squinting at me. "What are you doing?"

My heart slams into my throat. "I'm—" My voice cracks. I cough. "I'm taking out the trash," I lie. She doesn't have her glasses on; she can't tell what I'm holding. I imagine her panic when she finds my empty bed, my phone and wallet gone, how she'll hold her breath each time footsteps come falling down the hallway.

"Oh." She yawns. "All right." Then she mumbles something that sounds like *be careful*, but her voice slurs—the medication, probably— before dropping off. It has a deeper hold over her overnight. It'll be a few hours before she wakes up and realizes I lied.

. . .

Harry's car pulls into the lot just as I come out of the stairwell, and I am so happy to see him I feel weak. He leans over to unlock the passenger door. The air inside his car smells vaguely soapy, and his hair's still wet.

"Thank you," I say. I toss my bag into the back seat, buckle my seat belt and turn to face him. "Seriously, Harry, thank you. I owe you."

"Nah, don't worry about it."

I swallow. I wish I'd never told him about the election. "And look—I'm sorry about—"

He looks away. "Don't mention it."

I know he means it, that he'd rather I didn't. So I don't.

I'd almost forgotten how quickly he can change the mood. But he does it—he adjusts his rearview mirror, then holds up a brown paper bag with grease spots on the bottom. "It's your lucky day: I stopped at Donut Wheel on my way here."

I'm so flooded with gratitude for him, for everything, it takes effort to sound normal. "Excellent."

"Maple bar or cinnamon twist?"

"You pick."

He breaks both donuts in half, holding the bag out to me. I take the half maple bar and eat it while he backs out of the parking spot and onto the street. We're doing it; we're officially on the way. The donut is pillowy and sweet.

"So where am I going?" he says. "Do you have an address?"

"Yeah," I say, my mouth full. "It's a field station. Here." I reach for his phone, which is charging on the dashboard, and tap in his password and put the address in. "Eight hours. There's some traffic."

"You're sure she'll be there? You didn't call her or anything, did you?"

"No, I couldn't find a phone number, just the address. But I'm assuming she's just living there."

There's a sort of a sense of magic that can envelop you, a sense of destiny, that feels vulnerable to parsing everything out carefully or overthinking things. I wonder fleetingly if maybe that's what my dad always felt, and maybe that was his mistake—believing it would inoculate him. Whatever, though; that's the whole thing about that feeling, that you have to leave it intact so it doesn't evaporate on you. I change the subject. "Did you tell Regina you were coming?"

He doesn't answer right away. "No."

"How come?"

"I just didn't."

"What'd you tell your parents?"

"I didn't tell them anything yet. I just said I was going to school."

"Are you going to get in trouble?"

"Am I going to get in trouble?" he repeats, amused. "No, I think they'll be super cool with me cutting class—while I'm still grounded, no less—to drive to basically Oregon without telling anyone. They love that kind of thing. Love it. It'll be great."

"You're sure you want to do it?"

"I'm sure."

I should ask him why. I should ask him if he's really sure, maybe try to talk him out of it. The light changes, and we get onto the freeway.

"I could take the bus," I say. "Or—"

"It's fine. I wanted to come." He licks sugar off his fingers and appraises me. "You snuck out, too, didn't you? There's no way your parents would've let you go."

"Yeah, no, there's no way they would've let me."

"What are you going to do when they find out?"

"Nothing." My phone's stayed quiet—my mom's probably still asleep. "I figure we'll have at least an hour head start."

"Ah." He starts to say something else, reconsiders it, goes quiet.

I say, "What?"

"Nothing. It's just—ah, forget it."

"Should we do this a few more times before I tell you to just say it, or—"

"Like you never try to think before you say something. Okay, fine. It's like—so I got into Princeton, right, and I guess I always thought if I did, everything would be different, and I'd be this different person, and all that time I thought everything would fall into place if I'd just get in."

"And?"

"Nada. I feel nothing. So I was kind of glad you called," he says. "This morning. Because then it was like, oh, okay, right, Princeton or not, I still have to figure out who I'm going to be. You know?"

He holds out the bag with the rest of the cinnamon twist. My fingers brush against his, and there's a feeling like a pinwheel in my stomach, and then—something shifts.

All my life, I've always waited for signs. Like with art, like with everything, I've waited for things to fall into place and to feel right, to feel like the universe had given me its permission and its blessing.

But maybe you never really get that, or maybe only some of us do, if we're lucky, if we're born to the right people in the right circumstances at the right time, and even then, maybe not. And the rest of us—the world will tell you over and over you aren't good enough, in as many ways as it knows how. Maybe you have to fight for your place in it no matter what, no matter who you are. And I know this—I always worried I hadn't earned mine, that my sister should've taken it instead. But maybe she's been here all along, and maybe that doesn't mean anything so much as it creates an absence of meaning, a void I get to fill on my own. I know enough by now to know the rest of the world still goes on without you even if you try to retreat from it, that there's only so long you can hide out. But I also believe that, if you're lucky, what you share with someone can reshape the way the world contours itself around you. Or maybe it's not that—maybe it's just that it fortifies you so that you force the world to contort itself into new ways to fit you.

And Harry here like this, after I'd sort of given up on him, how he dropped everything and is risking getting massively in trouble for me: it is what it is. I feel the way I feel. Whatever it means, wherever it'll go, I'm in it. And I need to find out if it's at all like that for him, too.

·   ·   ·

For a long time when you drive through the bowels of the state it looks like nothing—flat and grassy, rural in a way people from out of state never associate with California, and it feels like you could drive for miles in any direction and find nothing at all.

We've been on the road for two and a half hours now and my parents still haven't called. My mom must be wiped out. Or maybe, because I left my door closed, she just thinks I'm asleep.

That's what I'm telling myself, anyway. That she's there, that she's safe, that when I get back they'll both be there, immigration agents miles and miles away.

For now, at least, the road is solid and open beneath us, and I'm here with Harry, and I can stow those thoughts away. We're on I-5 now, passing through small towns with names like Hershey and Harrington, towns that hide themselves off the highway so you feel like you could pull off the road and not find any of them. We hit Arbuckle, and Harry says, "Like Garfield," and it makes me laugh. "All right, loser," I say.

My nervousness is expanding with each mile we put behind us. If my parents were wrong and it isn't her—but I won't think about it. I know what it's like to be sketching out rough lines, shading and stippling and crumpling up each attempt; I know what it's like to watch something take shape in all the chaos. You learn to suspend the questions and give yourself over to the process. I do that now.

I feel hyperconscious of Harry next to me, the smooth outlines of his forearms, the scent of his shampoo. We're mostly—uncharacteristically—quiet. Once, in Orland, we both reach for the radio dial at the same time and our fingers touch. When my family lived in Austin, every year for the Fourth of July we'd drive out into the country roads with the Parker-McEvoys and buy sparklers from wooden stands and we'd light them when it got dark. That crackling and heady scent of smoke, the way the sparks arced through the night so loud and bright and hot they made your heart race—Harry's skin against mine feels just like that.

I keep trying to string the words together, what I'll say to him. But Mr. X won't leave me alone.

It's one thing to feel a funny way. It's another to put it out there in the open for everyone to have to see. You're asking him to do a disgusting thing with you. If he isn't funny about you the way you want him to be he won't be too hot about being around you after this, you sniffing around him with those hungry eyes of yours.

I don't care what hypothetical old white men think, I tell him. He tips back his head and laughs.

Hypothetical? You think you conjured me from nothing? I'm your neighbor. I'm your dentist. I'm your cop. I'm your congressman. I'm your boss. I'm your teacher. Don't think for a minute—

My phone rings. I jump.

"Your parents?" Harry says.

It rings again. "Yep."

"You going to answer it?"

"Yes?" I say. It rings again. "What else should I do, just ignore it?"

Ring. "I mean, what are you going to tell them? I won't pick up if my parents call."

The phone feels hot in my hand. It rings again. Then it stops, and I feel—inexplicably—desperate for it to be ringing again, to have the chance to answer still.

I wanted that, though, didn't I? Otherwise I would've just picked up.

On her voicemail, my mom is frantic. "Daniel, where are you? Pick up your phone. Call me right now. I'm going to call you again." She does. I silence it. There's a pit in my stomach.

And then the guilt comes flooding into the car, heady and loud, slinking around my shoulders like a cat. What if something happens to them while I'm gone? I could come back and find the apartment empty, and I'll be stuck forever with the image of her praying I'll pick up as the phone rings and rings.

I sink back against the seat. "I should've picked up."

"Call her back, then."

"I can't."

"How come?"

"I just—I can't." I crack the window. The air outside feels dusty and hot. I open up his glove compartment and stick my phone inside. I'll keep it off, let the messages I'm sure she's leaving pile up.

I shouldn't let them worry more than they need to. I know that. All the same, though—I'm not proud that the thought occurs to me the way it does, blaring neon in my mind, but all the same, there was a lot they let me worry about and mourn and believe. And none of it was ever true.

Traffic slows to a trickle as we lose a lane to construction, and then the road releases us back into open lanes and Harry sets his cruise control. In the distance you can see Mount Shasta starting to come into focus, towering over the valley. We drive toward it, the grasses and flatlands blurring past the windows.

It's funny about being in a car with someone—all those miles you plow into the road tie you to each other somehow, intertwine your fates at least temporarily, and they blur the borders between your two existences and etch away at whatever was keeping you so separate and distinct. I have a weirdly certain feeling that if I touched him again right now both of us would get shocked. I can feel the charge building up in the air, how it ratchets higher every time the road dips and we get jostled closer together. I know that feeling with him, what it's like when every time you touch the rest of your body stops existing and all of you funnels itself into that shivery point of contact.

I make a deal with myself: in five minutes, I'll say something. I won't practice or overthink it like I always do. I'll just start talking. The truth will come out.

But then five minutes go by—I watch them tick off on his dashboard—and I can't do it. I make the same deal with myself for ten minutes, then fifteen, holding it there in front of me the whole time we're talking. But I can't do it. What if he never wants to see me again?

Around Redding I start to get jittery. It's flatter out here, more fields and trees and open space than the Bay Area, and Mount Shasta has been expanding in the windshield a while now, massive and looming and covered in snow. We stop at an A&W, where a white man in a hat watches us openly and a white mom with her kids pretends not to, and get burgers and root beer floats. Harry doesn't finish his.

"I'm too amped," he says to me, clearing the table for us. "Your sister you didn't even know was alive, and you're going to see her—how are you even functional right now?"

It's twelve-forty-five by the time we leave, and it's supposed to be just three or four hours from here. We pass through an abandoned mining town, and soon the road drops down to two lanes. It's not like Redding felt especially crowded, but without all its buildings and roads the land starts to feel naked, kind of, and barren—long fields of dying grass pockmarked with trees. Here the trees are tall and huge and old and leafless, their branches wizened and sort of gothic-looking. The cars come fewer and fewer between, and even though I know it's not true, it feels like being in a place where no one's ever been.

We pass through Montgomery Creek, which isn't a town so much as a few old farmhouse-looking houses that overlook the highway and a speed limit that slows to fifty-five as you go through the fields. The fields give way to forest, and you feel small.

I lose a battle with myself and turn my phone on, wondering if it's worse if my parents have been calling and calling or worse if they haven't. Then there are seven new messages—I listen to each one, my mom crying by the last three—and that emphatically answers my question: it's worse that they did.

I imagine staying home with them next year, dodging endless awkward reunions at Target and Ranch 99, making up stupid excuses when people ask why I'm still here. I imagine being forty and telling everyone how once upon a time I had an acceptance to the best art school in the nation. And I imagine losing Harry. He'd call sometimes, probably, but he'd feel guilty and embarrassed about how crappy my life was turning out—he'd do that loud talking where he tries to get you to laugh, where there's no room in the conversation for any of your sadness to leak out, and he'd have his roommate and his fratty friends there and he'd be a reasonably short plane ride away from Regina and—

I have to stop. When I really let myself think about not being with him next year, about just fading out of his life, I can hardly breathe.

"I just wish they'd told me sooner," I say abruptly. "I spent literally my whole life being lied to. They should've been honest with me. And then maybe—"

He waits for me to finish, and when I don't he says, "And then maybe what?"

And then maybe I wouldn't have spent my whole life pierced by a grief I couldn't ever talk about; I wouldn't have carried the guilt of having outlived her with me everywhere. And then maybe I would've been more careful at school. And then maybe I would've understood why they were so panicked about the principal and I wouldn't have been as angry as I was, and then I would never have lost control driving. And then maybe it wouldn't feel like this now, this massive debt I'll never—because it's still my fault, I still have to blame myself—be able to pay back.

They shouldn't have lied to me. And if they're waiting at home right now, worried, frantic each time they get my voicemail—then maybe it makes them they wish they would've just told me the truth, too. I don't have it in me to spare them that.

But it doesn't matter, I guess, whether they regret it or not. It's all too late for that. I pull my seat belt tighter around myself. "Eh, it's not important. I'm going to withdraw from RISD."

"You're—wait, what, what the hell? Why are you withdrawing? Because of your parents?"

"Yes and no. It's because—" I hesitate. I thought I'd never tell anybody this. "It's because we wouldn't have gotten into the car accident if not for me. The accident was my fault."

"How was it your fault?"

I tell him. It sounds even worse when I say it out loud.

"You definitely can't withdraw," he says.

That surprises me, actually—I kind of expected he'd say *Yes, obviously, of course you don't deserve to go,* and also maybe *and get the hell out of my car.* "My parents are pretty fucked, Harry. And I made it so much worse. They had to give the police their car registration, and now they have no car, and my mom got hurt. I have to stay here."

"Danny—you didn't know."

"Yeah, well, when you deliberately crash a car it doesn't really matter what you know."

"I mean—okay, yes, I'll give you that. But what if—what if it really is your sister? If they have their daughter back, doesn't that make up for literally anything?"

I hadn't quite let myself form those thoughts. But they've been kindling, because as soon as he says it they catch flame. What if it is her? And what if she only knows a false version of the story and I tell her the truth, I tell her what really happened and how they've never stopped wishing for her back—can I balance that, somehow, that and all those years they lied to me, the anger I probably shouldn't feel but do, against my guilt?

"It doesn't change their situation," I say finally. "Even if it somehow makes up for some of it—they're still in the same boat. It doesn't change anything." This is the part I'll have to carry alone, though: that a part of me will always resent them for this. Always.

"That's literally been your dream for as long as I've known you, Danny."

"It has."

"You really think you can fix anything by not going? You honestly think that's better?"

Of course I don't think it's *better.* But you don't always get better—sometimes you just get less bad. Sometimes you just get right. "I don't know if I can fix anything no matter what. Neither one of them are perfect options, but if I just bail on my parents I don't think I can live with myself."

A lesser friend, I think, would try harder to talk me out of it whether or not he believed it, unfurling a safe, attractive future I could map myself into in order to make me feel better in the moment, so he could duck away from how it feels. Harry doesn't, though. He says, "Is."

"Excuse me?"

"Neither one of them *is* a perfect option." He reaches out and claps his hand against my thigh, and leaves it there. "Subject-verb."

Then he grins, holding it until, in spite of myself, and in spite of the fact that his eyes are sad, I smile back.

And I almost tell him then. I almost do.

I don't, though. He puts his hand back on the wheel, and the letdown that floods me, like a wave receding and then crashing back, makes me wonder if maybe I can't. Maybe I just won't ever. I try to tell myself I will, that I still have time—but time always almost feels like it belongs to you, like you can stretch and sculpt it to make it what you need it to be, but that's a lesson I hope I never need to learn again: you belong to it, and not the other way around.

▫   ▫   ▫

In Burney—a stretch of flat buildings lining the side of the road, a section carved out of the forest—we stop to get gas. A white woman in a pickup truck at the pump behind us scrutinizes us, leaning against her truck with her arms crossed, and I feel that old mixture—maybe it's not justified, but a lot of times it probably is—of defiance and pity and shame. She lifts her cigarette to her lips and I watch her cheeks hollow and then fill back in as she inhales.

Everything feels different when we start driving again. The clumps of trees thicken, mostly pine now, and as you climb higher sometimes you come through a bend and the trees open up and you can see small valleys spread out below you, blanketed in a green that stretches across to the tree line, peaks rising up bluish in the distance. The air's thinner up here and the sunlight streams through the sky differently, landing on the windshield in a way that looks clearer than how it does at home. Mostly, though, I think it feels different because I know that was our last stop, because the next time we get out of the car it'll be to find Joy.

My pulse has been higher ever since the gas station. I try to tell myself it's that there's less oxygen up here, but I know I'm just nervous. I can't quite sit still, either—I fiddle with the radio, tap my hands on my knees. I wish I'd brought my sketchbook, even though trying to draw in the car always makes me carsick. I would draw us, though, I think: me and Harry in the car. I'd draw the way the light keeps glancing off the rearview mirror and the way the world outside the window looks like a painting and the way inside the car we feel kind of buffered from it all, how really everything that matters is right here inside. For now, at least.

"So," I say, when we drive through Fall River Mills, a flat stretch with mountains that rise up in the distance, "I still haven't exactly put together a solid game plan. I was going to just kind of show up and try to talk to her."

"Sounds good to me."

"Does it really? Because it's starting to sound pretty bad to me."

He shrugs. "If it's her, do you really need a plan?"

My pulse picks up again, thudding in time to the bumps on the road. Outside a cluster of cows is grazing in a grass clearing. The sun is so bright it makes the grass look almost neon.

We could still turn around, I tell myself. There's nothing stopping us. "I don't know. Who knows. It could end up not being her. Or who even knows." Then I tell myself: I'm going to do it. Now. "Hey, Harry?"

"Yeah."

My heart is pounding so hard it feels impossible that he wouldn't hear it. My vision goes soft around the edges.

"Ah—never mind. Forgot what I was going to say."

◦ ˎ ◦

You see Alturas before you reach it. You come to a peak and there below you is the whole city clustered together in a pocket of valley, and as you drive into it you lose sight of it until you're practically there. The sky out here is huge. The land goes on and on, tall grasses that wave in the wind and pull your eyes along the horizon line, drawing them up the mountains hovering in the near distance. When we see a sign for Alturas, population 2,827, the nervousness hits me. My mouth goes dry and my hands are sweaty against the wheel. Harry reaches over and taps my knee; he can feel it, I think, what that sign means to me. Maybe it didn't feel real before this.

We stopped really talking thirty or forty minutes ago, not in a way that felt like things were done but more that we were leaving them suspended, balancing carefully above us so we'd tiptoe under their shadows without upending anything. Since then we've been mostly quiet.

And I still haven't said anything to him. What would happen if I just never do? I'll regret it forever, I know that. My life will radiate out and out from this moment and I'll always wish I could have it back to do over.

But then won't I feel that, too, if I tell him and it ruins everything?

We pass into the city limits. I take a deep breath and hold out my arms a little from my sides to see if I can feel anything different. Do my atoms know I'm here, this close to her? Could you measure something different in me? I let them back down.

"For whatever it's worth," Harry says, "I think it's a good thing you're doing."

"That doesn't always mean a good outcome, though."

"I know," he says. "That's the part about the world I never know how to live with. But it's not nothing, either."

We drive through town—it takes all of sixty seconds, old buildings with flat facades that remind me of the Gold Rush and squarish brick buildings mashed against the kind of newer building that masquerades as older, hastily built—and keep going out past town on a dirt road into the grasslands. I can barely swallow. But I try to watch everything carefully, not just for directions but also because this is the life my sister inhabits, because I want to collect all the texture and details.

It's seven or eight miles on the back roads, but it feels like longer because you can't go very fast. The grass is taller out here, in some stretches nearly as tall as the car, and it makes it look like the mountains behind it could be anywhere from five to five hundred miles away. There's a layer of dust building on the windshield. We don't pass a single other car, and more than once Harry says, "You're sure this is right?"

"I'm pretty sure. The map looks right." Besides that, I'm starting to feel it—some tingling in my limbs that means we're getting closer, something that brings me back to what it felt like in my dad's lab that morning all those years ago. And then we go up over a crest and then we see it in the clearing down below: the field station. Where my sister is.

The field station is two portables situated in a T. There are some trucks parked kind of haphazardly in front. All around is high yellow grass and occasionally trees, and it stretches about as far as you can see. Thirty or forty yards from the far portable is what I'm pretty sure from the map is the Pit River cutting through the grass, a wooden footbridge going across it.

The heat outside seeps into the car as soon as Harry cuts the engine. I drink some of the water we got at the gas station. When we get out my legs feel heavy after sitting so long, and the dried grass is brittle under our feet. It's hot out here, and so quiet—no cars, no planes, no city noises. The sun has an easier time finding you, too.

I both can't wait a second longer and would not feel ready if I had a hundred years. Harry says, "You ready?"

"Sort of."

I feel kind of dizzy. I close my eyes and try to reenvision the world as one where I'm brave, and ready, and can do this, a world where everything ends well. And I try to remember what it feels like in this moment, too, because I know it's one that'll define the rest of my life—sever everything into a distinct before and after.

"You okay?"

There's a buzzing in my ears. I keep my eyes closed. "Yeah."

Tell him, I order myself. Just do it. Do it now.

"You want me to wait in the car?"

I open my eyes again. It's so bright here I have to squint, the world constricting. "What? No."

He grins. "I was hoping you'd say that."

I'll tell him later, then. I feel blurred, like if you looked at me I'd be wavering, a heat mirage rising off the asphalt.

I go up the portable's two metal steps, my legs like gelatin. My footsteps are loud, and I cringe. I don't want anyone to come out before I'm ready, and it feels—even though we aren't—like sneaking around. No one comes out, though. I knock.

A white guy in his mid- to late twenties answers the door, and when I look behind him, my eyes scanning for her, there's no one but another guy about the same age sitting at a computer pushed against the wall.

"Uh, hi," he says. He glances back toward the other guy. They must not get many drop-in visitors here. "Can I help you?"

"Hi," I say. "I'm here to see Joy." When they look at me blankly, I say, "Joy Ballard?"

"You're here to see Joy?" the one at the computer says. Both guys look at me strangely, then at each other. "She know you're coming?"

"Kind of." He keeps looking at me, his eyebrows raised, so I say, "Probably not specifically today, though."

"Huh. Okay." He glances at the clock. "Well, she's out in the field, but I think she'll be back any minute now. You want to come inside?"

"Ah—" I glance back toward Harry. Already this is veering off of the scene I'd drawn out in my head. But that's fine, that's how life goes; you adapt. "We'll just hang out and wait out here. I don't want to bug you guys."

He shrugs. "All right, cool. She should be back soon."

I have a brief intuition (Regina's legacy in my life) that if they were women, this would be different—they'd vet me differently (/at all). I feel a twinge of annoyance at them for not doing that on her behalf. We're two random guys who showed up out of nowhere wanting to see Joy, and they don't blink an eye. But I can't exactly trust that annoyance in the same way I can't trust anything right now—because a bunch of different feelings are veering wildly all over the place inside me, tilting around like windmills. My muscles feel rubbery and soft.

Harry and I sit in the car with the doors open. There's a breeze that picks up every so often, but mostly the air is still. I feel bizarrely aware of my breath, like I have to keep paying attention to keep it going, and also just aware of all the invisible mechanisms going on to keep my lungs filled. I was as ready as I was ever going to be walking up those stairs, but the waiting feels harder, somehow, now that it's dragged into another round.

We hear her car before we see it. Harry sits up straighter. Then a Jeep pulls up from over the hill, heralded by dust, and I think even if there were other cars here, even if we weren't out in the far reaches of the state this way, I'd know it was her. A soft buzzing starts in my fingertips, radiates up through my arms and into my spine.

Harry turns to get out of the car.

"Wait," I say. "I need to tell you—I have to—"

I run out of words. I reach out and take his hand.

At first he kind of laughs and starts to take his hand back. But then he sees my face, and I'm sure it looks as nakedly uncertain as I feel, and he stops laughing. He looks down at our hands and then up at me again, a kind of understanding passing across his face. "Are you—"

I swallow. "Yes."

"You—" He lets go. My heart throws itself weakly against my rib cage and then slumps inside my chest. "Um," he says. A panic goes into his eyes. "Danny—"

Oh God. I can't breathe. But then a car door slams, and it breaks apart the moment, and we both get out of the car. Joy's parked in front of the portables. Harry smooths his hands over his thighs, refusing to look at me. My palms are sweating. And then Joy gets out of the car and there she is, less than ten feet from me.

She's wearing khaki pants and a long-sleeved shirt and a sun hat, lace-up hiking boots, small gold earrings. And in person I recognize her, not just because I've seen pictures, but in a way that makes me think I would've known her anywhere, in any context, and I feel certain then: it's her. She has my dad's forehead and my mom's cheekbones, my same mouth and eyes.

I think she knows who I am. I can see it in her face, the way that same recognition sparks, and also she looks less surprised than I would've expected. But she says, politely, "Can I help you?"

"I'm Danny," I say. "This is kind of a long story. But I think—I think we might be related."

"You think—oh." She takes off her hat and twists the brim in her fingers. "Wow, I wasn't . . . expecting you. Ah, and what brings you here?"

That should be obvious, shouldn't it? "I needed to talk to you."

"Right," she says again. She looks back toward the portable. Then she gives a little wave to Harry. "I'm Joy."

"Harry." He manufactures a smile and takes a step forward to extend his hand. "It's nice to meet you."

I thought the words would show up the same time we did—that when I saw her everything would click into place and I'd know what it was I was supposed to say. It's the opposite, though—it's like all the words I've ever known are slipping away from me, and I have to clutch at ones that fit.

"My dad is Tseng Huabo," I say. The sheer fact of her is dizzying. All this time she lived less than fifty miles from me. "Now he goes by Joseph Cheng and my mom goes by Anna Cheng. They had a daughter who was kidnapped in China about twenty-two years ago."

"Ah," she says. She looks around again. Aside from the two guys in the trailer, we could probably drive for twenty minutes before we encountered another human being. It feels the way it always did in Texas when there were lightning storms and you tried to get out of clearings and parking lots, make sure you weren't the tallest thing around.

"Okay, well—" I can sense her making a decision. "There's nowhere to really go here. Do you guys want to get dinner in town? I was going to go eat anyway."

My heart picks up, the beats like the wind catching and scattering a pile of leaves. "Yes, sure, definitely, that would be perfect. That would be great."

"Okay." She goes up the steps and opens the door and says into it, "I'm going into town. You guys want anything?" I can't hear their answer, but she says, "Yeah, I'm fine. I'll explain later. Maybe."

Her voice was different when she talked to them. Regina does that, too—she has a slightly higher-pitched voice in public, something smoother and a little more friendly-sounding, which is how Joy sounded with us.

Joy opens the door to one of the Jeeps. I open the passenger door and start to get in the back, but Harry motions to me to take the front seat. He's careful not to touch me as he gets in.

Joy takes a long time buckling her seat belt and adjusting the mirrors. She looks calm, but I keep getting a sense that she isn't, actually. I can't tell what she's thinking.

But it's her, right? It's her? She hasn't technically confirmed it, but she would've told me if it wasn't. I wonder if it would be different if Harry weren't here—if she doesn't want to say anything in front of him right away. Which is fair; she has no idea who he is.

To be fair, maybe I don't, entirely, either. I haven't been able to meet his eyes since the car. Pretending things are fine is a physical effort. If I ruined everything—but I won't think about that yet. I erase it from my mind, visualize scrubbing the eraser dust to wipe the paper clean, and focus on Joy. My sister. I can hardly breathe.

Joy starts the car and we pull out onto the dirt road. "Your car did okay on the way in?" she says pleasantly. "All of ours have all-wheel drive. It's pretty bumpy out here."

"Yeah, it was okay." I add, "It's really beautiful out here."

"It is, isn't it? It's also so dry. High desert. I get eczema." My mom does, too. "Unfortunately, ticks love it here too. All the grass. Byron—that was one of the guys you just met—got bitten last week and had to get tested for Lyme disease. Negative, fortunately."

She chatters about that, the ticks and the Lyme disease and the native grasses here, the whole ride back into town. I don't know what I expected her to be like—like me, maybe, or maybe like my parents—but it's odd fitting the reality of someone around your (unfounded) expectations. She's nice, though, talkative and self-assured, but she also seems on edge. Which I want her to not be. I want her to not be small-talking like we're strangers at a bus station, to not be creating a kind of hedge of pleasantries around herself so that it would be strange for me to bust past that with everything we actually need to talk about.

But maybe she's just nervous. It's hard to blame her. I mean, I'm nervous as hell. So I'm polite in return, and I tell myself that I'll wait until we're settled in the restaurant and then we'll talk, and then everything will be fine. There are years and years to catch up on.

By the time we've pulled back onto paved roads again I've learned more than I ever would've imagined myself knowing about the eco-system of the high desert up here, but basically nothing about Joy except that she's really into all this. There is—improbably—a Thai restaurant in the middle of downtown, and when we go in they exclaim over Joy (she must come a lot) and ask who her visitors are. She introduces us by name, not by description. When we sit down Joy says, "I'd recommend the drunken noodles. That's what I'm getting."

"You're getting—oh." Ordering a plate of noodles for yourself that way instead of family-style is something I've only ever seen white people do, and I don't know why that feels so jarring. I guess it's because for as much as she looks like me, I can still feel on the periphery all those little fractures I can't quite put my finger on. Like that Harry and I could speak Chinese in front of her (me crappily, but still) and for all I know Joy wouldn't understand a word, like all those missing commonalities I can't assume about her past.

It feels weird to get basically anything on the menu and eat it just by myself, but I don't want to try to negotiate splitting anything on the menu with Harry in front of her, or maybe at all. When the woman who greeted us comes back to take our orders I get a green curry, my mom's favorite, and Harry gets pad thai. And then the woman goes back, and then there's a lull.

I take a long breath and try to gather all the things I've been practicing saying. Exactly at the same time, though, Joy says, "So you're both in high school?"

"Yeah, seniors."

"And what are you doing next year?" The question's polite still, the way it would come from a friend of the family, an adult making conversation at the store.

Harry tips his head toward me. "Harry's going to Princeton," I say. "And I'm, ah, still deciding."

"Isn't the deadline pretty soon? My sister did the college application thing a few years ago, so it's fresh in my memory."

My sister. That aches. "Yeah, it's next week. I'm trying to figure some things out with family first, actually. Which is part of why—that's a big part of how I even found out about you."

Her expression shifts almost imperceptibly, fast enough that I only see the quick cover-up and not whatever's lying underneath. "It must be a huge choice!" she says brightly. "I remember trying to pick colleges. It's hard to picture what a place is really like until you actually go there. Everything looks so different in the brochures than in real life."

"Yeah. Look, Joy—my parents—it's kind of a complicated situation right now. They've had a rough year and we're all kind of trying to figure out what comes next, and—"

"I see." She reaches for her glass of water and drinks half of it. Her expression is anything but inviting, but I pretend not to notice.

"But they finally sat me down and told me the truth about everything that happened with their daughter that they lost and then with the Ballards. Which—it's you, right?"

"Excuse me." Joy stands abruptly, pushing back her chair so hard the arms get caught on the table, rattling it. Our waters slosh over the sides. She's out the door before I can mentally gather myself enough to stand up.

"Do you think she's leaving?" I say. "Crap." I should've led up to things better. Or I should've practiced this more, or maybe I should've said more in my message to her so this didn't feel as abrupt. I had eight hours in the car I could've been preparing.

"I don't know." Harry watches through the window, and for a second it feels like we always do, the two of us united against all the forces of the world. "No, she's just outside."

"Should I go after her?"

"I don't know. No, probably not. I think you should just give her some space."

"I can't just sit here, though. She's right there, and she's my *sister*. I'm sure it's her."

"I know, but—it isn't always better to be there, even if you're trying to help. Sometimes you just have to back off."

I feel my skin flush all the way down to my navel, a sick feeling worming into my stomach. How much am I supposed to read into that? "Yeah, but—" Whatever. I get up. I don't believe that. Because this is what I always hoped for my life when I thought my sister had died: that somehow by being the one who was still here I'd figure things out. That it does mean something to be there, that the world is intrinsically different by you being in it, and that whatever ways it spins around you, you can take something from that and make it better, somehow, than it was.

And maybe now that sounds like wanting to just get credit for showing up. But it's not nothing, right? Some people never show up. Or they start to and then they're gone, or they want something bigger or flashier and less steady than the work of putting yourself there even when it's not comfortable. I don't want that to be true about me.

I find Joy outside crouched on the ground, breathing into cupped hands. "Are you okay?"

"I'm fine."

"Do you need me to call someone?"

She closes her eyes. She looks so much like my mom when she does that, and without warning it makes me wish with all my heart my mom were here right now. She'd know what to say.

It's just me, though, and I have no idea. I crouch next to Joy. "Can I bring you some water? I can order you some tea."

"I don't need anything. It's just—you can't just show up out of the blue like this," she says. "Without any warning, without even asking—my God." She drops her hands and takes more long breaths.

Oh. There's a hollow spot in my chest where my heart should go. "I'm really sorry—I didn't mean—"

"I just need to breathe a little while." She does. There are a few people on the other side of the sidewalk outside what looks like a hardware store, and they're watching us. One calls, "You okay over there?" and Joy waves him off. This street we're on is basically the whole town and it makes it feel lonely here, kind of, way off on the edge of the world. Not a single car has driven by since we've been out here.

She takes two more long breaths and then she stands, unsteadily. I offer my hand to pull her up, but she ignores it, and I tuck it behind my back.

"I didn't mean to freak out on you. But I was just having a normal day at work, and then all of a sudden out of nowhere you show up to drag up all these extremely personal things about my past—"

"I'm really sorry. I really didn't mean for it to be like that for you. I thought—I guess I was just so excited to see you, and I thought you'd—"

She sighs. "They like me here," she says, and it takes me a few seconds to understand that she means the restaurant. "They always bring my orders out right away. Our food is probably ready. Let's just go back inside."

When we go back in our food has come, and Joy sits down, almost mechanically, and resolutely picks up her fork. I can tell somehow that it's important to her to pull herself together and sit through this meal, like maybe she'll look back on this as a moment she had to be strong, a shitty time she had to get through and she gathered herself together and pulled it off.

I feel loose, like all my joints and cartilage are in danger of splitting and just coming apart, rendering me into dust. I can't taste my curry. None of this is what I imagined. It didn't occur to me that it would be her and she wouldn't want to see me, that the sight of me would traumatize her.

All of us pick at our food, and Joy asks a little more about college. Everything I say she treats as mildly interesting trivia, roughly the same way Regina reacts when Harry sends her YouTube clips he thought were funny. Mostly, though, she talks to Harry, because apparently she considered doing a postdoc at Princeton and loved the area. And also I think because it's probably easier—Harry doesn't matter to her. Harry she'll never have to think about again.

I think about my parents waiting back at home, and I imagine telling them about this: *I went to see her and gave her a panic attack and then we came back.* When the check comes, I reach for it, but Joy takes it before I can. "I can—"

"No, no," she says breezily. "I'm a regular here." Which isn't exactly a reason, but—my Asianness fails me—I also don't have the energy to fight for it. Joy pays. In her car on the way back she turns on the radio just loud enough that you'd have to raise your voice to talk over it, so we don't.

When the paved road ends and we're back on the dirt and gravel the car jostles us around, and I lean my head against the backrest and close my eyes and try to unravel all the moments leading to this one, imagine what I could've done differently, what I could still do. Maybe if I tell her more about what it's been like for my parents, or if I tell her the whole story. Or maybe—

"Do you guys need anything for your drive back?" Joy says as we pull back in sight of the portables. "There's not much open right now in town, but we have some water bottles and Red Bulls and trail mix."

I say yes just to prolong things. How is it that I came all the way here and I'll leave with nothing? We follow her into the portable, where Byron (at least I think it's Byron; they're both white guys in their twenties with short hair) nods at us from where he's sitting in front of one of the computers wearing heavy-duty headphones. Joy pulls down a box from one of the plastic shelves and starts to rummage through it.

While we're standing there, a strange looks goes over Harry's face. I follow his gaze to the wall, and there next to a whiteboard is the portrait of my mom, the one I drew. It's an impossible feeling to see it here in this context. It stuns me in place. I must stare at it a good minute, the rest of the room fading out in the periphery.

"I was home visiting my parents and I thought I'd stop by your art showing. I read about it online," Joy says quietly.

I jump; I didn't even notice she'd come closer to me. "How did you even hear about it?"

"I was—" She glances back toward not-Byron. "I was looking you up. You really should be more careful about online privacy."

"You were looking me up?"

"I was curious. I'm a scientist. I was curious about any biological ties."

I was certain already, but hearing her say it is staggering nonetheless, too much and too big to absorb right away. I will replay that for the rest of my life.

"They would love to talk to you," I say. "I'm pretty sure they'd give anything at all just to hear your voice, even just for a few seconds. Anything you want to know or anything you want to say to them—I could call them right now if you want."

Byron/not-Byron are watching us with their arms crossed, and in the portable's small space I feel how little room there is right now for me. We've worn out our welcome, I know that.

She starts to say something, then stops herself. I can see her struggling. But I understand that struggle for what it is—she's not choosing between two different parts of herself, I don't think. She made her choice. The struggle now is just that she's a nice person and will feel bad if she hurts me, not because of who I am, but just because of who she is.

"I'm not open to talking to them," she says. "I'm sorry to hear they aren't doing well, and for your sake I hope things clear up soon."

She's gathered some water bottles and granola bars, a few cans of Red Bull, and she puts them in a bag now and hands it to me. I can sense her lightening, having nearly disposed of us. A part of my heart curls like a pencil shaving and peels off.

"Drive safely back," she says. "I'm glad to know you've been doing well. Really. You have a lot of talent. Good luck with everything. It was nice to meet you both."

TWENTY-EIGHT

The drive from San José to Modoc County feels striking and starkly beautiful on the way there, when you're full of hope and promise and the future, when you feel like you're the hero in your story. On the way back, though, when you've lost what you set out for, when you're beginning to understand how you screwed everything up and now you're left with nothing, it feels long and painful and impossible to begin.

I thought I'd have something to offer my parents.

I guess I still do, even though it's none of what I wanted. I'll tell them I'll stay here with them, figure out some kind of job here. Maybe they'll try to talk me out of it, but deep down I'm sure they know I can't go to Providence. They could be detained and I'd have no way of knowing. I wouldn't be able to visit or talk to them. And even if not, even if nothing happens, I can't leave them here alone in their awful apartment to panic whenever footsteps go by. I can't do that to them. They've lost too much already.

So that's my offer. And I have this, too, small as it is: all the anger and resentment I felt toward them are gone. When Joy closed the door behind us those things drained completely away.

We've left the city limits when, with a suddenness that arcs through me like a knife, it all clicks into place. His experiment, losing the house, all of it: my dad risked everything because that experiment was all he had left of her, because the emptiness he must have felt (must feel still) would eclipse anything I'm currently feeling, and all he had to fill that ocean-sized hole was the hope of some tangible, atomic connection to her that no part of their history and none of his choices could sever.

And that was why my mom hated the experiment so much. Because it exhumed everything she'd tried so hard to bury.

The sun is starting to dip down as we drive back. You never really notice how much you miss the daylight until it's slipping away. Driving with someone feels different at night—the dark locks you into the car and shrinks the world around you so all it is is you, and you feel how little you have left outside the car.

We make it to McArthur, eighty or ninety minutes, without talking. I'm too drained to worry about what that might mean. In the soft early night the rocks and scrub brush rise against us, hemming us to the road. Harry, who's been still and subdued, finally clears his throat.

"Well," he says, "at least you know, right?"

"I mean, whatever." So I know. But comparing how I feel right now to how I did just hours ago—I should've just let myself stay in limbo forever. It hurt a lot less.

"Maybe someday she'll change her—"

"She's not going to." If she felt nothing when I was there with her, if all the years I mourned her meant nothing to her, it's never going to be any different. I feel tears pricking at my eyes, and I reach up and swipe at them roughly. "You don't have to try to make it seem better. It sucks. End of story."

"I'm sorry."

"It's not your fault."

"I know. I'm just—I really wanted it to go differently."

"I know you did."

He shifts in his seat and looks around like he's afraid someone might overhear us. I know him well enough to guess what that means. I wish he'd just say nothing, though—I don't need a panicky, awkward speech where he tries to let me down gently.

"Listen," he says. He stares straight ahead at the road as it climbs an incline. "You're really important to me. I don't want you to think— damn it." He works his jaw and thuds his fist gently against the dashboard. "We're always going to be friends, right? We'll always—"

"You can stop."

Out of the corner of my eye I see him flinch. "I don't mean it like that. I swear."

"What do you mean it like, then?"

"I mean it like—I can't imagine what it'll be like next year without you. And I wish—"

He stops. I say, "You wish what?"

"Nothing. It doesn't matter. Wishes don't count." He lets his foot off the gas abruptly. When I glance at the speedometer it shows nearly ninety. He lets the needle drift back down to seventy. "You don't hate me, right? We're good?"

I turn my head away. "You know how I feel about you."

The road flattens, returning us to the hold of the earth again. There've been more cars the past ten or twenty miles, brake lights gleaming red like dragon eyes. I have never been so tired in my life.

"Can I ask you something?" he says.

Who cares anymore. "Yep."

"How long have you—how long?"

I think about lying, but there's no point. "Always."

He bites at his lip. "Really?"

I shrug. What else is there to say? Maybe someday I'll look back on this night, too, as something I wish I could have back. Maybe someday I'll dissect it a million times and trick myself into thinking if I just said something differently it could've changed everything. But the truth is that Harry knows me. There's nothing I haven't told him or shown him, and there's nothing else I have left to offer him. That was the rest of it.

I'm exhausted. I lean my head against the cool glass of the window and watch the night pass by.

*   *   *

My parents throw the door open before I even take out my key. They must have been spying from the peephole. I come in and then they both hover over me, not touching. I can feel their waiting pulsing in the room. My mom says, "Are you all right?"

"I'm fine. I—"

"We were so worried. We didn't know if you'd—"

Her voice breaks, and she puts her hands over her mouth. My dad drapes his arm around her shoulder. It's nearly three in the morning, and from the way they're both watching me I know that the whole time I was gone they were waiting for news, that likely neither of them slept or ate.

And I understand something else then, too, for the first time, something cocooned inside this mini welcome-home brigade of theirs: why both my parents treated me the way they did after the crash. I should've recognized sooner how intimately they understand guilt and how it's shaped them and shaped me, too, both the choices they've had to make and the stories they tell themselves. I've lived my whole life inside their guilt.

"I didn't mean to make you worry. I was all right. I just needed to see her. And I thought if I went to talk to her there—I thought it would change things."

My mom takes my face in her hands. "Daniel—"

"Wait. I also wanted to say how sorry I am about the crash. Um—" I can't look at either of them. "I know everything's so much worse because of that and because of me and I would do anything to take it back. And I know it's too late to change anything, but I think you made the wrong choice when you chose me over her. Over my sister, I mean."

"Daniel, you can't think of it that way," my dad says. He looks pained. "We never have."

Haven't they ever, in the dark moments they wouldn't tell someone else about? But if they have, I know, they'll take that to their graves. I say, "But—"

"No," my dad says firmly. "No. We are so lucky to have you. We've always felt that way."

The words in front of me waver and then fade, and my lungs expand again. I'll hold on to those words. I wish I had more to give them back in return.

I can give them this, at least: I tell them it's really her. And I try my best to turn it into something they might want to hear. I tell them she's happy. I tell my dad she's a scientist like he is, I tell my mom she's kind and polite like my mom is. I tell them that she looks like me.

My mom is crying, but trying to pretend she isn't. The look on her face—if I were to draw it the part I'd go after, I think, is the loneliness, like you could fill the whole city with people for her and it wouldn't be close to enough.

"Also," I say quickly, "there's something else. I'm withdrawing from RISD and I'm going to stay here."

"What? No," my mom says. "Of course you're going. You have to go. We are so happy you were accepted. You'll go."

"I can't. I'm not. I emailed them to ask how to withdraw."

"Don't be ridiculous," my dad says. "You've worked your whole life—"

"I'm not being ridiculous. I'm not going. I'd spend the whole time there worrying, anyway. It wouldn't be worth it even if I did. But also, just—I can't. Maybe I can take classes at community college here, and I'll get a job and help out. Maybe I could get a job at the mall with you, Ba. Or something. I'll figure something out."

My parents exchange a long look, and some understanding passes between them, something I can't interpret. "We'll speak about it later," my dad says.

"But—"

He quiets me. "I'm hungry. Aren't you hungry?"

"Yes," my mom says quickly, even though I know her appetite's been shot lately. "Me too. What do you feel like eating, Daniel? We're starving. Let's go get something to eat."

I am actually—in spite of everything—starving, too, so my parents have me get an Uber and we pay eight dollars for the guy to take us to a Jack in the Box and we go through the drive-through, and my mom insists I get a soda, which we never get, and we order a bagful of greasy food. Back in the apartment my mom spreads one of the thin bathroom towels on the floor and we have a picnic, and instead of talking about any of the things I think we all want to avoid, my parents start talking about when I was little. *Do you remember,* my mom says, a soft smile on her face, and then they're off and running. They tell stories about me as a toddler, me as a preschooler, me in grade school. And listening to them you'd think all the years were happy.

This won't last forever, I know that—the rest of the world is waiting, and there's only so long you can hold it at bay. All the same, though, I'm grateful. I understand this is a gift. I'll take it as long as it lasts.

I picture drawing us this way, my parents looking kind of awkward sitting cross-legged on the floor, the towel stained where some of the ketchup spilled. I hope someday, wherever life takes us, we'll look back on this as the worst time in our lives. That from the safety of a better future the way things feel right now will fade and we'll be left with just hazy vignettes: the time I drove to Alturas, the time we ate Jack in the Box together on the apartment floor.

The people who matter to you most—you aren't always going to occupy that same space in their lives, I guess. Maybe that's what I always loved most about art, that it was a way of multiplying myself so I could feel like I was always a part of more than I really was. I should hold on to the fact that Joy kept something I drew. Maybe that still means something, however small. And maybe life is when you gather all the things you can hold on to and carry with you, and cross your fingers it'll be enough.

* * *

I've never told anyone this. It's not a secret, it's just not something that was ever big enough to bring up or explain why it keeps playing through my head. But this is what I remember:

I was walking home with Sandra in eighth grade near the

beginning of the year back when we were friends still and she'd been kind of weird the whole way, quieter than usual, and distracted. We'd passed Columbus and the crowds of kids trudging down Bubb had thinned out a little when she looked around and said, apropos of nothing, "You know who I'm kind of into? I'm kind of into Ahmed."

"I knew it!" I'd crowed. I stopped in my tracks and she bumped into me, nearly knocking me over. I was grinning triumphantly. "I so knew it."

"No you didn't."

"Um, I *entirely* did." It's hard to remember there was ever a time when they weren't publicly and permanently linked, that it would've taken any kind of observation to see what there was between them, but I had known: she kept bringing him up gratuitously, finding ways to work him into conversation. I knew what that felt like. "You're really bad at keeping secrets. I knew it." I elbowed her. "Ask him out."

"Um, no thank you."

"Why not?"

"I just kind of have a thing for him. I'm not going to ask him *out*."

"Why? You're scared?"

And this was the moment—it was over in four seconds. It was fall and we were crunching through leaves and I was hungry, ready to be home, and Sandra said, "Other people don't exist just to be your happy ending, you know?"

I think about that now. She was right, of course, but still, sometimes people give you that. And it's a gift every time, something rare and important, not something you're ever guaranteed and not any pattern that might help you understand the world.

My mom comes into my room that night a few minutes after I've gotten into bed. She sits on my mattress across from me and says, "I want to ask you something."

I'm already half-asleep. "Mmph."

She waits until I'm mostly awake again. "Do you mean it about RISD, Daniel?"

I do mean it. I don't have a choice, not really. Anyway, I saw what it looked like for my dad to go after his dreams. Most people don't get to, he was right. "Yeah."

"What will make you change your mind?"

"Nothing."

"You're certain?"

I try to blink away the heaviness in my eyes. I am certain, and more than that, I know they understand that—they understand what it means for your life to orbit around a single choice, how everything that comes after will always originate from a single point. And they know the grief and regret that come with it, too. "Yeah."

She leans forward and rests her cheek against mine, then smooths my hair and kisses my cheek.

"You are such a good son, Daniel," she says. "We are very proud of you."

˲ ˳ ˳

That night I sleep what feels like a century. Around noon, when my phone rings, I wake up abruptly with what feels like a hangover. The sunlight splits through the dark curtains, illuminating all the dust motes suspended in the air.

I roll over and feel around for my phone charging on my nightstand. It's Regina. I try to clear the sleep from my voice. "Hello?"

"Hey," she says quietly. It sounds like she's been crying.

"You all right?"

"Yeah. I mean, no, but—yeah. Harry told me about your sister. I'm really sorry."

What is there to say? It feels like a death. "Thanks."

My phone buzzes with a message, and then another one. It's probably Harry. "I wish it had gone differently," Regina says.

"Yeah, well." I lay my head back against the pillow and close my eyes. "Hey, Reg, I should've called you after Mr. Denton had us in his office."

"It's all right."

"No, I should've—"

"I actually went and talked to the psychologist."

"You did?" I open my eyes again and shift until I'm sitting up. "How was it? You don't sound good."

"No, it was okay. It was good, actually. She was better than I expected. It's just been . . . kind of a long morning." I hear her get up and close her door. "Did you know Harry was the last person she talked to?"

She means Sandra, I know. "He never told me that."

"He never told anyone else."

"What did they talk about? When was it?"

She tells me: it was two hours before. Afterward, a few days after, when he was in a panic he couldn't come down from, Harry showed her the messages. He'd been at a tennis match and Sandra had written *You'll always be good to Regina, right?*

He was sweaty and thirsty and hurried, ready for his next set, checking his phone while he was getting water, which his coach always yelled at him about when he noticed. Sandra was a posses- sive, bossy friend—she'd always been—and they'd banter sometimes over whether he was a worthy boyfriend or not. She'd dole out numbers like an Olympian judge sometimes (8 for being a good date to a dance, 6 for being a less-than-stimulating lunch companion), and he always laughed, but I know it kind of bothered him, too; if he could've figured out a way to say so without sounding oversensitive, he would've done it.

The text struck him as kind of unusual, but there was another set to play—he was down—and so he didn't answer at first. Then he changed his mind and said, *I always am already.*

Sandra wrote back, *Good. Keep that promise*, and Harry put down his phone and went to play the rest of his match. He won.

My phone keeps buzzing. "When you told me about your parents," Regina says, "something—I don't know. Some part of me snapped out of something. I guess I just feel so guilty every time I'm happy, or every time I'm with anyone I care about. Like how can I just go on with all my friendships like everything didn't end for me last year?"

"Oh, Reg—"

"Anyway, I wanted to tell you I turned in my deposit for Northwestern."

"Wait, what, seriously? You did? Regina, that's great."

"My parents finally gave in. I think it was the tribute, actually—I think it really freaked my mom out." She pauses. "Honestly, though, I don't know if I can imagine going and like—I don't know, cramming for finals or studying abroad or passive-aggressively dumping my roommate's laundry on her bed or whatever you're supposed to do in college. Just doing all those things like that's all there is in my world."

"I know what you mean. I think it'll get there, though." At the very least those things will happen; you go through the motions and then it turns out you did them, even if you weren't entirely there for it as you did.

"Someday, maybe. We'll see. Also, I started going to my church again."

"Oh yeah? How's that been?"

"It's—complicated."

"Complicated good or complicated bad?"

"Complicated like—I couldn't bring myself to sing anything during worship and I was still furious at everyone who ever tried to tell me last year God works all things for good, but then during the message I just felt like God was reminding me that the whole history of the world is that it's fallen. He promises redemption someday, just not yet. And in the meantime whole decades' worth of the Bible is just grieving all these broken things."

"Well, that's—"

"Also, I broke up with Harry."

The world tilts sideways, wobbling on its axis. "Wait, what?"

"I did it just now."

I don't know what to say. "Why?"

"I should've done it a long time ago."

"You don't have feelings for him?"

"Of course I do. I love Harry, and I'll always love him, but not like that. But also—I don't think I was ever who he wanted."

The way she says it—I think she knew more than I realized, all this time. My phone buzzes again. "I don't know what to say. You're okay with it?"

"It's weird, definitely. And I'm sad. But I wasn't ever really in it. You know? At least not the way you're supposed to be. It feels so selfish and wrong to just try to have some kind of happy ending when—when not everyone gets one. With Harry at least I didn't have to feel guilty for doing that because it was never going to be happily ever after with him. We aren't right for each other. It felt less wrong that way." She hesitates. "I know you're not supposed to think like that—like, shutting down your own life because you feel guilty. But I guess you feel what you feel."

"And how do you feel now?"

"I wouldn't say better, but—righter, I guess. Maybe better will come."

*　　*　　*

There are so many messages when Regina and I hang up that I have to scroll back up to read them:

Yo, where you at
You up yet?
Pick up your phone
Pick it up
What are you doing are you sleeping still?
Pick up your damn phone
Danny
Dannnnyyyyyyyyyyyyyy
Danny stg if you don't pick up right this second
Okay don't pick up your phone, but
You know what you told me yesterday and I said I wish it could be different? It's different now
Can I come over?
PICK UP YOUR PHONE

I write back, *come over.*

I feel tingly all over. When I get up and put clothes on, my fingers feel thick and numb, and I fumble with the buttons on my shirt. It's quiet; my parents must still be asleep. My heart is percussive. I can't stop smiling.

When I open my door the living room is empty, and I don't hear anything from the bathroom. I peek out on the balcony and say, "Ma?" No answer. "Ba?" Still silence.

I tell myself they've just gone down to the laundry room or something, or maybe they went out to bring back some food, and I rummage through the mostly empty fridge and the cupboards. It's only after I give up and plop down on the couch/bed that I find the letter next to their phones lying on the TV stand. It's an envelope with my name on it, in my mom's writing, and inside the envelope there's three hundred dollars in cash.

Our beloved Daniel,

We have always believe in you.

We never want to burden you with our problem and mistake and we always dream of a much bigger life for you than this.

We know you will go on to do great thing as an artist. We will be always watching for your name.

Keep your same phone number always so we always know how to find you. Someday, when the time is right, you will hear from us again.

We love you more than you can ever dream.

鴛

You have known for years where she lives—the woman who gave birth to you. The woman who first cuddled you, who gave you your first name, taught you your first tongue. Who got on a plane and crossed an ocean without you like you were luggage that didn't fit. Whom you have tried and tried to discard, who haunts you every day of your life.

All your life you cupped this dream in your hands like a bird: that he would come. Your baby brother, your replacement. You've rehearsed all the things you'd say to him, how to reduce him to nothing in only a few sentences, how to summon all those years of your own anger and make your pain lash around so vicious and wild it would break his skin and lodge itself underneath. And then he could carry those wounds back to them and infect them, too. Pain multiplies exponentially. What you cannot fix you can continue to destroy.

And then there he was.

He was nothing like you expected. But you—you were everything you should've expected. All those years of your plotting crumbled and you felt your old familiar self rising up, rushing in to try to ease his way and make him feel better. All those same familiar urges that make you smile when men say *Smile!*, that made you go to the movies with your advisor one day because he said he was lonely even though you didn't want to, that made you worm yourself into bright Chinese dresses with your sister to take Christmas pictures your mom arranged each year growing up, that bring you home for every holiday. *Who are you in the face of someone else's pain?* demand the urges. *Who are you to withhold yourself?* And you didn't tell him, although you considered it, how six years ago (you work your way backward; he would've been about to start middle school) you went to see his father.

When you were younger your parents took you and your sister to join a group for girls adopted from China and their families. You'd go each week to one of the family's houses and watch documentaries about China, and the moms would all try to cook Chinese food and pass out red envelopes for Chinese New Year or they'd bring in books to try to teach you words in Mandarin. Each week, you'd look around at all the other girls and think how any one of them could have just as easily wound up your sister instead. Your life was shaped by the whims of overseas agencies, by paperwork and timing. Your sister loved those meetings, but you hated them; you begged your mom to let you stay at home. Culture was important. She never let you. After returning you'd get migraines, flashes of black-rimmed light that screamed across your vision and left you weak and ill.

When you don't live out the life you were born into, the idea that you might someday, somehow, understand is intoxicating. In undergrad you met other adoptees. It was easier, somehow, outside your family's eager, watchful eye. Your friend Tish, from Orinda and before that from Seoul, was in reunion with her first family. She claimed it was messy, and never easy, but before something's a reality it can be anything you wish. It can be not only easy but fulfilling and perfect, too; you can banish fear if you imagine only the most wonderful things.

When you were a junior in college you had found where your brother's father worked and a boy from your Animal Behavior class, who lived in San José, offered to drive you over Fourth of July weekend. You will never forget the particular sound of your footsteps in the linoleum hallway, the lights flickering overhead. He was in the laboratory, sitting at a computer by an otherwise unremarkable window that's forever seared into your memory, and when he saw you the earth stopped around him; you felt it happen, a disruption in the gravitational pull. You felt his whole life change.

He came out into the hallway. You were shy and hopeful and terrified all at once, happy in a way you couldn't quite control, and then he wouldn't talk with you. *You have a new family now,* he told you, and the whole world hardened against you, and you within it, petrified inside the stark truth of all the ugliness of a cold uncaring universe. *You must go back to them. It's not safe for you to be here. Go.*

You have nurtured your hatred ever since. You are small and pretty, with a lovely smile. You hide your hatred well.

For weeks and weeks you lie awake at night remembering your brother's visit, dissecting it and sliding it under a microscope in your mind. You think of it the nights your boyfriend comes to visit, the day your family drives up to surprise you, the day your sister calls from college in tears, homesick, and you settle back into those easy rhythms and unspoken sentences of siblinghood, the least fraught language you know and what now feels like your mother tongue.

You will admit this to yourself: when he was here, even against all your people-pleasing learned behaviors, you brought up your sister the way you did to hurt him. Or not to hurt him, maybe—although that's what it did; you saw it in his face—but to wall yourself off from him, to place markers around yourself and let all the space between you echo back at him. It was the way you did it, tossing her out there like you didn't know the implications. You knew them. Your sister is the one to whom you admit this, in fact, when you finally call her and tell her how he came. Ruth has always been different from you (she knows nothing of her first family, and yearns for answers): if it had been her, she would have hugged him and never let him go.

You have been watching his life unspool from a distance. Despite your warning, he makes no effort at privacy. He posted when he left for college, when he arrived. He posts pictures and videos of his dorm there, the art he's making, the things he does on weekends, the visits from the boy he brought to meet you who goes to Brown now (you'd thought he said Princeton, but maybe you were wrong), the two of them twined together lying on the grass looking so happy to be with each other it makes your teeth hurt. (Sometimes, though, in the pictures other people post of him, those ones he didn't curate personally, you think he looks deeply sad.) He posts a happy-anniversary message to his parents; he posts the details of his first studio exhibition with his classmates; he posts when he's going to be off campus. In fact he posts so much that it occurs to you more than once to wonder if he's doing it for the benefit of an audience—is it you? He has shifted his life onto screens, a narrative you can tune in to, so that every day, if you like (you do), you can check in on him and see that he's safe, that he's busy, that he's surrounded by people who like him and even some who love him. You think he must be doing it on purpose.

"Go see him," your sister tells you every time she calls. She knows how you watch him. She doesn't tell your parents. "Don't see them if you don't want, but at least go see him. You live basically on the edge of nowhere and I know from personal experience it's the most boring place in the world, so what else are you going to do? Just go."

You told no one this, not Mike from Animal Behavior who bought you a Slurpee and drove you back to campus, not Tish from your dorm who stayed up with you all that night and gave you a cool damp towel when you threw up, not the therapist who called 911 because she couldn't be sure the panic attack you had in her office wasn't something worse, not even Ruth. You got lost leaving your father's campus. You were dizzy and stricken and the hallway loomed unnavigable in front of you, branching off to a maze of so many other hallways whose sum total was far too great for you to ever find yourself. You walked back and forth and finally unseeingly stumbled down a flight of stairs that delivered you into the unsparing glare of the sun. That was where you saw him again.

He was crouched against the side of the building, weeping, wobbly, and trying to steady himself against the brick wall.

Still, you didn't understand until your brother came, and then it was clear; his father had been trying to protect him. Your brother had the unmistakable air of one who's been the very center of someone else's universe all his life, one formed of all those hopes and dreams and fears and pains and longings and regrets. You know what that feels like, you and Ruth both.

It is no longer possible to hate them. You miss the hatred. After a while it can start to feel like a friend. Or maybe it's just that the other things roiling underneath are unmasked now, and those things are harder things to feel. You are adrift. You cry a lot. You go drunk stargazing with Byron and Lance. Ruth sends you an Edible Arrangement and you eat the entire thing in one sitting. You go to see her and spend too much of your stipend taking her shopping and out to eat.

Like everything, it starts small. First you reread a post about his showing in December. Then you screenshot it, save it to your desktop. You let your eyes flick over your lab calendar and rest on the blank spots in between incubation and hatch.

You look up his campus on a map. You look up plane tickets to Rhode Island, just out of curiosity, just to see. You call a hotel with a forgiving cancellation policy. Finally you grow tired of pretending, and you book a flight.

You surrender yourself to momentum. On the plane you buy a miniature bottle of wine and let it blur away all the sharp corners of existence, and out the window you watch the landscape give way and give way, again and again, while you sail past it unscathed. You always feel most at home in the sky.

When the wheels touch down you feel the land returning to you, spreading like gangrene from that initial thud, and you have to take a

Xanax. The mountains you flew over are all siphoned from the land, all come to press against your lungs in a rush of pressure, and in the terminal you hunch over on a grimy chair, gasping for breath, forcing a smile and a nod for the woman who stoops to ask worriedly if you're all right. You want to grab her hand and beg her not to leave.

It takes you so long to find your way to campus and then to find the gallery space you're worried you've missed it, but the room is full still. You see the other boy first. He's leaning against the wall by the door watching, his eyes shining, and when you follow the direction of his small, private smile it leads you to your brother.

Your brother is standing by a painting talking to a woman you recognize from his posts as one of his professors. He's engrossed in their conversation and it's a few minutes before he looks up and sees you.

He's across the room still; there are people between you, and you aren't certain you won't turn and walk out. You stay close to the door and recite the mantra your sister made you repeat (*I am doing this for myself, I owe them nothing, I can always leave*). But then he says something to his professor and comes toward you. All the air in the room goes hot.

There are so many ways this could have gone, so many ways this still could go. But in that instant, the one where you saw that flash of recognition strike him like lightning, you felt what you came here to see if you'd feel: the same strike at the same time, an atomic pull you can't explain. You feel the distance between you as a physical entity, and you feel it compress with each of his steps.

And then he's in front of you, startled and unsure.

"Hi," he says. Something in his tone strikes you as brave. Maybe hope is always brave.

Ruth would hug him. You're not sure you will ever be able to. But you're there, and you can breathe still, and you say hi to him back.

RESOURCES

National Suicide Prevention Lifeline:
www.suicidepreventionlifeline.org
1-800-273-8255

Crisis Text Line:
www.crisistextline.org
Text HOME to 741741 from anywhere in the USA, anytime, about
any type of crisis.

United We Dream:
www.unitedwedream.org

ACKNOWLEDGMENTS

This book absolutely would not exist without the immense brilliance, patience, wisdom and talent of Laura Schreiber. Thank you eternally for shepherding it into being, for seeing and trusting and excavating the story lurking inside all the awful drafts, and for being an endless font of vision and clarity and support. Sometimes when the world feels heavy and dark, I think about people like you putting your whole selves into working to make real these books you believe in so that young people who might need them can find them, and that feels like a gift.

Thank you as always to Adriann Ranta, agent extraordinare, for believing in this book along its journey (and me, along mine) and for your unwavering confidence and insight. Thank you to Maria Elias for outfitting this story on its foray into the world and for all the care and creativity you bring to your work. Thank you to Adams Carvalho for the beautiful art. Thank you to Cassie McGinty for your endless enthusiasm and dedication. Thank you to Dina Sherman for all your magic in connecting books with the outside world. Thank you to Emily Meehan and the team at Hyperion for everything.

Thank you to Lee Kelly, Anna-Marie McLemore, Jen Brooks, and Charlotte Huang for your thoughtfulness and feedback on earlier versions of this story, and for encouraging me to believe there really was a story here. A million thanks to Mark O'Brien, Eric Smith, Ann Jacobus, Meredith Ireland, Tim Kim, and Sabaa Tahir for sharing your experience and expertise. And I am endlessly grateful and lucky to be a part of this writing community—thank you, thank you to all the incredible friends and colleagues I've made through it.

Thank you to all the librarians, educators, and booksellers for creating a literary universe for kids who so deeply need it right now, and for letting me be a part of it.

Thank you forever to all my friends and family, near and far, and to my church for the constant reminder and proof that there is beauty and hope in the world, and that it's worth telling about. (Also, for the group texts that keep me sane.)

For my family—thank you for all the traditions and values and inside jokes that make up the stories of who we are and who we come from. To my grandmothers, Helen Loy and Marge Gilbert, thank you for creating and shaping our families, for a lifetime of stories and support, and for always telling everyone who will listen about my books. To my parents, Kirk and Teri, thank you for always believing in me and for all your care and generosity in helping me balance the work of family and writing.

To Zach and Audrey, thank you for being the brightest, most blazing spots of joy in all my days, for giving me hope in the world and the future, and for happily letting me share so many stories with you. And to Jesse—thank you for everything, for the laughter and support and encouragement and steady belief in me, for our beautiful kids (who, admittedly, do not make books happen any sooner but who are funny and cute enough to make up for it anyway). My favorite story is our own.